A *Collision* *of* *Worlds*

A.J. Van–Rixtel

***

ALBAR
Publishing.

First Printing: September 2014
Second Edition

ALBAR
Publishing.

ISBN Paperback- **978-1500921897**

10 9 8 7 6 5 4 3 2

Acknowledgments.

My fantastic friend Winstion, you truly are the person who gave me the drive to put this book out there for others to read. After reading chapter 1 of my raw manuscript "Go, be an author!" were your words. Well here I am. Winstion I am an author.

Holly Jackson, the first person to read the whole of my novel and provide the critical feedback I needed. Whose guidance was invaluable.

Patti Geesey my editor, I must have driven you to distraction constantly asking questions. Thank you for getting it back to me on time for my deadline.

To Olly
Thank you for your support
I really hope you enjoy!

14/12/2017.

Map of Kaarth:

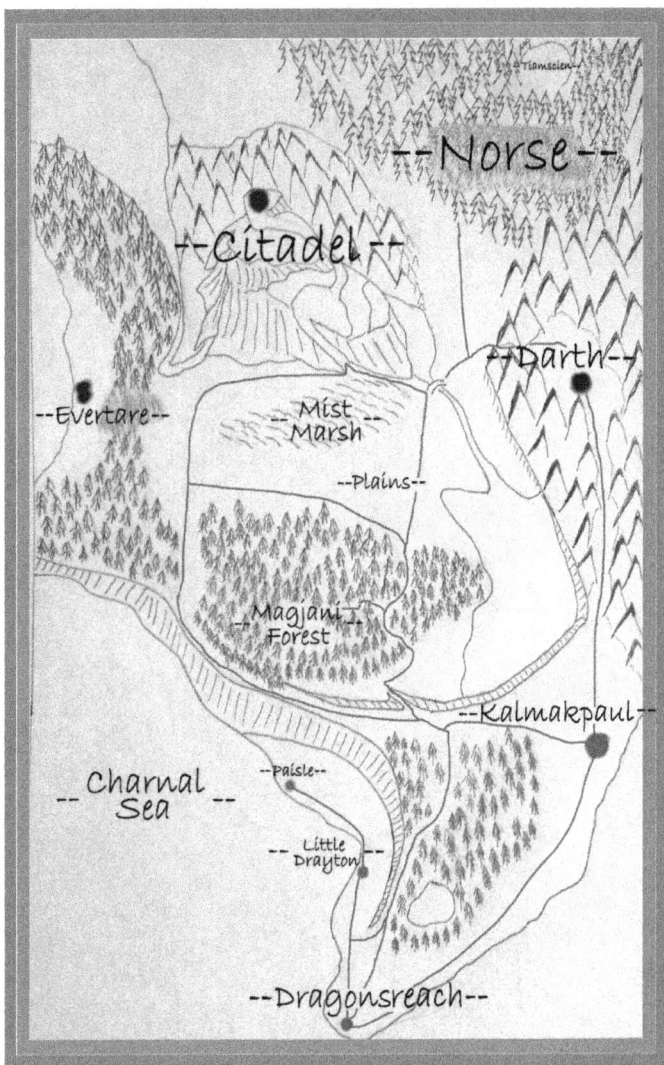

Map of Everglade:

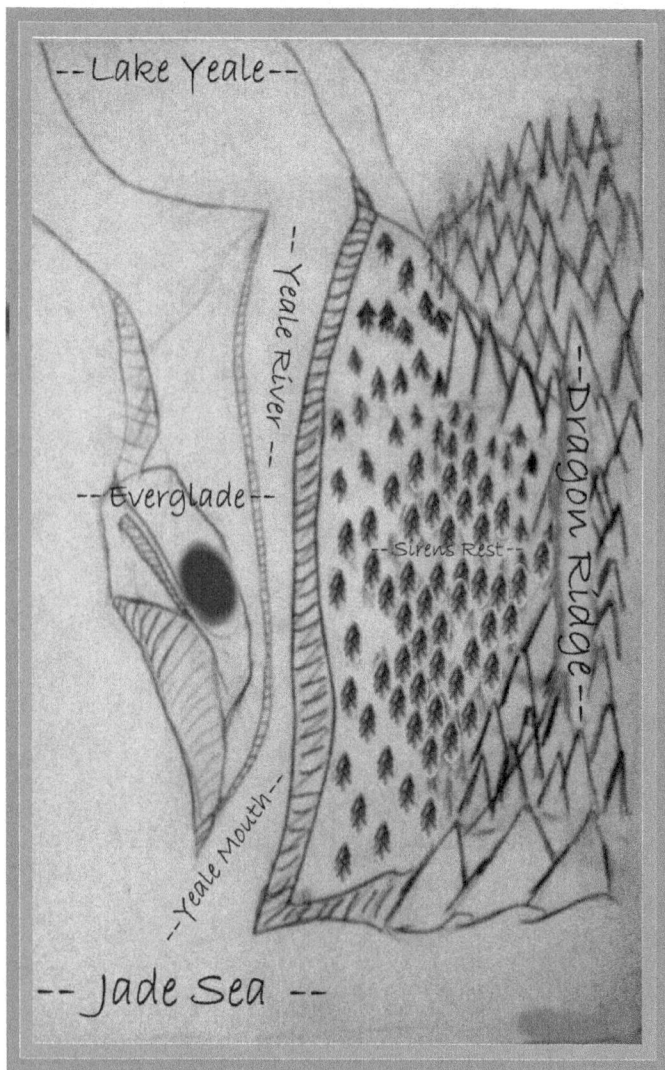

Lake Yeale

Yeale River

Everglade

Sirens Rest

Dragon Ridge

Yeale Mouth

Jade Sea

Part 1:

-The Binds Weaken-

Chapter 1

Morace Roccan looked into his Pa's fading eyes. Pa lay in bed, weakened since a mast fell on top of him. It happened on the ship they commanded together, a fishing vessel; now claimed by the sea due to the unruly weather. The loss of the ship was very much a loss to the family, as their livelihood had depended on it. *Wineria* lay at the bottom of the ocean like Pa lay on the bed. Sweat dripped from Pa's face and his eyes became weaker as his life drained from him.

Pa was in the spare room that Morace's eldest brothers had used when growing up. Lit with a single candle, the light just barely reached the corners of the room. The spherical glow created round shadows on the walls from the ornaments and furniture.

Pa was nearly ninety and he had lived a full life. Morace was the youngest of three brothers, and worried that he was not ready to look after his family. Despite being only twenty-one, it would be up to him to look after his mother and three sisters. A tear left his eye. He was the only male who still lived in his childhood home; his older brothers all had families of their own. With the weather the way it was, it would be a struggle to get help from them. They would be preoccupied.

The storm that had claimed their ship and probably soon his father had been brewing for a week. The entire community had become frenzied with panic. It was by far the worst weather they had ever had since the old Storm Days. It was not just this community feeling the effects; the rest of the world known as Kaarth also suffered. News had spread of the thick, rolling, black clouds of the super storm; hurricanes were nothing more than breezes in comparison to this.

An expedition to a neighbouring village that the storm had moved through revealed no remaining life. All the buildings had been levelled. Now the storm headed to Morace's little fishing village with what seemed like an intense determination to destroy it. The villagers had packed most of their belongings to flee and make their way to the Citadel, Kaarth's capital city.

The Citadel had once withstood the worst of what the weather had thrown at Kaarth during the Storm Days over a thousand years ago. Then the world had felt a perfect balance of the weather – but that all changed a year or so ago. Now, it looked as if the Storm Days had returned. The historians taught of the unruly weather that plagued the land; the weather that had brought sorrow and death. It was rumoured a race from another world had caused the issues.

Pa stirred for a moment. 'Morace?' he croaked.

'Yes, Pa.' He looked tearfully into his Pa's half-closed eyes.

'Don't you be a-fretting, boy. I am going to the great dock-yard in the sky and will be joining my brothers- you be a strong, good boy. You will be able to take care of the girls and Mama.'

'I don't know...'

'Boy, you can do it. You must. There is no hope for this little town; it will be in ruin. Your only hope to provide for our family is in the Citadel.'

'Pa... You can't mean us to move...'

'Not I, son,' Pa croaked. 'You must take the girls and Mama. I am too weak to travel to the Citadel and...' There was a long pause as Pa tried to get the words out of his mouth. Morace gave him some water to help. '...and you must take them. There is nothing here for them now, 'cept death, and I d'ant want that for them. Take them.' Pa's eyes begged his youngest son to do as he willed.

How could I ignore Pa's deathbed wishes?

'Yes, Pa, I will.' Morace looked at his Pa's eyes again and saw the last of his life flow away. After he closed his Pa's eyes, he wept until he fell asleep.

Lorett Roccan stood on the harbour pier looking out to sea. The sun had started to set. The colours melded together to create a warm glow on the horizon. Tears leaked from her eyes. It was a cold day, so she had wrapped up in her coat to ward off the chill in the air. The sea was choppy. A storm was brewing yet again, though this time it seemed to be much closer. To her right should have been the fishing vessel that her family owned, but it had been lost. Lorett turned to head back to the house. She needed to make sure her twin, Morace, was well and had not taken this too hard.

With solemn steps, she navigated her way back to her house through the market. Everyone knew who she was and what had happened. Every now and then one of the vendors would stop her to ask of her Pa's health. She responded politely enough even though she knew he might not make it. It was hard for her.

It had gotten quite late. Lorett also knew, too that Mama would be worried about her. *Dinner should be ready.*

She looked at the house that she had lived in all of her life. Home. Lorett walked up to the door and opened it. The squeak of the hinges sent a little shiver down her spine. Even though it was such a little thing, it was something that warmed her up. The sound reminded her that she was home.

'Lorett, there you are. Why were you out so late?' Mama asked. She was quite flustered.

'Sorry, Mama, I wanted to be alone for a while.' Lorett gave a reassuring smile.

Mama flapped her arms about to say it did not matter. 'Go get your brother, will you? He has not eaten since yesterday.'

Lorett went to fetch her brother. He had not left Pa's side since the incident.

She opened the door to Pa's room carefully, remembering that Pa disliked doors being opened too hard. Lorett saw her brother with his head resting on the bed next to Pa. She looked at Pa and knew instinctively that her hero had passed on. She cried quietly, needing a little time before waking Morace up.

When she was ready, she gently shook Morace awake.

When he was woken by his twin sister, Morace briefly forgot where he was until he saw the lifeless body of his Pa. He fought back the tears so that his sister would not see him weep. He gave her a drowsy smile, but knew it would not be convincing. The hairs on the back of his neck prickled as he felt his sister's arms wrap comfortingly around his shoulders. The smell of dinner that floated in from downstairs brought him back into the world. His stomach growled hungrily.

'Lorett.' He smiled not wanting her arms to leave him. 'We need to eat. Mama is probably going to send a search party.' They got up slowly and went to the dining room.

Morace sat at the table with his Mama and three sisters. In a sombre silence, they ate the food Mama had prepared.

After they had cleared everything away, they stood in the garden to lay their Pa's body to rest in the earth. Mama planted a pansy on top of the mound of dirt that her husband lay under; it was Pa's favourite flower.

'It's fitting that he should be buried here,' Mama said looking at her children. 'He liked this garden. It was the first thing he looked at when we viewed this home.' All four of her children hugged her.

Morace lit a resting candle then staked it in the ground above Pa's grave. He turned to face his family, determination set in his eyes. 'Tomorrow we shall leave for the Citadel. It's what Pa wanted for us.' Morace's attitude changed suddenly. It was as though he had become years older in an instant. Morace stood tall as the protector of his family.

'Aye, well we best be getting some sleep then. It's a long way,' said Mama. 'Run off to bed. Now!'

Late into the night, Morace sat at the desk in his Pa's study, with lit a candle. The candle's gaze illuminated the bookshelves and the maps that lay on the desk. The girls and Mama were all in bed asleep. Questions bounced around in his mind, which made it hard to sleep. He faced a task he did not know how to prepare for. It was one thing getting to the Citadel; it was another thing thriving there. They would be one of many families fleeing from the incoming storm. Was he really up for it?

Not 'bluddy' likely I tell ya.

'Oh, Pa, why did this have to happen? You were meant to live forever, not die. We were meant to rule the seas, not drown in them,' Morace said aloud.

'Morace?' He started at the voice in the doorway. Lorett looked ethereal in the dim light, her slender form covered by a white nightgown. Her face was furrowed with worry.

'Lorett, why are you not asleep? We have a lot of traveling to do. You know.'

Lorett moved into the light. Morace could see that she had been crying; her eyes were red. She sat on the sofa in the corner of the room. With her hand, she lightly patted the cushion next to her. 'I know, but it's the same reason you couldn't sleep. Can you sit with me on the sofa?'

Morace sat down with her. He could feel the warmth that radiated from her as she leant on him for comfort.

'Do you think he is watching us?' she asked.

'Yes, he will always watch us.'

She looked into his eyes to see if he actually believed his words, or whether he was just trying to ease her pain. She smiled knowing her brother was telling the truth.

'Good,' she said as she pressed her head against his body. 'I am going to miss him,' she added, muffled by her brother's strong sailor's chest.

'We will all miss him, Lorett, but he would want us to be happy and not sad. Remember what he used to say?'

She looked at him, puzzled.

'He used to say, "*Naw I d'ant want any of you teh be unhappy when I die. I want you teh remember me for me laughs...*"'

She smiled when the memory came to life in her mind. 'He was standing on a table when he said that at the Fisher Moon festival. He was very drunk.'

Morace pictured the scene. 'I also remember having to carry you home that night.' He winked. 'At fourteen you were very drunk too, and very flirty with Old Man Tubb's young boy.'

'I was not drunk, and besides, you were not so sober yourself.' She waved a finger accusingly as she spoke.

A sharp noise from outside gave them both a start.

'Wait here,' he said, keen to keep his sister safe.

She gave him a frustrated look. Morace knew what would be coming - he had seen that face many times before.

'No! What happens if you can't handle it? We go together,' she demanded.

Darn she is so stubborn, she won't accept no.

'Ok, but please be careful.'

They grabbed their coats and moved slowly to the door. Stepping outside, all they could see was fog. The sound of rain reached their ears; it was raining hard. A flash of lightning illuminated everything for a moment before it abruptly went dark again.

'See! What good would you have been, you on your own?'

She was right, only she could see clearly in fog, which was why Pa would take her on the voyages. He called her the Torchlight in the Storm; she could see much better than any of the crewmen.

Suddenly Morace felt a huge gust of wind rush towards them from the sea. Lorett pulled him out of the way of a tornadic waterspout. They lost their balance and fell to the ground, hard. As they looked up, they witnessed what could only be described as a nightmare.

The tornadic waterspout rushed passed them careening straight into the house. Their birth house. The house they had grew up in. The house their Mama and two sisters slept in. Their house was now a disintegrated wreck.

Lorett screamed and began to rush forwards but it was Morace's turn to grab hold of her. She fought his grip but was powerless against him. His twin began to sob in his arms.

'Hold still,' he cried, 'it's too dangerous.'

'But Mama and...'

'Gone.' The tears trickled down his face. They warmed his cheeks against the cold wind.

'How can you be so blunt?' Lorett stared at her brother. Tears now dropped from her eyes, too.

'I am sorry.' He held her as she wept, stroking her hair, singing until she slept in his arms.

The truth was, it killed him to be blunt. It broke him inside. He had to hold her back; to let her go in would have been fatal.

Morace held her still for a number of hours. He made his mind up. He decided he would take his sister to their eldest brother and tell him of the news. He needed to do something. Somehow, he could sense something unnatural. He was sure that the waterspout was no accident or some freak weather. He would let his sister know his intentions on visiting their brother in the morning, right now, she needed sleep and so did he.

He picked up her slumbering body and sought out shelter, so that they had protection from the cold. Sleep did not come well for him but he took what little he could.

Chapter 2

The twins awoke the following morning. They were stiff from sleeping in the cold. The nightmare had seemed to continue. As they walked the mud-clotted streets, it became apparent no one was alive. The whole of their fishing village had been wiped off the map, so to speak. They were the only survivors. Houses and shops had been levelled. Against the odds. Perhaps it was because they had become alerted to the disaster.

Morace found a horse and cart to take him and his sister to their brother in the mountains. It would take two weeks to travel to Darth, the city in which their elder brother lived. Morace had travelled there once or twice with Pa to sell their fish in the markets for a handsome profit. Those journeys had been filled with laughter and drinking - but not this one. Communication between Morace and Lorett had become quiet and abrupt. Morace knew that Lorett had taken this hard; she had been close to Mama.

They took the straight path through the woods of Stern; Morace hoped that they would find some game to catch. He knew that somewhere in the woods there was a pool of water he could fish in. Being the son of a fisherman, he could catch relatively well.

On the second day, he found the little pool. As he cast out his makeshift rod, he felt a stabbing pain in his heart. They had been due to travel to this lake not four weeks away from now, with his Pa.

After he cast out the rod four more times, Morace had to stop. It was too much for him, and he knew that in a couple of days they would reach an inn up the road.

***

Morace drew in the horse and cart at the stables of an inn they always stayed in on the way north. It had been four days since his fishing attempt, and they were both weary. They needed beds to sleep in and food to fill the emptiness in their bellies. Morace was relieved that Lorett lay asleep; at least she was not worrying about what might happen to them - as he was.

'Wake up. Lorett, it's time for a proper bed.'

Lorett gave her brother a weak but reassuring smile. She had forgiven him for being so abrupt. She had realised that Morace had done what he needed to save her.

'We will get a good meal here. We always do. Tavener always gives us his best steak,' said Morace.

'Yes, I am hungry. Let's go eat,' announced Lorett. She jumped off the cart, her slender form wrapped up in the long coat she favoured. Morace followed closely.

The smell of freshly cooked meals in the air led their noses. There had been little that they had been able to salvage in the way of food when they left their homestead. The tornadic waterspouts took away everything.

They entered the inn.

The tavern part of the inn had around a dozen tables. Only one had patrons sat to eat. The long bar had a few standing drinkers too. It was not that busy. Morace did not mind, seeing as he did not want much attention. It did still seem strange that there were only a small number of people. *Perhaps they have left due to the storms.*

As the twins entered, for a moment it seemed everyone looked up to see who had arrived. All noise disappeared in a vacuum of soundless judgement. There were people in the inn that recognised the two. They knew they were from the village south from here. They started to talk among themselves and a sudden commotion from the bar diverted their attention. It was Tavener Doc, the owner of the inn.

Tavener Doc studied the two who had just entered, his mouth hung open and trembled god praises.

'Great tankards! You're alive.' He was surprisingly agile for a man of his size. He rushed forwards to embrace them warmly. 'We thought any who dwelled in the village would be dead, yet here you are alive and well. I say you must be starvin'! Come into my private room. I will get Dacy to rustle you up some steak.'

'Thanks, Tavener. We knew we would be welcome.'

'Of course. I will sit with you in a minute, so you can get settled down.'

They sat in front of a huge fire to dry off. Its warmth touched every corner of the room. A maid gave them fresh clothes; being a hunting inn, they were brown leather suitable for tracking.

Hunting trophies hung around the fireplace. Tavener was a hunter through and through. The steak they ate was one of his latest kills - a great bear known as a Urak. It was quite a special kill if you managed to survive it, according to Dacy, who told them with pride for her master. Now the Urak's head rested above the dark mahogany surround.

'Enjoying your meal, I see,' said the innkeeper, who easily exceeded seven foot and more than likely sized the same as the Urak.

'Yes, thanks,' they both said in unison.

'I nearly lost my arm to her maw, but I was too smart for her.' Tavener attempted to make small talk to put them all at ease.

Suddenly, Lorett threw herself into the big man's arms. She hugged him tightly. Tears flooded from her eyes onto Tavener's tunic. As children, they used to come up to the inn and Tavener told them stories. Lorett had always been taken by them. The stories about her Pa had made her laugh. They were close.

Even though he was the size of a bear and she so small in comparison, it always amused Tavener that she was never scared of him. Every time they met, she would embrace him. Now she needed it more than ever.

'Hey, lass, it's okay. You're safe. Tell me, what happened down in the village?'

'It was horri...' she began to say, and then sobbed unable to continue. 'Everyone is dead,' she managed to get out.

'It was just like Dragonsreach, but this time it was even stranger, Tavener,' Morace said, sullen and tired.

Morace told Tavener everything.

Tavener gave them a room in a quieter part of the inn. It was a twin bed room so that Morace and Lorett could be together, just in case something happened during the night. The patrons received strict orders not to go making noise in the corridor where the twins slept peacefully and hopefully away from horrid dreams. No one dared to test Tavener's orders; they had been told that if they were caught they would face a night out in the wild. These parts of the woods were home to some frightful creatures much worse than the Urak. One of them, said to be Tavener himself.

Tavener shifted around as he gathered the things he would need for the journey. He could tell that Morace intended to leave his sister with his brother in Darth, but that would be wrong. Knowing that he and his sister were close, it would be unwise for them to separate. Tavener did not want them to fend for themselves. The image of them standing at the door haggard and near starvation was still strong in his mind. Tavener decided that he would accompany them to make sure they were safe.

Happy that he had all the stuff they would need for the journey, Tavener blew out the candle and settled for sleep.

Morace slept late into the morning. The autumn sun peeked through the curtains and light fell on his shut eyes. Opening his eyes slowly so that he did not become blinded, he looked around the room. His heart dropped. It had not been a dream. He had not woken at home, in his own bed.

He looked at his twin in the other bed sleeping peacefully, and brushed her hair away from her eyes. He smelt the remnants of breakfast wafting up the corridor, so he took to the kitchen once he had dressed.

As he wandered into the kitchen, he was greeted by the big form of Tavener who ushered him to sit down and gave him a plate of porridge. It was so thick that you could cut it with a knife. Tavener sat down with Morace, to eat his own probably fourth bowl of porridge. There was a silence between them.

'You have not told her yet, have you?' Tavener spoke first.

'What? Told who? What do you mean?' Morace looked taken aback.

'I mean that you are going to find out what is happening and you are to leave your sister behind with your brother.'

How did he know? Was it written on my face that plainly?

'Yes, and what of it?'

'Don't get snippy with me, boy. I have seen you grow up and Lorett too. There is be a bond between you that goes deeper than just being twins. You may not see it yet, but it's there.'

'What do you know? I need to keep her safe. Pa left it for me to...'

Tavener smiled. 'I know your Pa and he would have said that... but I have seen it. You and your sister need each other.' He looked out of the window. 'Do you remember when you were ten? You were in the woods on your own. You had fallen in the well?'

'Yes, and you found me? What of it?'

'Well, I did not know you had fallen. I was told, by your sister. She sensed something was wrong and she came to me welling up with worry.'

'I don't remember being told this. I just remember making loads of noise.'

'I remember the look on her face. She felt something when you were in trouble, and came darting to me to help you.'

'You mean?' Morace sighed. 'I can't. I have to protect her, and she must stay with my brother where it is safe.'

'And what if "safe" is with you? More harm can come from worry of the unknown and feeling the way she can, because she can feel you. Feeling the way she can, might be her own ruin. Then what? Is that keeping her safe?' Tavener gave him an earnest look. 'She has something in her that you may need. It's no good you needing it and her being a thousand leagues away.'

Morace looked at him hard trying to decipher any hidden meaning behind the words. He found none.

'There must be a reason why you two are the only survivors,' Tavener added.

'Do you know something? If so, what can you tell me?' he asked.

'Morace?' A voice came from behind. It was his sister's. 'There you are. I was worried when I woke to find you missing.'

'See, boy? Listen to what I said. Morning, Lorett. Sleep well, did you?'

Lorett hugged him and sat to her own plate of porridge.

'Just how I remember.' She smiled wearily. 'When do we leave for the north?'

'I don't know but it would be good to have two horses. The cart is too slow and we don't have much stuff to carry anyway.' Morace said. It hurt to say it, but it was the truth. 'We would be quicker if we rode on horses.' He turned to Tavener. 'Is that something you could help with?'

'Well, we would need three if I am coming with you,' Tavener remarked.

They both looked at him surprised and speechless.

'You can't come with us,' Morace said forcibly.

'Why not? This situation seems bad, and it's coming up the continent. We need to act fast and find out what it is. Besides, you are fisher children – not exactly trained in land hunting. You need all the help you can get.'

'Well, I welcome your company, Tavener.' Lorett shot a look at her brother, aghast at him. 'Even if my brother does not show it, I am sure he is grateful, too.'

'Ah, your brother is just burning from the conversation we had.'

'What conversation?' she asked.

'It's nothing. We just had a difference of opinion on something. Tavener, it would be great if you joined us, thank you.' Morace smiled weakly.

'That's settled then. I will ready the horses.'

Lorett shot her brother a look of confusion at the unspoken words she knew existed, and wondered what the issue between the two was.

Chapter 3

'No, you are doing it wrong. How do you ever expect to sit at the Everglade Council if you can't get it right?' Sellacia spoke ferociously at his pupil.

'I am not doing it wrong. I am improving it; it will be much better once I rid this incant of its dullness.'

'It's dullness? That sort of talk will get you blacklisted from the council. Then what will you do? You will be nothing and stripped of your magic,' said Sellacia, a stern, stone-faced elven mage with a long crooked nose and old eyes. He held a graceful elegance that came from being an elder housed under the Tree of Wisdom. His white ivory robes glided over the floor. He positioned himself in front of the impetuous young elf. He was getting ready to lecture the youth yet again.

'A mage who gets bored is a dangerous mage and is one that gets watched.'

'I know, I have heard this time and time again. We learn this in pre-mage.'

'But it is something I seem to have to repeat on a regular basis.' The old elf's hands dropped onto the desk where his pupil sat, making the papers jump with the impact.

The sundial shone on mid-day, which meant that it was the end of class for the day. The student closed his books and began to make his way to the door; with Sellacia still stood at the desk. His face softened a little.

'Lazon, you have gifts that any mage would envy. Use them wisely, and don't cause mischief.'

Lazon bowed, turned to the door and walked with a pace that could burn lines in the floor. He took his usual route to the Arcanedia to find his friend.

The Arcanedia was the hall where all the mages flocked to make a start on their private studies.

He came to the giant hall. It could easily hold over one thousand people. Its curved ceiling had mosaics depicting scenes from the Arcanedia's long and illustrious history. The ceiling was held up with pillars of obsidian and lit with arcfire. He scanned the room and saw that she was sat in their usual place.

'Shanrea, I am here! Old Sellacia was giving me a lecture on getting bored again and trying to improve the stupid incant he got me to perfect.'

Shanrea wore her academic robes having just come from class. Her long brown hair was braided like all the elven girls who studied at the university. It covered the points of her ears just slightly. Her face was sun browned, as she had recently been out to the country where the weather was hot and humid. Lazon had not seen her for nearly a month. He had been busy while she was away; working on something so huge, he burst to show her.

She stared at him with furious eyes. 'Lazon, you need to be careful! It is dangerous to meddle. You are still young and...'

'Careful, Shan, you are going to start sounding like Sellacia. Besides, I have something to show you today. I have been working on a little project.'

'What? Where? When did you have the time?' She sounded shocked and displeased. At the same time, she was eager to find out more.

'Hush, and follow me.'

They left the Arcanedia and he took her to an unknown part of the university.

'Where are we going?'

'It's not far now.'

He paused at a door and told her to wait for him to come back. When he returned a few moments later, he had a grin on his face.

'Ok, I think you are going to like this.' He took her hand to lead her through the door and she felt a chill overcome her body. Was it wind?

'Lazon, what...'

'Shush, I need to focus.'

'Focus on what?' Then she saw it. Her mouth hung open. 'Lazon, what have you done? Is this...?' Her brows turned to a frown.

'Yes, yes it is. It is the first Weather Working in nearly one thousand years! I have managed it.'

Before them was a storm; thick black clouds contained within a glass structure. Tornadic waterspouts created from nothing bashed against the glass.

'Is it not beautiful?' Lazon said.

'This is foolish, it's dangerous, too. You don't know what effect this will have.'

'Relax. It is contained.' He tried to reassure her, but she was not convinced.

'Weather Working is banned, and for good reasons.'

He looked aghast at Shanrea. She was meant to support him, not have doubt.

'Stop it now and never do it again," she insisted.

'I won't. I have been practicing this for nearly a year, and it will stay until I can get the information I need.'

'Well, have you taken into account the fact that last time the Weather Working affected not only our world but the other world too? What about that?'

Lazon gave her a look that scared and shocked her. He looked different... he looked obsessed.

'Get out!' he yelled furiously. He shot his head in her direction.

Shanrea saw something unrecognisable in his eyes. She fought to hold back tears for her friend.

'This will work. You will see, and then I will be known as the greatest mage to ever walk.' He continued to shout.

Shanrea slammed the door behind her. For a moment she could not move. Frozen, she stood with her hand on her heart fighting the pain that was forming there for her dearest friend.

The fool. What was he thinking? He is going to cause mayhem with this. I need to tell someone.

She knew where she should go, but instead she went to the one person she trusted; she went to her father. She had known Lazon since childhood, and she knew he became bored easily, but to actually attempt Weather Magic was insanity. He needed to be stopped. He needed to see the error in his ways. She picked up the pace and navigated her way back to the Arcanedia in search of her father.

She had to ask one of the stewards where he was. The steward, dressed in green robes, informed her that the council had been summoned and her father was in the meeting.

A council meeting this early in the day? Oh no! They must already know something is wrong.

She sped to the council meeting, met with little resistance, until she reached the huge carved out mahogany doors. They were etched with pictures depicting the opening of the council some thousand years ago.

The council had been formed then because of the first Weather Working scandal. It was their duty to ensure the same thing never happened again. For an entire year, Lazon had been working on his project.

They have failed to notice in all that time?

'Sorry, Miss, council business only,' one of the guards said. She knew him.

-21-

'This is council business, I think.' She was uncertain. She shook her head. This was too important though, and the council needed to know. 'Could you at least fetch my father, so I can speak to him?' She spoke with a determination the guards could not ignore. 'Please, I would not be here if I did not think it to be urgent.'

'Wait here. I will fetch your father, if he can be spared.'

The Steward on duty knocked loudly on the door. With permission granted for him to enter, he slipped through the doors into the room. It was ten minutes before he returned with her father. His face looked like thunder.

Grabbing his daughter by the arm, he pulled her into a dimly lit side room. He was not pleased.

'We are dealing with matters of high importance, Shanrea. What is it that you have to speak to me about that means I must leave my duties to tend to you?'

'It's Lazon, father,' she began.

Her father looked at her questioningly expecting more.

'I fear he has done something stupid and reckless. I did not know where to go, so I came to you.'

Her father sat down. 'Go on, what has he done? I think I might already know, but go on.' Her father had not much patience at this time.

'He has done a Working of the Weather; he has created a storm here in the university.'

'Then it is as I feared. There is a reason why Weather Magic was banned. It does not just affect our own world, but the world in which we coincide with. That world is not equipped to deal with that sort of magic. Where is he? Tell me.'

'He is in an isolated part of the university. I did not know it existed and...' She then realised that her father knew something was wrong before she had even said it. That was the reason why the council had been called. 'What has he done to the other world?'

'He has not done anything intentionally, but his ignorance has cost many lives. The treaty the council signed with Kaarth may be in ruin.' He looked hard and saddened. 'I am sorry. I know he is your friend, but I must ask that you step away from him and let the council deal with this situation.'

'Father, no, you mean?' She sat down unable to stand with the weight of what was on her shoulders. 'Will he get stupefied? Please father, tell me the truth.' Shanrea's eyes pleaded with him to say no.

She knew though, that if you committed a crime that showed a complete lack of integrity or decorum, you were stupefied to prevent the same from happening again. It was a horrific ritual. One that cut the soles of your feet and the palms of your hands, to drain you of all the magic you possessed. It was said the more powerful you were, the more pain you would be in when the ceremony took place.

'It may be even worse than that. I must go to speak with the council. They need to know. We will find him. Go home now.' He moved to the door but turned to look at his tearful daughter. 'Shanrea, don't do anything stupid. Please go home.' He left.

She was faced with a split-second decision. She left the small room and watched her father go back into the council hall. She ran, not to her home, but back to where Lazon was tempting his fate.

When she reached the room, she frantically searched for Lazon. When she could not see him straight away, she became worried. Once she found him, her eyes widened. Something was wrong... he was clearly panicked trying to contain the storm. It had grown so much. It looked as though it was trying to escape.

He had lost control.

The glass container suddenly shattered, sending glass in all directions. A shard cut Shanrea's cheek. It was not deep, but the storm's chilly winds made it sting. Blood started to drip from the wound. Over the roar of the wind, she tried to get Lazon's attention.

'Lazon!' she screamed. 'What's happening?'

Lazon turned to face her. Blood streamed out of his nose and mouth.

'Lazon, can you stop it?'

'I don't know. I think it's too late. I should have listened to you. I am sorry.'

A tornadic waterspout lashed out and sent him flying to the floor.

'I can't control it!' he yelled. 'Get out. I don't want you in here. If you die I would never forgive myself.'

Shanrea remained where she was. Her blood trickled down her face. With her mind, she focused.

What is this?

Shanrea could sense something within the storm. *A weak spot?* Something then surged through her and into the weak spot of the storm. Glass bottles that rested on the shelves fell to the floor as the room shook with the power she poured into the storm, an attempt to weaken the magic.

'Shan, what are you doing?'

'Shut up, I am concentrating.' Her focus returned to the storm but she began to fail.

Lazon suddenly felt the storm's weakness too. With a snap of his hand, he conjured some unmaking magic to pour into the rupture of the working. Together, the two young mages focused their efforts on the storm, their combined efforts weakening it quicker. After a few minutes of hard power aimed at the storm, it dissipated. It remained silent for a moment.

The Council burst through the door. Shanrea fell to the ground exhausted.

Chapter 4

Shanrea awoke with a pulsating headache. She tried to sit up, but every bone in her body ached. She felt broken inside. Her memory was a little hazy; she could not quite remember what had happened. Only fragments came back to her. Her eyesight adjusted slowly to the low arclight of the room.

Suddenly she flashed back. The whole scene came clear and she was in the room again fighting the storm. She screamed. A pother rushed in, closely followed by her father. He looked worried.

Dace tried hard to hide his distress. 'Why did you have to go back?' He perched himself at the end of her bed. He looked with sorrow at his broken daughter. With hard determination, he held back tears that threatened to reveal the depth of his sadness. He was not upset at the fact she went back to her friend, but now she looked like an accomplice in the most crucial of crimes, and a hearing would have to take place. He would have to be a witness and he would not be able to protect her.

She struggled to answer. 'I could not let him face it on his own. It's a good job I did go back, otherwise the storm would have gotten out of control. I was able to sense its power and its weakness. I stopped it.' Her eyes were beginning to fill with tears. 'Father, what will happen to Lazon?'

'I am more concerned about what will happen to you. You are now also tarred with this indiscretion. To the eyes of the council, you are as guilty as Lazon. You were both caught in the act as it were.'

She began to shake uncontrollably; fear struck her hard and fast. 'What? But I tried to help. I only found out what he had been doing that afternoon; he showed me for the first time. I was mortified.' She was using all her effort to fight the accusation against her.

'There is no need to claim your innocence to me. I know you would not be so foolish.' He looked at his daughter hard in the eyes. 'The council, however, is not so inclined to believe you have no part in this. You should have listened to me when I said to go home.' He sighed, then gently kissed his daughter on the forehead as he got up to leave. At the door, he was met with someone he would rather have avoided. He closed the door behind him not wanting his daughter to hear the conversation.

'That was quite a little story she spun you there.' The words were spoken by Gragio, the right hand of the council and its Justice Minister. He was a cruel man, one you would regret ever crossing. He had long black robes with the insignia of the home guard wrapped around his shoulders. With long, braided black hair, his presence was imposing and intimidating. He used his presence to great effect. Shanrea's father, however, was a strong elf himself, who was seldom intimidated by anyone. He was reputed to use great ruthlessness to get to the truth. Gragio though, knew ways of information extraction that would be considered inhumane.

'You cannot bully me, Gragio. I know my daughter is innocent. She rushed to us to let us know what she had found out, despite Lazon being her friend.' Standing strong, he looked into Gragio's dark eyes. They were cold and showed malice.

'Well, I will be the judge of that, Dace, won't I? I will have to question her, of course, to make sure she is not lying.' His words rang with a joy that stung - and Gragio knew it. He would enjoy making the girl suffer, just to get at her father. 'I have the full extent of the law at my disposal and you know what that means.' He almost licked his lips but stopped before he showed too much satisfaction.

'What do you want, Gragio? Or have you just come here to watch me squirm for my daughter? I shan't give you such satisfaction.'

He walked briskly down the corridor away from his enemy. He was worried for his daughter. If only she had listened to him in the first place, none of this would have happened.

Repeatedly he had told her that Lazon was too troublesome and he would lead her into trouble. Now she was in the most trouble any elf could be in. Dace pondered at what he could do to help his daughter. He was too emotional to concentrate. It was hopeless. Well, the only thing he could think of was an appeal to the king, but that would be difficult, especially for him, considering the nature of the crime his daughter was charged with.

A thought suddenly came to him. It was dangerous, but it might be his only option. If he went to the king, he would be laughed at and scorned. Instead, he would have to help Shanrea escape from here, but first he needed to attend a council meeting. His daughter was far too weak to try anything like that. She would need to get her strength back first.

Lazon sat isolated in the depths of jail, pondering on what had occurred. His hands were bound by cuffs infused with magic to prevent the use of his own. He was tired and hungry. He was not permitted to speak to Shanrea. She was in bed under house arrest.

Did that mean that she was also considered a criminal?

The thought chilled him to the bone. He did not think he would be able to live with himself if anything happened to her.

'Damn. Why did the old man Sell have to be right?' He played the event in his mind over and over, wondering when his trial would be.

If only I could see Shan. Her presence would help.

He looked up at the sound of a click on the door. It was time to face his punishment. Although, anything done to him would be nothing compared to the mental punishment he would endure if the same happened to Shan.

Inside the council chamber, Dace could feel the eyes of the council member's burn with intent. They were all elves of the highest order. All the eyes were judgmental of his current situation. Even though it would be his daughter in the trial hall, he would equally be on trial as her father. He would not see the last of this himself. He may even be ejected from the council for his daughter's transgressions.

In the exact centre was the accusation cage, forged from obsidian. Lazon was chained inside. Shanrea would have been too, had she been strong enough.

The chamber itself was a large circular room decorated with paintings of previous First Ministers of the Elven high council. When one left the office, their image would be added. So far the chamber had seen seventeen different elves in the chair. The one who occupied it now was an elf named Essle Diaane.

Essle Diaane had succeeded his father. His ancestry was known to sit in the chair. He was young, only in his thirties, and had occupied the chair for a mere few months. He wore ivory robes with gold stripes down the side, which signalled his power in office. His seat was a little higher than everyone else's was. With his arms folded, and his stony face giving no emotion, he too looked at Dace, studying him.

'Please, all be seated and we will begin,' Essle Diaane said standing up. He brought forward the first order of business. 'The weather has been disturbed in the other world. It has gotten out of control and I fear it may be too late to stop it.'

Muttering ensued and accusation flared. Dace could feel the allegations towards his daughter; people had already made up their minds. There might be nothing he could do.

'Order, elves! We shall not have accusations flying in my chamber, not when all the facts have not been accounted for.' At least Essle was a just elf, and would not condemn anyone before they had a chance to speak, despite what the evidence may suggest. 'What's more, we need solutions not–'

'What we need, Essle Diaane, is the people who have caused this brought to justice.' The elf who gave the outcry always spoke out in these meetings, particularly in favour for the Justice Minister. No doubt, they had words about this prior to this meeting.

'While I am speaking, you will not speak. Otherwise, I will have you removed from the chambers. Is that understood?'

Sitting back down, the Elf swallowed his thoughts and remained silent.

'We need to find a way to help our neighbouring world. Does anyone have any suggestions?'

No one answered. No one had faced anything like this before so they could not even fathom an idea.

'What do the histories say to this? The weather was once bad for them. We meddled with it before, and in our ignorance we were almost too late in finding out that it had consequences for our neighbours,' Essle Diaane said. The words stung but they were true. Their ignorance nearly cost a whole world of people. It was something the elves had worked hard at to rectify.

'I think we first need to send ambassadors to Kaarth and let them know we are there to help them.' The suggestion made by a tall and elegant elf called Sal Fain who normally spoke wise words. 'We also need to feel the earth and see exactly what the extent of the damage is.' He looked at the council, then to Essle Diaane, 'I will take lead on this. I know of Kaarth's history.'

'Very well Sal Fain, I will select the people you will take, I will have to ponder on this of course.'

Sal Fain inclined his head in respect. He gathered his robes and sat back down.

'If we are going to the other world, we need to inform them that those who have brought this destruction have been caught, and are facing the extent of our laws,' another elf pointed out; another one of Gragio's followers.

'Of course we will tell them that, but we cannot act in hast. There are sketchy details that need to be addressed. I will be leading the investigation.'

'What?' This outcry came from Gragio almost in disgust. Heads turned to the Justice Minister, who was usually reserved and not one to shout out. 'Surely you mean that I will be investigating this travesty? Seeing as I am the Justice Minister.' Gragio did not just stand up, he moved to the desk to air his protest. As he did, he slammed his hands in front of the First Minister.

'Sit back down, Gragio.'

Staying where he was, Gragio exhibited his disapproval at the announcement. 'I will not sit down while you make stupid decisions. I was appointed this position by your father for a reason. If you are to not use me in situations like these then what use am I?'

'I will not have this conversation here, Gragio. If you have concerns about my decisions you know where to air them, but I should warn you I have already spoken to the king on this matter, and he has granted me his acceptance on it.' He raised an eyebrow daring Gragio to challenge him. 'And I am not my father. Whatever reasons he had to have you in the council are not needed here. This brings me to my second item today, Gragio: your removal from office.'

Dace's heart almost leapt from his chest at the news. It meant his daughter was saved from certain torture at the hand of Gragio.

The whole Chamber was in an uproar with this announcement, and Gragio looked mortified. This was not meant to happen. He was about to protest yet again but Essle stopped him by raising his hand.

'I would not bother protesting; again, I have the king's full backing.' He requested the guards to remove Gragio from the council chambers and they followed the orders given. 'Now where were we?' The other council elves were still a little shocked, and confused. 'You are all probably after the reason why Gragio has been removed? Well, my next item will shed some light.

'When a Justice Minister is appointed to tackle problems such as we are facing, would it not be more fitting to also look at why it took nearly a year to find the issue?' The other ministers looked at the First Minister and suddenly realised what he meant. 'And the only reason we know the cause and place of this travesty, was because of our new Justice Minister's daughter, who, by the way, is what I would call a hero.'

It took a few moments for this news to sink in before realisation set in around the chamber.

'I am sorry... did you just appoint me Justice Minister?' Dace asked, shocked and confused.

'That is what I said. Your daughter, despite knowing that she would be tarnished as Lazon's accomplice, went to stop him. She found a way to stop the storm. I also think there is something more she can do, which is why she will be accompanying Sal Fain to Kaarth.' He turned to the council in the chamber.

Lazon listened quietly, waiting to hear what was going to happen to him. He was happy that Shanrea had been called a hero and would not be tarnished in this whole situation.

'I have decided that Lazon will also go to Kaarth, so that he can learn for himself the reason why we don't dabble in Weather Workings any more. I think that is all that is needed to be said. I will open the floor to questions.'

Lazon looked at the First Minister then to Shanrea's father. Dace was relieved that his daughter's life was safe. Lazon's mind then wandered over to his own position as the cage was lowered and his chains removed. Free.

How did this happen? Surely, I was to lose my power. That is what should have happened.

Naturally, there were many questions and debates to be had, but if there was to be a change in the decision, it would not come soon. There would be a little time before the ambassadors were due to embark on their journey, for Shanrea needed to make a full recovery first. The pother said that it could take a few days for her to regain her full strength. In the meantime, Dace was required to meet with the First Minister in his private study to discuss matters of great importance.

Chapter 5

'Replace me? I will show them what happens if they replace me. Now all my work has been for nothing.' A bitter Gragio paced the length of his office in his home in the country. He had travelled there to get some space and collect on his thoughts. For years, he had been working his way into the council. He had finally managed to convince Essle's father that he needed him. His plan to become the First Minister had taken a leap forward. He was being recognised as a great mage both within the council and outside of it, but now...now his name would be smeared with this forceful removal.

A knock on the door stopped him in his paces. He slammed his hands on the table.

'I told you I was not to be disturbed,' he yelled to the door.

'S-Sir...' His servant stuttered. 'He was quite insistent he speak to you now.'

'I did not have to enter this way, Lord Lengan, but I thought it would be more pleasing than just appearing to you.' The voice was cold; it sent a chill down Gragio's spine. He knew who, or a better word what, this was.

'Ok, let him in.'

The servant returned to his duties. He hated to admit it but he was a little scared for his master.

The figure stood by the window. Gragio looked at it with intense, fearful eyes. It seemed as though parts of this creature were there and others were not; they looked to be held together by shadow. The figure wore a cloak as dark as the night sky. Its green eyes were the things that let you know it could see. It inclined its head to the only chair in the room.

'Sit down,' it said. Gragio had no choice but to do so. You did whatever an Agent of the Shadows told you. That one was here meant either his imminent death or they wanted him for something. 'We would like to enlist your services within the shadows, Lord Lengan.' It skirted around the dimness of the office. The shadow in the room seemed to get even larger so its form could use more of the space. It seemed to Gragio as though the Shadow Agent was marking its territory with each glided movement.

Soon enough the whole room was smothered with a thick foreboding darkness. The room was now set for the creature to begin its enlisting of the elf that sat before him. Gragio trembled a little, intimidated by the presence. If he did not please the shadows now, he would die. He knew his life depended on what happened next.

'How can I help the Shadow Empress?' Gragio asked.

The thing shot its head at the elf. It hissed at him as though he should not have spoken. 'The world is changing. All of the worlds are. Times must change. With change, there is only room for one world. The worlds must meet in the middle. Whoever is the strongest at the end, will have power over the rest. You like power?' The agent waited for what seemed an impossible amount of time for an answer. Time froze on the last word.

It rang through the ears of the elf. The Empress wanted him for her bidding. The agent's words made his mind work overtime.

Power was a word the former Justice Minister was moved by. He craved power as a beast craves meat. It fed him, nourishing his body to the extent of bursting. This Shadow Agent knew the words to use to make Gragio hungry. Images of him on top of everything fed his hunger for more.

Power, I need power.

The Shadow Agent licked his lips. The elf was now blind to his will. To make this man a pawn to use in the Empress's business would be easy. The enticement had begun with the show of power he had exhibited at the start. People like this elf were all the same; easy to manipulate for the Mistress's will. Too easy.

'Power.' The elf's head peeked up, nodding with agreement before anything had been said. 'Power would be granted to those who help the Shadows gain their rightful place in the new world. That is something you crave, right?' The agent dangled an imaginary carrot in front of the elven fool. 'Or has my Mistress chosen unwisely?'

Gragio fell forward off his chair as the carrot fell from his mind. The shadows in the room began to recoil threatening to disappear as soon as the last word left its lips. Gragio clung to them. 'No, your mistress has not chosen unwisely. I am the one for this. I can help. I want power. Please. Give it to me.' The elf on the floor in front of the agent grovelled. He did not realise that if others saw him now they would simply see a weak pathetic elf praying to the shadows.

The agent knew he had accomplished what he needed. He let the shadows fall once again round the whole room, this time enveloping the elven pawn.

'Good,' the agent hissed. 'We need more like you, willing to embrace the Empress.'

A shiver ran down Gragio's spine. A question worked its way out of his mouth. 'So what must I do?'

'You will wait.'

Gragio's heart sank. *Have I not pleased you?*

'Wait for me to arrive again. The next time I won't come through the door.' With that, the Shadow Agent disappeared and the natural shadows returned.

Gragio sat back in his chair heaving. Then he vomited until all that remained was bile. He staggered to the cabinet where he stored his drinks and drank a bottle of brandy.

Whenever he shut his eyes, Gragio's dreams became consumed with shadows that he could not escape. A persistent nightmare kept coming back - a woman's voice and a scream that curdled his blood. He awoke four or five times during the night, becoming so disorientated that soon he was unable to tell whether the dreams were real or not.

-Travel- Kaarth- Highlands-Pool of Shadow's

Waking up in the morning with the autumn light on his face, he struggled to get up and out of his four-posted bed due to weariness. After much effort, he eventually forced himself to get dressed in the black robes he took to wearing when he was in office. He glanced at the empty bottle of brandy he had left of the table and held his head.

Must have been a booze-filled dream. Pool of Shadows... the whole thing seems like nonsense.

His servant had prepared breakfast but Gragio did not feel like eating anything. He was revolted by the idea, to the point where vomit reached the back of his throat again.

'I think I need some fresh air. No one is to disturb me. Understand?'

'Yes sir.'

The route he took brought him to the woods within the grounds of his estate. The bird song and the sounds of the brook running through the woods rang through his hungover head. He made his way to the weeping willow tree he did the majority of his thinking under. He thought hard about what he needed to do. He rubbed his eyes. It seemed as though they were playing tricks on him.

Slowly, the branches blackened as if they were plagued with tree rot. They swarmed around Gragio catching him at the wrists and ankles. He was bound to the tree, just like he had bound himself to the Shadows the night before. He heard a voice. A female voice.

'You should not dismiss the Empress, the Shadows have eyes, we come to you when everrrr.'

'What is happ...' One of the willow's long strands wrapped itself round Gragio's mouth before he could finish what he was going to say.

'Time is not for you to talk, my puppet. You agreed to do my bidding. You appear to have ignored my minion's message... So I must come to you directly which displeases me... go to Kaarth and to the Pool of Shadows... and do so swiftly. I do not wait for too long.'

With sudden swift motions, the tree's grasp released him. He fell to the ground hard. In pain, he picked himself up, his eyes fixed on the tree. Its leaves were still blighted. The tree fell to pieces before him. Real. Not some foolishness as he had originally thought.

'I am watching, Gragio; I have been here all this time. Do not make choosing you mean I have chosen poorly.'

That night Gragio packed everything he would need ready to go to Kaarth.

Chapter 6

A bitter coldness had chased Morace, Lorett and Tavener for over three days after they had left the inn. The cold had such a force that it killed all but one of their horses. They had been unprepared for the harshness of the snap. The only surviving horse was Tavener's own, as it was bred to withstand high levels of cold. Drido, strong willed like his owner, was a pure black beast with a size that would intimidate even the keenest of riders. Its strength surprised even Tavener at times. Tavener had this stallion since its birth, and Drido trusted him only.

They had yet to find anywhere to put up camp. Tavener looked at the snowy clouds. It soon would be deep into the night.

'It 'as never been this bad. It be by far teh worst I'ave ever encountered. What be most worrisome is all the game has scurried off into hiding. I'm finding it 'ard to hunt in this. There is nothing.' Tavener looked in the likely places where there should be even just a rabbit. There was nothing. 'It's like they felt the coming cold and just fled.'

Their situation was dire. All of the provisions they had taken with them were too frozen to eat. They would ruin if they tried to warm them up, and then would poison them if they tried to eat them.

Lorett had been given the first ride on Dridio as she was beginning to feel the effects of the lack of food. This was much to the horse's distress, but Tavener won that battle.

A pine forest materialised out of the snow and fog. Tavener recognised it instantly. He took out a map and realised that they had taken the wrong track. They had been heading into a place he had hoped to avoid. He studied the map to see if they could retrace their path. Tavener sighed. They could, but it would delay them. They needed to eat, too. It was too late now to change the direction. He decided to continue to at least the edge of the forest, so that it would provide adequate protection for the rest of the night. Lorett noticed Tavener's distress. He spoke to answer the question she was about to ask, almost as though he was reading her mind.

'This is the Magjani forest, so be wary. Stories talk of timber pine trolls within its depths. We shall stay on the outskirts, no fire at all.'

Lorett looked at her brother. She missed the warmth and felt as though the wind cut through her every time it breezed. It felt like it was alive. It was too intense. She welcomed the shelter of the forest, but the idea of these trolls frightened her. She could sense something with the wind, as though they were being watched. There was something Tavener was not telling them.

'Tavener, what's wrong? There is something on your face giving you away.' She could always do that. She could look at someone's face and know if they had just lied or hidden something, no matter how well they concealed it.

'This is not teh route I intended to take; this forest is nothing but bad news.' There was no point trying to hide it. She would weed out the truth in the end. 'Look, we must keep on and rest. I am wanting to get to the plains before the end of the next day.'

They continued. Lorett grew even more uneasy with the winds passing. It felt as though they had eyes.

They made it to the edge of the woods by the end of the day. Tavener had to call a halt. The snow had picked up and he could not see the way. Even Lorett had trouble finding a way.

Morace could not sleep. His thoughts raced. He had become a secluded figure through the whole journey. He was thinking on too many things at once. Things that he could not change but wished he could. Hindsight was playing like a bitch, making him dwell on the things he should have done instead. What the hardest thing for him to bear was in the mere hours he had been charged with the protection of his family, he had lost three of them.

I should have woken them up. I should not have left the house to investigate.

Unconsciously, he was kicking the dirt under his foot in his frustration. A twig snapped making his eyes look up suddenly.

'Morace?' The silence was broken, his thoughts turned onto the voice of his sister.

'Lorett, why are you awake? You need to sleep.' He could see her angry eyes.

'And you don't?' She held his hand. 'Why are you beating yourself up over the past? I know it is hard, but it was not your fault.'

'It was Lorett, It bleddy well was my fault. I failed Pa...' He let her rest her head on his shoulder, and sighed. 'I failed Mama and our sisters, and for what? I said I would look for the cause of this weather, didn't I? I bet I won't. I should have just stayed at the inn...'

Lorett's head picked up. The back of her neck prickled with a sense that something was not right. 'Something is watching us. I felt it earlier in the wind and it is here again,' she said.

Morace stood up withdrawing the knife Tavener had given him.

'I don't think that will cut it,' Lorett suggested. 'Besides, it is just watching. I don't think it will harm us.' Lorett smiled and kissed him on the forehead. 'Brother, go to sleep. You need rest.'

Suddenly without warning, both were lifted into the air. Morace dropped to the ground hard. Lorett was caught by whatever it was, and placed on a fallen log. Morace got up stiffly, brushed the needles off and searched for his sister. He found her on the fallen log some ten feet away.

'What was that?' he called out to her.

'I don't know, but I don't want to find–'

A roar bellowed from the trees. In a swift but cumbersome motion, a large, snowy, wood-like creature appeared in front of them.

'Troll!' Tavener was awake and up. He put himself in front of the troll. It dwarfed even him. He pulled out his crossbow and began cranking it. It took too long almost. Eventually it fired. It hit the troll in its barky chest, but the creature shrugged it off, unaffected. Tossing the crossbow aside, he drew his great sword. Tavener ducked and dived, chunks of bark from the troll's limbs fell off.

The troll caught him in the sternum, sending Tavener into a tree twenty feet away with such force it knocked him out. The troll turned and charged at Morace, catching him unaware. Morace flew into another tree.

Lorett, now alone, looked at the troll.

It had knocked her brother flying, but had caught her and placed her on the log. She was sure it had been the troll. Lorett looked at her two fallen companions. She trembled not with fear but with a sudden courage.

The troll paced around. It did not attack, but sniffed the air around Lorett. Lorett stood still looking at the creature. Why had it not attacked yet? *There must be a reason.*

The troll moved closer to her and she could make out the rough shape of its face. She saw what looked like a mouth. Sounds came out of it. She realised it was actually singing.

'What are you? Can you understand me?' She realised she did not speak these words but sung them instead. The troll bowed its head towards Lorett, and sung back.

'Siren, I am here. These men will not harm you any longer. No longer shall you be their captive'

'Captive? You think I be a captive? One of them is my brother, the other my friend'

The troll looked at the fallen men.

'You called me a Siren? They are long since gone if I remember the stories. I think you are mistaken.'

It shook its head no.

'Be mistaken? I am not, for you can sing the woodland song.'

Morace and Tavener came to their senses and regrouped. Tavener witnessed that what he had never seen but had heard stories about. Morace was horrified. He went forward to his sister only to be halted by Tavener. Tavener grabbed Morace by the shoulders to stop him grabbing his sword.

Morace rounded on him with fury in his eyes. 'That's my sister, we need to help her.' Morace struggled to free himself. He did not see or hear the forest around him. All he could think of was his sister's safety.

'Your sister is fine. Now listen, will you, to the trees and the air...'

Morace listened carefully not hearing anything at first. After a few moments, he heard the song. It was not words.

The trees rang with the sounds of the forest song. Morace's eyes widened as he heard his sister's voice bounce off the trees followed by the troll in answer. His body tingled with a warm sensation. His sister's voice was beautiful.

'Is she singing?'

His sister always had a great song voice, one that could enchant and cause any man to fall head over heels for her. Morace recalled a night that had gotten out of hand a couple years back.

They had gone out together, to the tavern in the other village. The village had a reputation for being rough, and drunken people roamed the streets every night. One heavily drunken man in the tavern had taken a liking to Lorett, but a dislike to Morace. Morace had left the room to relieve himself and the man had decided to make his move on Lorett.

'Heh Mishi, wanna leave this place and find a room?'

Lorett, about to object, was grabbed by the arm. Morace had returned just in time, and asked the man to leave her alone.

The man in turn had decided to take a swing at Morace, but before it landed Lorett held the man's face and looked into his eyes.

'I am sorry. I said I cannot go with you.' She smiled as she said the words. The man forgot his quarrel with Morace.

Morace remembered this incident completely, because he was certain that Lorett had a hint of a song to the words she spoke to the man. It was as if he had fallen under her spell.

'She is not just singing, Morace, she is talking with nature. Your sister is not a normal girl. Your sister is a Siren.'

'A Siren?'

'Please tell me you have heard of the Sirens, boy?'

He had not, but he felt now like he should have. 'No, it was always Lorett who was interested in learning about that stuff. I never really cared for it. The past is the past.'

'Well, let me tell you something about Sirens; don't anger them, they make bad enemies.'

The song went on for an hour. Morace and Tavener sat cross-legged in the pines to watch. The song between Lorett and the troll filled the air with its beauty. By the end of their song, four more trolls had arrived as well as other creatures of the forest that were even more unusual than the trolls. Some were tall and thin that looked like they could be trees. Ents, Tavener called them. A tear fell from the seven footer's eye.

At the end, the trees still swayed with the remnants of the song. The troll who had conversed with Lorett turned to leave through the hedgerows, followed by its kin. The ents pointed at Tavener and an understanding came to him, even though no verbal communication was made. Ents were said to give guidance and wisdom to those who came to pass them on their journeys, but that was said a long time ago, way before his time, even generations before. He had heard myths of the knowledge that ents would pass on.

Lorett sat on the fallen log. She buzzed with the song she sang with the troll.

I am a Siren, a creature of the forest... and my brother... he does not know what he is and I can't tell him until he is ready.

'We have to go,' she announced. 'We can go through the forest. The creatures won't harm us.'

Lorett led them through to the centre of the forest with a swift pace. Morace looked at his sister; her presence had changed. Morace could sense it.

Chapter 7

Towards the centre of the forest, the snow had not touched the floor. Lorett took them further in with every step. They had travelled for hours in this direction, but something kept them going and they felt no weariness at all. Lorett sang along the way and the birds in the trees tuned in the chorus. Tavener's sense of fear for the forest had disappeared. *A Siren is a powerful creature; their return to the world must mean something big is happening. To walk with one, even though it is the girl he had watched grow up, is something even more amazing.*

Morace noticed that Lorett's manner changed also. She stood tall and powerful. She had developed a grace of something majestic. However, he was concerned that they had not had a chance to speak since the encounter with the troll.

'Lorett, where are we heading? Are we nearly there yet?' The irony pinged him. She always used to ask that of Pa when they travelled somewhere secret. There was no response from his sister. Morace worried that she was on the way to becoming a different person with this new turn in their life.

They came upon a clearing in the forest. Lorett abruptly stopped, causing them to almost knock into each other. She looked into the exact centre of the clearing then started to sing another beautiful melody to the trees. Within the clearing, a floral display peaked up. A dance with petals created what looked like a mirror. Lorett let ripples flow from the touch of her finger. Its surface was not solid, but you could not see clearly through it. She then sat down cross-legged. To the others, it looked like she was waiting for something to happen.

Morace's stomach rumbled hungrily. He had not eaten for many hours and all the walking had made him thirsty, too. He did not know what the time was, but it must have gotten late into the evening. Watching his sister for movement, he saw nothing at all. It was as if she was meditating. Weariness bested him, so he lay down in the pines on the floor and slept.

'It will happen now. We need to act to save the worlds,' he said.

Two girls looked up at him for the courage.

'Will it hurt?'

'I do not know but I promise you this, when it is done, you will be able to grow into the women you wish to become.'

'It's time. We need to do this now.'

The two girls held hands. A spark ignited between them. The worlds seemed to spin. The girl that never aged and the girl that aged rapidly, to help the world grow, brought together by fate. The light shone brightly. The ground started to shake.

The three elves selected for the journey to Kaarth, stood waiting for the portal that would take them to Kaarth, to materialise. Lazon looked at Shanrea. They had had little chance to speak on what had happened, and was about to happen, Shanrea studied him too. The elf before her was a fragment of his former self. He had withdrawn since the incident that nearly cost them their lives.

Lazon had nightmares in the days that had passed. They had stayed in Sal Fain's house, so that he could teach them the ways of Kaarth. Frequently during the night Lazon would call out screaming that his body was on fire. Shanrea thought that it could be an effect of the Weather Magic.

Lazon had been forbidden to use it but his body craved to feel it again. In the year he had been using the taboo magic he had become addicted. He now suffered from withdrawal. He would not tell Shanrea what plagued his mind or how he felt. They used to be so close.

If it was not for Shanrea I would be dead. I could have destroyed everything.

He had to battle the surges of power that wanted to burst out and create the weather. It was tiring but he had to stay awake. This meant he got very little sleep.

'The portal is coming.' Sal Fain urged the two of them to stand up. The floor began to shake and Shanrea linked fingers with Lazon to feel safe. The Wayward mirror had been created by the dwarves thousands of years ago. They were the last relics that remained of the dwarves who had been wiped out by the dragon wars. Both Kaarth and the Everglade had once been plagued by dragons. The dwarves had been butchered by the dragons, who had then picked on their bones. That had been their undoing. The dwarves had learnt that the dragons were unable to be wiped out through normal means, so in their alchemy labs they devised a powerful poultice and drank it. This poultice corrupted the dwarve's blood turning them into a poison for the dragons. The dragon's numbers, after years of battle, were just as few as the dwarves were. Their greed had killed them all off. For when they had feasted on the bones of the dead dwarves, the corruption of the dragons started. Two great races perished.

The Wayward mirror now stood in front of them. Its water-like substance rippled with the touch of the wind. Its frame was crafted out of hard obsidian, pure dark purple, mined from the lava mines.

The elves were all wearing the expedition clothes of their race. Elven leathers were given to them by the quartermaster. They were each also equipped with hunting knives, just in case they came across unfriendly creatures. Sal Fain had forgone the leathers, deciding instead that since this was a humbling venture, he had dressed in his finery to demonstrate that he was someone with authority within the elven nation. He had been waiting for this moment; not the moment when the elven race had to go on their knees to the humans once again, but the chance to walk among the humans. He had studied them. He had become a bit of an expert in their ways, their culture, and habits.

'We have to time this right,' Sal Fain said.

Just as Lazon was about to form a question, a commotion outside the portal room gave him pause.

'Hold it.' There was no doubt. The Prince himself appeared. Lazon looked at the prince, stunned. He was not wearing his usual high order robes either, but traveller leathers. 'I will be accompanying you on this journey to Kaarth, seeing as our nation is the cause of this.' He looked at Lazon with intent. Lazon's heart pounded. Shanrea's hand squeezed his own to remind him that he was not alone. She was with him.

'Is this approved?' Sal Fain asked.

'Well, I am here, am I not, Lord Fain?' The prince shrugged the challenge off easily. 'We shall also have four elves from the Royal Legion accompanying us.' The Prince of the Elves, Horacio Wylennd stood tall to face the elves that were to accompany him. 'I have studied what happens when you step through the mirror; it shall take us to the other world where we will represent our people to the people of Kaarth, even though we come with bad tidings.' He looked at Lazon again. 'We are to hold ourselves with the dignity of the elves.' Horacio looked at Sal Fain. 'Is it time?'

Sal nodded yes. As he passed Shanrea, the prince acknowledged her with a nod. 'It pleases me that we are to be accompanied by the one true person here who would sacrifice herself, even knowing the consequences she might face. Our kingdom is in your debt.' He looked at Lazon and gave no word.

He stepped through the mirror, and with a light, he disappeared. Two of the guards followed. Sal Fain stepped through next.

Holding hands, Shanrea and Lazon went together. The third guard proceeded.

As the fourth guard started to follow, his eyes widened as his heart was stabbed by a long black blade. He fell to the floor, dead.

Gragio stepped from the shadows he had created with magic. He pulled out a glowing orb from within his black robes and touched it to the Wayward Mirror. As he stepped through, the Wayward Mirror shattered into fragments. Destroyed.

The mirror in the clearing glowed brightly, blinding those around it. Figures appeared, indistinguishable due to the brightness. Morace got up to watch, withdrawing the knife he had been handed. He was ready to fight if the need presented itself.

'Put that down, boy, otherwise you might hurt yourself,' Tavener said, as he looked at him from the corner of his eye. 'There will be no trouble here.'

'But...' Morace protested but in the end lost out. As he put the knife back in its hold, he saw the figures more clearly. They were elves.

Once all the elves had appeared through the portal, Lorett stood to greet them first. An elven man clad in light armour and a cloak knelt to her.

'Siren, may I ask your name?' he asked in his own tongue.

Lorett touched him on his forehead. 'My name is Lorett, and you are Prince of your people, you bring tidings of the elves?'

The Elven Prince spoke words Tavener and Morace now understood.

Lorett must have put magic on them, Morace thought.

'We do bring news. Also we hope to come in the aid of your world.' The prince looked at Lazon. *Nothing good will come of throwing him to this world and letting him be ripped apart by the wolves, as his father had suggested. I am not my father, I must show compassion.* 'I have brought seven companions with me. Is it far to the Citadel? I must speak with your leaders.'

Tavener spoke up. 'You say seven of you? I see only six.'

The elves looked around counting their numbers.

'He is right. Where is Breso? He was the last to come through the mirror.' Horacio looked at his followers. They could only speculate, which was not going to get them anywhere. 'We must press on Lorett, these men, are they with you?'

'Yes, they are. One is my brother and the other an old friend.'

'Dead?' Dace's hard eyes looked at the guard who gave him the news concerning one of the elves that had been given selected to be part of the group to Kaarth.

'Yes sir. There was not a person in sight. I found him not twenty minutes since the group left.'

Dace's eyes widened with fear...*his daughter.* 'There was only one body, you are sure?'

'I am.' The guard shifted uneasily. He knew he had to mention all the details. 'Sir, there is more.'

Dace grew impatient. He did not like waiting for information to be presented to him. The Elven Guard hesitated. He did not want to be shot as the messenger.

'Well, go on. Don't expect me to wait all day.'

'The guard on duty was found asleep,' he said. Dace's eyebrow raised waiting. 'We have him under arrest for sleeping on duty.'

'Good. I shall speak to him in the afternoon. Make sure he is secure.'

Dace had to make a report directly to the king. The conversation he had had with the Prime Minister before the party had left him with a sense of unease. He knew the prince had also expressed an intent to travel to the world ravaged by the weather. This was the reason Dace had been required to attend a secret council.

They had wanted to keep it quiet. They had wanted a quiet departure, so not even the three original members had been told until the very last minute. Dace was now worried that something may have befallen the group. He wanted to mount a second party into Kaarth, but the news that the gate had been destroyed caused that idea to dissolve as quickly as it came.

'We need to move on,' the Elven Prince protested as Lorett's attempt at resting became persuasive.

Lorett had felt different ever since the song with the troll. She did not want to become someone else from this experience, but it felt as though it might already be too late. She really wanted to speak to her brother, but did not know where to start. Time pressed fast, and knowing this also made her fret. This made it almost impossible to stop and speak with the one person she owed an explanation. She could sense her brother's worry, which he was right to, of course. He had just learned that his sister had become a creature of magic. *I must speak to him soon.*

'Yes, we need to press on, but at the moment we must rest and this, I fear... this will be the best place for it. I doubt we will get much chance later.' She looked at her brother. He nodded in understanding.

Tavener lit a fire since the forest now posed no threat to them. Lorett took her brother to one side, down a little path to a stream. She explained what was going on, apologised for not speaking, promised she would not be completely changed, and hugged him tightly.

She told him that it was the elves who had triggered the wild weather. They had come to help solve the issue, but first they must present themselves to the land's ruler out of courtesy.

His sister's, the Siren's role in this was uncertain, but one thing was for sure; their lives had changed and more change was to follow, but in what way again was undetermined.

Morace held onto his sister for as long as he could.

'Lorett, I will be here with you. That you can count on.' He looked into her eyes. They changed colour with her mood. All throughout her childhood, her eyes gave her away. Morace could tell better than anyone what mood she was in, being her twin. At that moment they were a shade of grey, meaning she was scared for someone.

'I know you will, Morace, you always have.' *But you won't be here for too long, not with what you have to do, and I don't know if you can do it or bring yourself to do it.* 'Can I lay with you like we did when we were children? When it was cold or I was scared? I need the comfort.'

'Yes you can.'

Lorett sang through the night in her dreams. It was not a song of beauty. She had gone to sleep with much on her mind; the thoughts raced across her mind like horses running a paddock. Morace slept next to her an arm around her, her protector. Her brother. Twins at birth and twins until the end.

The troll had warned her, that although their relationship would stay strong and their connection kept, their paths would split.

Morning came too swiftly for Morace. He found the elves sat around the fire. They cooked some of the food they had brought with them.

Tavener ate with them. 'My name is Tavener,' he said to a young male. The elf was clad in leathers with a hunting knife tucked in his cloak. He looked up from his meal, his eyes full of sorrow. It was a little hard for Tavener to see someone so young so sad.

'My name is Lazon Delafrey.' There was sorrow in his voice, too.

'Why are you so sad, young elf? A boy on an adventure must surely be happy?'

'I don't have much cause to be happy at a time like this,' Lazon said.

'Why not?'

'Your world is being ravaged by the weather, and our people are the cause.' *I have not been permitted to tell him that I am the cause, but I want to so badly.* He took a mouthful of his food.

'Yes, but you act as though you yourself are the cause. At least you have come to help us. You have not left us to fend for ourselves.'

That stung Lazon like a wasp. The man had no idea, and he had to lie to his face. *This must be my true punishment. What am I to do? Have everyone thank me for coming to help when I am the cause?*

'Sorry, Tavener, I have not had much chance at sleep.'

Lazon picked himself up. Tavener watched as the young elf found the girl elf who were around the same age as the twins. He sat down with her.

'There is a lot of youth here, isn't there, Tavener?' It was the taller elf who spoke with an aged wisdom. 'My name is Sal Fain.' He outstretched his hand; a typical greeting he remembered from his studies. He sat next to Tavener.

'Indeed there is. Do you see those two over there?' He pointed to Lorett and Morace who had sat with the Elven Royal Legion members to have their breakfast. 'They are twins. They share everything, and now their life is changed completely.' He looked into the eyes of the elf and studied them with intensity. 'I will not see them hurt. They have been through enough. They have lost both their parents, and their two sisters to the storms, and what's more, they are entwined in this.'

'I can see that they mean a great deal to you, Tavener. We also understand that this is our fault, and that is why we are here.'

'Well let me tell you what you are in for then, so that you know what you may face when we reach the Citadel.' Tavener was upset that the causes of all the weather destruction was nothing to do with their world or the people from it, but outside sources. The elves had caused this. 'Three of our villages have been wiped clean off Kaarth due to the storms; one of them being the twins' home. They witnessed the destruction of their entire family in one night. Many others have perished in the storms.'

Sal Fain had known that arriving here with the knowledge that the elves - or one in particular - had caused problems to this world would be difficult for them all. Knowing that the issues so horrifically affected two of the people they were with made matters worse. It would be tricky to manage. *Lazon must be feeling terrible now. I will speak with the Prince on this. He needs to know.*

'Thank you, Tavener. You are right. We should know what has befallen the world due to the elves, and how it has affected you.'

After breakfast, they all packed ready to set off on the long travels ahead. Lorett let Tavener take the lead once they reached the edge of the forest, for he knew the plains better than she. Lorett took Morace's hand; she walked with him for the majority of the journey. It was to be a long walk and the plains were dangerous.

Lorett sang softly a song of protection, so they could be warned if danger approached.

For five days they walked like this, on and on, the same sight. The plains were huge and empty. The heat was getting to them; another effect of the Weather Magic. Heads and bodies dripped with sweat. They had not found a water source and their reserves ran low. Everyone became agitated and closely watched how much water one another were consuming.

Lazon saw first-hand the effects his meddling had cost. *The Prime Minister must be a cruel man. This is true punishment.*

On the sixth day, they found their salvation in the form of a pool of fresh water, in a copse of trees. They refilled their skins and used the chance to rest a little. Lorett chose to sit by Lazon, which caught the attention of Sal Fain. With the knowledge he had of what happened to the twins he felt uneasy. Lorett took Lazon's hand in hers. As she bent in close to him, she whispered in his ear.

'Don't threat on what happened, Lazon,' she said. He looked puzzled. 'It was inevitable. The havoc your people put our world thousands of years ago was already too much, and this would have happened without your help. If anything, my friend, you using the magic when you did now means that we can do something to help.'

He looked at her. *What was she talking about? Had someone told her that it was him?*

'Did someone tell you it was I who used the magic which messed up the weather of your world?'

'No.'

'Then how did you know?'

'I just do. I can read it in your eyes. No one can keep secrets from me.' She hugged him and kissed him lightly on the head. She returned to her brother, but glanced back at him again, to give him her best smile.

Lazon pondered over the girl. The Siren. Lorett, her name was. He thought of her for a while and he began to feel positive about what had happened. It chilled him, however, that she knew what he had done without being told of it.

Shanrea had watched the Siren speak to Lazon. She wanted to know what had been said, as he seemed a little happier after the encounter. Shanrea sat and asked him. He told her what was said.

This is strange, Shanrea thought *Something deeper is happening here and no one truly knows what is going on now except for this Siren.*

A chill swept over Lorett; something had come too close. Lorett looked up. It was too late. The song she had sung to warn of danger had not worked fast enough. She still needed to learn about herself.

A male screamed loudly. Everything went silent.

Chapter 8

Gragio landed in a swamp filled with stenches that offended his nostrils. When he took out his map of this world, he saw that he was two days away from his intended destination. He folded the map and put it back in his robes. As he set off, he paid close attention to where he stepped. Anything could be alive within this swamp, ready to grab him. He wandered in the same direction for about an hour. The stench worsened and he had to pull a handkerchief out of his pocket to hold over his nose.

He was worried. Should he have accepted this task? The Shadow Empress was indeed a force to be reckoned with.

Did I truly have another option? Or was my fate already sealed when the agent appeared at my house?

There clearly was no turning back now. Gragio had already killed for the cause and it seemed definite that he needed to do this for his own survival. When the willow tried to kill him, it became even clearer.

He lost concentration for a moment due to his dark thoughts, and he stepped into a pool of sludge. His foot became stuck in the thick, green, putrid stuff. As he tried in vain to pull out his foot, he realised it was increasingly harder to move it; the sludge got thicker every time he moved. It had started to rise too; it was now up to his knee.

'Well, would you look at what the limo caught, eh?' A cocky voice from nowhere licked the air.

Gragio looked around trying to find its source; no luck. *What is a limo?*

'I would suggest you stop moving,' continued the voice. 'Be here soon, it will. More movement does not increase your chance of survival.'

'Who are you? Show yourself,' demanded Gragio.

'What, and miss the show? No thanks. I am fine right here.' It chuckled.

Gragio heard a thump to the ground with a little squelch, then another and another.

'It's coming. Be prepared.'

'Prepared for what? You're just going to watch me get killed?'

'Pretty much. It would make my day.'

Gragio then saw it; dark green with bits of goo dripping from it. It had no distinguishable features.

'The limo is coming. Take this.' From thin air, a bottle flung itself at Gragio. 'Now pour it on the limo juice.'

Gragio did as instructed. What did he have to lose? He felt the goo loosen its grip and he freed his foot.

'Now get up a tree.'

In a rush, he scrambled up the nearest tree to watch the limo bounce its way across the path.

'A limo?' Gragio jumped down from the tree, took a stick and prodded the sludge. It had appeared to have gone back to its normal consistency. 'This might come in handy.' He took out a container to scoop up some of the sludge. He looked around for whoever had thrown the potion. 'Where are you? Are you not going to show yourself?' His black robes flapped as he looked around.

'I will in good time. I just need to know if you are the one I was sent for.'

Sent for? What did he mean?

'Now just keep going about your business. Go on, I will watch.' The voice started to hum a little tune.

Reluctantly, Gragio walked on ever more vigilant for the limo juice. He did not intend to be stuck again. He was concerned about the invisible companion he had acquired; he wondered what it intended to do to him.

Gragio started to work out an anti-concealment spell, so that he could locate the follower. He muttered the incantation under his breath. His elven magic flowed through him. As he got to the last syllable and was ready to release the magic. The creature interrupted the silence.

'Oh, that won't work, my friend. Hehe...' the voice said mischievously. 'My advice to you is to not even try. End in your hurt, it would.'

Gragio tried anyway. With a flash, he was lifted off the ground and flung into a tree. He nearly had his head cracked open.

'See, I told you, and now your pride is hurt as well as your body.'

Gragio picked himself up, frustrated. 'Show yourself.'

What is this thing? How is it able to become invisible and disable a clairvoyant spell as powerful as the one I had conjured? The elf became riled to the point of distraction. He was even more desperate to know what this thing was, now that he had learnt it possessed magic. 'Tell me what you are!'

'Now, now. I don't think that's how a power battle works, is it Mr Elf? The one who has the power must not reveal, you are very puny it might make you jealous.'

Gragio heard it chuckling, and could almost imagine someone rolling around on the floor.

'I am a very powerful mage, thank you, and I don't take kindly to insults.'

'Ha, look who is all riled and upset, about to wet his pants, eh?'

The joyous tone of the voice was too much for Gragio to bear any longer. He was ready to burst with rage. He started to walk with strides that were long and fast. *I can't see this thing, but maybe I could out-walk it...? I hope.*

'Walking away won't help you get rid of me. Besides, I am almost linked to you now.'

What did that mean - linked to me?

Gragio moved uncomfortably, feeling invaded by the presence that was with him, taunting him. 'Why are you here? What are you? Tell me now.'

'Ok,' it said plain as day. 'I was getting a little bored anyway. Elves always are a little dull, especially the power hungry ones. Hehe.'

Gragio stopped in his tracks, waiting for whatever it was to make its appearance. He waited for a while, but there was nothing but empty air and silence.

For what seemed like an hour, he waited.

'I thought you were going to show yourself? Or was that just another ploy?' Gragio started as he heard a grunt.

'Oh, sorry. I dozed off. You bored me too much. Hehe.'

Gragio heard a rustle behind him. A bush seemed to have been moved by something unseen. The elf looked in front of him to find nothing still.

'Well, I am sorry, Mr Elf, but if you are going to just look straight ahead then you will be greatly disappointed.'

Gragio looked down and hurriedly stepped back. He could make out a pointy face with a goatee and sharp eyes. There was a purple tint to the face of the creature. It stood on two legs with brown sack pants that hung loose. Its chest was bare and hairy.

'What are you?'

'What am I? What am I?' It screeched, disgusted. 'You bastard. I am a Pwca, and not just any; I am Twak.'

'What is a Pwca?'

The creature gave another disgusted look. 'I am a faery-of the woodland distinction, to be precise. This was once my home, before it became smelly.'

Gragio stared at the creature. It was his mid-height, and he noticed what looked like the start of horns.

'Did you not get taught, you, that it is rude to stare?' the creature said as he pointed at Gragio.

'Well it is just as rude to point. It is just you look a lot like a faun.'

If the pigments in the Pwca's face could have, they would have turned red. 'I am no faun. They are disgusting and deceitful. We Pwca are a noble race of illusionists.' He put his hand to his hairy chest with pride.

'Illusionists, eh? Sounds like tricksters to me, but your magic is strong and already I have failed against you. So it looks like I am to put up with you.'

'You put up with me? More like I you.'

Gragio looked at the creature again. 'So why are you here, trickster?'

'Insurance. The Empress says hello.' Twak looked at his charge, *I don't see what is seen in this fool, but the Empress rules supreme, so what. Time to fly.* 'Ok, stand back, fool.'

Gragio did not take kindly to being called a fool, but stood back anyway. He saw something he did not expect. The woodland faery shifted; his skin started to crawl and churn with bubbles forming. Wings sprouted out from its shoulder blades, long, with brown feathers. As he flapped them, his body lengthened and he leapt onto four legs instead of the two. His head started to form a beak. The little Pwca had turned into a griffon before Gragio's very eyes.

'Hop on, fool. Can't be waiting for you all day, can we? If we waited for you to walk, then nothing would get done. We are working to a very tight deadline here...'

Reluctantly, Gragio got on the back of Twak. Twak took off with such speed that Gragio had to hold on tightly, otherwise he might have fallen and tumbled to his death.

Chapter 9

One of the elven guards flew in front of the party.

Lorett ran to him. 'His neck is broken!'

Lorett felt the earth beneath her rumble a little. *Was it an earthquake?* She shot a glance in the direction the elf had flown. It was hard to make out at first, but then she could see it. A huge black form was headed straight for the group. It was trying to build momentum.

'It's a juggernaut,' Tavener said out loud. 'They run large distances to build up momentum. Once they get enough speed they can't be stopped.' He looked at the elves who gave a nod. They took out their swords and stood ready.

The juggernaut got closer. Just in time, the party dived out the way before it hit them. Its bulky form careened into a tree, which disintegrated it into splinters. In the time it took for the juggernaut to slow down and turn around, the group had managed to recover enough composure. They quickly planned a strategy.

Horacio led the assault on the juggernaut. His sword was a long double-handed cleaver. He readied himself for the battle. The two elven guards that remained did the same. One of guards, the smaller of the two, wielded two short swords, and the other a long thin sword.

Morace looked on as the juggernaut readied to charge again. He felt strange; a weird sensation caused his hand to tingle. He presumed it to be nerves and got out his knife.

It had gained yards on them now. It almost reached the prince, who jumped above its head just as contact was to be made. The prince slashed with precise strokes to the back of the neck and head of the juggernaut, but the attempt was futile. The beast had thick armoured skin. The sword would not sink in.

The elf who held the long thin sword was not quick enough to dodge it. When he was hit, like his comrade, he flew high into the air then landed in a heap on the floor, his life taken out of him.

Morace felt his hand tingle again. It felt weird. He stuffed his hands into his pockets trying to get rid of the feeling. It did not work, the sensation was still there. His fingers twitched with the heat.

What is happening? It feels like burning in my hands, something is strange here.

Lorett sensed the surge of power. She looked at her brother. Her brother was to face his destiny soon, but she knew the other set had not arrived yet. That was meant to be the order of things. The troll said that two others with power would appear before all the powers were together. Lorett's eyes widened as she realised what this meant. *So that would mean...* She looked at the two younger elves.

'Lorett, look out!' The call that saved her life was almost too late. She was only just able to dive aside before the force of the juggernaut crushed her. This time, however, the beast had not reached full momentum, and was able to stop sooner. It was now on its way back.

Morace leapt up instinctively to protect his twin. Now between the beast and his sister a green light started to form. It was instinct. The power no longer burnt his hand. It had become a part of him. With hidden control, he sent the green light forward and it spiralled into the sternum of the beast. The beast stumbled and fell to the ground. Morace fell, too, with exhaustion.

Lorett ran to him. 'I am sorry. I could not tell you... not until you were ready. You had to *need* it to be able to use it.'

'Lorett,' he croaked. 'What am I?'

Morace fell into a deep slumber. The dreams from the previous night returned, but this time he could see himself more clearly and he could use this green light. He developed a fever, which caused Lorett to despair, as she could not find a remedy. She knew, however, this was her brother's own battle. His existence had started to make a change, and his body with it. The dormant power he held since his birth coursed through him. Every now and then, he would turn rigid and shake.

Lorett sang to him with a song to soothe him. The convulsions seemed to lessen.

Tavener did not quite know what to make of this. The two kids he had known had already changed so much, and now this? Morace with magic? It was insane.

Haste was still needed. The elves were eager to reach the Citadel, so Tavener looked for signs of a settlement and something that could be used to carry Morace whilst he recovered. There was no luck in either.

'I should have brought the horse with me,' Tavener said. 'It is not far now. If we were to take turns in carrying him... that might work.'

'Do you truly know how far the Citadel is? We could think it is not far, but we are stuck without water and carrying a dead weight,' the prince spoke harshly, but truthfully.

'That dead weight you are talking about happens to be my brother. Just because you are a prince does not mean you can be rude.' Lorett looked intensely at the Elven Prince. Even though she was a siren, here to guide the races together, her brother was number one on her list of priorities.

The prince looked back at the siren, agitated. He wanted to be on his way. This waste of time did not help, but he needed the siren as his father had told him. -*The elves, son, are guided by the sirens when they enter the world of Kaarth.* - He had no choice but to do what the siren did.

For three days, they waited for Morace to recover enough to be able to walk on his own. He was still drowsy and talked incoherently. Lorett knew that as time came to pass the effects of his new magic would become less harsh. It would not take as much of a toll on his body. Every now and then Morace would stumble, but Tavener would be there to pick him up again to continue their slow pace. The Elven Prince became more impatient.

Lorett knew, however, that Morace would need to get to the Citadel with the elves. He should not have found his power yet. She looked over to the two young elves with them. Are *they the same age? They look like it; they have only announced each other as good friends.* The male looked at her when he realised he was being watched, such hurt was on his face. He was still angry with himself but he would come to learn soon that what he did in fact was save the worlds, or at least the people in them.

As dusk fell on the fourth day, they had been able to walk again. The golden rays of the sun created a pretty horizon. Their shadows became longer with every step. They walked hard for the whole day. They had been able to pick up their pace as Morace had recovered fully. He talked a lot more. It seemed as though he had a new lease of life within him, his strides were long and meaningful.

While he was in his slumber state he had encountered more dreams, ones that gave him answers to questions he had sought. He had also encountered the two girls again, but this time he used his power with their own. What's more, he knew that he needed to go elsewhere before the Citadel. It would be pointless for him to go to the Citadel – for any of them. However, tradition dictated that the elves would need to present themselves on Kaarth before they proceeded with their business.

Morace decided that he would stay with his sister until the last possible moment before he embarked on his journey. He believed his sister knew already that they would be separated. This was the reason why she was so focused at the start of her new discovery. It would have been hard on the both of them to talk about their separation.

They set up a camp fire for the night. The temperature of the plains had dropped considerably over the last few days and they needed warmth. They also slept closer to one another to keep the chilling air away.

'One more day and we will be at the Citadel,' Tavener announced to the group who had sat down to eat a boar they happened across. Tavener had shot it with his crossbow to give them a good meal for the night. 'The last leg of the journey will be a challenge. It's the wraith marches, said no wraiths be with us now, but,' he paused to look at Lorett, 'if this past week has taught me anything, is that anything can happen.'

Lorett smiled. This was great news. They were nearly there and ready to speak to the King of Kaarth.

Chapter 10

The marshes were riddled with thick mists, which made it hard to see. Morace held onto Lorett's hand as they navigated through. There was a stench in the hot air, which every now and then blew noisily through pockets in the earth. Lorett's hand squeezed her brother's tightly.

They had travelled for half the morning with no change in the scenery. They stopped to eat to keep their morale up. The plains they had previously walked through were not a patch on the marshes, which challenged them mentally. Sometimes adamant voices could be heard, and screams, too.

Lazon walked with Shanrea, they held hands to give each other comfort. Lazon puzzled over his conversation with the siren; what had her words meant?

Suddenly Shanrea let out a scream, holding her head in her hands she fell to her knees.

Shanrea a voice whispered in her head. *You must bring them to me, all of them, so that I can see them for myself. To the Wraith of the Marsh you must go.*

Fighting the confusion, Shanrea felt light headed as she started to walk again beside Lazon, who tried to talk to her. She gave no response.

'Shanrea, are you ok?' There was still no reply from her. 'Shanrea, answer me!' He was slightly frantic at the lack of acknowledgement. She had only been down for a few seconds but still it was enough to cause him worry. He grabbed her shoulders and spun her around so their eyes would meet, hoping it would snap her into reality. 'Shanrea, are you ok?'

Her eyes widened as she heard his voice. 'Yes, sorry, I was thinking.'

'Everyone stop and stand back, something is wrong with Shanrea.' Lazon saw that her eyes had turned a milky colour as though she had gone blind.

Shanrea then spoke quietly. 'We must get on, we need to find it.'

'Find what?'

'The Wraith of the Marsh, we need it to speak to us.' Her eyes returned to their usual hazelnut colour.

The Wraith of the Marsh was a creature one should not have to voluntarily seek out, but it would seem that they had to.

'Who told you this?'

'We must head on to the Citadel first,' Horacio exclaimed. 'We need to do what is proper, as is bound by blood.'

'We will! But first we must come this way.' Shanrea led them onwards, picking up her pace.

The mist became even thicker. The prince was unhappy with the unexpected change in direction. He protested with every step that they took further in the wrong direction.

'I knew she should not have come. Now we are going the wrong way,' Horacio muttered. His father was insistent that they appeared to the King first, as that was the law.

Shanrea stepped in front of the Prince stopping everyone in their tracks. 'We must do this first. We will be given knowledge to present to the King of Kaarth. The wraith knows something and must speak with us.'

'I am sorry, lass, but the prince is not the only one with concerns about this detour. The wraiths were said to plague the country for many years. I am not happy about this.' Tavener spoke like he was scared, this seldom happened.

Shanrea now took his face in her hands gently. 'I know you have concerns.' She looked out to the others, 'You all do, but the wraiths are of the old world and have all but become extinct. There are old wives tales about how they steal your children in the middle of the night.' She looked at them with determination in her eyes. 'Trust me, we need to go here first, and then present ourselves to the King of Kaarth.'

She turned around before any objections could be sent her way and started a steady pace again.

After about another half an hour hard walk they saw the way was lit with fire. The fires became more frequent as they continued. The mists had also started to recede slightly. Little shacks could be seen faintly in the distance.

'People actually live here?' Tavener asked in shock

'Not people, Tavener. Wraiths.'

Tavener shuddered at the thought. 'I was not expecting them to live in houses.'

'What did you expect them to live in?' Shanrea shot a look at Tavener. 'A grave yard?'

'Well, yeah, I did actually.'

They continued on. The shacks were a single room with one window. None of them had any doors. They were solid wood all the way around.

How do they get in? Tavener thought.

Tavener started to circle one of the shacks they passed. With curious eyes, he inspected the wood. His hand touched the surface which was cold and moist. *Almost rotten*, he thought. He closed his hand to a fist. Lightly he wrapped his knuckles to the wooden shack.

'What is it you want, flesh sack?' A harsh voice hissed out of the air. Tavener looked around in search of the voice. When he looked back at the shack, a pale face had appeared, sharp and hard looking. 'You humans think you can just come and pound on my house.'

Tavener took a step back, shocked. His hand fell on the hilt of his sword. He let go when he realised it would be futile against a wraith. 'Oh I am sorry, I erm did not realise any one was in.'

The wraith shrank back into its house, hissing venomous words.

'See, I told you, lass,' Tavener said to Shanrea.

'You knocked on his house for no reason other than curiosity, Tavener, of course he was a little peeved off.'

Taken aback from the scolding by the elven girl, Tavener looked at Lorett and Morace who tried in vain to contain their laughter.

'Tavener, are you scared of a few wraiths? You're the man who has slain a beast that rivalled his own size?' Lorett probed.

'These creatures have no blood, child. I can't simply cut them down if they attack.'

'Do not worry, Tavener, we will not harm you, you simply just met a wraith who is a grouch,' the Wraith of the Marsh whispered.

They had reached their destination. They were greeted by a form; a presence that sent a chill down their spine, but somehow gave them hope when they saw it.

Morace could feel the power of living (or not) for many years. He had felt changes all over. The mists in the marsh were not natural. They would not have stumbled on this place accidentally; it was certain that they had been led here. What's more, he could feel the changes in the company he kept. Lorett and the elf girl, Shanrea, most of all. Magic. He could also feel the change himself, yet he still did not know what he was.

'All of you must be hungry. Wraiths don't eat; we are in and out of this world or all worlds, and have no need of it. We have laid out a feast for you all.'

'Thank you, master wraith.' Shanrea curtsied in appreciation and respect for the wraith.

They were led to a large banquet table laden with all sorts of food and drink.

'Enjoy yourselves and then we shall speak.'

Despite the cold misty setting, there was food, drink, banter, flirting and song during the evening. Even the hard-faced prince smiled and joined in with the song. Lorett sung her favourite songs and danced with all who would, as was in her nature. Morace watched her dance with everyone and remembered times of when they were younger. He smiled. His hands were taken by those that were warm and soft to the touch; they were Shanrea's. He stared into her hazel eyes. They were eyes of beauty and grace that he had not noticed at first, but as he looked into them, he could see warmth. Her face enchanted him; it was smooth and slender. He could just make out the points of her elven ears through her hair.

She smiled at him, which seemed to penetrate his skin and head straight for his heart.

'For the elves, when a girl takes your hands it means she would like a dance, Morace.'

His face flushed and he felt strange inside. This was new. He stood up and placed his hand on her hip and they danced to the voice of his sister. The moon shone high in the sky and everything seemed to slow down a little.

Shanrea took Morace to a quieter place. 'We need to see the Wraith of the Marsh, together first, before the others do.'

Morace's heart almost leapt out of his chest. *Is this what all the dancing was about, to bring me to meet the wraith? Although why did I even care?* He looked at the elven girl in front of him as she urged him to come on. Did he like her? He had felt a warmth when she held his hand to dance. He shook his head no. Now was not the time to have feelings for anyone, not when there was so much happening.

He walked on, trying to push away the feelings he had for Shanrea.

They entered a cave illuminated with flames in pits of rock. The cave tunnelled for a bit, then came upon an opening to reveal a large cavernous area with bookshelves around the edges. *The wraiths liked to read?* Morace looked at Shanrea who did not say a thing, which suggested to him that he should keep his mouth shut. They walked into the exact centre of the room, where the stone had deep carvings etched in them, the lines filled with moss.

The wraith appeared suddenly giving Morace and Shanrea a start. For something that was not alive in the sense of flesh and blood, he looked remarkably well. Wisps of ethereal white robes whipped the air lightly. It gave the wraith a grace, but somehow Morace knew this wraith would be a force to be reckoned with. He pointed at chairs so they could sit. He took a stone chair by the round table and sat with Morace and Shanrea.

'I have asked you here today, as you will carry a great burden.' His voice was raspy, with an aged tone. 'You will both need to accept this, as you will need to work with each other.'

'Sorry what...' Morace was cut short.

'This will try you to the maximum. You have already been challenged.' The wraith took a book that appeared on the table from nowhere. He handed it over to Morace. 'This book will tell you all you need about who and what you are.'

'What...' Another question cut off.

'Read it together and you will see. I will speak to you once it is done.'

Morace watched the wraith depart through the wall. *How could something like that walk through a wall and yet hold a book in the same instance?* Morace puzzled over this for a moment before looking at the book.

It was a journal, bound in leather. It looked quite old and battered.

'What is it, Morace?' Shanrea asked.

'It looks old,' he responded.

She pulled up her chair close to Morace, and leaned in so their shoulders touched. Morace did not feel like an invasion of space, but welcomed the warmth. Even with all the fires, it still felt cold.

'It's a journal. I can't tell from the front who wrote it. The name is scratched out.' He showed her.

'Open it, Morace.'

'He did slowly, not wanting to rush lest it crumbled due to its age. Luckily the pages were still firm as though they had been preserved, *with magic?*

Morace began to read the first few lines.

> *I am a Druid. Whoever reads this passage or this journal will be reading it because I have handed it to you in my ethereal form. I will soon have to pass this world and enter the next stage of consciousness. If you are reading this it means that as I feared the worlds have started to fall apart and we must act fast. I say we, but what I actually mean is you, for I can no longer influence the worlds any more. I can only ensure that the measures I put in place are put into motion. The first one is by handing you the journal you are now reading; my journal.*

I want to let you know that you two are Druids, or will be once you learn to harness your power. I need you to know this because without your guidance, everything will become unwoven.

Now put this book down, so that I know you have read up to this point.

Shanrea and Morace looked at each other. Both had the exact same thought. *Druids? This journal was talking to us and it said we were Druids, how is that even possible?*

'Wait a minute. Are you thinking the same thing that I am thinking?'

'That you are normal and nothing special?'

'Yes,' Morace replied.

'Your display with the juggernaut showed you are more than just a normal person.' Shanrea had a sense of admiration for the feat that Morace had performed against the creature that had attacked them.

'And how about you, Shanrea. What have you done? There must be something.'

Shanrea considered. Had she had done anything different from any other mage in the university or the Everglade for that matter? For a moment she completely forgot that she had stopped the storm; the same storm that had caused the death of Morace's family.

'I stopped the storm when it got out of control. I don't know what happened to me. I could feel what was right to do. I could feel the power within me.'

It had been the same for Morace who had felt the power manifest itself in him.

'Good, I can see the understanding between you two.'

The wraith had appeared suddenly giving them yet another start. This time, his being was less; he had faded in the minutes that had passed from their last encounter.

'Understanding is good; you will need it. It will help you start to trust each other.'

'Wraith, are you dying?' Shanrea asked.

'I am fading, but not dying. I am merely transcending to another existence.'

Morace looked at the druid. He was about to speak, but the wraith spoke instead.

'I cannot stay long. The process is nearly complete, and there are more things I need to tell you before I depart.' The wraith took to his seat. 'You must read the entire journal; all of it. Soon you will have choices to make one of them will be your duty.' He looked at Shanrea for that. 'But there may be consequences. The other choice will be haste to get the job done, but again, there are more consequences for that. I cannot tell you what these are, for I do not know. However, think wisely and you will know what is best when the time comes.'

'Wraith, are you to leave us now?'

'You, yes, but you have the journal. I must now speak with Lorett the siren briefly, as she is still awake. Rest now and remember to read the journal.'

With a flash, the wraith disappeared. He left the two of them to ponder over the meanings of his words. They looked at the journal hopeful that all their questions would be answered within its pages. They started to read the journal together. Both of them were eager but also scared to read about what their fate could entail.

'You must let them do what they think best, Lorett. It will be up to them to decide.'

'How is so much at stake? They do not know the consequences for what their actions will bring,' Lorett protested.

'They would not be able to make the decision if they know what the consequences will entail. They must go into this ignorant of what the outcome is to be.'

'Well I still protest. Morace is my brother... but I understand of what you mean.'

'Would you have prefer not know what the consequences will be?'

'I would have preferred there to be no consequences at all,' Lorett added with a fierce determination as a true human would. She still showed that she was brought up by humans, even though she was much more than a human.

'All actions have consequences, Lorett. A consequence might not necessarily be bad, as it can also be good.'

'I suppose you are right. We must hope that the path they chose has a good consequence. I wish though you could tell me which path would lead to which.'

'I can't. No being should know this. I have worked to forget it so that I can't accidentally let it be known.' He pointed a finger to the bed. 'Child, you must rest and be ready for the morning.'

The wraith disappeared with a flash as before. Lorett felt weary so took to the bed and fell into a slumber.

The following morning, the mists let them pass out of the marshes. Within an hour, they had reached the gates of the Citadel.

Chapter 11

The foreboding iron gates of the Citadel opened slowly to let them in the huge white walls of stone. The guards noticed the elves, and they began to mutter. One of them, a stout fat man, ran to prevent them going any further. He held out a spear, and his helmet fell across his eyes clumsily.

'Sirs.' He looked and saw the women with them too. 'Madams,' he added. 'And you are elves, some of you. I have never seen an elf before.' He looked at the elves intently. 'What business brings you to Kaarth?'

'Boris!' A sharp voice turned his head. 'What have you been told? All visitors must report to the guardhouse. Why are you continuing to commune with these wayfarers?'

'Captain, some of them are elves.'

The tall, slender guard looked at the visitors properly for the first time. He walked the steps down from the tower where he stood.

'Elves, you say? You know where the elves are to go, Boris. Take them to the king, but first make sure they are relieved of their weapons.' The officer stood and looked at them hard and with ice. He wore black finery showing his stature in the capital. 'Most of these are children, nothing more. Tell me, have you come to help us in our time of need?'

The prince stepped forward. 'I am Prince Horacio Wylennd. I am here to represent the elves in this crisis. The elves offer their service in aiding. As per the treaty signed by the elves and men of old, we came to the Citadel first when arriving in your land.'

The Guard Captain looked at the Elven Prince and nodded. 'I will escort you to the palace to present you to the king.'

Before anything else could be said, the head guard turned around and started to pace towards the palace. The others followed, watched by the stallholders in the market area. The patrons stopped to stare too, muttering amongst themselves.

The Citadel had been built up into different levels. As it rose up the hillside, there was the market district which you walked through upon arrival into the city. This area had parts covered by towering marble pillars with a canopy on top to offer some shelter. The buildings of this district were made of white marble. They were neatly laid out, showing careful planning. In the centre of the district was a huge clock tower made of black marble, laced with white.

This large area brought in the majority of the coin, with shops and market stalls that bustled every day - except the last day of the week, when the masters and mistresses of the stalls rested and took stock of their earnings. This section was prosperous and made nice for the whole of the world to come and marvel at the masonry. They were heading to the palace.

The palace stood at the top and overlooked the epic city.

The masons who made this must have been skilled in their craft, thought Shanrea, who had been thinking that the university back home was beautiful, but this was some master-level masonry.

Morace and Lorett had been to the Citadel three or four times as children and had always been taken in by its grandeur. The district they walked in now was the residential district. This was where all the wealthy people lived, the landlords and land owners. As a child, Morace had remembered another part of the Citadel; one not so grand.

The district Morace remembered was called the scrubs. It was not so elegant, but cleverly hidden from view from those who were ignorant of its existence. The Guard Captain was not about to take the elves through those parts. Who would show visitors the parts of the city which weren't up to the same standard? Morace knew there were such parts. He remembered them well because his Pa would go there when he could spare some of his catches. He would take Morace with him to show that despite appearances, there were places that people tried to hide. That the poor were normally hidden, but could be found if need be.

They had reached the palace grounds. It was still a long walk through the grounds to the doors of the palace. The grounds were rich with plant life and water features. The King of Kaarth was well known for his gardens and wanted it to be the first impression anyone had of him. He had even opened them up to the general population. What was the point in a garden if no one else could see it? That was the king's philosophy on gardens at least.

Two large guards stood sentry at the palace doors, and when they saw the Guard Captain, they stood to attention.

The company sat in the holding room and waited to be summoned by the steward to assemble in front of the king. The prince grew impatient. He looked at Sal Fain, who had been rather quiet. Sal Fain had briefed the prince on the etiquette of the humans about ten times over.

'Remember, humans don't like to be made fools of, Prince.' Sal Fain started to speak again.

'I know, believe it or not, Sal Fain, I am not like some people who do not pay attention to important words or even laws.' The last part was meant for Lazon.

Lazon had sat quietly next to Shanrea, who held his hand. This was to be the hardest part for Lazon to bear. The humans may call for his life. His mind raced over what could happen. All of it made worse by the fact that he knew Shanrea would put herself at risk if he were to have a death penalty. *It may have been better for me to have died with the elves.*

Morace started to read the journal with Shanrea while they waited. This had been the first opportunity they had since they received it. It told them that the druid who wrote it, who was now the wraith but soon to be something else, had foretold that the weather would soon get worse. That it would be triggered by the elves. That it may be their saving, for it would warn them before it would become too late to do something about it. However, only if they would act quickly. Before they could read further, they had been summoned.

The Hall of Order was large. It was filled with people of the Kaarthean Council. There had been a session, so some business had been already been taken care of. It was part way through the morning. At the top of the room sat the one who must have been the king. He sat upon on a raised platform in a throne made of white stone, marble it looked like.

The king looked aged and haggard. He moved his old frame so that he stood up. The king raised his hands to make silence fall within the hall of order. Within minutes, the hall became still. Despite his appearance, the king held a presence that it would appear no one dared to question.

'Bring the elves and their company forward to the podium. Let this prince speak to me.' The king did not sound amused. He eyed them. He took judgment with each and every one them as they walked up to the podium. His eyes stopped on Lazon.

It was as if he could feel the burn from the stare. Lazon looked up at the king. A smile crept over the king's face.

'I am King Jewws Ingud, and the elves have never appeared within Kaarth for nigh on one thousand years ever since the treaty was signed. Something to do with guilt, I would suspect.' He shot a look at the ones who were not elves. 'And you, who are you to be with elves? Something tells me you did not just stumble upon them out in some woods. What are you in all this? Where do you fit?'

The king had decided to speak to those he had not expected to see with the elves, as this was the thing that was on his mind for the time being.

Morace stepped up to the podium to speak to the king and the council.

'My name is Morace Roccan. I am from this world. I have also found out that I am a druid.' All the eyes of the council hall showed that they were stunned at the announcement. He continued as though what he just told them was a normal thing. Morace told them the reason why they were here and what had happened. He left out the encounter with the wraith, for it was still too fresh in his mind for him to figure that out. He stepped down and looked at Shanrea to see if she understood. He walked up to stand by her. He felt like he needed stand with her.

After Morace spoke his piece, the king looked at him. 'So at the moment, Morace, your brothers are none the wiser about their parents' fate or their sisters'?'

'Aye, yes your highness.'

'Very well. We must see to that.' He looked at his steward. 'See to it that messages are sent to the brothers that their parents have passed on into the next world.' The steward bowed and left through a side door.

'Now, elf, tell me why is it you have felt it necessary to venture into Kaarth?'

The prince was just about to take the podium. He cleared his throat ready to speak when the king put his hand up to stop him.

'No, not you. I don't want a prepared speech tailored to what you think I want to hear. No, I want *him* to speak to me and the council.' His finger pointed to Lazon.

Lazon was shocked and did not know what to say or do. He had not prepared to speak. He moved gingerly to the podium and stood on it. It was bad enough when the King of Kaarth had stared at him, but now the whole of the council hall had eyes on him.

'Tell me, boy, why they would bring the likes of you to the world of Kaarth in the middle of its plight? Where death and destruction have suddenly happened, of which something that we had not seen since the last time the elves admitted to their use of a now-forbidden magic?'

The king must have seen it, that Lazon had had something to do with all of this. Lazon did not know what to say, so he thought the truth would have to be the only way to go.

He looked at Morace. He had not told him that his indiscretion had caused half of his family to be wiped away. He was just about to speak when he felt his bones turn weak, and he fell to the floor. Attempting to get up, he felt woozy. He did not know what had come over him.

Morace's hand tingled with the magic he had just conjured. He knew already that Lazon was the one who started the Weather Magic again, but it would not accomplish anything him admitting it now in front of the king. He could read the king; he was after the one responsible for this.

Horacio took the podium in place of Lazon.

'We are sorry for the destruction the weather has brought upon your people and we, as the entire Elven nation, express our deepest regrets on the loss of lives it has caused. We clearly had let our rules slack, and we have had full investigations into this and that is why we're here now; to aid you in what we can for your people.'

'So you admit your race has something to do with all this destruction? All the death? All the sorrow? Despite the laws, we had come up with. My ancestor was there when the treaty was written. It's your magic that has caused this.' He stood up and looked straight at the elves. 'An apology is not enough for our people, and we would now hope to seek retribution.' He shot glances at the guards who had begun to move into the company. 'Arrest all the elves, and if the others try to stop you, arrest them, too, for treason.'

Things got bad fast, and now it was time to act. Sal Fain was the first to be apprehended and brought down to the ground as he was only an arm's reach to the nearest guard.

Morace leant into Shanrea so that his lips pressed her ear. He whispered the plan he had come up with. She nodded in acknowledgement and let an arclight begin to form in her hand. Faced with nerves, Morace knew this decision was a reckless one. They did need to get out of this situation though.

Morace also lit the arclight within his hand. The two druids then worked in unison together to throw light into the air. The two lights that they had created collided together. They seemed to shatter, and a bright light engulfed the room. Morace grabbed the closest person to him he could and pulled them to a run, so did Shanrea. All were blinded in the confusion. The two druids shielded their eyes as they ran to the outside with the comrades they had managed to grab. Once out of the palace, Morace thought hard of a place they could go. He remembered the place where there would be little patrol. They ran to the scrubs.

Chapter 12

Morace had found a quiet part of the scrubs. They hid for the best part of a week so that they could figure out how to free the others from the king. In the confusion, they had only managed to get the last elven guard out. Tavener had managed to keep his wits about him and make an escape, too. The one Shanrea had managed to grab was actually one of the king's guards, so they quickly left him unconscious in the street. That meant that the prince, Sal Fain, Lazon, and Lorett, much to Morace's despair, were held captive. They needed to find a way to free them.

They managed to find scraps of food to keep their strength up. Morace, Tavener, and the elven guard discussed the best plans to get everyone out. It did not help that they were now the most wanted people in the Citadel, and all the guards had been given descriptions of them.

'There may be a way,' Tavener said one night with hesitation. He decided that all the options would need to be addressed, so proceeded to explain. 'Some of the people I do dealings with for the inn may not be the most honest of people. One of them in particular might be able to help us.' He scratched his head to think. 'Only I don't recall him saying when he would be next in the Citadel. He is a hard man to find because of his transgressions.'

Morace looked at Tavener. A plan started to form in his head.

'How well do you know him? I think we need all the help we can get.' Morace was unsure, but felt that anything they had was better than nothing. 'Please, Tavener, we must just see if he is willing to help.'

'I have to find him first though. There is no guarantee he is in the Citadel. Besides, we are wanted for treason; he might not want to be washed up in that. Perhaps I should not have mentioned it.'

'But you have, and we need to try. Please, Tavener. If not for me, for my sister.'

Tavener always had a soft spot for Lorett. He had seen her grow up and listened to all her songs. Perhaps it was the siren's magic even then; she must have had some of it as a young girl.

'Aye. That I will, boy.' He left the room they had dubbed the planning room. It had a table with half-finished plans jotted down. It felt like they were getting somewhere now at least.

Morace had not read a bit of the journal since they were in hiding. He could feel its weight in his pocket, but he was busy looking at the plans.

Shanrea came to the doorway, and leant against the frame. She watched him for a while and smiled. He was so focused on the plans in front of him he had not noticed her. He felt guilty for the predicament they were in. There were decisions to be made, ones that would have consequences, but he could not determine them from overthinking. The guilt manifested into frustration. Shanrea had seen it with Lazon; it would get worse if she let it continue.

A mage, or even a druid as it turned out they were, should not let frustration take a grip on them. She did admire him though. Like her with Lazon days ago, he had managed to make a split decision, so quick he was. He must have sensed what she had. The king of this land was not about to accept some too-late apology from a race that should have known better.

Oh, Lazon, what did you do?

Even though it was true, she had read in the diary that the events with Lazon could have saved more lives... *Why did it have to be us? I was having a great time.*

She had seen enough of Morace beating himself up over what had happened, and decided to put his mind on other things.

Still unnoticed, Shanrea silently crept up behind him and placed a hand on his shoulder. He looked up at her with no leap in his heart at a sudden change. He just smiled. Shanrea could see the smile in a dusty mirror ahead of them. *He has a nice smile. He should smile more.*

Morace put his hand on top of hers and gave it a squeeze. He took the strength that he needed from her. She was to be able to do that. When everything seemed so hopeless she was there. *Is that what the wraith made happen?*

'Morace, you should smile more. You look better this way.'

'I don't know what to do. It's in Tavener's hands now; he must find this person...'

Shanrea shushed him.

'You have been working hard trying to figure things out. Getting frustrated about it won't help. You need rest.' She took his hand and led him to a bench in the corner. She sat him down away from the table and put her arms around him. 'If you don't rest, your magic will consume you, and then you will be no good to anyone.'

'My magic is perfectly fine, thank you.'

'It's not. It's rising and falling with your emotions. I can feel it, Morace.' She sat next to him. Morace started to feel calmer with her presence.

'We need to continue reading the journal,' Morace suggested.

'No, we don't. Your mind needs to relax right now. Reading the journal won't help that.' She leant closer into him and put her arms around his waist. He put his around her shoulders. Her head nuzzled into his strong chest. All thoughts suddenly escaped him, and he felt free of all the burdens his mind had given him. He let his hand stroke Shanrea's hair; it was still well kept despite all the trials they had faced.

From his chest, Shanrea looked up to see if he was relaxed and no longer on a mission of self-destruction. She straightened up so that their eyes met.

Morace could feel his heart pound in his chest. It reminded him of the time he and Shanrea danced together. He had danced with many girls during the fishing and harvest festivals. None had ever made him feel the way he did now. He smiled. He could see the kindness in Shanrea's eyes. They were truly beautiful. While he became enticed by the gaze Shanrea had, he felt her move in even closer.

Shanrea closed her eyes as she pressed her lips onto his. As he kissed back, her heart started to pound. Both their lips were moist. Their love began to form from this moment. Their fingers interlaced as they continued to kiss one another. She had just started to pull up his tunic when there was a knock at the door. They stopped suddenly and straightened up.

'Sorry, ma'am for bothering you.' It was the last remaining elven guard. He saw them on the bench. Their faces flushed. 'I have just heard on the wind that Sal Fain has been killed.'

Shanrea looked at the elven comrade, shocked. 'Killed? You mean they killed him?'

'Yes, some of the scrub kids were talking about it.' He looked saddened by the news. 'At noon, it was. Hung from a rope, still hanging, he is.' The guard left them on their own again.

'This is bad. We came here peacefully, and your king has killed one of us.' She looked at Morace hard.

'This is my fault! This is to try and draw us out. It must be.' Then he thought about his sister. What would become of her? He could not bear it if she was killed too. 'We need to act fast now, but with caution. My actions, it would appear, have had dire consequences.'

'It gets worse. If news gets back to our people, they might declare war on your land. Despite it being partly our fault, there was no need for your king to...' Shanrea was thinking forward. She remembered what the prince had said about his father. His father, the king of the elves, had wanted to get this over quickly. He had wanted to throw Lazon to the people of Kaarth. *Would he be quick to send the elves to war?*

'I think it may be too late for that,' he said. 'You heard our king; he said he sought retribution for this. He has already intended war, whether the elves want it or not.'

'We have to find a way to stop this, as well as stopping the weather from getting out of control.'

Morace took the journal out of his tunic. 'Let's start by finishing this.'

Shanrea nodded in agreement.

Tavener had to find of a way to get word to the person he hoped could help them. *What was it he said?* He racked his brain to think of it.

'Tavener, my friend, if you are ever in need of assistance and are in the Citadel, head over to the Bolted Crossbow and ask for room thirteen.'

Tavener remembered the strong northern accent. He had almost struggled to understand what had been said. He knew the inn was somewhere here in the scrubs, but exactly where, he could not think. He would have to ask, and that would be risky; especially with him being a seven-foot-tall man. It would be hard to be inconspicuous.

Perhaps Morace could help with that, or the elven lass? Mayhap they have some form of magic they can use?

He went to see them in the planning room. The young druids had fallen asleep in each other's arms while they crammed in the knowledge of the journal they had been given. So he decided to leave it for the night. Sleep, at this time, was more important.

He moved out of the room and into the smaller space where the elven guard sat. Tavener sat in a vacant chair. He looked at the elf.

The elven guard was small and looked to be agile. He might not be the best in a face on face fight, but certainly when stealth or agility were to be involved, would get the advantage.

They chatted for a while. They exchanged names and what sort of training they had in the ways of keeping safe. The elf's name was Zaan, and was he was a keen hunter like Tavener. He took pride in telling Tavener in the ways he had outsmarted his kills.

Tavener told him of the biggest kill he had ever made and how it had made him feel. They talked of which countries they liked to hunt in; Tavener favouring more open woodland to engage in the beasts he hunted, and Zaan preferring the denser woods his homeland provided, so that he could ambush his prey better. Tavener and Zaan continued to talk well into the night, until they finally fell asleep.

Chapter 13

Morace sat with Shanrea in a huge hall, overlooking two girls who were learning their powers. This was Morace's dream. He did not know whether Shanrea was having the same dream or not; it was the first one she had appeared in. The two girls spoke of the weather, how it was getting worse, and how even the elves had started to feel its effects. It was affecting both their worlds now.

'If the war breaks out between the humans and the elves, they would not be able to stand the onslaught of the...'

'Why are we sitting here, Shanrea, while my sister is captured? We need to rescue her and your brother.'

'Brother? What do you mean? I have no brother.' Morace looked at her. *'You don't know, do you? Yes, a brother. Well, a twin in fact, like me and my sister.'*

One of the girls looked shocked. 'No! You were not meant to tell her yet.' She jumped at Morace, who held her by the shoulders. Then darkness fell. The sound of drums called, and the air became heavy...

Morning had come. Shanrea was the first to wake up with the sun on her face; its warmth intensified with yet another heat wave. She felt strange at first, realising that she had fallen asleep with Morace, but she realised that it gave her comfort and that despite all the hardship they had faced, she had someone with her that she could face it with. She could feel the rise and fall of his chest as he breathed. Before she got up, she let her head remain where it was. She might not get much comfort after this, so she stole every moment of it she could.

Her mind wandered to the dream she had. It was a strange one and she did not know what to make of it. There had been two girls. Morace had been in it too. It had felt oddly real, but it must have been just a dream, for there had been mention of her having a brother who was captured.

Morace started to jerk about. He twisted and turned. Sweat started to pour down his face. Shanrea jumped up shocked, scared for Morace. His eyes opened sharply, staring into hers.

'Shanrea?'

'Yes, Morace, I am here. What is it?'

'A dream turned into a nightmare. The sounds of drums were deafening and then there was darkness. I fear there may be more to this than terrific weather, Shanrea. Much more.'

'Tell me of your nightmare. I had a similar dream myself, or at least I think it was a dream.'

They told each other of what their dreams had contained while they held each other. They discovered their dreams had been the same.

'This is too strange to be coincidental,' Morace stated. 'Is this the first time you have had dreams like these?'

'Yes, what about you?'

He shook his head. 'It isn't. I have had these since, well, I don't know when they first started.' He looked hard at the wall studying the detail in an effort to remember it. 'They became clearer the first time I used my magic, more purposeful. There must be a reason for them,' Morace added.

'Maybe the answer is in the journal?' Shanrea suggested.

'Let's take a look.' Morace picked it up from the table and flicked through its pages to see if there was anything on dreams. He flicked through the journal a few times before he spotted the word dreams in the near middle of the book.

It fell under the word somnium; a word neither of them were familiar with. Morace read the passage aloud.

> **Somnium:** *a dream state that a druid slips into and communicates with their other voices. It is a place where they can find knowledge that may be hidden from them. If contact is made with another of their kind, then they will share the same dream.*

'So does that mean I shared your... somnium?'
Morace nodded. 'There is more, Shanrea.'

> *Sometimes the knowledge received may not be whole, so a warning to those who seek it must be wise to the fact that it may not be wholesome.*

'The passage ends there, Shanrea, but what does it mean?'

No answer came to her. She mulled over the dream again, especially the bit about her having a brother. It said that Morace knew of him. But how? That must be an unwholesome fact. Could it mean that she had a brother or even a twin? Who could he be, and did she have to find him?

'I have no idea, Morace. It is strange that you and Lorett are twins, and I am also supposed to have a twin.'

He looked at her, shifting to get a little more comfortable. 'I think it means we have a whole many more questions that I would like answered,' he said. 'But I have no idea where I could get those answers.' He kissed her. 'If Lorett was here she would put us on the right path. She could always think clearer than me.'

Shanrea got up, leaving Morace's embrace. 'We need action. Where is Tavener?'

Morace shrugged. *Where is the other elven guard?*

They left the room together, entered the smaller living room and saw the two asleep in chairs. Morace moved over to Tavener's chair.

'Tavener, wake up.' Lightly, he shook him awake.

'What..? What is it?' Tavener, for as long as Morace could always remember, was never the best of people in the mornings and really did not appreciate being woken. Morace remembered Pa taking him on a visit, when he was eight years old with his sister. They had woken up rather early and Tavener was still in bed snoring like a troll. Lorett had decided it would be fun to play a game. Somehow, she always managed to get louder and louder with her joyful squeals. This time was no different. They started to play and about halfway through their game, they ended up in front of Tavener's room without realising.

They both jumped out of their skin at the response Tavener gave for being woken up. A seven-foot-tall hunter, no matter how friendly he was normally, was still a scary sight when he was angry. At least for two little eight year olds. They hightailed it out of the inn and hid themselves in the barn, not daring to venture out. It took Pa a few hours to find them. Never again did they play that game.

'Tavener, have you managed to find your friend?'

Still groggy, but able to string a sentence together, Tavener got up out of the chair. 'I have not yet, but I know how we can find him. There is a tavern called the Bolted Crossbow, and if we give the right phrase he will meet us, but...' Tavener looked unsure about the whole idea.

'But what?' Morace asked.

'But... I fear I can't really go out into the street and look any sort inconspicuous. I am just too big. Someone else would have to go, but it would be risky.'

'I know the risk if we are seen by the guards. They will aim to catch us.'

Tavener shook his head. 'It's not that. I don't know what the reaction would be if someone other than me gave the code.'

'So what are you suggesting, Tavener?' Shanrea asked. 'That we forget this idea and think of a new one?'

'I will go,' Morace said. 'I have some power. I know I have not had much chance to use it, but it's the only option we have.'

Shanrea looked at him. She knew that he was right but she still did not like this idea. 'It looks like it's a must.'

Morace looked at her face. It gave away a little too much of her thoughts at the worries she had for the course of action. He kissed her.

'Come back safe, and don't do anything foolish,' she said.

Tavener noticed the affection between the young druids. *It looks like young Morace has found love.*

Morace gave Tavener a quick hug then left for the door.

Morace kept to the shadows the buildings provided. He managed to remain undetected on his journey to the Bolted Crossbow, which bode well for the sneaking skills he had learnt whilst trying to hunt food with Tavener. After an hour or so, he found the tavern.

The sign to the Bolted Crossbow hung off its chain. The wooden structure looked to be in disrepair, unlikely to last much longer. He entered quietly trying not to draw attention to himself, but as soon as he opened the door, it made the longest, loudest creak you could ever wish to make. Despite it being morning, there were many patrons about. All eyes fell on the newcomer. He may as well have yelled out that he was a fugitive.

All these people looked desperate. It was quite likely that somebody would run out and fetch the guard for a few bits of coin. Morace walked up to the bar and asked for room thirteen. The barman studied him up and down then gestured for him to follow. He went through a door but everything was black. The door locked with a click. Morace was trapped.

Chapter 14

Morace's eldest brother, Lento Roccan, sat in his home in the mountains. He had heard reports that the weather had turned dire. The news chilled him, but the reports that his childhood hometown had been wiped off the earth near froze him solid.

Pa and Mama. Were they ok? My brother and sisters too?

The earth shook again with the tremors that had ravaged the mountains for the past month. He had concluded there must be a connection between the storms and the heat wave, and now their own situation.

It seemed to him the world had started to tear itself apart. The blame was pointed to the Elven nation. History dictated that the elven weather magic had caused the near destruction of the world. Kaarth had nearly been swallowed up before it was discovered what the cause was and preventive measures taken into effect.

Had the elves gone back on their word after nearly a thousand years?

A frantic knock on the door took Lento out of his ponderous moment, so he got up to answer the knock.

'Master Roccan, it's happening again, but this time there are miners trapped in the mines.'

'Fools. I told them not to go in there! I told them that the tremors meant there will be worse yet to come.'

Furiously, Lento pulled on his cloak and took to the cobbled streets in the city of Darth, a prosperous mining city. However, its prosperity was also its downside, for the more they gained in the mines, the greedier they became. Now it was up to the Guard Captain to bail them out.

Lento had been awarded the command of the City Guard and its twenty thousand men a year ago, when he had been thrust into the limelight. He had saved the city from almost certain annihilation by stopping a landslide in the mountain that Darth had been carved into. He was known to be an honest man. He was someone who spoke what he thought, regardless of what other people wanted to hear. This gave him an edge. It also made people feel uneasy. He was particularly vocal about the miners going back with all the tremors.

'They will never learn. Their greed will get the better of them,' he thundered with anger.

Darth mined some of the finest minerals and metals ever to be found in Kaarth. It gave them a rich treasury. The governor of Darth was also the owner of the mines. With his money, he gained the power to govern the city. He and Lento conversed often, both before and after he was appointed Guard Captain. They were friends, and Lento could talk frankly with him on matters that concerned the city and the land it looked after. It was the governor Lento had spoken to about the stupidity that was sending the miners back into the mines.

'I told you, Kane, but you would not listen.'

'Father,' his daughter's voice called out. A sixteen-year-old girl ran to her father and stopped in front of him. Her long, red hair a mess, clearly she had just be practicing in the training yard. *She must have heard about the mine collapse and come running to help.*

'Nythe, I need to get going to mount a rescue mission.' As he started to walk again so did she, matching his place so she did not slow him down. She was like her father, determined to do the right thing and make sure it was done. She had trained as a healer and she would follow her father to offer her services.

It comforted him that his daughter took such a strong lead from him. She wanted to help as much as he did. She was stubborn like him, and like his Pa. His stubbornness had been one of the reasons why he left his childhood home. Once he had left, his relationship with Pa had improved. Whenever Pa had visited, he had spoken of how proud he was of his son, for getting to where he had.

Lento's heart panged when he thought the same could happen with his daughter. She would marry, eventually, and then go to live with her husband and birth children with him, but that would be a while yet he hoped. He had spotted her and the governor's son flirting and dancing so it might come sooner rather than later, but at least if it was with him he would still get to see her. In the corner of his eye, he looked at her. She was too much of a free spirit to join with someone in marriage. At this moment, there was determination on her face to do the right thing. *That's my girl.*

They arrived at the collapsed entrance to the mine. Dust was everywhere. He could see people frantically trying to aid those trapped. They had not paid attention to the fact that there was a whole mountainside unstable. He had to stop them.

'Stand back,' he boomed. Everyone fell silent; they knew to stop when he shouted. 'If you continue, you will bring the whole mountain down on yourselves. Is that what you want?'

They stared blindly at the Guard Captain, clearly a little scared. They did not want to do anything else wrong.

Lento took charge. He organised groups of people with different jobs. After a whole day of rescue, they managed to bring out the majority of the workforce. They lost ten men down the mine.

If only I had got down here sooner.

Now it was the time for council with the governor; a conversation he would be blunt with. His greed now had killed ten people.

Lento stormed through the doors of the manor where the governor lived. A servant looked at him, terrified. Lento's face was like thunder and the servant, like the miners, dared not cross him.

'Bring your master here, now!' Lento demanded. He was a lean man, built to fight. He trained every day. He knew how to handle himself; it again was another reason why he was picked as Guard Captain.

The servant ran to get Kane. A little time later he was back with him. Kane did not look happy.

'Come into the study, Lento,' he said calmly.

Lento did not need to be shown the way as he had spent many a time in there in council with the governor.

'Lead the way.' He respected the governor enough to follow him into the study. He closed the door behind him.

The study was filled with books on the history of Kaarth and the elves' land of the Everglade. It was a passion of Kane's.

'Sit down, Lento.' He pointed to the chair in front of the desk.

'Thanks, but I would prefer to stand. It's late and I am tired. I will be quick.'

'I think you should sit, Lento. I have grave news for you.' His face looked stricken with grief.

'Grave news? What are you on about?'

'It's your father, mother, and sisters. They have perished due to the storms on the coast. I am sorry.'

Kane was right. He did need to sit down. All of a sudden, he felt empty and sunk to the floor.

Kane poured him a glass of brandy then handed it to him. 'I am truly sorry. You know how fond I was of your father.'

'How do you know this? And what of Morace? Is there no mention of my brother?'

'That is another part of the news I have. Lorett has survived, but sits in the cells underneath the Citadel. Apparently, Lorett and Morace have conspired with the elves. The king has declared war on the elves for their part in the weather and for breaking the treaty. Morace tried to flee with them but some were left behind in the confusion. Lorett was one of them.' He poured out some more brandy for Lento to drink. 'A messenger arrived just this evening with the news.'

Lento did not know what to make of this. How had his brother and sister become entangled with elves? Why had they gone to the Citadel rather than to him or Caser, their other brother who was still alive? His face turned white. *Oh, no. Caser.*

Caser was a live wire and had left the family home as soon as he could. Would word have been dispatched to him, too? He had many followers and who surely would try to get Lorett out of the cells in the Citadel.

'I need to find my brother Caser. He will no doubt have word of this and be looking to surely set free my captive sister without thought or caution. His head will not see the right way without proper counsel.'

'Then leave and take some men. I will see that your daughter is looked after while you are gone.'

Lento set off at dawn the next morning with six men he trusted under his command.

If the king harms my sister, I will hold him responsible.

They were all competent riders, able to ride with haste. Lento had decided to ride to the Citadel, as he would be able to head Caser off if he was to get involved. Caser would then be forced to listen to him and come to his senses. There was, of course, the chance that Caser would already be of a calm mind about the situation and not come out for a fight.

They rode well into the day and would ride many more days to reach the Citadel. Hopefully it would not be too late.

Chapter 15

Lorett sat with the captured elves in the cell they had occupied for a couple of days. She had been told she could leave, but she refused. She was adamant that since the elves had come to help her people, she would help them now.

Lazon was particularly quiet. *I should be the only one here, not everyone else. If only they would let me take the blame for it all.*

Lorett looked at him and smiled.

How can she smile? What is she up to? What does she know that we all don't?

The fact was she could smile because ever since they had been captured she had been singing a song so faint and inaudible no one could tell she was singing it. The effects of the song, however, would soon become evident. There had been six changes of guard since their capture and they were back with the first she had sung the song to.

Men were said to be enchanted by the siren's call. If the siren could get it right, it would mean that she could persuade the man to follow her every beck and call - except a druid. They were immune. The song she had sung was now embedded in the guards' minds, and all she had to do was wait. She was still troubled that Sal Fain had been killed before he could be rescued, which caused her to have to fight back tears, but she kept on going. She hoped that Morace was ready with some form of help, for it would be hard to remain undetected once they were out in the main part of the castle.

Horacio stared at the wall. He had not said a word to Lorett, but he had studied her. It was almost as if he knew what she was up to and decided not to pursue a conversation.

'When we leave, Lazon, you and I need to depart, but first we need to collect something from your world,' Lorett said this suddenly and without warning. Lazon looked at her puzzled. Lorett continued. 'Your magic runs strong. In your woods there is a form of magic that we will need to bring to your sister and my brother, once they find the halls of knowledge.'

Sister? Lazon looked at Lorett. 'Sister? I don't have a sister. I am an only child.'

Lorett shook her head. 'You and Shanrea are of the same age. You have been told of different birthdays but that is not the case. Both of you were orphaned as children. You grew up together, yes, but you are twins. You and Shanrea were simply raised by different people.'

'What? You mean... How do you know this?'

Lorett looked at him intently. 'A troll told me, but I only worked out recently of yours and Shan's heritage.'

A troll told her?

'Just like he told me of what happened with you and your magic, and that if you hadn't used your magic, the worlds would have faced much worse peril.'

'Wait...' Lazon started to ask another question.

She put a finger on Lazon's lips to silence him. Lorett looked out of the window. 'Ok, this is the moment where my brother is to make a decision which will impact what happens next in the chain of events. This will have consequences.' She fell silent.

***

Morace waited in the dark for what seemed like ages. He was beginning to think that Tavener's fears were substantial; that because someone had used the code that had not been anticipated, he could be dispatched.

'Who are you and how do you know of the shadows?' The voice startled him. It seemed to be all around the room. 'Well, don't keep me waiting, boy. You did bring me here.'

'My name is Morace Roccan. I was told that I could come here if I required assistance by my friend Tavener, who met up with either you or someone you know that can help us.'

'The shadows do not help strangers, but it would appear you have something we want.'

'What is it you want of me?'

'You are a druid, are you not?'

'Well yes, but I have just discovered this.'

'Well, then you may know there is a place where the druids once stored all their knowledge, in order for us to help rescue your sister, Lorett her name is, right?'

'How do you know of my sister?' *Or rather how did they know she needed rescuing? Tavener, what is this?*

'Morace, we are the shadows. We know everything. Now, you do not want to fail your sister, do you? Like you failed your mother, father and your other sisters?'

Morace's guilt soared at the words that almost crippled him.

'That's it; remember the emotions you felt when that happened? How bad would it be if your last sister were to die too? Your twin?'

The shadow agent worked his wicked tongue on the mind of the young druid, drawing him into his own will. Throughout his time as an Agent of the Shadows, he had been able to tempt the young druids to do his mistress's bidding. However, since there were other wiser druids about back then, he had been unable to find the strong-hold of the druids and learn from their repository of knowledge.

I have ambitions to finally replace the Empress, but she has other plans. I can sense them, but she refuses to relay them to me. That will be her undoing. Now my time has come to seize power.

'Morace, I would ask that when you have found the re-pository of knowledge, you will send word to me, and al-low me entry into its halls.'

Morace considered. Was this really his decision to make? His thought wandered over to his sister and her current predicament.

The shadow agent honed in again. 'You don't want your sister to have the same fate, do you?'

'No, I don't. I will find this stronghold and take you to it, if you promise to help me free my sister.'

'Good choice. Wait at the sewer near the foot of the wall. Be there for midnight of the next day.'

The shadow agent disappeared before Morace could acknowledge the last words said. He felt uneasy about the whole encounter. *Have I made a mistake?*

What also did not help was this person did not show themselves; they could have something to hide. Hindsight was once again playing on his mind. *There is nothing I can do now.* He would speak with Shanrea on this. He had thought a lot about Shanrea. She was a druid too and they had managed to bond. He knew he had feelings for her, but what did that mean? More questions ran through his mind; he really did need to sort them out.

Shanrea waited patiently for Morace to return. Four days drifted by slowly, and her worry grew. *I should have gone with him. I should have given him back up.*

Tavener could see her concern. 'You love him, don't you?' He asked out right.

'I have feelings for him, yes. Perhaps it's because we are the same.'

He looked at her and smiled. 'He likes you. I can tell.'

Before the conversation went further, Morace burst through the door, startling them all. He heaved and vomited on the floor, then again.

'I have a bad feeling that what I have done mayhap be the wrong decision,' he said.

'What do you mean? What happened?' Shanrea asked.

He explained what had happened in detail.

'That sounds like a shadow agent to me.' Zaan looked as if he was about to vomit too. He explained who they served, and that nothing was ever simple or clear cut with them. 'I had not realised they were in both worlds.' Zaan started to pace the room. 'I need to go back and inform the council on this matter. They need to know. I also need to inform them of the death of Sal Fain. They need to decide on what action to take.'

'I understand, but we should wait until we have rescued everyone from the cells. So we need to be at the sewer for midnight the next day?' Shanrea looked at Morace for the answer to her question.

'Yes, that's what it said, but we shan't all go. Tavener can come, we will be under cover of darkness and you two can stay here and wait for us.'

Shanrea looked up sharply. She did not agree with the decision that was made. It was the same face Lorett always made when Morace went to do a task on his own. Morace knew it well.

'No, I will not wait around this time for you to potentially be led into a trap.' She kissed him. 'I am coming with you this time.' She gave him no chance to object by kissing him again. She stood next to him and linked her fingers with his.

Damn, she is just like Lorett, but that saved me before.

Zaan spoke next. 'And I most certainly will not be sitting around doing nothing while the prince is a captive, and as the last of the guards, it is my duty to make sure he is safe.' He moved to their side too.

This was not what Morace had planned. He wanted someone to remain here in case something went wrong.

They slept for the last time in the little hut in the scrubs. Despite it being quite grotty, they had grown fond of the little place.

In the morning, they packed and prepared themselves. They had time to relax a short while. Shanrea and Morace took to a room on their own to sit together and read a little more of the journal. They took in some of the incantations that may be useful to them.

By midnight, they were waiting by the sewer.

There had been silence within the cell, but suddenly there was commotion and noise of death. The guard fell to the floor and a shadow fell over them. Suddenly the King of Kaarth appeared. Lorett looked at him puzzled. *Why is the king here at such a late hour?*

The king entered the cell. Slowly he withdrew a short knife. He backed the prince into a corner, and before the prince could do anything, the king slashed the knife across the prince's throat. The prince gasped his last breath then fell to the floor, his life flowing out of him. The wall and the floor were painted with his blood.

The shadow appeared again, this time over the King of Kaarth. He fell to the floor, lying motionless. He was now dead, too.

The shadow disappeared and Lorett looked at Lazon. *Morace what have you done? This may have bad consequences for us all.*

'Lazon, we need to go. The guards will change soon and I lost concentration long enough for my song to disappear. I was not expecting this.'

'The prince is dead, so is your king.' He did not bear thinking about what this meant for the worlds in which they lived. There had been so much death already and there would surely be more to come.

They fled the scene of which someone would surely discover soon. They needed to find somewhere to flee. Where could they go?

Lorett took Lazon's hand and pulled him in a direction. Somehow, she knew where to go and which turns to take. *I need to find a way to conceal us.* As soon as she thought it, the words of the song came out from her mouth. They were concealed.

Once it had passed midnight Morace began to pace. The shadow had told him to be prompt and now there was nothing. Then he heard the patter of feet on a hard floor as they echoed out of one of the sewer pipes. He searched the entrances of them all and found which one was giving off the sounds. He looked into it and saw shadows move. He shuddered.

Only two people were in the tunnels. His heart dropped for a moment thinking that Lorett had not made it. Then he heard her song. *So who was not with them?* As they came closer, it was apparent that the prince was missing.

When Lazon and Lorett escaped the mouth of the pipe, they were buffeted by questions.

'Where is the prince?' Zaan asked who had immediately stepped forward.

'He did not make it.' Lorett struggled to speak. She was worried since it was the king who had killed him. What consequences would that have? 'The guards could start looking for us. We need to get out of here, really.'

They decided to leave the Citadel. It was not an option to stay there now. Once the king was found dead, there would be no place for them to hide. Just as they were about to depart, they heard a horse.

'Morace, Lorett I have found you.'

Lorett looked at the horseman and knew instantly who it was. Their eldest brother Lento was here. *To save them?*

'The prince was slain by the king's hand?' Lento looked puzzled at this, 'the king might have just declared war with the elves.'

Lento had taken them to a small farmhouse that he used when he visited this part of the country, owned by the governor.

'The king was then killed by a shadow,' Lorett added to the story.

A shadow?

Morace's heart skipped a beat. *I should never have agreed to this. It was* stupid. 'It's all my fault, I have now possibly caused a war between the elves and the humans with my stupidity.'

'You were not stupid, just young. The shadow agent probably played you; played to your need to protect your family, to protect me.' Lorett finished, hoping her words helped a little.

'So what do we do now?' Tavener asked.

Zaan spoke first. 'I must head back to the Everglade. I have failed in my task. I must report to the king and the council on what has happened.' He spoke sadly. Despite the elves being the apparent cause of Kaarth's plight, their prince and heir to the throne had been slain in Kaarth while he sat in his cell. It would be seen by the council that although they offered a hand to help the humans, it had been thrown back at them. It would be hard for him but he would try to persuade the council that the humans had acted under a cloud of suffering and were not thinking straight.

'There is something that Lazon and I must do in the Everglade. So we shall travel there. We would enjoy your company for a while, Zaan, if you would let us?' Lorett looked at Zaan with tired eyes. She had rested while in the cells and her mind raced with thoughts that she did not quite understand. Morace shifted uncomfortably at the idea. What if the elves sought to gain retribution by taking her life? He knew though that he would not be able to travel with her, because he and Shanrea had to find this repository of knowledge. They had found the location written in the journal so now they had to get there.

'Shanrea and I must travel to the Norse, to find something that will help us and let us learn how to tackle this problem.'

Lorett looked at her brother. He had grown quite mature in the past weeks and so had she with this thrust at them. They had no choice but to be.

'Well, mine and Lazon's task is going to somehow aid you once you have found your knowledge so we will meet soon.'

Tavener was torn. Should he go with the druids or venture into the Everglade with Lorett and Lazon? Perhaps Lorett and Lazon could benefit from his help on their journey. Morace and Shanrea were druids and had magic to command that was very powerful.

'I will venture with Lorett and Lazon.' Tavener looked at Morace. 'I would love to travel the Norse, but I will have time to do that later. I might never get the chance to venture into the Everglade again. I would like to see that.' He embraced Morace strongly. 'Good luck, and I will see you soon, no doubt.'

They set off, two parties in different directions. Morace and Shanrea headed to the far north. Lorett, Lazon, Zaan, and Tavener went back to the forest where they had met the elves.

Morace looked back as his sister slowly faded into the distance, a tear in his eye. 'I do hope she is okay. I would hate for something to happen to her.'

Shanrea took his hand giving it a squeeze. 'She will be fine. Lazon will look after her.' She was worried about Lazon. So much had been revealed and she had not had a chance to speak with him about it. She still had to muddle over it in her mind, anyway. This would give her time.

Gragio had been told to wait for Twak, who apparently needed to go on an errand all of a sudden. The Pwca returned on the fifth night. Soon after, they found it - the pool of shadows. Dark rock surrounded a black pool of water that was as still as ice. *So what now? Do I wait for what...something to happen?*

'Twak, what do I do now?'

'We wait!' The forest creature had gone back into the form it had first appeared to Gragio in. The small stunted creature was ugly and smarmy.

Twak took out a flute and began to play tunes. With the tunes, the water began to bubble and shadows began to emit from within the pool.

Twak stopped playing the tune and pointed at Gragio. 'Now it's time for you to play with some magic. Create a storm with thunder. You must have it in you, I am sure; otherwise the Shadow Empress would not have chosen you.'

Gragio was unsure about this. Was this not the cause of all the strife in the world? He was about to protest.

'Summon the storm,' Twak said with impatience.

The creature was quite forceful and Gragio agreed with reluctance. He looked within himself and found the incants. Within minutes, the storm had been summoned and the thunderbolt struck the centre of the pool. The water churned and a Wayward Gate opened up, its black obsidian shining with the storm.

'Great, the Empress was right about you.'

'Why have we created a gate?'

'Why so many questions?' the woodland creature asked jokingly.

Gragio could then hear the sound of drums from within the gate. Figures started to form in the gap between. It was a man. No, not a man but a dwarf, clad in armour made out of a black metal. It looked so strong. More appeared. The first took its battle-axe and swung it around his head. Before Gragio knew what happened, his head rolled around on the floor.

'Finally! I wanted him gone for a while.' The woodland faery then began to transform again and became Gragio.

'You keep bad company, Twak. Elves are arrogant,' the dwarf said as he held up Gragio's head and spat at it.

'I can still use his body. Give it here.'

Chapter 16

Twak stood in his Gragio transformation and looked at 'his' army that had come through the portal; one hundred thousand strong dwarves. Their General stood next to him clad in black armour smoking a pipe.

The General's face was scrunched up with a scowl. His black beard was pleated along with his long black hair. The axe that took off the head of Gragio rested on his shoulder.

'For many a year I have waited for what was promised to us by the Shadow Empress,' he said with a deep voice. 'We pretend to be wiped out by dragons and we have to wait over a thousand years for what is rightly ours. My ancestors have passed the stories on to me through our entire bloodline.' He started to pace.

'We did have a little problem,' Twak said. 'We had to get you out a little before we were completely ready, for the Weather Magic was triggered before it was meant to.'

The General spat on the floor. 'Bleddy elves always meddling in that which should be left.'

Twak looked at him. He fed on the hate that was being emitted from the dwarf. 'But all is not lost, for we have been able to formulate a new plan. One that might suit us... I mean, you better.'

The dwarf looked at the faery creature who masqueraded as the elf. 'I do say, you had better tell me this plan of yours before I become entangled with a rage I cannot stop.' He was unhappy with the news he had received that the plan had changed.

'The plan is set straight now. Sooner or later the elves and humans will wage a war with one another, by a design of the shadow's making. The elves have lost their prince and the humans their king.' The forest creature salivated as he relayed the new plan. There would be so much hatred and so much terror. He relished it. 'So that will mean shortly they will be at a war with each other.'

The dwarf's eyebrow rose. He knew what would happen once the war started. 'You mean for them to fight for a while, do you?'

Twak nodded.

'Then we will come and wipe both their races off the face of both worlds?' The dwarf ventured. He liked the idea of the dwarves wiping out yet another two races.

'Not entirely, unless you mean for the dwarves to do the menial tasks that you don't think your mighty race ought to do?'

'You mean us to rule these people? As what, an overlord?'

'I do, and a fine overlord you would make, too. Don't you think?'

'That does sound a fitting new beginning, instead of us sitting in the shadows waiting for our rise.' The dwarf was taken in yet again.

The dwarves had made a deal with the Shadow Empress through one of her agents who was now a forgotten memory thanks to Twak. The dwarves made this pact when they realised that they faced their extinction. The empress had sent the agent to his ancestor and they made a deal. This was to be the deal now coming into fruition.

'We shall wait for the races of man and elf to almost finish themselves off before we come to pick up the pieces.' The dwarf stood proud as he looked upon his army. 'There is one thing that has been puzzling me however.' The dwarf broke his moment of joy. Twak thought he knew what would be asked next, but he waited for the dwarf to say it. 'What is it that the empress will get out of all of this?'

'Oh, the empress gets to witness something completely epic unfold before her.' A half-truth he gave to the dwarf. Twak knew exactly what would happen. The elves and men would battle, and the hatred would form the energy for the empress to become stronger. The dwarves then would get involved meaning more energy for his empress. The empress gained her power from hatred, envy and death. She revelled in it. It was how she had lived for so long. The two worlds created much hatred that fed her; it had sustained her for thousands of years.

All of this was unknown to the races. Most people had no knowledge of the shadows and their empress- except for one, but he was long gone, dispatched by the empress herself. They had been lovers, the stories stated for those who had heard of them. The powerful man met with a beautiful woman on his travels and they fell madly in love with one another. He had come from the Norse, it was said; a cold, perilous place unless you knew how to handle yourself. Both looked for power, and looked to gain more. However, for the empress it had become an obsession that came to consume her. This was before she became the empress of the shadows.

She had discovered how to gain from the negative aspects of the world; all its hate, anger and frustration made her ever more powerful. When the man she had fallen in love with discovered this, he realised it would end badly. No one should have that amount of hate and anger flowing through them. It would surely corrupt her. He watched her become more and more consumed by it. He gradually lost the woman he had fallen in love with. She started to refuse to venture into the light. She receded into the shadows whenever she could.

It reached the point where she screamed with hurt if the light touched her. He hatched a plan. He knew things would get worse if he did not do anything. The plan worked as he intended. He knew he would not be powerful enough to completely unmake her, which would destroy everything about her. She was much too powerful for that. He managed to weaken her enough to then hold her. She would still be sustained by the hatred of the worlds, but at least she could not do anything with it.

There was only one problem. He would have to leave the world he currently existed in. However, before he did, he wrote a journal to give to people who would follow him. He also knew that if something happened large enough to trigger a whole flurry of hate, she might just become powerful enough to rise again.

That was Twak's purpose now; to bring the empress back into the world as a force to be reckoned with. The humans, elves, and dwarves were all pawns in this. Soon the shadows would return.

'General, you shall have what you were destined for, I assure you.' Twak still had to make sure he had the dwarves' trust - at least until they were no longer needed.

Chapter 17

The Norse was true to form. Cold winds ravaged the two druids. They made little headway once they had reached its start. It had been two weeks of hard travel, and that was with the horses given to them by Morace's brother. The temperature dropped rapidly as they neared the colder lands in the north. They made the decision to leave the horses behind and continue on foot.

They were now on their fourth day without the horses. They ventured into a taiga pine forest. Its trees were taller than either of them had ever seen. Luckily, they had discovered the magic they could use to keep warm but it drained them, so they could only use it in short bursts. When they walked, they struggled to sustain the magic that took away the chilly air on their bones and joints.

'It's getting late. We need to rest.' Morace stated.

They caught some game that lived in the forest. They slept side by side, over the past weeks they had become closer than ever, as they only had each other for company. Morace stroked back Shanrea's hair and smoothed it around her ear. It was something she liked. He knew it gave her comfort.

It did not give her comfort if he did it while she slept; it meant that he was not sleeping, that he was thinking. Shanrea attempted to make him comfortable so that he could sleep better.

Morace regretted the deal he made with the shadow agent. It looked like two races were likely to go to war with one another. They were so far away from everything;

away from the problems he had caused. A king and a prince had died because of him.

'Go to sleep, Morace. It is late.' She kissed him and then turned over to sleep.

'Nairia, I think these might be the two we were told to look out for.' A monkey then screeched quietly. The wraith stood in between the trees. He waited for the monkey to decide what he should do next. As he watched the two that slept before him, he smiled. 'Everything appears to be going to plan.'

The monkey then moved forward to the boy; a human, child, almost. With tentativeness, Nairia moved even closer. She had started to track the boy and the girl ever since they entered the Norse. As she sniffed the air around her, she looked at the wraith who urged her on. Lightly, she walked on to the chest of the boy. It was now morning. She started to tap him on the face.

Morace woke to a tap on his face. His chest thumped. He could hear a little noise. His eyes opened slowly. They widened with shock as they met a pair of large eyes. The thing they belonged to knocked him on his head. Its furry tail flicked his face a couple of times. It was a little monkey. Morace sat up and the monkey moved to sit upon his head. It flicked its tail across his face.

Using his hand closest to Shanrea, he shook her lightly to wake her from her slumber. She yawned as she stretched away the stiffness that had developed while she had slept.

'What, what is it?' She could not see through her sleep-filled eyes.

'Shanrea, there is a monkey on my head.'

Shanrea looked at his head. She was speechless at the sight of a monkey perched on his head. She suppressed a laugh at Morace's expense.

'Aw, is it not the cutest little thing?' Shanrea asked jokingly.

'It would be if it had not woken me up by hitting me on the head, and don't laugh, I can see your mouth curving.'

Shanrea could not help it. She burst into laughter unable to contain it anymore, rolling around on the frosted floor.

'It is a little funny, you have to admit; and look at your face; it's a picture.' Shanrea put her arm around Morace, and the monkey ran up and perched itself on her shoulder. She gave it some leftover food from the night before, and stroked its head. As she packed everything away, Morace watched her go about the camp as though having a monkey on your shoulder was normal. The monkey looked at him and Morace was certain it stuck its tongue out at him.

'Nairia does not normally take so well to strangers.' A voice from within the woods called out giving Morace and Shanrea a start. 'Unless there is magic involved.'

The monkey jumped off Shanrea and ran through the trees, to the voice's source. In the next instant, a man built almost the same size as Tavener appeared. He wore white furs and almost blended in with the snow, except for the brown form of the monkey on his shoulder. His hair was white as the snow. He was perfectly camouflaged for an ambush.

Was this an ambush? Morace suddenly thought. He scanned for more of these men.

'You don't need to be worrying, little druid. There is only I here.'

'How do you know that we are Druids?' Shanrea asked. 'Have you been following us? Who are you?'

'My name is really of no importance. I am here just to guide you, or have you not yet reached that part of the journal?'

They had not. They had set off for the Norse with such a focused determination that they had not had the chance to read much further.

'I thought as much,' he said.

Shanrea had a sudden thought. 'You are one of them, aren't you? You are a wraith, but you are more whole.'

The man nodded. 'I am indeed a wraith, although not contained to the marshes, young elf. We have a few more days of travel to reach Tiamscien, the knowledge repository.' He waited for them to finish gathering their stuff before setting off with him.

The wraith's pace was fast. Morace and Shanrea managed to keep up for most of the morning before they needed to stop to eat. The monkey grew attached to Shanrea and sat on her shoulder while they walked, her tail brushing across her back.

'I hope you don't plan on keeping that,' Morace said with a little disgust in his voice.

'Why not?' Shanrea looked at him with her sharp eyes.

'Well, erm, it's just, well, it's a little smelly and it did try to attack me.'

The Nairia screeched at him.

'Smelly? Attack?' Shanrea's mouth cracked open a little smile. 'Morace. She did not attack you. She merely gave you a wakeup call.'

Morace turned back to his breakfast. He mumbled under his breath. 'Did too attack me.'

Once they had eaten, they were set on route again. While they travelled, Morace's mind constantly wondered what Lorett was doing and how she fared.

Lorett had said that she needed to get something from the elven world, and then bring it to them once they had found the place they were looking for. They were twins. They used to do everything together as they grew up. Ever since Pa had died, all that happened was change. *Why can't things not just be the way they were meant to be?*

'Morace, it's okay.' It would appear that Shanrea could tell when his mind worked over something.

'Is it? So far all there has been is death and destruction; what more is there to be?'

The wraith stopped them suddenly. 'Change happens all the time, young druid. Sometimes what may seem bad could be the opposite in the long run. It takes time.' He started to walk. 'What may seem good at the time could turn out to be bad.' Nairia made a noise in agreement.

'How long have we left?' Morace asked.

'Patience, young druid. We will arrive by nightfall.'

'Great, we need to hurry. I still need to figure out what needs to be done.' Morace looked at Shanrea. 'Then we can call for Lorett. I am sure she would have finished what she needed to do by now.'

'Do you even know how you would do that?'

Morace had not really put much thought to it, actually. He would have to look in the journal for advice.

They reached a more enclosed part of the forest and something in the air did not sit right for Shanrea. It all felt a little odd. She could sense the change in the air. There was a clear presence of magic within this part of the forest. It was magic like hers and Morace's.

'Can you feel it too?' she asked Morace.

'I can. We are close to what we are looking for. The magic here is strong.'

They continued to walk. The twilight created a dark glow by the time they reached two rows of trees that created a tunnel. Once they got to the end, Morace looked up at the sight in front of him.

There was a huge structure. It was a building so grand in size that Morace could scarcely believe it existed in the forest without being seen. *It must be the magic.* It must be warded against unwanted eyes. All knowledge of it must have been kept secret for thousands of years. *That must be some powerful magic right there.* The masonry work on the building was immense; it must have taken some talented hands to create all the workings on it. It was dark, though, and you could tell it had not seen anyone for a while.

'Welcome, young druids. It has been a while since anyone living has ventured down the path we have just taken. It feels good to see it now. Go forth and immerse yourselves in what you need. Oh, and look after the monkey for me. I would be grateful.'

The monkey made a little noise in what Morace thought must have been a goodbye to the wraith.

'Where will you go now?' Morace asked, but the wraith had gone.

Chapter 18

Lorett, along with Lazon and Tavener, had spent the better part of a week to get to the world of the elves. It took another week once on Everglade to find the area they needed. Both Lorett and Tavener marvelled at the Everglade's beauty. It truly was a beautiful place with lush forests that hid gorges where the water ran into magnificent valleys. There was so much plant life that Lorett had never seen in her life before. Had she had the time to study them, she would have. The trees were huge; the magnitude of their colour suggested that autumn was here. The shades of reds and oranges caught her eye wherever she turned. Being a siren, she felt more in tune with the nature of this world then her own, which saddened her. Did that mean that she might want to stay here once this was all over? Did she have a choice? She looked at Lazon. *Where do you fit in all of this?*

He had some power. Perhaps was meant to trigger the change that was coming. He certainly had the ability to do so.

'I know this place,' Lazon said suddenly as they entered a clearing with a little stream and a gate. The gate was a strange sight for them to see. What was it doing here? 'This is Alk-Mea, The Resting. In your tongue, it's the laying place for the sirens.'

Lorett looked at him. 'This is where the sirens go when they depart from the worlds?

'Yes, and no living siren has ever set foot here. No living being, that is for that matter. It is forbidden in fact.'

Lorett looked at him a little unnerved. 'Well it is here I was told to go, to collect something that we will need.'

Lorett strode into the centre of the clearing and touched the gate. Its metal was stone cold, and with her touch it lit up. She began to sing a song with complex lyrics, ones she had not even known she knew. It was an innate magic that took her by surprise. She understood what needed to be done. With the words sung, orbs of lights started to zip from the gate, until there were seven lights around Lorett.

Tavener placed his hand on his crossbow. Not knowing if he would be able to protect them from the orbs.

'I don't like this,' Tavener said.

The orbs started to get bigger then longer. They took the shape of something humanoid. They started to walk towards Lorett. When they started to circle her, she stood still and continued to sing to them.

One of them turned to Lazon who stood to the side, in awe at the sight before him. It stretched out its hand. Another reached out to Lorett.

They were close enough now to touch. Their hands clasped onto the shoulders of Lazon and Lorett.

A bright flash blinded Tavener. When he regained his sight, he saw that Lazon and Lorett lay on the floor. The light forms had disappeared. *Damn I was meant to be protecting them.* He went to check their bodies; they were still alive. He was relieved. He tried to wake them but nothing he did worked. At a loss at what to do, he sat down with his crossbow across his knees and waited. *If anything, I can protect them from harm this way.*

'Where are we?' Lazon asked. 'Are we dead?'

'No we are not dead, but if we do die here, we will die in the outer world too.'

The thought of that chilled him to the bone.

Lorett got up to walk. There were lights all around them. It looked like they were still in the forest clearing. The gate was there but everything was lighter and slightly fuzzy.

'This is the clearing, but where is Tavener?' wondered Lazon.

'He was left behind. Only beings of magic are permitted to enter,' Lorett said. 'We have now truly entered Alk-Mea.'

Lazon did not know it but she still sang quietly. The song she sang was to find what the resting sirens looked after. Time seemed as though it would be endless in this place, but Lorett knew that they did not have long in this state of consciousness. Their bodies would also be defenceless and prone to outside attack. Luckily, they had Tavener with them and he could protect them. That gave Lorett some reassurance. However, what concerned her most was the harm that this exposure would give to their minds, especially since they were alive when they entered.

'The Alk-Mea is a tree, Lazon, and inside it there will be three stones. There will be magic warding it. I will need you to break the wards so that I can retrieve the stones.'

'Stones? But how will I know what to do?'

'The same way I do. You already have the knowledge deep within you.'

They came across another clearing that featured a large willow tree. It was bent over with age. Lorett explained that the tree was dying. It was the reason for the world's plight, not Lazon's go at weather magic, although the elves use of weather magic caused the tree to slowly lose its life.

'Why didn't anyone stop us all those years ago?'

'The sirens tried, but the elves refused to listen,' Lorett returned.

'So now it is up to us to save what is left of the races after the war that will more than likely ensue?' he asked.

'Pretty much,' she responded sadly. 'But there is one thing that concerns me. There seems to be something stirring the pot between the races; something that hopes to gain from this war.' She looked at him hard. 'Do you remember the shadows in the cell? They were too unnatural for my liking.' She remembered also the description that Morace gave of his encounter in the Bolted Crossbow.

'What do you mean?'

'I mean that someone wants us destroyed and it is up to us to find out who.' They had walked under the willow, its long tendrils brushed over their heads. 'I would not have been able to do that on my own.'

What did she mean?

'You mean that I did some sort of magic?'

'You did, yes.'

She put her hands in a hollow in the tree. Her eyes widened with surprise.

It had dropped on Lorett's body from the trees, and it took a moment or two for Tavener to realise what it was doing. A spider the size of a small dog, with red and black legs worked its way from her legs to her head. It then sunk its fangs into the back of her neck before Tavener had time to load the crossbow. Once he had, he shot the spider off her sleeping body. It writhed and curled up around the bolt. Tavener dropped the crossbow as he ran to her to look at the wound in her neck.

It had already started to go white round the holes where the spider's fangs had penetrated her skin. She started to shake violently and her temperature plummeted. Tavener was at a loss what to do. He did not even know what type of spider it was. *There is nothing like this on Kaarth.*

He remembered what he did when Morace was bitten by a venomous snake as a child. *Perhaps this works the same way?* He applied pressure around the bite then began to suck out the venom. As he spat out the vile stuff, he hoped it had not already begun to corrupt her body.

Lazon saw Lorett shake, and caught her as she collapsed. He gently guided her to the floor and saw the marks form on her neck. It looked like a spider bite. He suddenly realised what spider it was: a shaku. He knew that unless they acted fast, Lorett would die. Out of instinct, he started to do the exact same thing Tavener had done. His magic exploded and he could feel it work. Lorett began to stir.

Lorett is sitting in the Alk-Mea. There is a dance in her favour. Has she saved the world and entered the resting with sirens past? Is it all over? Had she done enough?

An older siren comes over to her, smiling; long silver hair caught in an invisible wind.

'Sit with me, child.'

Lorett obeys.

'You know you are a siren?'

Lorett nods.

'You know not yet of your heritage however.'

'I am a fisherman's daughter and twin to a druid?'

'You are more than just that. A diary will reveal all. It was my brother's'

'You know of the diary?'

'I do, take heed of what it says, child, and who it is signed by also.'

'I have to go back now, don't I?'

'You do.'

Lorett goes back to the ground and lies down.

The redness from Lorett's neck started to dissipate and Tavener emptied his mouth of the vile stuff once more, relieved. Her body became still, her temperature returned to normal. He collected his crossbow from the ground and watched for more of the spiders. He was more vigilant this time. He focused on one spot for no more than a second. His eyes darted at every angle to find what may be hidden.

The flash happened again suddenly, which blinded him. He hated not being able to see; it was his biggest fear. It would mean that he could not hunt.

The flash slowly fizzled out. Tavener's eyes managed to adjust again to the light. He saw the same humanoid forms once again above the bodies of Lorett and Lazon.

Lorett and Lazon started to stir as they came back to their senses. They sat up, and the forms then disappeared.

Tavener moved to Lorett. She started to get up but as she got to her feet, she wobbled in a daze. She was still weak. Tavener caught her as she lost all buoyancy and almost crumpled to the floor.

'She is weak. She needs rest.' Tavener was worried. He did not know if she still had some of the spider's venom inside her. 'There was a spider, I killed it but...'

'The chances are, Tavener, she still has some of the venom in her. I think I was able to weaken its effects with my magic, but there is a healer who specialises with these spiders in the university. They travelled to the university arriving the morning of the next day.

Lorett sat propped up in bed, awake and alert. A day spent in the university infirmary allowed her to fight off the rest of the affliction she had received. Tavener brought her news of the elves' discussion about the situation with their prince. The king was livid. The fact that the king of Kaarth's own hand slew his son made matters worse. He held a council meeting for a week.

'They have decided that they will go to war, Lorett.' His face looked saddened. She knew that Tavener disliked war. Some people relish a fight for their land but not Tavener. He liked to hunt for his thrills rather than going through a battle with people it would be better to bash tankards with.

Lorett got up suddenly. She was nearly out of the room before Tavener could protest. She had made up her mind to go and speak to the king of the elves, and she did not care for people who would try to stop her. Despite still being a little weak, she looked as though she could throw thunder.

The elves on guard let her pass. Perhaps it was the fact she was a siren and even the elves would respect a siren.

She made her way to the king using a song to seek him out, which she muttered to herself. She made it to the huge, black, iron doors before the guards then prevented her access.

'The king has asked to not be disturbed, Miss.'

Lorett looked at them. She stopped the seeking song. 'I must see your king!' she demanded. The elves were a little cautious. They had never seen such determination from someone so young. 'I am a siren. You will let me enter, now!' The guards looked at one another. She had put a little song behind the words, which would force the elves to listen. She had hoped not to have to use it on them, but they left her no choice. This was important. She needed to see the king.

The guards opened the door to give entry to Lorett. All of her weariness from the bite of the spider was gone with the adrenaline that pumped through her. The king turned to greet her with no shock at the interruption.

'I have been expecting you, siren. Lorett, is it not?' He pointed to a chair.

She took it, ready to talk to the king of the elves.

Chapter 19

'The king has agreed to talk with whoever is leading the people of Kaarth when we return.' Lorett looked happy and delighted at the breakthrough. 'He will only do it if I am there, and he will not visit the Citadel.' She spoke to Tavener who sat down in front of her. He still felt bad for not protecting her. *If she had died, we would have been doomed.* His mind raced from scenario to scenario of what could have happened if she had died; if he had failed her.

'Hmm... did he not seem too calm about the situation?' Tavener asked suspiciously. It seemed too easy for this to be a legitimate attempt at making peace, if you considered all that had gone on. Despite being what she was, Lorett was still young and could easily misread things.

'It's okay, Tavener. We will meet at Darth where my brother is so that he can be present too.' She hugged him. 'Tavener, it will be okay.' She walked out of the room. As she closed the door behind her, a thought crossed her mind.

I hope it's going to be okay. I could read nothing from the king of the elves; he was closed.

She was uncomfortable with the way the king felt, but his face looked sincere. She searched for Lazon; she wanted to speak to him for a while.

It was early evening and Lazon had gone to a tavern to relax for a bit. Lorett found him by using the tracking song once again.

'Can I sit?'

Lazon was staring into his empty beer glass. He looked up at her when she spoke, startled at her sudden appearance. He nodded at the empty stool and she took it.

'It looks like we go back now to find out the fate of this war, eh?' Lazon still blamed himself, despite Lorett's persistence that he had helped save the worlds. He had even seen the tree and its life was draining already.

'Lazon, you must believe that you are not to blame for this.'

'I know, but... I think of you and your family.'

She looked at him hard and intense. 'My family fell victim to a storm, that's all. It could have happened anytime.' She tried hard to make him feel better. 'It would have happened...'

'You don't know that,' he retorted.

'Actually it *was* going to happen. I discovered weeks back.' She looked at Lazon again with piercing eyes. She leaned into him and kissed him. He was shocked at first but then he leaned in and kissed her back. Once they pulled apart, he spoke first.

'Why would you do that?'

'Kiss you?'

'Yes.'

'Why do people normally kiss?' She said jokingly. She kissed him again then walked out of the tavern. He looked after her, perplexed. He had not much experience with women. The only one he properly knew was like a sister to him. It turned out that she *was* his sister. That reminded him - he still had questions about that and it would seem that Lorett could answer them.

Lazon ran after Lorett. When he caught up with her, he pulled her to the side by the arm.

'I need answers, Lorett. You know about Shanrea and me being twins.'

'Yes, it's true, Lazon. I have no idea of its significance however.' She started to walk again and he followed.

'You don't truly know?'

'I don't know. I wish I did so that it would be easier for me to think on what needs doing, but I am sorry, I just don't have all the answers.' *Everyone expects me to have the answers.*

'That is something that plays on your mind a lot, is it not?'

'Yes. I do get frustrated at the fact I don't know all the answers.'

It was something she could not change. One thing that she wanted to find more out about was the druids and their role in the whole thing. There was more to this than she could decipher on her own. There were shadows and forces that she could not hope to contend with, but she remained focused on what needed to be done.

They had reached the place in which they were to stay for their last night in the Everglade before they headed back to Kaarth. She turned to Lazon, kissed him goodnight, and went to bed.

Her dreams were troubled and she tossed and turned throughout the night. Something plagued her mind like a tic she could not scratch. She woke up at the same point in each dream; every time the problem was about to be revealed. She screamed once and Tavener burst in to find out what was wrong. She did not know why, but she soon fell back to sleep with Tavener watching over her.

Once Tavener left the room he was approached by Lazon.

'It could be the spider. Once they have bitten someone, they can cause things like this.' What he did not say was that the spider's influence played on the things running in the person's mind. 'Once it is finally out of her system she will be fine.' He smiled and went back to bed himself.

Dawn approached and it was an early start for them. They had washed and eaten breakfast before the first light had appeared and the bird song chirped in the air. Lazon met up with Tavener and Lorett, who stood together. A message had to be sent to the new king of Kaarth to inform them of what will happen and that they must make preparations to travel.

Lorett watched as Lazon approached. She did not know why she had had the urge to kiss him the night before. Perhaps she pitied him for feeling responsible. *Do I have feelings for him? Or was it just something to make him feel better about the death of my family?* The truth was that she did hold him somewhat responsible, but he was important in this and they needed him on board. Lorett took his hand and gave it a squeeze. *He needs me for this, to show that he is not alone and that he is not blamed for what happened.*

'When we get to Darth, you can stay in my brother's house.' She did not want him around the talks with the kings, not after what happened the last time. She felt he would self-implode with guilt if he were bombarded with these talks as well.

They walked to the gate room to begin their journey back to Kaarth, to discover what was to happen in the worlds. They called for the gate to appear. They stood perplexed; it had not appeared. Lorett looked at the elven guard who tended to the gate. The guard shifted uncomfortably.

'Something happened on the first venture into your world. One member of the company was found dead and the gate destroyed. I kept it quiet. I had fallen asleep on duty so did not say anything.'

Lorett moved over to the place where the gate should have stood.

'That explains what happened to the missing guard that came with us.' Lazon said.

'There was powerful magic here. We will just have to use the gate we came in from instead, won't we?'

At the clearing, this time a few of the elven guard accompanied them.

'Looks like the makers of these gates made some more.'

The gate rose. They were a complete replica of the one they were trying to go through to have the talks.

These talks would affect everything they knew and held close to them. They had to go well. Otherwise, she and the rest of them would have a struggle on their hands to do what was needed.

It had been decided that Lorett, Lazon, and Tavener would travel first to bring word to the new king that his presence would be needed in Darth to have talks with the elven king. It had been a week or so since Lorett had been on Kaarth; she had missed it but she had felt strongly drawn to the elven land. Perhaps it was the fact that she was a siren and their resting place was in that world. If she departed from the worlds, she would end up there. That thought sent a chill down her spine.

They walked through the gate.

Once they stepped through, they were met by the Citadel Home Guard and placed under arrest for the murder of the king. Lorett was almost in shock but then realised that they were still fugitives on the run in this world. They were taken to an encampment and kept under guard. Patrols were stationed by the gate to capture or kill any elves that were to pass through.

It's a good job the king of the elves did not come through with us. Lorett tried to talk to the guard who was on duty at the time. There were about a hundred men at the camp; it was a few clicks away from the gateway.

'Please, I must speak to whoever is in command of this unit,' Lorett pleaded with their captors.

'Silence, girl!' said the guard with venom in his voice. Clearly, his orders were to not speak to her. Did he know what she was? What her powers could do? She shifted uncomfortably. Time was now truly of the essence here. 'You will have your time in front of the king soon enough.' He looked at her. 'But not at the Citadel, we head for Darth.'

That was good they were headed to the one place she wanted to go. Her brother would help with her case to put to the king.

They next morning they started riding towards Darth. Lorett, Lazon, and Tavener sat in a portable cell with their hands bound. Given the situation they were in, Lorett was rather happy and content. She knew that her brother would not accept this and would be looking to speak to the king immediately, as soon as news reached him on this.

A messenger had been dispatched to Darth to advise of the captives, and to ready the council hall for a trial. A small unit of guards had been set to move with the cell. They left the main bulk of the unit behind to watch for more activity from the location of the gate.

Lorett sang on the journey to pass the time, which annoyed the guards. They gagged her mouth to stop her spirit from rising too much. They felt she should be sad and upset about the situation she was in, not singing about it.

At midday, they had a break for food and water. The captives were kept in the cell. Lorett's gag was removed so she could drink.

'Why are you so cheerful, Lorett?' Lazon asked.

'We are being taken exactly where we need to go,' she said as though being in a cell did not matter. 'The king *of my people* will meet us there and we can begin the council meeting as soon as the elven king arrives.'

'Yes, but...' Lazon was cut short.

'But what? All we need to do is speak to the king, to advise him who will be next out of the gate, and they will be brought too.' Lorett could see her plan clearly in her head. It surely could not fail.

Tavener still felt uneasy. 'You seem very certain of this, Lorett. How do you know it won't turn sour?' It was Tavener's turn to question her happiness.

'Because, Tavener, of who I am. I can sing, remember?'

Lazon looked at her, shocked. 'You can't force people to change their ways like that, Lorett.'

'Why not? I have the power, don't I?' Lorett now tread dangerous waters. She became defensive.

Lazon's face dropped. 'It's immoral.'

'If I have the power to make the world safe from war then surely I should use it?'

'Yes, but not like this. You cannot take away the free will of people and make their decisions for them, otherwise it will be false.' Tavener became stern. He did not like the way she was handling her power; if she continued, she would become corrupted.

It would take at least another day to reach Darth. Lorett would consider what action to take and when to take it during the travel. It would be so much easier to just use her powers on everyone, and then there would be no cause for concern with war.

Chapter 20

Lento sat in his study with papers that detailed his plans for the battle with the elves. There had been previous wars before between the elves and men, so it was not something the worlds had not seen before. The only problem was, it had been nearly two thousand years since the last Great War, so he read the histories once again. He needed to find some sort of advantage for the battle.

He had already found that only the elves had the magic to open the gateways, since the dwarves had been wiped off the planet. This gave them a disadvantage. They would not be able to mount an attack without either capturing an elf or using Lazon or even Shanrea's elven magic. He would hate to ask it of the two that were with them. Besides, it was clear that Morace and Shanrea were in love. He had realised that as soon as he had met with them near the Citadel.

Lazon was a puzzle of his own. He had not had the chance to talk to Lazon, but he could see the elf's frustration.

A knock on the door caused him to stop his thoughts and drop his pen.

'Yes, enter,' he said, quite displeased.

The summoned maid curtsied.

'What is it? I specifically advised not to be disturbed unless absolutely necessary.'

'A messenger has come with news. He says he must present it to you straight away.'

Lento stared at her with stern eyes, waiting. 'Is that all? Bring in this messenger.'

A few moments later, the skinny messenger stood before him. He bowed.

'Are you going to make me stand here all day? Or will you actually speak?' Lento's patience had almost run dry.

'Sorry, Master Lento. Sir, I bring you news of the king's murderers. They have been apprehended and are headed our way.'

'Thank you for informing me. You may leave.' Lento tried to swallow some of the fear that had built up. He knew who was being blamed for the death of the king, two of them being the twins. He now needed to plan what to do if it was one of them captured. He would have to be cautious about it because he did not want others to think him as corrupt.

He went about the plans for war at his desk. The moment the captives arrived in the city could not come soon enough for him.

It did not take as long as he thought for them to arrive. The message came to him as soon as they were spotted from the towers as they headed up from the south. It was more than likely Lorett and Lazon, which might make it a little easier. If it were Morace with his newfound powers, he would find it harder to claim their innocence.

Once they arrived into the city courtyard, Lento strode up to the mobile cell. He saw that his sister was gagged. Lento knew what she was; did the guards know, too?

'Why is this prisoner gagged?'

'She was singing,' said one of the guards. He was almost proud for a moment but then seeing the look on Lento's face, he suddenly felt uneasy.

'So it's a crime now to sing, is it?' Lento said furiously at the guards. 'If she wants to sing then what would be the harm in it?' He looked at the guard. They mentioned nothing of her being a siren so they must not have known. 'Well it does not matter now. Take them to the cells, but I will see this one in my study.' He pointed to Lorett.

The guards obediently took Tavener and Lazon to the cells and took Lorett to Lento's study. She was dirty, the cloths she wore were torn and ragged.

'Sister, what has happened? Tell me what news you bring.' He was both eager and scared to hear.

'The king of the elves does want war. I have managed to speak to him and he has agreed to come and see our new king.' She moved to hug him but he stopped her. A look in Lorett's eyes spoke of the pain she felt. She craved for a hug from her brother.

'If they come in now they would wonder why I am hugging you. I have to play this carefully.' He looked at her. He knew the new king; he had trained with him for some years.

Since there was no more on the royal bloodline, it came to the next high family to take the throne. The new king was roughly the same age as him, anxious to prove himself. He might try to use these captives to prove to the council that he was the right choice.

They discussed in length what they should do. He sent her to the castle jailhouse, reluctantly.

The next task would be speaking to the king to get a pardon for the captives.

The king would be in the castle with the governor by now, so Lento hastily took the most direct route to the castle. This route took him through the busy market. Luckily, because of who he was, the crowds of people let him through. He was greeted by the guard, who let him through without question.

'Good day, isn't it?' the guard asked.

'It would be under better circumstances.' He said no more but continued to walk to the governor's office.

He spoke to the governor's steward who told him where they were. It was not the study but a meeting room he and the governor had many a word in. He made his way to the room.

'The king has specifically asked not to be disturbed,' one of the guards said. It was a king's guard and not one of his own. It would be more difficult to gain entry.

'Yes, I understand. I say it all the time to my guards but it usually means that if something important comes up, then we can be interrupted.'

The guards looked at one another.

'Something important?' the other said.

'Tell us, and we shall see if it is deemed important enough to disturb the king.

Lento looked at them. 'I am Darth's city Guard Captain. I also command its army, which means that on the potential eve of war I am probably the most important man to speak with the king.'

The guards muttered amongst themselves. They knocked on the door and opened it just enough to speak to the rooms occupants. The guard looked back at Lento, and opened the door wider to let him in.

'Your Majesty,' he bowed.

'Lento,' the governor said as he took his hand in greeting.

'I felt it pressing that I be here while we look into this situation. I expect that the men I command will be in the battle.' Lento looked at the king to gauge his mood, and to show that if there was a war then he would be there. 'I have been looking into the previous wars.'

'Really.' The king sounded impressed. 'What have you found?'

Lento informed the king that they would not be able to use the gates to mount an attack on their enemy's homeland. The king looked hard at Lento, and then his eyes lit up with the realisation of who he was sitting with.

'I remember you, Lento. We trained together, years back.'

This was good for Lento. If the king remembered him then he would be able to talk with him on the matters concerning his sister. 'I seem to remember that you were very good at knocking me on my arse.' The king laughed a little.

'Well, you would insist on making that same mistake every time we sparred. What else was I meant to do?' He recalled that every time he had sparred with the king, he had been predictable. He needed to learn what would happen if he kept it up. If he had done so in battle, he would have died. Others in the training courtyard were not as honest and they reluctantly sparred properly, with someone so high up in stature. 'You had to learn and the others were too scared to show you what could happen.'

'Yes. His honesty is one of the reasons why he is appointed where he is now. He can be trusted to speak the truth.'

That could not have been better placed for Lento. The governor really knew how to say things in the right place.

'That's good,' said the king. 'We need people we can trust. It would be great to have you.'

Lento had waited for the best opportunity to talk about the captives. *There is no time like now.* 'I have some things I would like to discuss with you; it's about the captives we have charged for the death of the king.' The king's eyebrows rose. 'As you are probably aware, I did speak to one of them before I came here, the girl. You see, I have reasons for this... the girl you hold captive is my sister. Until recently, she thought that she was a normal girl - until she discovered something. After our parents were killed by the storms she discovered she is a siren.'

He explained the story in detail, emphasising the fact that she would not have committed the murder of the king. She *had* been a witness, and he repeated what she had told him. 'It would seem that there are other stranger things going on here that at the moment can't be explained fully.'

The king looked at him intently. 'I do not know what to say. I believe you are indeed a man of integrity and that what you say is what you believe to be true.' This was starting to sound good for Lorett and hopefully the others too. 'But' and there was hesitation. 'You are emotionally attached to your sister, Lento. You would be more inclined to believe...'

'Your Majesty, I have known Lento for as long as I can remember. He is not a man who would be easily swayed by his emotions.' The governor added.

The king had not taken his eyes off Lento for the entire time.

'My sister has been working hard to find a way to help us. She has come with news from the elves that they are inclined to go to war. She has managed to work out a deal with them to try to bring talks instead of war. Their king has agreed to speak with us on such terms, to see if there is a way to avoid war.'

'I will speak with your sister on this matter, until such time, I can't make any sort of decision seeing as I have only one man's word for it.' He got up and began to move out of the room. He looked back. 'I shall speak with her after lunch, for all this talk has made me hungry.'

Once the king had left, the governor looked at Lento.

'Lorett is one of the captives? When did you find out?'

Lento looked at him. 'Once they were brought in. I had my suspicions that one of the twins would be amongst them.' He was glad that it was Lorett, since Morace had used magic in the council hall in the Citadel to escape. It would have been harder to prove him innocent through words alone.

The governor offered Lento some whisky, which he accepted. 'I have done all I can to help her. Tell me you do have a plan if we are forced to go to war?'

Lento looked at his friend and leader. 'I have the formation of a plan; I just hope it will work.'

Lorett and the king spoke during the evening. The king decided that her story was more than likely to be true. She told him that the elven king would be arriving soon, and suggested that it would do better for him to not be considered a criminal. A messenger was sent immediately to receive the king of the elves. The king agreed to her being present at the talks as mediator. Lorett had used no songs to do this.

Chapter 21

It was late evening, and Morace cradled his glass of whisky. They had spent four days in the repository, investigating its secrets. Shanrea sat cross-legged with a book rested on her knees. It spoke of the history of the dwarven race; a race now extinct. Their engineering had rivalled any of the races. It was the dwarves who had created the gates (with the help of the elven-mages and their magic).

They had crafted the gates from obsidian, using a skill that had taken thousands of years to develop.

Obsidian was a dense material. It took hours to cut even a single shard. Each shard was cut precisely in accordance to the designs of the gate. If there were one groove out of place then the portal would be destroyed when the elven magic touched it. Shanrea saw that there were not just the gates in the forest of Kaarth, but also others dotted around both worlds.

'There are more of these gates. I wonder if the elves knew of them. Looks like the dwarves were building a network.'

'Why would they do that?' Morace asked.

'I don't know, but the druids caught wind of this and put a stop to it,' Shanrea added, reading the next passage in the book.

'So the druids felt as though the dwarves were up to something?' Morace suggested.

'It does not say, but why would they stop them?' Shanrea and Morace puzzled over this for some time.

When they arrived at Tiamscien, they sought new clothes to wear as they had worn the same ones for some time. Morace chose to wear a dark midnight blue set of robes.

Apparently the druids preferred to wear robes. Shanrea had gone for something a little less dark, and her robes licked her ankles.

Despite years of inactivity, all the furnishings and fabrics were kept as if they had just been made. Shanrea was also happy to be able to get a hot bath, as was Morace for that matter, once they had found the large bathroom.

They decided to have a later dinner. Morace caught a goose and Shanrea had found a room within the building that housed a vast garden that was overgrown with many vegetables. She gathered up some potatoes and carrots. She was even able to find some peas.

Morace began to cook the goose; it was large and would feed them for a couple of days. While he cooked on the big open fire pit, he found it quite peaceful. He imagined what it would have been like when there were more people to roam the corridors and cooks in the kitchen.

Shanrea came into the kitchen with the vegetables she had managed to harvest. Once everything was cooked they sat to eat. There was little conversation as they were still hungry from their travels. This was the first proper meal they had eaten for a week or so.

They talked for an hour or so about their childhoods. Morace had come from a large family but Shanrea was orphaned and had been adopted by a wealthy, powerful family. She had grown up in the same orphanage as Lazon. They had not known that they were twins. They had grown up as best friends.

Lazon had not been adopted, so he had grown up in the orphanage until he was old enough to leave. Shanrea had led a different life. She did, however, manage to keep in contact with Lazon, much to her new family's despair. They had not wanted her to see the boy that was now not of her class. There was a bond though, stronger than words of discouragement could break between them.

Now she knew why.

'Is there anything in the journal about why twins are so significant? I mean you are a twin as am I.

'I don't know.'

Morace's thoughts had also been preoccupied with the decision to not guide the shadow agent to the doors of the repository. He wondered how that bode for the worlds; the shadows had tricked and fooled him into accepting a deal that plunged the worlds into a war.

Two nations now faced a battle that no one could truly win, but would cost all. He was safe from all that here, except from his conscience that cut him like a knife.

'I shall read it tomorrow. It is too late to try to read it now. The language is old and it makes my head hurt,' he said as he rubbed his eyes.

They headed off to the bed they now shared. Shanrea kissed him as they entered the room and began to undo the tunic under his robes. She ran her warm hands over his strong chest. She took his robes off then his tunic. She pushed him onto the bed, landing on top of him. He returned her kisses, their fingers entwined.

Morning came and Morace woke up to find that Shanrea was not beside him in their bed. He shot up instantly to look for her. He put on a robe and took for the stairs down the hall. First he went to the kitchen. She was not there. Where was she? Panic began to set in; it felt strange as though something was not right at all.

He suddenly had a thought and began to run down a corridor. He seemed to run for a while getting nowhere fast. He felt dizzy, and had to stop. He vomited then fell into a door.

It opened up into a room that was dark with pinewood furnishings. In the exact centre of the room was a table made out of obsidian with stone fused in patterns of extreme elegance. It stood strong and powerful.

He found her sitting down at the table, smiling at what she had found. Her neck then opened up, blood spewing out of her throat and onto the floor. Her lifeless body was thrown to the ground.

He woke up sweat pouring from his forehead. He sat bolt upright then turned to Shanrea's body as she lay asleep. He checked that she was alive. Her chest moved up and down as she breathed. He gave a sigh of relief.

'What's up?' Shanrea had stirred awake.

'I am sorry for waking you.'

'I was awake anyway. You shouted my name in your sleep.' She looked concerned. 'What happened?'

'I lost you. It was a strange. I just could not find you and I felt sick to the stomach.' He gave her a hug. He did not want to let her go for a moment. Dawn still had yet to break, but he could not get back to sleep now, and neither could she.

He remembered the room in the dream. It felt very different to the other rooms in Tiamscien. He had a notion that was where they had to go.

'There was a room, but it felt very strange. Something happened in my dream in that room that I care not to re-live.'

Shanrea stared at his eyes, which were fear stricken. She knew that he would not tell her so as not to pass that fear onto her. She decided not to venture onto the subject with him; he would tell her in time. She knew that much from him. She put her arm around his bare shoulders for comfort. He had looked away for a moment in thought. She leant in and kissed him.

'Let's find this room.' She got up. Her brown hair fell gracefully across her shoulders as though she had already combed it. Her pointed ears peaked through her hair. Morace was transfixed by her beauty for a while. Once he realised he was in a trance he shook his head to snap out of it.

He put on some fresh clothes. She did the same.

'So where was this room that you found?'

'I remember running down a really long corridor.'

She looked at him. They would need more helpful information. When none came, she just laughed.

'Why are you laughing?'

'You are a noddy head,' she said jokingly.

'I am not, I answered your question.' He did not look amused by the comment at all.

'It's just that this place is huge… There are many long corridors with a lot of doors on them.' She lay back down on the made bed.

'What are you doing?' he asked.

'I am thinking.'

'On what?'

'I am thinking we have been here for what, this is the fifth day now, right?'

'Yes, your point being?' He lay next to her and held her hand.

'My point is that we have only been down one of these corridors to check the room out. Which room were you in before you found the room?' She looked at him and patiently waited for him to respond.

'Well, I woke up.' He looked up at the ceiling for inspiration. It was always hard to remember a dream. He could never truly reflect on what happened in it, especially one of those that you tried to forget because you didn't like the contents. He remembered the bit where he woke up to find that Shanrea was not there and putting on his robe to find her and going down to the kitchen.

'So you went to the kitchen?'

'Yeah.' The dream started to come back to him better now. They started to retrace the steps in the dreams to see if that helped. It did also mean that they could grab something to eat while they walked around.

Morace began to remember more and started to pick up his pace a little. He then went into a full on sprint as he remembered where the room was. He stopped at a door, breathless. Shanrea caught up with him.

'Why did you dash off?'

'I remembered, sorry.' He kissed her. 'But this is it.'

She put her hand to the door. There was power in there. She could feel it pulsate against the door, against the walls, too.

'Shall we go in?'

The door creaked as they entered.

The room was how Morace remembered it, except it was less dark and he did not feel dizzy. Now that he was more with his senses, Morace could see that the room was large and circular.

In the centre was the obsidian table Shanrea had sat at in his dream. He walked up to the table and could see a stone tablet that showed three circles. They were linked with wavy lines in the centre. There were wooden chairs and wooden panelled walls.

At least Shanrea is with me this time, so there is no way that something will happen the way the dream showed. He still looked out for shadows, however. He did not want to tell her that part of the dream either. He was having trouble with it himself.

They looked around the room some more. They found many books on certain events of history in both the worlds.

'There is too much for just us to read and learn from.'

Shanrea agreed with him.

'Look at the wall. It's the same stone as the one on the table.' There were swirls engraved on the stone in the wall. Shards of obsidian framed it.

'It's warm to the touch.' Morace gestured to Shanrea to touch its surface. She recoiled from it, as if it burnt her.

'That's where the power is coming from. Did you feel that surge?'

'Yes, there is strong magic in this.' Morace looked at her hand. He knew that this was not druid magic alone. 'There is siren magic in here too, mixed in with the druids'.'

She looked at him. 'So the sirens and the druids worked together?'

He nodded. 'It's what we are doing now, isn't it? Lorett is the siren; we are the druids.' So that gave the three of them a purpose in all this.

But what about Lazon? What was his purpose? Has that purpose shown itself already?

'What about Lazon? There must have been a purpose for him,' Shanrea remarked.

'He is raw power; he is more powerful than all of us put together.' Morace slowly began to understand. It seemed that this room cleared his mind. It allowed for complete concentration on these matters. 'He is like a catalyst in this, I think.' Morace was still not sure. He did not want to speak on it too much just in case it put the wrong ideas into their heads.

'I really like this room. I feel clear to think on things in here. Maybe we should use this room to read through everything we have?' suggested Shanrea.

Morace had to agree he felt the same. He started to pick through some of the history books on the worlds.

'I think sometimes the best place to start might be the histories. Do you agree?'

He was right. Sometimes to look to the future, it helped to look at the past, to get a sense of the direction you needed to go. To have a look at what others did before you. The reasons why those decisions were made will become apparent. It also looked like the druids may have had an inclination on what was going to unfold.

They picked up a number of books and began to read through them in the little room. They had found their starting point.

Chapter 22

Talks between the new king of Kaarth and the elven king broke down into a complete row. Lorett's attempts at discussing peace between the two had not worked. Even her songs to try and soothe the situation failed. The kings had come into the chamber filled with too much hatred. Lorett's voice had become strained as she tried to calm the situation.

'My son was killed in your cells. We had come on a peaceful mission to help you with your plight.' The elven king had put this point across many times already.

The king of Kaarth, true to form, would rebuttal with the same argument. 'You came to help with a problem that your race caused through your complete lack of judgment.'

Lorett, who was normally calm, became agitated at the two men who behaved like children. As the talks were taking place, they received reports that the elven world had started to lose towns the same way Kaarth had.

'Stop this bickering.' Lorett stood in the centre of the room. She realised she had gotten herself in between them. 'I understand that both sides have suffered great losses at mayhap the hand of the other; I was there. I can't prove it, but I am sure there was more to what I saw, rather than just a king killing a captive in his cell.'

They looked at her. They both remembered that she was a siren. They had been told this before they entered the talks, but their hate had consumed them enough to brush it aside.

'Clap your tongue, siren,' Kaarth's king thundered. 'In fact I am closing this session. Who knows what you have done to tarnish this meeting?'

'I have done nothing except sit and watch you two tear each other apart with words,' she said with tear-filled eyes. *It would be so much easier if they stopped bickering between each other, but it looks like they have just taken the opportunity to point blame and not look at the bigger picture. Give me strength.* 'Our worlds are at stake here. We need to find a way to–'

'Silence, girl. Else I will have you thrown in the cells.'

Lorett turned on her heels. She could tell that it was the end of these talks. Frustrated, she stormed towards the door. She was disheartened that the two behind her were not level headed enough to realise that there was more at stake.

She had dreamt the night before that a darkness would fall if things continued the way they were going. The troll she had sung to spoke to her in song once more. He told her that it was up to her to stop the darkness. She looked back at them as she was about to close the door.

'Please see past this and look to the future of both our worlds.' She slammed the door on the two kings, angry and frustrated.

They looked at the closed door for a moment and started to argue again.

Lorett sped down the corridor. She was on a tunnel vision dash to her brother and did not notice the servant she nearly knocked over. Housed in Darth, she had been here enough to know her way without help. Talks had begun in council halls then quickly regressed into a one on one meeting, as there were too many heads with different opinions and agendas.

Lorett was chosen as negotiator to be in the room with them, despite her youth. Now she headed for her brother's office to lay down some of her frustration. It was better to let off steam with someone who knew her.

She missed her twin. It was hard to wait for him to find the place they needed. Somehow, she knew they were close to it and they would soon call for her. She hated that she might need to leave things in the state that they were in and wondered what state the worlds would be in once they returned.

When she reached her brother's office in Darth's castle, she hugged her brother who had gotten up to receive her. Lorett brushed the tears from her eyes. He knew it would be hard for her. She had so much knowledge about what was to happen, but she struggled with how much of that she could give. It was too much of a burden on her.

'I take it things did not go well?' he asked, holding her in his arms.

'No, and I fear me being there made things worse,' she said deflated.

'These are proud men. One of them took the throne just a week ago.' Lento ruffled her hair. She always made a fuss when he did that to her. She patted it down to make it neat again. A weak smile appeared on her face. Her brother knew how to make her laugh if needed.

'You always did that when I was growing up.'

'And Pa would always scold me for it afterwards for winding you up so.' They laughed for a moment.

'Well, I am older now and can handle myself better, so there will be no more ruffling of my hair; I won't allow it.'

Lento smiled at his determined sister. 'Ha. That's my sister, all right. You always were spirited, Wildflower.' He sat back down at his desk and took out a paper and quill. 'Now it looks like the men I command will be required and I must make sure they are prepared. You can stay for a while...' This meant she could, but must remain silent as a dormouse. It also meant that like when they were children, she could help if she felt she could.

'So what plan do you have?' she asked.

'I plan on not having to go to battle if anything can be done about it, but if that fails I have not a clue.' He cast a weary smile. 'Magic is messy business, Lorett, and somehow you have become involved. I always knew there was something about you.' He winked. 'Little Torchlight, Pa used to call you.'

'Well it looks like a plan two will have to be made. If only we could talk them out of their anger.'

'It's difficult, Wildflower, to talk stubborn people out of what they think to be right. It sometimes means they have to admit that they can be wrong.' He shrugged. 'That's the reason why I am here. I tried to talk Pa, who was stubborn and stuck in his ways, into something different. Neither of us could see the other side, so I left.'

Lento's leaving had been one of the hardest days in Lorett's life; she loved her brother and had always looked up to him. She had always felt that she was his favourite sister despite him never saying it. Sometimes she thought that she annoyed him by being around and butting into his business at all possible times. She knew that he would never tell her to go away though.

'Would you like to come down to the training room with me? I will show you some things you can do. I have seen you carry your sword, and I think you will thank me for giving you some training with it.'

In an instant, she was at the door ready to go. She loved it when he taught her new things and jumped on the chance. It also gave them a moment, even if it would be brief, to forget about the dire situation.

'You never know, brother, I might meet a nice barracks man while I am there.'

He looked at her, confounded. 'I doubt it. I will have everyone know you are off limits.' He smiled.

'You will do no such thing, brother. I am a woman who
can handle herself.' She stood with pride.

The truth hurt him a little. She had grown so much in the
years he had been gone, and that was one of the things he
regretted. He had not seen her grow up into the woman
she had become.

'We shall see, shall we? In the courtyard.'

They made their way to the yard and he handed her a
training blade. They practiced for a good three hours without realising how much time had passed. With each strike,
Lorett became better and hit harder.

She is going to leave me with bruises.

Lento studied her. She would make quite the little fighter,
but he did not want that for her. Once finished, they
clasped hands then hugged.

'Phew, you smell of sweat, Wildflower. Go to my home
and wash. The maid will help you.'

She went through the town square past all the shops. She
wondered whether the bookshop that she used to visit
was still there. She walked to where she remembered it
and there it was. Going inside, the door chimed with the
little bell; it always did when someone walked in.

'Ah, Lorett. It's been awhile since your last visit. Tell me,
what news do you bring from the coast?'

*He honestly did not know? Had no one told him? Did any-
one out here know?* Her face turned cold with what she had
to say.

'It's gone. Destroyed by the weather.'

He looked taken aback. 'What do you mean gone?'

'I mean every structure around the coast has been destroyed.' She held back the tears. 'My Pa and mother died,
and so did my sisters. Our house was destroyed!'

'I am so very sorry to hear that my dear, but that is not all that is bothering you I can see.' The keeper of the store was an old one. He had lived many years and had seen her many times. Every time she visited Darth, she went to the bookstore and bought enough books to last her to the next visit. Still she did not want this conversation with him so she changed the subject.

'Any new books in?' Then she changed her mind. 'Actually no. Do you have any books on the druids?'

'The druids? Ah... I have many a fantasy book on them.'

'No, not fantasy, but a book on their kind? You know the ones who used to walk Kaarth thousands of years ago.'

'Don't be foolish, girl. The druids are a legend; some fantasy, not some actual beings.' He stood steadfast.

'There is not even one? Written by someone who believed in them just to see what they found out about them?'

He looked at her. He puzzled over the question.

She had slipped a little song to her voice when she asked again. One that was subtle. She had attempted to use her power to persuade once again. A little pang in her heart let her know that it was wrong.

'Well there was one person who drove himself damn near insane in the belief that they truly existed. He wrote down all of his finds. He eventually ventured into the Norse and never returned.' The keeper turned around. He disappeared to the back, presumably to find it. The keeper did not return for a while but when he did, he brought back a thick, dust-covered book. 'Now this book was given to me by the man who wrote it. He said to keep it safe, so I did. This man was also my brother.' He handed her the book. 'Now I don't want you chasing myths and legends; not like my brother did.'

Lorett took the book. 'How much would you like for it?'

'Oh, nothing. You can have it, as long as you don't ruin yourself on it.'

She began walking back to Lento's house. She was greeted by the maid upon arrival and she requested a bath be run. The maid curtsied, which felt a little weird for Lorett, then walked off to fill the tub.

Once she had bathed and was clean again, she decided to have a read of the book. As the time passed by, she completely forgot that there was a world out there and a struggle, then her stomach grumbled hungrily. Lorett placed the book on the mantle above a huge, beautiful fireplace and walked to the kitchen.

Lorett knew the way to the kitchen in her brother's house. It was along one of her favourite corridors in the estate. The walls were decorated with paintings that created a wonderful feast for everyone's eyes. Lorett always took her time when she walked this corridor. There was a particular painting she always loved to see. This time though it was hard.

She stopped as she saw it. She stared, unable to move for a moment. The painting was of the house that was destroyed weeks ago. Her whole family, even Caser, stood at the front with smiles on their faces. She was only five years old. Once she had stared at it for long enough, she continued to the kitchen.

'Is there any food?' she asked the cook. The cook gave her some soup to eat. Once all that was eaten, she took to the garden with the book and began to read once again.

An hour or so later the maid appeared, running in a panic. She had a message to pass on to Lorett.

'I have news, Miss. The elves attacked the castle.'

Lorett was concerned her brother must be there. 'Attacked, how? What news of my brother? Show me.'

'Your brother is fine, Miss, but you are unsafe. We need to get you and Lazon out of here.'

Lorett watched the maid as she ran towards the kitchen. When the maid returned a moment later she held a long sword and a short sword. With the straps, she attached them to her back.

The maid looked at Lorett. 'Your brother trains all of his staff, Miss.' She had stripped down to reveal leather greaves and tunic. 'He also said we should be prepared for a quick exit. Now let's go find your elven friend.'

Lazon had remained in his room in Lento's house for the entire time they spent in Darth. He fondled the stones they had acquired from the forest. As he heard the commotion from outside, he snapped out of his melancholy.

With Lorett and Lazon in tow, the maid took the route to where Lento said he would meet them.

They found Tavener who had been waiting for news on the talks.

Chapter 23

Lento met up with Lorett, Lazon, and Tavener when they were out of the city. His family, including his daughter stood by his side.

Lorett tried to focus. *I just can't seem to figure this out.*

Nythe noticed that Lorett was deep in thought. She slowed her pace to walk alongside her and gave her a hug.

Lorett felt a little stronger after the hug. Her niece was full of the energy that a young person should have. She missed that. She could feel herself getting more tired each passing day. She struggled to sleep at night for it. *Morace, where are you? I need you in this struggle.*

'How are you, Aunt?' Nythe asked.

'I am good, just sad is all.'

'I think you are amazing.' Nythe always was able to cheer people up. At sixteen, her energy spread to those around her. 'Father said he was able to come up with a plan while you were reading.' She smiled. 'He was very busy. He managed to form the army of men he commands and make sure they were ready.'

'Sorry, what?'

'Father saw that things were not getting better so he had the army prepare. Some stayed in the castle to mount a defence while people left. He sent the rest to wait for him.'

So he had thought of something then? Had that also been what the training had been about? Had he known that the elves and men would not put this aside? He must have trained me so that I could do something.

'Come, you two, stop dawdling.' Lento had noticed that Lorett and Nythe had fallen behind with their chatter.

Nythe turned to look round. 'I heard something.'

An arrow suddenly struck the ground before her. Nythe jumped instinctively and ran forward.

'That's an elven arrow,' Lazon called.

'Damn. They found us,' Lento said, frustrated.

Suddenly, three elven hunters appeared with bows. Tavener readied the crossbow and took out two in quick succession, the third fell to a thrown knife. *Thrown by whom?* Lorett looked around. She saw a belt of knives around Nythe's waist. *Looks like someone else trains, too.*

Three more hunters appeared with hunting knives. As they caught up with the group, Lorett was the first they met. She dispatched of the first easily enough. *He must not have been expecting me to be trained.*

The second met the same fate, but was more of a challenge for he had realised that she was more formidable than he first anticipated. The last proved yet more of a challenge. He knocked her to the ground. She thought she was about to see the end of her life as the elven hunter raised his blade above his head for the killer blow. His eyes widened as his body suddenly began to glow. When he crumpled to the floor, Lorett looked up. She remained there, stunned at what she had seen in his elven eyes for the moment he was glowing.

As she came to her senses, she looked for the magic's source. It was the only reasonable explanation. She realised it must have been Lazon who had summoned that power. It was such raw power it had scared her. Who knew what the elven hunter must have felt. She shivered at the thought. It was not normal elven magic, that was for sure.

'Lorett, are you okay?' Nythe asked concerned for her cousin.

'Yes I am.'

'Those were some fighting skills, Wildflower. I only spent three hours with you.'

She looked at her brother and grinned. 'Well it just shows you are a great tutor.'

'It takes a willing student to learn,' he replied.

'I hate to break up this little mushy moment, Father and Aunt, but the elves chased us. Does that not mean they could come back?'

It was true, of course, so they started to make their way to where their army awaited them.

Lorett sat in her brother's tent pondering over the attack by the elves. There must have been more gates for them to travel through. It was an oversight of course. She had forgotten that they needed to use a different gate to get back to Kaarth. *How could I forget?* They were at a major disadvantage now and serious thought had to be put forward for this. She knew that they needed to find these gateways, otherwise they would be dead before her and her brother had time to act.

A noise from outside the tent alerted her to Lento's arrival.

'Sister, no need to stand,' he said when she had started to get up to greet him. 'The rest of the army has regrouped and we are to march to the Citadel.' He looked at her with concern. She realised that the elven king had only pretended to attempt peace talks. It was clearly just a ruse to get to the king of Kaarth under false colours. Lorett blamed herself.

'We need to find these other gates,' she said with a determination that shocked Lento.

When had this little girl grown up so?

'We need to remove the advantage the elves have over us.'

She had hoped not to have to talk like this and that a war would not happen. 'So what will you do?'

'I am waiting for Morace to summon me regarding where he has ventured these weeks gone.'

Lorett was holding the stones she had gotten from the Everglade and hoped for some inspiration. She suddenly decided that she would sing. Lorett cleared her throat and let her voice travel the air. The more she sang, the further the song went until the whole camp was immersed in her lyrics. Some of the men knew the words and started to sing and the song was soon sung by all the men and women around.

Lento felt warmed by the atmosphere the song created.

As the evening became late, everyone started to dance around the fires. For a while, the camp did not feel the pressure of the coming war. The men started to move onto other songs.

Lorett changed her key just slightly and the stones glowed brightly. Stunned by this, she looked into them. What she saw inside them shocked her even more. It was Morace and Shanrea in a room filled with books.

The wall began to glow suddenly. Morace and Shanrea had heard the singing ring through the room that they occupied as they read through the tombs of knowledge. It was Shanrea who realised that there was a face on the wall. She pointed at the wall and tapped Morace on the shoulder.

'Morace, look. It's Lorett.'

Morace abandoned his book. 'How has she done that?'

'I don't know. I wonder if she can hear us.'

Morace got up and walked to the wall. 'Lorett, can you hear me?' There was no response from her, but he could tell she looked puzzled. He could also sense a lot of magic was being used. 'Lorett...'

'Morace? Is that you?' Lorett's voice reached his ears. She had heard him and vice versa.

'It is, Lorett. Were you able to find what you were looking for?'

'Yes, I believe so, but I bring grave news on the situation.' Lorett took some time to explain what had happened in detail.

He did not say anything while she spoke, but he was growing concerned at the amount of magic the stones were using. He thought it best to end the conversation.

'I will look into these stones. There must be something on them in here. There is so much to go through.'

A flash ended their communication.

Morace and Shanrea had looked over most of the repository and had noticed that the druids were very thorough with their record keeping. He went straight to the section that dealt with talismans. He found a book about siren sigil stones. He had glanced through this book a few days back so knew where it was. He then took it to the table where Shanrea waited for him.

'This is the book I was thinking of. I knew I should have paid more attention to it.' He flipped it open to a page he vaguely remembered as something of interest and there they were. The Siren Stones. He compared Lorett's description to that in the book.

'Strange. She said she had three stones.'

'Yes, that's right.'

'Well there is meant to be four of them. Looks like one is missing.'

'Missing, but how?'

Morace looked at her. 'I don't know, but these stones do more than just communicate.' He had read on. 'They allow someone to travel great distances too.' He continued to read. 'I got that wrong. Lorett could have come through to us by herself. That was a portal opened up by the siren's song. All she had to do was change her pitch and she would have come through the portal.' He put the book down aren't the only ones who created the means to travel.' Shanrea studied the pictures in the books. 'I have seen one of those stones before.'

'How? They should have all been in the tree Lorett took them out of.'

'I can't remember - but I do remember it was stolen by someone.' Shanrea took the book from him. 'Yes, I am certain. I wonder who now has the stone.'

'I am now wondering if whoever has the stone, has overheard our conversation.'

The thought sent a chill down Shanrea's spine. 'We need to be more vigilant. We are all new to this level of magic. Heck. I have never used magic until a month or so ago, now we are wielding it as though we have held this power for years.' She gave him back the book. 'Let's go get something to eat and rest. It's late. We need to sleep.' She touched his face with soft fingers that sent a tingle down his spine. He smiled, got up and kissed her lips.

The two druids had taken the time to learn about each other; their lives, their likes, and dislikes. They had grown much closer. Perhaps this was the way forward. The worlds were set to change, and the two of them were to lead them into it.

Twak fumbled with the stone that had glowed in his pocket. The news that he had learned from the druid and the siren's conversation was good. He knew that his attempt to manipulate the young druid boy into taking him to the hall of knowledge would in all likely fail. This was why he had the stone. His plan was coming into full force.

The elves were finally at war with man once again, after nearly two thousand years of silence.

Soon the dwarves would become involved and his power would grow even more. He had to get into the druid sanctuary because while his power grew so did the empress's. He needed to gain that advantage. He had to wait for the Siren to step up the pitch of her song to go through the portal. It was sure to happen.

But oh how the siren's voice punctured his ears; the mess that was her song. He spat. Then spat again. *Dirty, filthy siren. I thought your kind had been wiped off this world.*

He still wore the guise of the elven fool he had managed to trick to do his bidding, another thing that disgusted him, but necessary to aid his cause. *Disgusting, vile creatures, the lot of them, and now I have to meddle with the dwarves.* He spat again. 'Use them, I will; every last one of them until their destruction.'

A dwarf steward ran up to him while he was in mid rage, catching the words he had spewed about the dwarves.

Damn. Now that steward has heard me. 'What are you doing here? Eavesdropping, no doubt.' He made himself look a lot bigger and a cruel scowl formed on his face, sharp teeth bared.

'N...No sir. I just came to see if you needed anything.'

'Well I don't and now I have going to have to kill you for your stupidity.'

The dwarf looked stunned. His face would burn in the memory of Twak forever. The dwarf was struck by overpowering fear.

Stupid little fool, I will relish in snapping your neck and eating your soul. 'Now what's your name?'

'D. Dannell, sir.'

'Good. I like to know the names of the people I kill. I remember them all.' He walked slowly to the young dwarf, who was paralyzed with fear. Twak put one hand on the dwarf's chin and the other behind his neck. He twisted to hear the snap as the spinal cord broke in two. He opened his mouth to devour the dwarf's soul. The body turned into a wrinkled wreck of its former self. 'Darn the dwarves. Just don't fill me up enough.' He licked his lips. Under a bush, he hid the body.

It's time to explain the plan to the leader of the dwarves.

With purpose he went to find the leader of the dwarves. If anyone could hear his mind, all they would hear was laughter.

Lento saw Lorett as she threw up and ordered her to lie down on the bed. He gave her a bucket to vomit in further if needed and left her to rest for the night.

After a dreamless sleep, she woke up fresh and ready to tackle anything.

Lento greeted her in the morning and asked how she felt. They had breakfast together along with Lazon and Nythe.

Lazon fascinated Nythe. She had never met someone from the Everglade before. Every time he looked at her, she snapped her head away, as if she was a child fixed on something new.

Once breakfast had finished, Nythe headed to the tent where they kept the wounded. Her mind was transfixed on the elven man. As she rounded another tent, thoughts still on Lazon, she did not notice the cabinet of medical supplies. She crashed straight into it and the collision knocked all the supplies to the ground.

Mortified, Nythe started to pick up the supplies. As she went to grab some medicine, someone else picked it up first, his hand brushing against hers. Shyly she looked up. It was Lazon. Dumbstruck she backed away, tripping over the ropes of the tent. Her face glowed red with embarrassment. She was unable to string two words together.

'Nythe, isn't it?'

She nodded yes; she tried to speak but nothing came out.

He laughed a little. 'Are you nervous of me?'

She gave another nod.

'Why?' he asked.

The truth was, she did not really know. She had gone through her life with not a care in the world. She was seldom shy or unable to speak for herself, but in Lazon's case, she felt as though her insides turned to liquid.

Once all the supplies were picked up she managed a slight thank you and began to walk on. Lazon followed. They were both headed towards the medical tent.

Nythe started to go about her rounds, tending to the men who had become injured in the flight of Darth. She then came to Lazon who sat on a bed waiting to be seen. Her heart started to beat faster and she could not speak once again. *Come on Nythe, you are strong.* With the little pep talk, she composed herself. She stood in front of her next patient. *That's right it does not matter who it is. He is just another patient.*

'How can I help you?' she asked, surprised that she was able to string a sentence together.

'I have had a burning sensation in my arm since the battle with the elves on the way up here.' He started to take off his tunic that had been given him by Lento.

Then she knew it, the reason why she was like a little girl again around him. He had saved her life on that journey and she did not know how to act. She had never experienced anything like it before; she was still young and had nearly faced death. Impulsively she leant in and kissed him.

'What was that for?'

'Saving my life.' Now she had realised why she was so shy she lost all of the pent up feelings towards him. 'Sorry, I did not know the best way to say thank you.'

'It's okay.' He laughed a little. He thought about Lorett's kiss. This was different. It had left him tingling, but he could not put his finger on the reason why.

Lento had walked by, and saw the kiss his daughter had planted on the elven boy. *My little girl does appear to be growing up.* It brought a tear to his eye. He did not want to embarrass her so he swiftly moved on. Perhaps now she would settle down a little.

Lento had to have talks with the king and governor. They all needed to be kept informed of how things were progressing. Lento had been given a new position since his display in Darth saved many of his people. He had been given command over the whole effort.

The king, however, was still angry about the attempted ambush and blamed the siren for some of it. If they had not listened to her, they would not be stuck without a city defence. The king believed that she must have been taken in by the elven king's grandeur and that's why she was suckered in.

The king waited in his own tent for Lento and the governor to arrive to discuss what was next to happen.

They spoke for the better part of an hour. Eventually, they came up with a decision to head for the best place to mount a defence, which was the Citadel.

They started the trek to the Citadel.

Lorett had decided to go on a different route. She wanted to visit somewhere before they headed out to the Citadel.

Tavener chose to stay with the fighting effort this time since he was well versed with ambush tactics. He would be a valuable asset to the effort.

Lazon would travel with Lorett. It would feel weird for him being on a battle ground with the men against his elven kindred, even if he had already killed one. The shock came when Nythe announced she wanted to go with them too.

'No.' Lento outright refused. 'You are too young for this; you don't know what you are getting yourself into.'

'Father, I am nearly seventeen. I am a young woman now. Please let me go.'

'This is no walk in the park, this is real, and we are not in the training courtyard now.' He looked at her youthful face framed by her long, braided auburn hair. *When had she braided her hair?* He saw that Lorett's hair was held in braids too. She was another young one who should be singing, dancing and flirting, not trying to save the worlds. He sighed. He could not dwell on these thoughts. They needed to get a move on. 'Okay you can go,' he said with reluctance. *It's probably better this way anyway. Lorett plans to meet up with Morace.* 'But only if Lorett allows it and you remember your training.'

'Yes, father, of course I remember my training.'

Lorett agreed, happy to have another female on the journey. 'I will look after her, don't worry brother.'

They departed with hugs and began their journey south.

Lorett wanted to head back to her destroyed home. She had been feeling nostalgic and wanted to go back to where it all started. Perhaps she could think clearer on the way. She started to sing, Nythe and Lazon also joined in the chorus and soon they had sung about ten different songs.

Nythe had never felt so free. She was out in the open, away from the confines of life in a city. She had never had the chance to see her father's home village, and she would never see how it was before all the destruction. That was the thing with the brewing war - people had forgotten the true issue at hand. That was to stop the weather that tore apart the world.

Before they had left, they had heard reports that parts of Kaarth were now inhospitable. The weather had killed off anything that was trying to thrive in it. Lorett knew what her part in all of this was. As a siren she had to try and unite the nations of men, elves and dwarves. She had to make them forget that they were different and that if they worked together they would be able to thrive.

The sirens of the past had failed. The dwarves had all gone. The elves and men were too different. Lorett, through it all, had failed to prevent the war.

Perhaps it was because she was talked out of using her magic to control the situation. Would a faked peace be that bad? A marriage made into what seemed real. An illusion. *No, the others were right. That would eventually fail, too.*

It drew towards the end of the day. The sun had begun to drop in to let the moon shine above Kaarth. There were two moons. That was strange.

Nythe noticed it too. 'Since when did Kaarth have two moons?'

'It doesn't,' Lorett said.

'Well it looks like there is.' Lazon looked up. This second moon appeared closer than the other one, then he realised. 'That's not a moon. It's a planet. It's Everglade, my home world, it's getting closer...'

'Closer?' Nythe asked.

Then it struck Lorett. Alk-Mea was the anchor that kept the worlds apart, but in sync. The weather magic had weakened the tree's grip on the worlds. As it died, the tether lost strength.

'What happens when a boat breaks its anchor without people knowing about it?'

'It drifts,' Nythe suggested.

'Exactly. What happens to the water? It moves and no longer stays still.' Lorett realised now what was happening with the worlds. She did not know if it could be stopped. She explained about how the moon controlled the weather and the tides of the oceans. Storms were birthed from the ocean and now the world faced too much change at once. As the Everglade moved closer, it effectively became a second moon. It was the elven home world; the place where the weather magic was created. It caused the world to be sent to Kaarth. It was the trigger. *I have been wrong this whole time.*

'I am not on a mission to prevent it. I am on a mission to save our and your people from annihilation.' She looked at Lazon, hard. 'The worlds are going to collide. It was inevitable. Granted you sped up the process a little, Lazon. It was going to happen regardless of what you did, but we have been alerted to what we have to do before the destruction needs can take place.'

'So you doing what you did has hopefully saved us all. It's just the stubborn ways of our peoples that has us facing war.' Nythe added.

'Precisely,' Lorett agreed.

Lazon understood what had happened with the worlds. *I am not the cause of all this.* He was sure Lorett and Nythe were right. *Why did the leaders of the elves lead me to believe I was all to blame? It is almost as if they wanted to hide from the truth. They must have known.* Then a thought chilled him, he should have been put to death for what he had done but something had prevented that. Perhaps this was all meant to happen in the end.

Lorett took out the stones from the pocket in her tunic. 'I am going to speak to my brother. Now may be the time to return to him.' *I was right, heading to where this all started did help.*

She sang the same song to the stones as before and they began to glow again as she changed key. She saw the form of her brother and started to speak.

Morace told her of his concerns that their previous conversation may have been overheard. He then told her that he had studied up on the stones about how they can make the person who uses them ill, by draining them of their energy.

The next thing he suggested shocked her. He asked her to change the pitch of the song to open a portal. He told her to let the others through, then to follow.

Lorett did as he instructed. She closed her eyes. As she took Nythe and Lazon's hand, she warned them not to let go. The pitch of the song changed. Wind gushed. One moment they were there the next they were not. Thousands of miles, they travelled in an instant. Lorett opened her eyes - her brother stood in front of her with a smile on his face.

Shanrea embraced her twin with a hug. She smiled too as she turned to Morace, who was embracing his sister.

'That is siren magic,' Morace said. 'Very powerful.'

As she smiled, Lorett's eyes widened. Her body crumpled to the floor.

A shadow crept past them as they looked on Lorett who had fallen. It was not the siren's magic that caused her plight, but in fact the shadow agent's presence in using the stone. When she opened the portal, he had managed to slip through unnoticed. Now he was in the place he needed to be to gain the knowledge on how to become the most powerful presence the worlds would ever see. He had accomplished his goal.

He remained hidden for a while, looking for what he needed. He was unsure about leaving the dwarves for this endeavour, but it had to be done. He needed the power. He did not just need it. He craved it.

Twak roamed free.

Chapter 24

Surrounded by a vast, never ending darkness, Lorett tried to look for light. Is this what death is? 'Am I dead?'

'No.' Out of the darkness, a voice responded.

'Then where...'

'Of a dream you shall learn.'

'Who are you?'

'Of no importance I am, young siren.'

The darkness lifted. Lorett's eyes adjusted to the new light. Sitting at a long table there was cake, biscuits and tea laid out before her. A tea party.

Lorett recalled a book she once read. It was old. She had bought it from the book keeper when she was twelve. Lorett pictured the front cover. It was tattered, with part of the title scrubbed out. This scene was from that book.

Adventures in Wonderland.

The book was titled.

'This is the Hatter's tea party,' Lorett said to the voice.

'Correct. I used this since it was one of your favourite scenes in that book. It is in the acts of total madness that the truth will be revealed.

'Truth?'

'Yes, truth.'

Lorett could see the speaker clearly now. He wore a top hat, his eyes had a crazy look about him.

'Are you the Hatter?'

'No and yes- for now I am, but also not.' The Hatter ran onto the table towards Lorett and looked into her eyes. 'You *did not travel alone, by that I mean your company. Something else came through.'*

'Wait! What do you mean?'

'I mean what I said. Now let's dance- Sirens have wonderful voices to dance along to.'

Lorett began to sing. They danced for hours. The Hatter stopped suddenly.

'It's time for you to wake. I give you one last truth. This book is from very far away, like the elves, but even further.'

Lorett watched the Hatter's hat get bigger; the Hatter stepped inside of it.

Lorett woke up to find Morace staring at her, his eyes wide with fear for her wellbeing. She lay in a bed with the covers pulled up to her chin. They were brown, embroidered with nice patterns and swirls. She coughed a little and tried to get up, but she was still weak from the affliction she had.

A monkey? Lorett could see it as it hung from the light fitting in her room. It stared at her. It looked oddly familiar.

It had been nearly two weeks since they had arrived. Lorett had been asleep for all that time. Opening the portal had drained her. She thought it should not have. *There was no reason for it.* She shuddered then went still for a moment.

Morace realised she had woken. His hand held hers as it had done for most of the time she was asleep. 'Lorett, are you okay?' His heart dropped when he looked into her eyes. They looked weak.

She struggled to string a sentence together.

Morace grew more concerned. While she had been in the deep sleep state, he had read up on the portal. He found a book on it, hidden away in an old, deep underground part of the repository that spoke of the stones.

'I think I am okay.' She had lost all of her weakness suddenly. Lorett sat bolt upright. She stared into Morace's eyes. 'It's here,' she said suddenly.

Morace had not a clue what she was talking about. 'What's here?' He tried to get her to lie down once more but she refused, stubbornly. 'Lorett, you need to rest.'

'How long have I been out for?' she asked with despair in her eyes.

'I don't know,' he said. Morace had lost all track of time since Lorett had come to them. He was unable to contain his worry for her any longer. 'Please, Lorett. We are still unsure what has happened to you.'

'There is no time to worry about me. There is something among us now that could cause us trouble.'

Morace gave her a confused look. 'What are you talking about, Lorett? What something?'

Shanrea walked past the door and heard the raised voice of Lorett as she tried to plead with her brother. When she heard Morace try to get her back into the bed she sighed and walked into the room.

Both Lorett and Morace turned to see who had entered the room.

'Lorett, it is good to see you awake. You look well now.' Shanrea went over to hug her. 'It has been nearly two weeks since you came to us.'

'Nearly two weeks! It has had time to roam around undetected for two weeks?' Frantically Lorett tried to get up out of the bed. 'Where is Lazon? Is he alone? Nythe?' Shanrea looked at Morace, concerned now also.

To them Lorett seemed to act crazed. She was not herself. Morace felt he had no choice. He called for his druid magic and summoned an enchantment to calm her so she could slip into a dreamy state.

They left the room quietly, closing the door behind them. A tear fell down Morace's face. Shanrea wrapped her arms around his body to comfort.

'She looks crazed,' Morace said quietly. 'It's like she has gone out of her mind.'

'We did not know what would happen when she called on that magic, Morace.' She looked hard at him. Shanrea knew that he blamed himself for his sister's affliction. 'Something must have gone wrong at the time.'

'No, wait. She said something was here with us.' He had a sudden rush of panic. 'She is crazed, but she is right. Shanrea, it's the shadow agent. He has managed to find a way here.' He took to the room with the portal in it. 'The shadows have caused her affliction, and once again it's because of my decision to agree to its terms.'

'Morace, you don't know that.'

'Yes, I do. She is talking some sense when she says something is here, but she is still crazed.' He remembered the first time Lorett had woken up. He had needed to use his magic to send her to sleep then. She had become a garbled wreck, speaking incoherently. But every time she had woken, she made more and more sense.

'Morace, if she is right and something from the shadows is with us, we had better find it,' Shanrea said.

'First, let's all get together. We need someone around Lorett. I don't want the filthy creature to get my sister.'

Shanrea nodded in agreement. 'I think Lazon said he was going to ask Nythe for a walk. She seems quite taken with him.'

Morace had been surprised when he saw that Nythe had come with Lorett and Lazon. It had soon became apparent that there was more to just adventure on Nythe's mind; she was entranced with Lazon, someone who was unusual.

'Don't worry, Uncle,' she had said, knowing that he hated being called Uncle because of their age gap. 'I am nearly seventeen in years. I know what I am doing.' Lorett had agreed that she could come so he took no more notice of it.

'Where were they going to walk?' he asked her.

'I think maybe the vegetable garden,' Shanrea responded.

Shanrea had done a bit of work in there since their arrival to make it more manageable. It would seem that even though there was magic in the walls, there were still some things that it could not influence. This was a comfort to Morace at least, who did not enjoy using magic.

He could feel it everywhere in this place. It was built with it. He did know that before this was all over, he would have to use a lot more magic. That much he could tell. He kissed Shanrea as they started to head down to the garden. The monkey followed leaping onto Shanrea's shoulder.

They could not find Nythe and Lazon at all at first. They called a few times before they got a response. They were sat underneath a willow tree, both with books in their laps.

Nythe's book was on the elves. Lazon's was about Weather Magic and its effects on the worlds.

'What's wrong? Has Lorett woken up?' Nythe asked with concern over her face.

'She did, but I had to send her to sleep again. She was very frantic.'

Nythe's heart had leapt for a moment, but when the disappointment of the bad news set in, it sank again.

'There is something here that could cause us harm,' Shanrea said. 'We need to be vigilant and try not to be on our own.'

'So while we are talking now, who is with Lorett?' Nythe asked suddenly as soon as the thought came to her.

A look of horror slipped onto Morace's face. *We should not have left her on her own.*

Nairia jumped off Shanrea's shoulders. Unknown to the elven girl, she had become attached too. The monkey felt a little stupid at the fact she left the girl alone. *The stupid man's twin.* Nairia took all the short cuts to the chamber where the siren rested. She smelled nice. *I had better be careful though. Don't want to have to try and explain what I am to them.* The flames leapt behind her. *The intruder?*

'There is no one.' Morace's heart turned to ice. He raced to Lorett's room. *One of us should have stayed with her.*

He had to go through the kitchen to get to her but when he arrived it was on fire. Smoke filled the air and he stopped to put his hand on his throat as he choked. Morace was quickly joined by the others.

'It has set the kitchen on fire.'

They tried to contain the fire. It seemed that every time it looked like they were succeeding, the fire flared up again, almost burning them.

Shanrea saw a figure behind the fire. It smiled wickedly. *I recognise that person.* It was Gragio.

Twak watched from behind the fire in his Gragio guise. He stared straight at the elven girl. He had never met her, but thanks to Gragio's memories, he knew her name. Gragio had held resentment for her; she had been the so-called saviour of the Everglade, whilst he was cast aside like a rusty broom handle, all broken. *Ooh such strong emotion against this girl.*

Twak turned towards the door that led to the Siren, marvelling at what he had done to separate them from her. *That will keep them occupied for a bit.* Now it was time to rid the world of the despicable creature that is a siren. He had kept count of all the sirens he had killed when they were a prominent race. Oh, how he despised them. They were so despicable with their songs, and now he was going to be able to kill the last one. He relished this thought. Twak, the siren slayer, would rise above his stupid empress and become the Emperor of the Shadows. *With the knowledge I have, I know how I can do it.*

For a thousand years, I have waited for this moment; to claim my rightful place in the shadows. Not be some pitiful servant to someone as foolish as the shadow empress.

He had already been to the siren's room and watched her sleep. Even then, she had managed to sing to protect herself, but now that the druid had induced her sleep, he was able to intervene and kill whatever life she had left.

He no longer tried to remain undetected; he skulked around the shadows, his manner bold and determined to finish his goal. Twak took his time. A murderer in the shadows. He stretched out his hand, ready to turn the handle on the door. He felt warmth flow into his hand.

Twak felt a strange pain in his hand. He looked at it for a moment. When he looked ahead, he could see that Lorett stood in front of him awake and... she sang. Twak knew that the power was too strong for him to combat; he had never felt such natural power. He transformed into the griffon he had been once before. His wings beat down the narrow corridor towards a large window that overlooked the forest, and smashed through it.

Lorett had managed to wake up, thanks to Nairia's timely arrival, and conjure a song of protection before the creature attack. This time after using such power, she did not crumple to the floor, but stood strong. She had managed to get rid of the creature, but it had taken away with it knowledge that it should not possess.

As Morace made his way onto the corridor, he heard his sister sing. He had seen the griffon just as it flew out of the window. The cold air hit his cheeks.

Lorett had a glow around her that caused Morace some concern. He ignored the fact that the air was chilly in the corridor and ran to his sister.

The glow had dissipated now, but Lorett looked quite pale.

'Lorett, are you okay?'

She started to dance wildly and sing. She spoke random nonsense. It would seem that she had lost all sense inside her head once more. *Not another consequence from the deal I had made, surely?*

Nairia sat perched on Lorett's shoulder. The monkey was happy that she had saved the siren.

Shanrea looked at the monkey. Perhaps there was more to this monkey?

'Don't get comfortable. You are here for my bidding.'

Nairia was the only one who heard the voice. It spoke only to her.

'Good girl, Nairia. Thank you.'

Morace put his sister to sleep once again.

On the eve of war, Lento looked out from the Citadel walls. The elven army amassed and took form before his eyes. Morace had managed to send word, to warn him that there were more gates for the elves to use. He was glad of his decision to use the Citadel as the place to mount their defence. He turned to within the walls.

Men and women underwent preparations within the walls. They were hurried but did not panic, yet.

Lento started to see to his own preparation. Since he was now in command of the whole army effort, he needed to be prepared. He asked his steward to bring his suit of armour so that he could check it over to make sure there were no kinks.

Once the steward had brought the armour, he looked it over. He preferred light armour so that he could move fluidly. The suit of armour was recently made for him because of his new position, and so was his sword. He took it out of its scabbard and swung it about to test its motion. The sword was perfectly balanced and was his preferred sword type. The blade was an exact length to his arm. He had been measured for it once he had entered the Citadel. Its hilt was decorated plainly, because again that was how he preferred it. A weapon needed nothing extra than the care to make the blade, so the hilt was just black leather strips for the grip.

Lento detested the need to use force like this in battle, but if the need came of it, it was a must.

'I would prefer diplomacy over force but that is not going to happen,' he said to himself.

'Sometimes there is no other way,' Tavener said as he came beside him. Lento was a little startled at the sudden appearance of Tavener. 'That's a great fit for you.'

Lento turned to the man he held a huge respect for. Tavener had been with the twins almost from the start of this whole trial. He had agreed to go with Lorett into the Everglade with the elven boy, Lazon. 'Aye, it is a good fit, isn't it? It's just a shame it has come to this though, eh?'

'It is. There are too many young'uns in this whole thing.' The response was riddled with sorrow.

'Could you help me with this damn armour?'

Tavener helped Lento get the armour on. Once the armour was in place, he tested to ensure it was fluid enough to let him swing his sword.

'I plan on going to the training ground; it would be great if you could join me, Tavener?'

'Sure, let me grab some armour myself.'

The two men headed for the training ground. The men who were already there to practice stood to attention as

Lento walked by. He became irritated. *Time to show them who is in command.*

'Tell me; would you stand to attention on the battlefield?' he said. 'I know that you may have been told in the past to stand when someone of authority passes by.'

The men did not know what to do. All they knew was order and routine. Lento sighed.

It was not the men's fault, but he had little time to prepare them. There had not been a war in their lifetime; little scuffles, but nothing on this scale.

'When we are in the training yard, this is a battle ground. No formality here except for when I am giving my orders, is that understood?'

'Yes sir,' the men said.

Lento strode to one of the training squares, took a wooden sword and asked someone to go first.

The man who took up the challenge to face Lento was large and plain. He was young too. He looked as though he had been in a few scuffles during his life. *A good fighter? Maybe.* The scars on his face suggested he had come too close to the wrong end of a blade more than once. He wielded a larger training sword. *Looks like he prefers heavier weapons.* He went to shake hands with Lento, out of respect.

Lento kicked the dirt on the floor into the man's eyes. There was no etiquette in war. The big man was angered by this. Some of the onlookers gasped too.

Tavener raised an eyebrow. *This is going to be interesting.*

'Rule one in war my friends, anything counts. Drop your guard for a second and you will have your blood painting the ground.'

After the initial shock of the dirt in the face, the training fight began. In the first assault, Lento masterfully swung his sword in an arc, parried the coming blow, sidestepped and placed his foot, just to apply some pressure, to the back of the man's knee.

The man fell to on his knees.

This was repeated four or five times.

He is just like the new king was, all those years ago.

'You are just moving in lines. This is not good enough,' Lento shouted. He had put his sword to the back of the big guy's neck for the fifth time now. 'It would have been a fifth killing blow.' Lento let the man get back up.

'You play dirty. There's no honour in your fight.' He spat at the ground.

'I don't play. I will show you what it is really like out there.' They started to circle round and stared each other out. 'Most of you are respected in the community, but we are no longer against Citadel delinquents. This is a real fight.' *One that could have been avoided, but real nonetheless.* 'Treat training as if it is real. Just don't apply the finishing blow.' Lento had finished, he turned to exit the training ring.

The big man started to run heavy footed, angry at being humiliated in front of everyone. When he got to a sword's length away, Lento ducked and twisted around to strike his sword at the man's stomach. *He does learn. But he still would be dead.*

'Good you are learning my friend, but don't let your anger give you away.'

The young man brushed the sword aside. He swore as he stormed off.

'This is the training ground; here anything goes just like in the battlefield. Remember that and you will get on fine.' Lento finished. *I hope.*

The men were unsure as to whether or not to move, or go back about their own training.

Tavener followed Lento. *They may learn yet.* 'You are a hard teacher. I heard you taught your family, and the girls too. They must be formidable.'

Lento looked at Tavener. 'I have to teach them real. Not some fake pampered training. How will it help if I do not?'

'I have the same sentiment my friend. Hopefully we will get to drink together some time again.'

'We must. I need to have council with the king. We shall meet when this is over.'

Lento went to the king's study. He sat at the table, still in his armour. The king was yet to arrive. *Where is he? We really do need to talk.*

Finally the king entered. Lento stood out of respect. When the king took his seat, Lento sat back down.

'Lento.' The king looked tired already and the fight had not even started yet. 'Thank you for agreeing to be our commander. Now tell me, what plans have you for this fight?'

'I plan to win it,' Lento said. 'I also feel that our best way to defend ourselves is to use the Citadel. Their numbers are large but...' He did not know if this would be a good idea, but it might need to be called for. The king still had to agree to it. Both sides had to agree to it and he did not know if they would. He had to try.

'But what, Lento? If there is something you think will give us the advantage, then I must hear it.' The king's eyes pleaded with Lento to tell him anything that could give them the edge.

Perhaps the king would agree to what he had planned for this. Well there was no harm in trying. What was the worst that could happen?

'There may be more people we can call on,' Lento started. 'But they might not agree.'

'If they are Kaarthean, then they must agree. This is about the future of our world.'

'Well they are not what you would call honourable.' Lento kept an eye on the king's reaction, filled with anticipation and anguish.

'Go on.'

'There is a large group of people, who did not like the way this country was being run. I expect you have been told of them.' Lento started to pace. He often did this when he needed to say something that was difficult to say.

'Are you talking about the dryaks?' The king looked hard at Lento. He had heard of them. He also knew who their leader was. Lento would at least be able to speak to their leader but he was needed here.

'I am.' Lento looked up. It would be a challenge. His brother Caser led the dryaks. Lento was not on the best of terms with him, but perhaps they could talk like men. The need was great. A messenger would have to be sent.

Chapter 25

She lay unable to move, completely scared and afraid. She tried to move her limbs, her arms first and then her legs, but nothing. No movement... Her mind raced at the predicament she was in. At least her mind wasn't frozen. Her eyes. They could move, but looking all around she could see nothing. Nothing at all. If she could feel, she would have felt herself shiver at the thought.

Her frustration at the state she was in began to muster. She managed to keep it at bay, keep calm. She knew she had to work her way free of these invisible bonds. Find a way she must. The space she was in was still empty, black with nothing to see but...

A swirling mist began to form in front of her eyes. In disbelief she would have rubbed her eyes. She then found herself doing it... Her hands were free. What was this mist?

'Child of the earth, do not worry' a distinct voice whispered.

'Child of the earth you will be free' another voice whispered.

'Child of the earth you must find us' a third voice said.

The voices were the mist she thought. She tried to communicate back but to no avail. Child of the earth? That must be her.

Her hands were now free, were her legs? She tried them and they were. She was no longer a prisoner. But where was she?

'Dream.'

'Dream.'

'Dream.'

The voices again. Answering her thoughts?

'Yes.'
'Yes.'
'Yes.'
How?
'We are you.'
'We are you.'
'We are you.'
Can't you just talk in one?
'Yes.'
Where do I go now?
'The direction is yours to take, straight on, backwards, left or right, yours to take.'
But how do I know where to go?
'No one knows truly where to go or where their path will take them.'
A road does.
'A road is a physical journey; we talk only of the mind.'
'You will know where to go, siren.'
'You shall let the mind reveal what will happen. It will form the physical path.'
The siren began to walk, not knowing if it was the right direction. The voices had gone. She walked for a good hour it seemed. Maybe time did not count for anything here? Or maybe it did? She certainly did not feel tired at all.
After what seemed like another hour of walking, the darkness seemed to lighten. Sunlight?
'Yes.'
'Yes.'
'Yes.'
The voices were back.
Where are we? And please just one answer.
'The garden.'
'We need to awaken your mind before you head back.'
'It is still shackled to the agent of the shadow.'

She shuddered. She still felt a little foolish; she should have known not to use the stones when one was missing. She would have been more use and able to help. Not receded into her mind, booted out by some clod shot creature...

Her mind should have been left her own. She held a resentment for the creature.

'Please don't bring bitterness to the garden.'

'Please don't bring anger to the garden.'

'Please do not bring resentment to the garden.'

Silence for a moment.

Why?

More silence...

Why?

'Healing of the mind will amplify emotion.'

'You would be reminded to minimise those emotions going in.'

'It will be less painful, for you and every one.'

She understood what her mind-set must be going into this... It worried her though... She did not know if she could stop the waves of emotion that would threaten her healing of the mind...

She breathed in and started to walk. The sunlight blinded her as she moved into a desert. Garden? This is not a garden; it is a barren, lifeless landscape... She looked around seeing the dust; there was not even any desert vegetation in sight. No water, nothing.

Her bare feet touched the cold floor.

Cold floor, but the sun is so hot and bright? This is too queer. She continued walking not noticing at first that with every step new life began to form underneath her feet.

Then the ground changed before she had even placed her foot upon the green, lush, grassy meadow. She could feel the grass between her toes, and drew comfort from its gentle brush. Then it struck her.

This is my mind.

And it had become barren when the creature had invaded.
Blood seemed to move faster at coming to this conclusion,
anger. She had let the creature in...
'No, anger is not advisable.'
'It is too late.'
'It comes to do battle.'
Fire. It's source flying high above her head. Then she saw
it. Black wings. Long scaly tail. A deafening roar. A dragon.
In her mind. A creature of darkness no doubt.
'The battle must begin.'
'She must win.'
'Will she die?'

Morace looked in horror unable to do anything. Lorett his twin had gone deathly pale. There seemed to be no remedy to solve this and his frustration began to overwhelm him. *I have all this power, but I can't do anything to help.* Then it struck him, mayhap he *could* help. He might be able to give her some of his power, to help her fight whatever it was she was up against. There was no harm in trying. Who knows, it might just bring her back.

'*Shorai.*' His eyes lit up with the incant. He channelled the energy through his hands into his sister's heart. *I hope this works...*

There was no response from his sister who still slept soundly. *Nothing at all.* He continued with what he felt needed to be done. 'Shorai' He repeated the same incant for a safe amount of time, before his own life would be subject to jeopardy.

Tears fell from his eyes... Not another member of his family dead, surely? Not on his watch again.

He had to stop now but he did not want to. He could not just give up, not now, not while he still had life in his body that he could give to his sister. Darkness started to envelop him and his life force became less stable.

He felt arms wrap around his chest and pull him free. Morace was taken out of the room.

Shanrea spun him round to look into her fierce eyes. With anger and sadness, she slapped him.

'What were you thinking? Are you a noddy head?'

'I was trying to save my sister,' he said back, angry at the interruption.

'And what if you did, but in the end gave yourself up for dead?' Her eyes locked onto his. 'Your sister would wake up to you not being here. I would have to tell her you died to give her life.'

'I had to try.'

'Yes you did, to the limits that you could give. If that was not enough nothing would have been.'

'I know, but...'

'If you were to die, doing what you did it would have been pointless. You gave her all you needed to give for her to survive this, your death would not accomplish anything.' Her eyes had not gone off his. He was scared; he had never seen Shanrea like this.

'You don't know that.'

'I do. I have read about it, more deeply.' She kissed him to calm him and herself. 'Look, dinner is ready. She will survive this; Lorett is stronger than you think.'

'I know. I just feel so helpless.' He kissed her back.

'Well, don't.'

They headed towards the dining room to eat their dinner and talk on matters concerning the fate of the worlds.

She began to feel power she never knew she had inside her. Something different. Not of nature but of druids. Morace. She could feel him in her heart. He was with her but how? He didn't? Not Shorai. Please tell me he stopped before his life was taken... He has given me a lot. She felt the power surge through her bones, her veins, and her skin. Her hand began to tingle with power. It formed at the tips of her fingers burning to get out.

She released it towards the dragon ravaging her mind. Pure power - druid power. It struck the dragon with such force the waves pushed her over. She fell to the floor.

When she woke, everything was green and colourful. Everything looked normal.

Chapter 26

On the morning of the war, Lento lay on his bed reflecting what had and might happen. The night before the war granted little sleep. Lento was woken up frequently by dreams filled with death and scenes of horror. People he knew, even faces of people he did not know, were his true nightmares. He wished that his daughter were here. She was the one that gave him strength when he needed it, the one whose opinion he valued the most, even though she was young in years. The innocence of a child was sometimes the thing that drove everything forward. To protect it.

Sure, his daughter Nythe had been trained to protect herself at a young age. She wielded a fine blade, but he did not want that for her. He wanted her to marry and live a normal life. Whenever he looked in her eyes, he could tell that she longed for adventure, not marriage. It was for that reason he let her go with his siblings to the druid stronghold. Besides, it would be the safest place for her.

Now out of bed, Lento called for his steward to help him with his armour. It was nearly sun up and he wanted to be ready. The rest of the army would be on track for their preparations.

Once he was in his armour, he asked for breakfast. He ate then took for the king's chamber.

The king was on the balcony that overlooked the vast elven army. Unable to hold the gate in the woods, they could not prevent its use by the elves. They had not found any of the other hidden gates that Morace had told them about. The elven nation had plenty of time for them to get their army through the gates. They had plenty of ways to position themselves in idyllic locations.

He put his hand on the king's shoulder.

'This will be the day. We must start.' Lento spoke first.

'I know, there was no other way.'

There was another way, but you chose to be a proud person and not accept the discussion with the elven king.

'Well now we must battle. I have sent word to my brother in the west. There is no guarantee that he will come.'

The king shuddered a little.

Lento had once spent a couple of years in the Citadel training, and the king and he had become friends. Then his brother had turned up out of the blue, and had followed in Lento's footsteps. He was a hot head and soon enough had managed to get Lento into trouble. The now king had managed to persuade Lento to lose his brother or he would lose the standing he had gained in the Citadel.

A confrontation between the king and his brother left the latter wounded and bitter. He left the Citadel and took to the west.

'I know you don't like him but he may be our only salvation from this.'

'I know. I just hope he does not bear grudges.'

Like you? You mean with the display you did for the elven king because of the death of ours?

A horn sounded. The elves had begun to march on the Citadel and soon enough arrows started to flurry.

Lento went to the archers. Two thousand strong they were, some of the finest in the land.

'On my mark,' he yelled. He held up his arm 'Notch your arrows.'

The company of bowmen readied their first arrow.

'Draw.' In unison they drew their bows. Lento's hand then dropped. 'Engage.'

Lento's ears filled with the twang of two thousand released bowstrings. The elves in the front rows dropped to the ground, dead. This made the ones behind yell and drive forward faster. Anger filled the air. The anger fuelled the unknown forces.

A storm began to muster from behind the elves.

Weather Magic? Were the elves using weather magic in this fight? The thing that had caused this turmoil in the first place? Lightning struck at the one of the towers, which began to collapse. The men on the tower fell to their demise. Lento watched, helpless to do anything to prevent it.

More lightning struck but this time at the elves. Not Weather Magic, then? Lento struggled to understand for a moment what had happened. Then he saw that the elves were momentarily out of their senses due to the lightning.

'Now it's for our advantage.' Lento had already ordered for the gates to be opened so that the army within the walls could be dispatched once he arrived. His horse was ready for him. He mounted and ordered the men to follow. Obediently, the army chased the front of the elven army who had just started to regain their senses after being struck at by the lightning.

Lento's sword met with the sword of the elven warrior. The clang of metal rang through the plains where the battle ensued. Lento jumped off his horse to fight a lean elven sword wielder on foot, which he preferred. The first elf of many he knew he would have to battle with was a formidable opponent, but Lento shrugged off the challenge in little more than minutes. Many more elves fell to his blade, their blood mixed together right down to the hilt. This was the most he had killed and he did not like how this felt.

The morning wore on. Many on both sides had fallen. Then Lento saw the general of the elven army. He was taller than the other elves, and lean. He killed with a brutish sword. This elf lived to fight; the others used him as a weapon. He also commanded the elves. He swung his sword with such ferocity it took heads clean off.

Lento knew that the elves would be getting some valour from this elven general; it would lend them a terrible blow to dispatch of this elf. Lento determinedly charged at the elf, bloodied sword drawn, ready to add more. Clashing blades, they swapped parried blows. Lento started to tire, the elven swordsman kicked him to the ground hard. He had him pinned with his foot and he took Lento's helmet off. He raised his sword ready to strike.

Tavener had little or no trouble with the elves he faced. *I have killed the urak.* He swung a broadsword, with clear strikes, taking off the limbs of elves. He was yet to be scratched from any blade that came his way. It was without warning that the howling beast came for him.

A huge grey wolf bound to him, with yellow teeth bared from its wide maw. It had picked up a wicked pace as it ran to kill his intended prey. It struck with full force at the largest man it had ever seen. It slashed at Tavener's back, tearing at the armour.

Tavener was taken off his feet. They were now at the edge of the forest that bordered the plains of where the battle was in full swing.

Tavener was face down in the grime, the back of his armour in tatters. He could hear the anger growl from behind. It was as if it was daring him to play hunter. Tavener, who had hunted all of his life, now had the role reversed. He got up and turned to face the wolf which had stopped advancing and waited.

'Go on, Mr Hunter, Run.'

Tavener did not give himself time to think. He bolted. He then realised that the wolf had in fact just spoken. Told him to run.

Is this a game to it? He looked back. He could not see it anywhere. A mist had developed making it harder to see the trees. Angrily, he bumped into a couple but managed to proceed.

'This is ridiculous; I am a hunter of creatures of this sort, why am I running away?'

The wolf howled in answer. Tavener started to run once again. Away from the battle.

Twak watched on from the sky in a hawk form. What he saw, he liked. It was nearly time for his plan to come to fruition. He winged his way back to the dwarves' encampment, where half of the dwarves stayed with their general. The others had made their way to the other side of the elves to flank them. He turned into Gragio, for the last time he hoped.

'It is time. The elves and men are weak. We need to strike now.' The general nodded in impatient agreement.

'It's time.' He ordered at top of his voice. 'We go to war.'

The sound of the Horn of Dalrun rang through the encampment. The call reached the ears of the dwarves on the elven flank. They know knew that it was their turn to battle.

The dwarves marched, heavy and with purpose; a uniformed army, an immovable force. The ground shook as each foot hit the floor. This was how the dwarves always went into battle. They were like machines relentlessly moving forward, ready to fight for their cause. The horn blew again and the elves and humans heard its call. They had no idea what the noise was from until it was almost too late.

Lento looked into the eyes of the elven general who still held the sword in his hand. It was almost as if they communicated by thought because the elf dropped his arm and let Lento up.

'This is much too strange for us to continue in this fight we need to band together.'

The elves and men around them could see this communication and understood.

With a shake of hands, Lento and the elven general ordered the men and elves to battle the dwarves together.

The dwarves were now merely feet away from the two armies. Then the engagement ensued. The dwarves were strong and powerful, and they moved surprisingly swiftly. They ploughed through the front lines. The message had not got through to all the men and elves who still fought each other and not against this new enemy. They were butchered.

Lento dispatched a messenger to the king to advise him of what was happening then moved straight to the right flank to engage with the dwarves.

They were strong and wore armour laced with obsidian no doubt. It looked like the stories were true, they *were* a formidable race. He battled hard with them; it was a challenge with each one.

They wielded axes and maces. Crossbows shot bolts out into the armies. It was a true battle and one they had not expected.

Darkness set in over the field and a cold and chilly feeling fell over the vast space. It caused the men, elves and dwarves to stop suddenly. Ravens flew from the black clouds that unfolded. The griffon that was Twak soared overhead. *It's time to show these fools what this war was all about.* Laughter echoed from the clouds of black. The armies were enveloped by shadows. The griffon flew down into the centre of the hoard of men, elves and dwarves.

Tall and strong, the shadows seemed to emit from the beast itself.

'What is that?' Lento looked at the creature, as black as night and formidable. It would take a lot to kill something like that. Lento had known that the fight would be difficult with the elves, but then he had to fight with the dwarves, and now this thing. Things had happened that he could not believe. It was difficult for him to decide what needed to be done.

The griffon slashed at everything, man and elf. It appeared to be sided with the dwarves. The griffin then transformed - it got bigger, massive, and it changed into a two legged creature. It had become a giant. Its skin was black. It wielded a club and smashed at the armies.

'Retreat!' Lento called to his men and blew the horn he carried to sound the retreat. The elves followed suit and the dwarves chased down the men and elves as they retreated to the Citadel.

The gates to the Citadel were open for the survivors. The elves came in with them, allied in this fight.

Looks like my brother is not coming...

Chapter 27

A cannon was fired and the ball hit the giant in the chest, making it stagger. Another shot made it fall, landing on the surrounding dwarves. It let out a huge cry of pain and began to clamber back up.

Strong and powerful horsemen rode out to the field from the forest of Dalrun.

Lento took out his spyglass and looked at them. *Brother, you command this? What happened to the rebels you commanded?* It appeared to him that his brother was not in command of riff raff, but of an army that looked organised and powerful. What a surprise it was to see this new battle unfold. They attacked like raiders but they were effective. They killed ten or so dwarves with each attack. The forest was used for cover. The dwarves had no chance.

The cannon kept the dwarves and the creature at bay. *Where did they find that? Or how did they find out how to make one?*

'Hello, brother.'

Lento turned around to find his younger brother sat on the battlements with a grin.

Long auburn hair framed his face, with threads of silver peeking through. They clasped hands and embraced each other. He felt strong, not the sickly looking young man he remembered. He wore a long, all-weather coat that licked his ankles.

'You took your bleddy time,' Lento jested. 'Could have done with you at the start of all this.'

His brother shrugged. 'We were here. We just wanted to see what the king's army could do. We watched you in the thick of it.' Caser sat on a box he found. 'I was not expecting you to be in command.'

'Yeah, well it is good you appeared when you did, but this force is much too big for us to handle. We need magic,' Lento said. 'And you would never guess who that magic may come from, brother!'

'Who?'

'The twins.'

His brother looked at him, shocked. Caser got up and grabbed his brother's shoulders and looked hard into his face. 'The twins?'

'Yes, brother. Lorett is a siren and Morace, a druid.'

'What does Pa say to this?'

Lento shook his head. *He does not know Pa is dead. How do I tell him?* 'He died weeks back, brother, as did Mama and our sisters. We...'

'And no one thought to message me, to let me know?' Caser cut in. His wild temperament came through.

'It has been intense, brother.'

'Don't give me this brother bullshit.' Caser turned away and walked out of the Citadel.

Lento watched his brother ride to the forest around the dwarves, who were still occupied by the army. No more horses came, but they had done so much damage to the dwarves that another assault would not succeed. His brother had gone and his army with him.

Lento had not noticed, but as the dark shadow encroached over the Citadel, black forms began to take shape all around the city in strategic positions. Lento turned to find himself face to face with one of them. Its face was gnarled. He cut at it with his blade. Its arm fell off but it laughed a cruel and unforgiving laugh. He knew there was nothing to it. He had to run. Lento head-butted the creature and it stumbled but still laughed.

Lento began to run. Run where he did not know, but he let his legs carry him. He needed to regroup and think on this. He found somewhere quiet to hide and waited.

Noise came from women and children and men who tried to fight. Then he heard a voice over them all.

'I see you all have my attention now.'

A deathly silence and stillness fell over the Citadel. Lento looked for where the voice came from. It was the palace, and the voice was emitted by a little creature with goat-like legs.

'People of the worlds - the shadows have finally come. We are here to take our rightful place and cast our long shadow across the lands.'

The creature's voice was powerful and cutting. 'This is your king.' He held up the limp body of the King of Kaarth. With one strike, he took his head off. A shocked silence followed. 'Now I am your king.' Twak discarded the head on the floor. He turned to the palace, its white walls turned black with the clouds.

Lento looked up in shock. He started when he was touched on the shoulder. Ready to draw his sword, he turned his head. It was the elven general he had allied in battle with. They moved together into the lower parts of the city to hide and plan their next steps.

Caser was furious at his brother, and at his so-called family. *Lento, I could understand, but Morace and Lorett? I at least thought they would want to seek me out, tell me what happened.* His horse galloped hard into the trees. He knew he pushed her hard but also knew that she could handle it. He travelled for some time. He had learnt that some time ago that he was a little too rash. *Perhaps they thought I could not handle the news?*

His horse panted now. He stopped at a little pool allowing her to drink.

'It's okay, you can transform now.'

The horse transformed slowly; it became smaller, and humanoid. A bright light flashed and before him was the one he loved. She had become his wife some years ago.

'I am sorry I drove you so hard. It was unkind.'

Her bright eyes looked into his own, and he felt himself melt. Her white hair fell past her naked shoulders to cover her exposed breasts. Her face was youthful, despite her age being twice his own. 'Do not fret, Caser. It was my will also to travel that fast and hard. You needed it, and so did I.' They embraced. They sat on a rock by the pool of water, and he took out her robes he carried in his bag.

'What am I to do, my love?' he asked, looking for answers.

'What is your will?' she asked.

'To rule, to change this world. To make it what I want,' he answered, standing up with confidence.

'Then I will be here to help guide you, to lend you strength as you once did for me.' She cocked her head a little, waiting for his response to her pledge.

With a suddenness that still always shocked him, her eyes turned milky white.

> *Three worlds, one world, fire and water,*
> *death and rebirth, shadow and light.*

Her eyes turned back to their normal colour, she looked at Caser with a smile. *What you seek might come sooner than you think.*

'I have just had a vision, Caser. Something will happen very soon, something that I think will help.'

'What? Tell me of what you saw.'

'Three worlds will come to an end. One world will sit in its place. There will be fire and water, life and death.' The woman took his hand and looked into his eyes. They kissed. 'We shall mould this new world into what we want, Caser.'

Lorett shot up out of her bed. She locked eyes with Morace. He had not moved from her side since they had encountered the creature that must have caused Lorett to fall into this state.

'We need to do something, Morace.' She seemed focused and determined, not someone who had just been in a long slumber. 'It has happened... my worst fears.'

'What are you talking about, Lorett?' Morace asked even more concerned. 'Lay down, Lorett. You are not ready for this.'

'There is no time to lie down. The shadows have taken the Citadel.'

'How can you know this? We are miles away from the Citadel.'

'I can see the creature. He is more powerful than we could imagine and he gains more power with every bit of anger. It feeds him.' She looked with tear-filled eyes.

'You are still talking nonsense. You can't possibly know this. We are too far away.'

'But I do. I can see what he sees if I allow it and right now he has just killed the king. He has taken residence in the palace.'

With her hand, she touched his forehead. 'Look, brother. See what I see.'

His mind was whisked to the Citadel. Its former white walls and towers were no more; they were now black with the shadows. The sky was filled with black clouds.

Morace was horrified at what he saw. 'How are we meant to fight this? It seems an impossible task.'

'I don't know, but we must find a way. I fear that something much worse is coming; the empress of the shadows herself.'

'How?'

'Like this creature, she grows stronger with the rage and anger.'

She let go of the touch on his forehead and he sat back in his chair, exhausted.

Laughter came from deep inside her prison. The empress had begun to stir, enough energy given to her to form once more.

'The druids will pay for their treachery. Where is my servant?'

The empress was still too weak to do anything but wait for more anger and rage to feed her.

'I will return to rid this land of hope...'

Part 2:

-The Shadows Lengthen-

Chapter 28

Deep in the south of Kaarth, where the weather had left its trail of destruction, an unknown Wayward gate stood untouched. The landscape had once been a lush and thriving woodland, home to animals and people of a village known as Dragonsreach. The village was now destroyed and the bodies decomposed. Only skeletal figures remained and soon the bones would turn to dust. It had been two years since this little village met its doom. It lay forgotten; its people forgotten. No one had travelled this far south for fear that they may become sealed with the same fate. The buildings seemed like the ruins of an ancient city left to decay into dust.

The only movement came from the harsh tail winds of the storm that roamed the south. It seemed to want to ensure that it destroyed everything. It was as if the storm had a mind of its own.

It was now over a little fishing village for the sixth time. One that had been levelled in one night. It had killed most of its population. Vermin picked at the remains. They tried to find food but there was so little. Soon they would have to move on, otherwise their bellies would not fill. Death would chase even the vermin.

Two skinny rats fought over a piece of cloth they found. They bared their teeth as the potential source of food for the day lay in front of them. They fought in the shadow of the Wayward mirror.

It had not moved in centuries. It stood still, as no one had the desire to use it. Its purpose had been forgotten to all who once lived here.

As the shadows disappeared, the rats became illuminated in light. The mirror became active once more. Frightened at being seen and destroyed, the rats ran off. They still fought over the piece of cloth.

The mirror's glare reached out and bounced off trees in the evening light.

Out stepped a tall, lean man, who held a sword over his shoulder ready to fight if it became needed. His long black coat brushed the muddy floor. He looked up at the sky to study what it said.

'Magic!' he spat.

'Oi, move out of the way, will you? I can't see anything because you are so big.'

The man stepped out of the way. As he helped the young girl down from the mirror's platform, he patted her head. 'Marrisai, we have come.'

The girl wore all black. Her long, dark hair fell in braids against her back. She was dwarfed by the man who she accompanied; the man who adopted her.

'Great. So where do we go now, old man?'

'Less of the old man, girl. I do not yet know.' He looked deep into his daughter's eyes. He had been with her for twelve years but her appearance had remained the same. 'We are here for a purpose but it is not clear to me. We must wait until nightfall so we can read the stars.' The man picked her up by her shoulders and placed her on a fallen log. 'I will find shelter. It looks like there is a storm. It may come this way.'

Marrisai folded her arms in protest. She hated being left behind. It aggravated her when he treated her like a child. She looked like a twelve year old but she was not. She had lived a long time. She hated it. *It does have its advantages though.*

'Don't be long, old man. I am getting hungry.'

He looked at her and smiled. He smiled rarely these days, ever since he was given the mission from the stars. 'I saw some rats when I came out of the portal. Perhaps you can find them? They seem to like cloth.

'Humph. Try and find something a little more appetizing while you are looking for shelter.'

He ruffled her hair -she hated it when he did that- and disappeared into the shadows.

The man walked on for almost an hour looking for shelter. He sighed. *There is nothing here. Everything is dead, or destroyed. Just what has happened here?* He thought back to Marrisai. She was in a place destroyed when he had found her. It had seemed like she was the centre of it though. She looked back then like she did now. *I will never forget that night.*

The wind had howled harsh and strong. It sent a shiver down his spine. He had been walking for five days in the same direction as the stars told him to. He needed to find something but it was not revealed to him. He got to the woods as the stars told him he would. The trees became less dense as he moved further in. Some were uprooted. He reached a little village inside the trees. It had been destroyed; nothing survived. Bodies lay on the floor, all dead. They were disfigured, some even dismembered. Then he saw her.

A young girl. She looked like she was twelve years old. Her long dark hair hung over her naked body. The girl stood frozen on the spot perplexed at what had happened. She looked like she had walked in on a surprise party but the surprise was rather more sinister than what was expected.

Swiftly he walked over to her. He was still a little apprehensive. He took out a blanket he carried and put it over her naked shoulders. She was hot. Too hot to touch even.

He thought perhaps her cloths had been scorched off. His blanket remained safe however; he thought he might have lost it to her heat.

'Girl, what is your name?' he asked.

She did not reply.

'Girl, are you okay? Are you harmed?'

She pointed to her body at this point and shook her head to say no. To her head, she pointed and shrugged her shoulders. The man looked into her eyes. They were bright and powerful. He could almost feel the power that flowed from her. *Who is this girl? Was she the one I was meant to find?*

'Girl, where are your parents?'

She pointed at two of the dismembered bodies on the floor.

He took a step back from her.

'I am sorry.'

'Don't be,' she responded with words finally.

'Why not? Your parents are dead. What was the cause?'

'I was. They tried to kill me. So did the other villagers. I am not normal. You should leave me alone.'

He could feel some sort of force pushing him back. He fought it, determined to stay with the girl. She was so young; she needed to be looked after.

'I cannot leave, girl. I think I am bound to you. The stars have told me this,' he said gently.

The power seemed to lessen a little. It was still there pushing him away, but perhaps he was getting some-where with the girl.

'The stars? Are you sure?'

'I am.'

'Then prove it. If you indeed are, you will be bound to me by blood. Take this knife.' She threw him a knife. Instinc-tively he knew what to do. He took it to his hand and slashed it. The cut welled up with blood. He looked at her. She had done the same.

The force between them became more powerful. His test now began. With all his strength, he pushed his body. He was tired; he was weary from the days of travel to this place. His hand stung with the gash he had opened up to prove himself. Her hand was outstretched and ready to clasp his if he was indeed who he claimed to be.

When he made it, she smiled as their blood formed together. He was her guardian, her adopted father...

'Geez, you have been walking for hours, old man. Have you not found any shelter yet?'

He turned to see his daughter who sat atop a tree. He frowned. 'I told you to wait, Marrisai. Why do you never listen?'

'Well if I waited for you to come back I would be hungry. I went looking for those rats but they would not come out. So I came looking for you instead.' Marrisai jumped from the tree and landed in front of her father.

'Well, it helps really; although, I do wish you listened to me sometimes.' He started to walk again and she followed. 'There is no shelter here. We have to move on.'

'Oh, how long are we going to have to walk for? I am tired.'

He sighed. 'Jump onto my back. I will carry you.'

'Weehee.' Despite how they met, she still held onto some of those childlike instances. She was easily at least in her twenties. He let her have these moments. She thought of him as a father and he thought of her as his daughter. He had taught her how to fight and survive.

She was amazing with most of the weapons she picked up. What she favoured most was a long and short katana. It was also his favourite. She had even managed to learn how to keep the weapons hidden from view and how to summon them when needed. He was truly proud of her.

'Aieee. Why have you stopped walking?'

He had not realised that he had stopped. He stood staring ahead. Another village. A fishing village destroyed. He had seen sights like this before. This did not perturb him. What did, however, was the smell. He could smell the magic of druids. He pointed almost in a trance.

'Druids, Marrisai.' He spat on the floor.

'Oh, are you going to do something about it?'

'Of course. I am going to kill them. Every last one of them. I thought I already had, but clearly, I was wrong. Damn meddlesome fiends.'

'So this is why we have come?'

'I believe so. Come let's find shelter here.'

He had created it; the crucible from where he plotted his torture and toyed with his reluctant subjects. A subject. That's all they were to him, to poke and prod, dismantle and cause inflict, pain. He enjoyed it, being the top. The head and the one they feared. He relished the power he had over them; the weak and needy needed someone to rule them with cruelty. He was that man, that creature, that thing. Truth was they did not know what he was, except that he was dark, and evil.

It had been a year since he had arrived on the first and last day of the battle with the elves. He had come with his dwarven army, who were just as ruthless. Each day they brought him a subject to torture and leave mindless and lost.

His crucible stirred as someone entered. They were two dwarves, *despicable creatures*. He had not cared to learn their names. What was the point? They would soon outlive their usefulness and be killed. He just needed to bide his time while his army was born and then he could be rid of mortal flesh finally. The dwarves, the elves and man would bow down to his supremacy.

No one will stop me I will be an immovable force.

The dwarves looked at him, their faces reflecting the fear that the crucible was designed to create. *Good. Fear will rule them and keep them at bay.*

'You are meant to bring me a subject. You have also been tasked with finding and bringing the leader of the rebellion to me, either way you have brought me nothing. Why are you here empty handed?'

'We are sorry my lord.'

'Sorry does not cut it.' One of the dwarves fell to the floor dead; a red line across his throat had formed. 'That will do for now.' His retribution fulfilled for the moment, he shot a dark look at the other. He had bent to his knees.

Twak had taken his natural form; his goatish legs and strong chest. He was small, but in that, size was immense power.

The dwarves feared him but could not do anything about it. This was not what they expected when they came back to this land. They had been tricked and they knew it.

'He was a traitor. You knew of this?' An accusation was woven in with a question.

The young dwarf swallowed. 'I. I...'

'Do not think that you can lie to me. My mind is superior to yours.' He stood. Despite his size, the shadows made him look much bigger. *Time to toy with this little pup.* 'Well, answer me with the truth, for I require it.'

'I am not a traitor; I am loyal to you.'

'If you were loyal, then you would not have failed me... But you have. I do not expect failure; you will die now.'

Like the other, the dwarf fell to the floor dead, with a single thought.

Damn irritant. I need results not this continued failure.

He sat back in his throne. It was crafted out of a dark twisted wood from the swampland he had once called his home. The wood was embedded with a magic that sustained his life. *I actually miss that swamp a little.* Twak summoned his favourite drink from thin air. He sipped it with purpose. He needed to find these leaders of the rebels and put a stop to them. Not that they could actually do anything to him; he was impervious against mortal blades but he knew of the siren and her brother the druid.

They would be a thorn in my side until I can put a spear through their hearts.

He was unable to find the location of the druids' repository. He lost it in his flight from there the first time; he lost the stone, too. He had not a chance to find it again. He hoped that the druids had not discovered the stone, so that they would know it was lost to the one they hid. Hid like little mice from a cat. *I will find them and when I catch them, I will tear them apart.*

'I need to eat. Where is my latest subject?'

A dwarf dragged a young woman into the Crucible. The girl shrieked with terror. He enjoyed it better this way. Terror was like nectar to him, as well as the soul. He raised his hand for the dwarves to leave. He rose with a sadistic steadiness that hinted that he was going to enjoy the next few minutes. His prey was in front of him. He could smell the terror on her, and she stank with it.

'Tell me your name,' he commanded.

The girl gave no response.

'Do you fear me?'

She shook her head no.

'Really? I think you lie.'

'I won't give you the gratification of my fear. You are a monster. There is a storm coming and you will not survive. Your arrogance of your power will be your downfall.'

If he was taken aback, it was not shown. He remained emotionless, as he looked into the eyes of his captive. 'You think to cause me a quiver? That I will squirm at your words? You are a fool to think this.' He held her by the hair to force her to look up at him. She had no fear, she was right. *Why did you scream on entry to the crucible?* She started to smile at him, a smile he had not seen a mortal make for a long time. 'Why do you smile?' Suddenly all the fear he could smell disappeared. *Deception?*

'I smile because I unnerve you.' She was cocky.

He slapped her hard across the face. The sound rebounded off the walls of the hall.

'I will devour your soul. You know that, right? You should be trembling with fear, not sitting here cocky, bitch.'

'There are powers much greater than yours coming. You can't hope to survive.'

'I think differently. You and your hope are a tiny insect, a fly, and you can't hope to overturn my reign.' Twak watched the tears run down her face. His grip was tight on her hair.

They were tears that she could not control; they were there because she was in pain, not because she was sad.

'You are a fool, you know,' she said with arrogance.

'Please tell me more. I am loving this.' *This is even better than I thought... She is totally addled to think that I will be overthrown.* 'Please continue.'

'I am not from any settlement of this world, or the others.'

'Then where are you from?'

'I am from the shadows like you, but not as powerful.' She took his hand, his grip loosened on her hair. She smiled. 'I bring a message, one that you won't like to hear.'

'You can't. It's impossible.'

'She has awoken and she knows your intent. You are a fool to think that she would not seek vengeance.' The girl had power in her but it only stunned him. It would not be lethal. There was only one whose power was greater than his own. *If she starts to stir, I will be in trouble...*

The girl stood up. 'I was only giving you a message, and a chance to redeem yourself. Come to her holding and speak to her.' She flung him across the room like a discarded toy and walked out of the Crucible. The dwarves that tried to stop her flew, just like their master.

Time to fly. She turned into a dove and took to the sky.

The girl in dove form did not head straight back to her mistress. She wanted to feel the air around her wings; it was the first time since her creation that she was able to fly around without having a real purpose. She knew where Twak, the traitor, called his home for many years. She took to see and find out what she could. Even though the empress was powerful, she had been away from the worlds and had not seen its change for many years. The girl knew she would need to gain some sort of knowledge to pass on.

It took a day for her to fly to her destination. The swamp smelt putrid and gaseous. She came back to being a girl in a black cloak; the shadows enveloped her, to protect her from the nastiness about her.

She found the former dwelling of the shadow agent with ease. *The empress told me he was messy, sometimes reverting to the animal in himself.* When she entered the dilapidated shack that Twak called home, she found that there were scribbles on scraps of paper. Mad scribbles, she could see. He had turned crazy. All he had to do was wait, and bide his time in this swamp. His notes showed that he was still focused and determined, but he had chosen to go against his mistress. He thought he could be more powerful.

She felt sorrow for the creature. It was not his fault, but he should not have betrayed the one who gave him power.

Now it was her task to aid the empress and exact a punishment that would fit accordingly.

The girl continued to read through the notes. She could tell that Twak housed a deep disdain for sirens which could be used to her advantage. If there was a siren, could she enlist her? Could she gain her help in this quest to destroy the fool? She knew she was not nearly powerful enough to dispatch of the traitor herself, but if she found enough power from others around her, she could take him out.

She would become great, and have even more standing with her empress, which was the only thing that mattered.

Once she had all she needed from this despicable abode, she took to the sky once again. She flew towards the place where her mistress waited for her return. She would speak to her of the idea she had and gain approval from the shadows to fulfil what she needed to do.

Twak had picked himself up from the floor where he had been dumped by the shadow girl. He had never in all of his life been thrown like that. She held more power than he had realised. With the power he had gained from devoured victims, he had managed to travel great distances with nothing but a thought. *I need to clear up my past.*

He started to walk to the doorway out of the Crucible, then with a thought he simply disappeared.

His thought took him to his beginnings, where he was first seen by the now dead elven fool that he had used and threw away like a discarded puppet. That's all the people of this world were to him. Puppets.

Twak found his hut quickly. He noticed something quite unexpected. *Looks like my little visitor has digressed on a different path, one of the empress's choosing? No probably not.*

After some hours, Twak was in his true form. He looked around. He remembered the notes he had written. *Had she read them? Found out what he hated the most?* He found one piece of paper with the word siren written on it. Smelling it, he could still feel the trace of magic used to relieve memories. Then he shuddered.

I am in trouble it would appear.

Chapter 29

Marrisai lay in the little shelter her father had found. He stood on watch to make sure that there were no interruptions to her sleep. He was ready to wake her up if needed. While she slept, he watched her breathe and remembered how his life was before he had met her. He had wandered aimlessly for at least one hundred years. His life had been a blur. Perhaps he was old now, too old to follow the stars.

The stars first spoke to him nearly twenty years ago. To find this girl he now called daughter was his first mission. It had taken him a long time to find her. He knew that for sure. That was partly due to the fact that he had never heard the stars talk to him before, so he did not know what they meant. He needed to find someone who understood them first. He needed to be taught. For the first time in one hundred years, he had a direction at least.

Before that, he was known as the Aimless Wanderer. Sometimes his appearance brought good fortune and other times it was not so great.

Now he had been asked to come here to another world through a portal. To do what? He did not know. He looked up to the stars for the answers to his question.

He noticed instantly that they were different patterns to the stars in the world he and Marrisai had come from. This did not stop him from trying to understand them. The swirls of the reading began to form. The story of the stars unfolded for him. Then he saw it; the picture of his former master. In his world, he was known as a wraith. His picture was so clear here. *Did he come here too?* A memory stirred in his mind.

'I must leave this world. I was wrong to come here. Do not worry they will be safe.' A door had slammed. This was his master's voice but he could not see anything.

He returned to reality and the memory faded. *I remember this.*

The warm glow of the sun began to peek over the horizon. A warm dawn had arrived. This was their first dawn in this world.

'Oh my, isn't the sunrise beautiful here?' Marrisai looked out from the shelter.

'Indeed.' He looked at her. Despite just waking up, her beauty was ever present. Her hair did not seem to fall out of place. 'We need to get moving. The stars have spoken again. I know where we must go.'

'Great. Can I bathe first?'

'No, we leave now.'

'But I have not even had breakfast.'

He snapped his head towards her. 'We must leave now. Pack your things, child. Do not test my patience.'

Marrisai stormed back into her shelter and packed what little she had. He always got like this once he had read the stars. *Well I am going to bathe first. No matter what.*

'I will be right back. I am going to bathe.' Before he could protest she ran off to the sea.

The old man looked on as she ran off. *That damn child. She is so full of spirit.* He could never be angry with her for long, especially after what she had been through. Besides, it did mean he could enjoy the sunrise once more. Due to the smog that had developed in his own world, there was little chance to see the sunrise. *Damn those dwarves. They destroyed the world then left suddenly.*

Marrisai stripped naked to swim in the sea. She loved to swim; it made her free of everything, any worries she had. She dove under the water. She wanted swim for longer than what she would be allowed to. Marrisai really wanted to settle. Her love for her father was strong and what she craved most was to be able to settle with him and stay in one place. To live the rest of her days in the same place.

Even under the water, she could hear it. The explosion was that loud. The shockwaves came next and the ripples in the water hit her quite by surprise.

The old man had noticed the blackness in the sky creep over the morning glow. Everything had become cast in a dark shadow. The black forms came out of the shadow to subdue him. Grotesque creatures.

Marrisai. Damn girl. Why did she have to run off like that? With a suddenness that seemed to quell the advance of the dark form, he withdrew from the palm of his hand his long katana. There were at least eight of these black forms, but more could quite easily come.

Two advanced at the same time, to test what he was and what he could do. Once they got in reach, he could see their deformed faces closely. They smelt like a tar pit and caused him to feel nauseous. He held back the vomit that came to the top of his throat. He was in his ready stance, about to strike at the first one.

He had not noticed the shadow behind him take form. An ambush. It grabbed his arms with such force that he dropped his sword. His arms were pinned by his side and he was unable to draw out another weapon. The shadow creature put pressure on the back of his knees to take him down to the ground. He was subdued.

Marrisai crept behind a tree to see everything unfold. A tear began to form in her eyes. There were too many for her to take on. They had planned this ambush. They had sent enough to show that maybe her father had stood a chance. Then while his back was turned, the ambush took place. There was easily around fifty of them. There was nothing she could do but watch the event unfold. She was alone.

As she watched, she kept her cool. It would not do any good to rush to save him. She would have to play this right.

'Father, I will save you,' she declared under her breath.

'What is your name?'

They all looked the same to him, but he could tell this was the leader, as it stood tall above the rest. The others slouched, almost like cavemen. He remained silent long enough to piss the leader off. If they got angry, he might stand a chance. He focused on himself and nothing else. There was no knowing if these creatures held power over the mind. He did not think so but he did not want to take the chance. If his mind wandered over to his daughter, she might be in peril, if they could read minds. Over one hundred years of life trained you for most things. Still, they did catch him off guard with the ambush.

'Speak to me. Tell me of your name?' The creature slapped him across the face. They had tied him up with his hands behind his back.

'Truth be told I do not have a fixed name, creature.' He looked hard into what he imagined was the creature's eyes. 'I have once been called the Aimless Wanderer, but even that was a long time ago.'

'Don't lie to me. Every one of you pieces of flesh has a name.'

'Well I don't. Now if you will untie me I might spare your fifty or so followers.'

The creature howled with laughter. 'Spare us? Your arrogance would entertain our master.'

'You think me arrogant? How many years training have you had?'

'I was created yesterday.'

Now it was the man's turn to laugh. 'So you have not even had a day of training?'

'No. We do not require training. The memories of the past shadows are imprinted into me.' It slapped him once again across the face. His head dropped but then started to shake a little. An hysterical laughter filled the space.

'I have trained for at least one hundred years. I have seen a lot.'

The shadow creature tried to take a step back but he could not move. He was stuck frozen in place. A strange sensation swept over it; one the entire shadows had not felt before. It paralyzed them all.

'What is this? What have you done to us?' The enraged creature still tried to move backwards.

'Fear.' The man's eyes burned on the creature's face. 'You have been paralyzed by pure fear.' He waited for the words to sink in.

'The shadows have no fear.'

'Clearly that is a lie, shadow creature.'

'The shadows have no fear,' it repeated.

'Oh really? Then why do you have the need to repeat what you have just said? To repeat your words shows me that you indeed have fear. I told you, over one hundred years of training.' The man smiled.

Marrisai could feel the pressure her father had created. These creatures felt fear. It was now her turn. She crept up behind the nearest creatures. They could not move. Frozen with fear. She swiftly dispatched of nearly thirty of the creatures. She knew the hold her father had on them

-225-

would not last that long. The others began to be able to move stiffly. Another five fell to her blade before they could lift their blade to battle her.

That left around ten not including their leader. These ones had lost most of the fear her father had created. The first one came at her with an axe as dark as the night. She dodged its cumbersome swing and it struck the ground. The creature was stuck as it attempted to get the axe out of the ground. Before she could dispatch of it, however, two more of the creatures came at her with swords. She turned with grace like in a dance. She ducked and jumped as she embedded the two attackers; one with her long sword the other with the short sword. Marrisai threw the latter at the shadow creature who still tried to get its axe out of the ground. It struck the back of its neck with precision.

The shadows then once again became a little stuck with fear. Marrisai had trained with her father for a long time. He had taught her how to fight with fear; to use its power to quell most resistance.

The girl with the twelve-year-old appearance continued to kill the way she had started. She used the fear to quell the resistance she had in front of her. Marrisai had left only the leader of the party alive. All the others had fallen to her blade one way or the other.

'Get on your knees,' she said to the creature. With obedience, it did as told. Marrisai rested the long sword on the creature's shoulder. The short sword formed from the air as she summoned it from the creature she slew earlier and rested in on the other shoulder. 'It looks like you underestimated us.'

'I. I am...'

'Shut up,' she spat. 'You shall speak when asked a question. Father, have you untied yourself yet?'

'I have been untied for a while, daughter.' He stood by her side; there was a clear difference in their height. 'I am proud of you, daughter.'

'Pride can come later, father. Is there anything you want to ask of this creature?'

'I do not think there is anything this creature can give us. It was only created yesterday. All it has are the memories of the previously deceased of its race.' He patted his daughter's head. 'It would be good to find out how the memories get passed on.' He got onto one knee to look into the creature's cold eyes. 'Tell me creature, do you pass your memories on now? Or would you need to go back to your master?'

It remained silent for a moment. It sighed. 'If I die here today, they will not know of you.'

'Good. Marrisai what do you think? Should we let a potential enemy know we exist by releasing this creature now? Or should we kill it and keep our presence hidden?'

Marrisai looked at her father's eyes. She knew that this was a test from him. 'I would prefer not to have the leader of this creature alerted to our presence.'

He stood up and turned away. He rested his hand on her shoulder and gave it a squeeze. She knew what this meant. He walked away to get their bags.

The head of the creature rolled on the floor.

'We need to move now. Despite them not having the memories of us, I am sure that whatever creature created these beasts will have felt the numbers disappear from its presence.' The old man grabbed his bag. He tossed it at her, she caught it and strapped it over her back.

'Why do you say that all the time?' she asked.

'Say what?'

'That you do not have a name?' She had stopped and stared with a determination in her eyes. 'I gave you one. Remember? Like you gave to me.'

'Fear is stronger when it is nameless. When you fight with fear, to not give your name gives you the edge.' He smiled at her. 'Have I not taught you that, child?'

'I am sorry. It just cuts me when you say you do not have one.' She looked at the ground a little ashamed at herself. 'Can you please say it, just so I know that you do care that you have a name?'

He walked over to her and held her face in his hands. With a smile, he kissed her forehead. 'I do care, I am grateful for the fact that I have been given a name. My name is Danai given by you, my daughter, Marrisai.'

Marrisai hugged him hard. Deep down she was still a child needing comfort, despite what she had just done to the shadows. Her graceful dance had defeated nearly fifty creatures that she had never encountered before, but she was still just a girl. She had not lived long enough to become cold like he was.

He had softened a little though, when he became her father. She reminded him what it was like to be a man.

'We must walk now. We have stayed here long enough.' They walked a road that had not seen much use in the past year or so. Danai had skill as a tracker. He knew it had been last used by a horse and cart, in heavy rain. The tracks ran deep. *Maybe someone survived? I wonder if I can find them. I am sure they are involved in what is happening in this land. I bet it has something to do with druids.*

Chapter 30

Danai kept the pace fast and relentless. He carried his daughter on his back so that they could keep walking. She was so light she did not encumber him at all; it gave him a little comfort. They continued their walk up the road they had travelled for three days. Danai had not stopped even during the nights. Danai did not need to sleep. His training meant that he could stay awake for extreme periods of time.

The road they travelled took them to an inn. *Perhaps Marrisai will benefit from a bed to sleep in.*

'Hey girl, wake up there is an inn to rest in.'

Marrisai woke up, her head positioned between his shoulders. She had been comfortable. She yawned and looked at the building. 'Oh, I was comfortable on your back.'

'I thought you might benefit from a bed to sleep in and a little food.' He jabbed at her ribs. 'You are looking a little thin. Besides I can keep going without much sleep but without food my endurance will not last long.' He let her slide from his shoulders. 'Hold my hand, so that not many questions are asked. They walked up the steps of the inn. A bell rang as they entered through the door.

Heads turned to see who had arrived at such a late hour. *Oh right, it might not be normal for two travellers to come in, especially from this far south, at such a late hour.*

'I am sorry to be of trouble at this late hour.' He could see the only people who were left in the inn at this time were drunkards who would probably forget the visitors after more beer. 'My name is Danai and this is my daughter

Marrisai. We have come from the far south looking for a place to stay.' *A name does come in handy. It might have looked strange saying I had no name, or calling myself the Aimless Wanderer. I must thank my daughter for the name.* 'Who is the owner of this establishment?'

A woman looked up from the counter of the bar. 'The master has been away for some time. I am Dacy I am looking after the inn in his stead.' She came out from behind the bar to inspect the two travellers. Danai was quite handsome in her eye, with a streak of grey in his long auburn hair. She went to help take his coat but he refused.

'I am sorry; I have not had a chance to change my clothes for some time. I would feel better not to take them off in the eyes, or smell of others.'

In front of him, Dacy inclined her head in acknowledgment. 'It is a little late for dinner; I will give you the two rooms at the far end of the inn for your privacy.'

'That would be greatly appreciated, Miss. Could you run a bath for my daughter?'

Dacy ushered one of the waitresses to do this.

'Thank you, you have been kind.'

'Not a problem, sir. You and your daughter can have your privacy. Would you like a drink first?' She pointed to the beer taps on the bar.

'No, thank you. Could you show us to our rooms?'

Once they had bathed, they took to their separate rooms. Dacy had been right; they were a little out the way, which satisfied Danai. This meant he could think in peace. He stood in front of the door to Marrisai's room and knocked.

'Who is it?'

'It's me, are you decent?'

'I am. Come in.'

He pushed the door open and entered. She wore a long nightgown and looked ready to sleep. He had put back on his clothes, as he did not need sleep. Marrisai had been half way through brushing her hair. He took the brush from her and began to brush it for her.

'Remember when I first found you?'

'I do, it was the best day of my life.' She liked it when he did these fatherly things. It made her feel normal. 'Do you think one day we will have this?'

'What do you mean?'

'I mean, at the moment it almost feels as though this is normal. Like we could be in our own home.' She turned around and looked at him with an intense fierce look in her eyes. He had seen this look before from her, when she was determined that something was going to happen.

'I have already made that promise. Once the stars stop talking to me we can look to what we want.'

She hugged him. 'I worry about you.'

'There is no need to worry about me, child. I am strong, I have lived many years. I should like to think I would live many more. I see us settled.'

She hugged him with strong arms. Despite her appearance, she was strong. Her grip on him showed that she willed them to never be apart.

At first, he had tried not to be too attached to her. That became impossible. She was twelve at the time but as the years passed, his fondness for her grew. He loved her as a father would any daughter. They trained together every day. She had learnt from him everything she knew in fighting and the use of fear. He felt pride for her.

'It is time for you to sleep. I do not want to stay here for long. I will wake you in the morning.'

In the morning that followed, it was actually her that woke him. She had been up for nearly an hour before he even stirred. Marrisai had decided that if he had fallen asleep then he needed it.

He was not happy at the fact that he had allowed himself to fall asleep and he was moody for the remainder of the morning. It was when he woke up that he sensed it however.

Druid's magic.

How did I not sense this last night? Damn, I must have been tired.

He looked at the bed he had just slept in. He was certain now that he had slept in a bed that a druid had slept in. This was not the same though. It was like an unconscious druid and it was very faint. *The druid must have not realised what it was at this time. It was so long ago though, over a year, maybe?*

In the breakfast hall, they ate porridge. Danai called Dacy over to speak with her on the matter of the druid that once slept here.

'Don't be so silly. There is no such thing as druids. They are a myth. A legend.'

So in this world there are no druids? Perhaps they hide in secret. In the shadows?

'Marrisai, we need to go. Now!' Danai had gotten up and was ready to leave.

'But food?'

'You have enough.'

She shook her head. 'No, I mean we need to buy or get supplies, remember?'

'You're right. Dacy?'

Dacy turned her head to look at the man she might have fallen in love with. She had never heard an accent like his and it made him seem strange.

'Yes, Danai.' Even his name made her melt.

'We will need some supplies. Is there anything you can spare?'

'I am sure there is something I can find for you.' She trotted off to the storeroom. Eventually she came back laden with a number of foods; bread, cheeses and other items that Danai had never set his eyes on. He put his hands in his pocket and pulled out a gold ring.

'I hope this payment will be enough for the food?'

'More than enough.'

Danai opened up his bag and Dacy put the food inside it with care.

'Thank you, Dacy. You have been kind to me and my daughter. If I am ever back in the south I will certainly stay here once more.'

'You and your daughter will always be welcome.'

They started their walk down the road when they heard Dacy come after them. 'Wait, wait.' They turned round to see her standing with her hands on her knees to catch her breath. She looked up at them and smiled. 'Where are you two heading?'

'North,' Danai said unhelpfully.

'I know that. This road only goes north or south, I mean your destination.'

'That does not concern you.' Danai began to walk on with Marrisai in tow.

'Wait. I forgot to give you something.' Dacy put her hand on his shoulder. Danai turned around to see Dacy's face close to his own. She planted a kiss on his lips then ran off down the road back to the inn. 'You must come back,' she said before finally going back into the inn. Danai started to walk again. He did not look back.

Marrisai turned on him. 'You just let her kiss you.' She looked fierce, almost betrayed.

'It was a kiss, nothing more. She just had a little crush and felt it needed doing. The feeling was not reciprocated.' He touched where he had been kissed for a moment.

'You're lying. You like her too.'

'I do not. She provided us with hospitality that is all. There is nothing more to it.'

She scowled at him. *I will not let some woman get in between us.*

He stopped in front of her and turned. Marrisai straightened her face quickly. 'You're jealous.' He laughed. 'You think that I would like to make house with this woman, is that it?'

Her face flushed red. 'No. I just. I don't know. Any way weren't we in a rush to get going? You said something about druids?'

'Yes I did. One or more stayed at that inn some time ago. They did not know what they were at that time. They were still very young. I think I can use this to track them. There was something more though. Something I have never sensed before.'

'What do you mean?'

'There was another creature of magic with them. Its magic trace was sweet and pleasant. I think it was what we call entrice in our world. I will need to be careful.'

'Why just you?'

'Because they entice men. Last I saw you were a woman or girl. Not a man.'

Her cheeks turned red. 'Well, I will not let you get enticed. I am the only girl in your life as you are the only man in mine.'

'I know. You know, one day you may fall in love with someone and want to be with them.' He ruffled her hair.

'Well I have a slight problem there, don't I?'

'Which is?' he asked, completely oblivious to the fact.

'Who is going to fall in love with a twenty-six year old who looks like she is twelve? I don't even know if I am ever going to age physically.' She sat on a log that had fallen.

Danai sat with her. 'I am sorry. I should have realised.' He put his arm around her for the comfort he knew she needed.

Tears welled up in her eyes.

Danai remembered when he discovered he did not age. He had been older however when a similar thing happened to him. When he was around forty he realised he had not aged at all. He looked exactly the same. He did not know how or why. Only that it happened. For Marrisai, this happened while she was still young.

Marrisai sighed as Danai wiped away her tears.

'I know that you want a normal life. I promise you we will find a way to stop this and allow you to grow and become a woman as is your age.'

She looked into his eyes and found the comfort she needed. 'Thank you. It would mean the world to me. I promise you one thing - when I grow up, you will always be my father, no matter how much I grow.'

Before he could let the tears in his eyes form, he got up off the log. 'We must continue.'

'Bring me the prisoner.' Caser sat at the end of the long hall, deep in the city in the west. He called it Evertere. In a language, he read it meant overturn, which is what he wanted to do. The city he had created had been crafted out of the forest that let them live in its hollows. He sat in the long hall where he conducted his business. He had not needed cells for some years. The people respected him much so that he ordered their sealing.

When his horsemen found the man in their wood almost dead, he ordered the cells reopened. Especially with the war.

Caser knew the man. He remembered him from his childhood. A hunter in the south, who lived in an inn. The king of the people of Evertere would try to enlist him this night. He had tried four times already. Four times over the year, he held him captive. *No doubt, this man came from the battlefield.*

There was commotion. The prisoner was outside. Caser waited with anticipation. Despite him calling the cells a name that sounded horrid and beneath the citizens of his city, he kept them nice and clean. They were almost like luxury cells to make the prisoner feel comfortable. Most of Caser's followers had spent some time in the cells before he closed them off.

The doors to the hall opened up. Caser got up from the cushion he sat on at the end of the table. He walked over with purpose to the man he remembered from his childhood.

'Tavener-Doc, how do you fair?' He embraced him with warmth. Caser liked Tavener. He was a good fighter and an honest man.

'It would be better if I was not prisoner,' Tavener said with a little venom to his words.

'Well you needn't be. I already told you four times you can join us.' Caser sat back down on the cushion and patted the one next to him for Tavener to sit with him. 'Please take off his shackles. He is a free man if he chooses.'

With reluctance, the guard took off the shackles.

'You want to know why I am so kind to you, Tavener?' He studied the big man who took a cushion next to him and helped himself to a leg of chicken.

'Because I helped your brother and sister.' Tavener filled a glass up with wine. He sipped it eyeing the man he saw grow up.

'That is correct. If it was not for you I am sure they would be dead.' He handed Tavener the bowl of roasted potatoes.

'I am sure they would have been fine without me. Considering what they are.' Tavener took some of the potatoes and hauled them onto his plate.

'Are the guards treating you well? With respect?'

'They treat me fine, thank you. I would like to get back to see what has happened to the twins.'

'Oh, and you will. But I need to know I have you onside first.' Caser stood up. He was tall and wore a long, elegant coat that reached the floor. It was designed intricately. Tavener had not seen the design anywhere in this land.

'Caser. Your coat. It is of a design I do not recognise. Where did you find it?'

'Ah, that is a story worth telling; remember the stories that I lorded over a band of ruffians? Well this is not the case. I left a man I thought to be a friend in charge while I travelled over the Desert of the Lost Kings. While I travelled, I found a city deep within the desert forgotten by Kaarth. It had become prosperous. I bought this coat from there.'

'It is good. It looks expensive.'

'The country I went to does not trade with coin.'

'Then what did you trade for it?' Tavener asked with interest. He thought he would like to see this city.

'I traded them a home to live. You see, while I was searching the desert to see what was on the other side, my former friend followed me and threatened to take over the little country. He managed to bring over a small force with him.' Caser looked saddened. 'I had to kill him.'

Tavener put his hand on Caser's shoulder. 'Boy, you did the right thing.'

'Their city was destroyed because I could not control one man. He was greedy. Almost half of the people here are people from that city. I did not get this coat by trading. I got it because I am the leader of my people and theirs. We thrive together in this new country. We have become one people.'

'You have done a good job here. I am surprised at what you have managed to do, to be honest. One man has managed to create all of this.'

'Not just me. My men have helped me. I want to live in peace.'

Tavener shifted uncomfortably. He did not know how to explain that their existence may be threatened by the shadows. *I do not think they will stay out of the shadows' gaze.*

'Caser, I thank you for looking after me this year. I am sorry I was so reluctant to receive you. I saw you at the battle in the Citadel. I saw you run off too.'

'That is true, I did. I came to see what was happening. I heard about Lorett and Morace. Lorett had been captured. I came to help.' He looked out onto the woodland before him. 'I found out that my Pa had died and no one had thought to tell me.'

A knock on the door took Caser out of his thoughts. With a powerful grace, he strode to the door and opened it. A servant stood at the threshold.

'Master, your wife is giving birth.'

'What now? Surely it is too early for that?'

Tavener followed the frantic king of Evertere to his wife's side. The room was purified white. She was on a bed in the middle. The pain of the contractions were audible. Her screams bounced off the walls.

Caser said to the birth mother, 'It's too early.'

'Caser, it is fine. It is not too early for a Seiser.' The birth mother assured him. He took the seat next to his wife's bed. She took his hand in his.

'Caser, our son will be born soon and then we can fashion this world.'

'Don't talk, my love. Focus on the birth.'

The last contraction was the most extreme for her, but then the birth mother said she could see the head. An instant later, she could see the whole baby. Their son was on its mother's chest suckling her breast.

'The rebirth has taken place. A future king sits in my arms, Caser.

'Galian, he is beautiful,' Caser spoke to his wife.

The birth mother inspected the child, unsure for a moment. 'Sire, madam, this child is not male. It is female.'

Caser picked up the baby and inspected it. Sure enough, she was female. 'I thought it was to be a son?'

'It would seem that in the future, Caser, Evertere will be ruled by a queen,' Galian said before she fell into a deep sleep.

'Everyone out. My wife needs to sleep.'

Tavener began to leave the room with everyone else.

'Except you, Tavener. I still need to speak to you. My child is young to this world and I fear that there is war and danger. I also fear that it will come here and we will have no choice but to fight it.'

Tavener thought he could see where this conversation was going to take a turn. He shifted uncomfortably.

'I want you to take my daughter and protect her. In six weeks, I would like you to take her. Take her to the twins. They will know what to do.'

'What? I can't. The twins are up north in the Norse. The cold will surely kill the child.'

'Your job will be to protect her.' Caser was insistent. He had a determined look in his eyes.

'You have kept me in a cell for about a year.'

'I would trust no one else with this task, Tavener. Galian and I have already discussed this. You must take her. One day, she will tell you her name.'

'But Caser, I am in no position to...'

'It needs to be done, Tavener. Now please, leave this chamber so that I can be with my wife.'

Tavener left the room. He attempted to figure out what had happened. *Look after a baby?* He was unable to think about how he could do this in the current circumstances. He knew that Caser was serious though.

Chapter 31

'Look at that really huge city. What it is called?' Marrisai asked Danai. They had been travelling for six weeks. They had lost the trail of the druids all of a sudden.

Something clearly has happened here that is beyond normal reasoning.

'Marrisai, get down for a moment I need to think. I can't find the trail at all.' He let her off his back. Marrisai stretched her legs.

'Are we lost?'

'No.'

'Are you sure? We look lost to me.'

'No. I just can't find the trail I was following. Wait.' He held up hand. She stopped suddenly.

'What is it?'

'Shush, it can't be. He has gone?' Danai seemed to talk to himself. Marrisai watched her father turn crazy before her eyes.

'What is it?'

'The wraith; he has gone. My former master has left all the worlds.'

'Wait, you mean the one who taught you all you know?'

'Well, all I know about using fear to unnerve my foe. I have had other trainers. But this one was the strangest of the lot.'

'So are we going to that city over there?' she said, pointing at the city in the distance.

'No, probably not yet.'

'Why not?'

'Because, girl, look at what is over that city.'

Marrisai looked hard. She was unable to see anything, until she realised it was hidden in the thick clouds she thought to be a thunderstorm.

'That is a Crucible. It is a druid's most powerful weapon. It is used to create fear forever and destroy hope. It looks like the druids here are just as bad at the ones back in our world.'

Marrisai stared hard at the blackness that surrounded the city. It also touched some of the woodland to the west and the plains below. She had a feeling that they would have to go all the way around to reach their destination.

After a brief respite, Marrisai held onto the back of Danai so that her legs would not buckle under the strain.

The plains were an endless barren land. They were cold, not what she thought they would be like. There was no life around, which chilled her. No life. She had seen places with little life before, but for there to be no life at all seemed truly wrong. *So this is the true power of the druids. How can something or someone create an atmosphere like this?*

Almost as though he heard what she had been thinking, Danai stopped. 'Druid magic has killed this land. It clearly has driven fear. But it is strange. I cannot quite tell what it is yet.'

Danai took them towards the east, away from what he had dubbed the city of fear. He did not think there would be anything alive there at this time anyway. Every now and then he would ask Marrisai if she was all right, usually just as she was about to fall asleep.

Marrisai slipped into a deep dream. She found herself on a huge boat captained by her father. Not Danai, but her true father. He was a ghost though, not true to this world. His form was ethereal in the light of the moon. A girl was there,

*too. She was young, maybe in her twenties. The girl walked
over to her.*

*'Marrisai, we are ready. The portal will soon take us to sal-
vation. We will defeat the shadows. I am sorry Dan...'*

'Wake up, Marrisai, please.' Danai's hands shook her gently.

When she awoke, Marrisai realised she was on the
ground. Her eyes opened to a blurry scene of two men
looking down at her. As her eyes adjusted to the light she
could see one was Danai. The other looked a little like
Danai, he had silver streaks in his hair. She started to sit
up, which was a bad idea. Her head rang with a headache.

'My head hurts,' she said as the two men stopped her
from getting up.

'It will do, you fell off my back and hit your head. You
have been out cold for three days.'

'Three days?'

'You also talked in your sleep, about your father.' He
looked at her with a frown. 'I think it was about your true
father, Marrisai.'

'Why do you say that? And I told you my "true father" is
you, not that bastard.'

'Yes, you called him a bastard. That's how I know you
were not talking to me.' Danai helped her into a sitting position so that she could take some water. They were no
longer in the plains but in what appeared to be some sort
of camp.

'Wait, if I have been out for three days why am I still on
the floor?' she asked suspiciously.

'I just got here. This man Lento found us and helped me
carry you to their encampment. He has told me what has
happened to this land.' He hugged her so that her ear was
near his mouth. 'I told him we were from the Deep South.'
Gently he put her back on the ground. He had basically

told her not to tell them who they were, or where they came from.

'Uh, can I go back to sleep now?'

'No, not yet.' Lento spoke for the first time. 'I would like our doctor to check you over. You too, Danai. You have travelled the plains and they are dangerous. Although there appears to be no life, the creature of the Crucible sends out diseases every now and then.'

Danai obliged and picked up his daughter to be led to the tent where the doctor worked.

'I can walk, you know,' Marrisai protested.

Danai kept hold of her. 'I would prefer to hold you.'

Marrisai understood. She knew that Danai would be a little wary of the strangers around.

Lento looked at his second in command who stood like a sentinel next to him. 'Keep an eye on them, Kyle. They seem suspicious. Neither one of them have any weapons, yet from what he told me they have travelled all the way from the south. It does not sit right with me.'

'Aye, your Majesty.'

Lento walked away from the entrance of the camp to his tent. *Who are these people? From deep in the south? I thought that was all but destroyed.* He sat in the chair at his desk. He had tried to outwit the shadows for little over a year. Since the battle with the elves, he had become King of the Kaartheans. Lento had been determined the strongest out of the survivors. He also led the elves with the help of the general he had faced in battle and then with the emergence of the dwarves, quickly became allied with.

The elf would wait for him. Lento had yet to report on his return from a mission to scout the area that he had set out on. They had not expected to find anything but they did. They found a man and a twelve-year-old girl out in the plains. Lento needed to relay this to Sail-Ro, who would be impatient to hear the report.

The Elven General Sail-Ro, stood up to receive Lento.

'I hope your scouting mission was uneventful, Lento,' the elven general asked. He had already heard of some of the things that had happened.

'For the most part. Please take a seat and some wine.'

The elf obliged. 'Tell me of the travellers you found.'

Lento relayed the story. He mentioned the fact that they had no weapons, despite where they claimed to have come from.

'This is very strange. You say they claim to have travelled from the Deep South?'

'Yes, and that land has all but been destroyed by the weather.'

'I have asked the doctor to take a look at them both and see if he can find out anything about them. I don't think they are from this world. I have never seen anyone like them. Could you look at them too, and see if they are from the Everglade?'

The elf looked at him with hard eyes. 'You think them elven?'

'I do not know, but it can't hurt to find out, can it?' Lento leaned forward a little closer. 'Do you remember the stories of the Dal-Mai-Sai?'

'You think them to be of the ancients? If they are, then I wonder what this means!' The elf got up suddenly, now intrigued. He wrapped his light cloak around his body as he turned to leave.

'Sail, not a word of this to anyone, not yet,' Lento warned. He left the tent.

Sail-Ro walked past tents and carts to see the doctor as she worked on her patients. He recalled what happened in the battle, how when everything changed the unspoken communication between him and Lento was strong. They had become fast friends and fantastic allies. Once they had realised the elves could not return to the Everglade as the shadows occupied every Wayward Mirror, they were pretty much stuck. They had planned to get reinforcements to help aid the Kaartheans. This could no longer happen.

The Dal-Mai-Sai? If they had truly returned, what could this mean? He had heard stories of this race. They were formally from the Everglade. They were advanced, and had the use of some awesome technology that almost rivalled that of the dwarves. They had been reclusive and had only looked out for themselves. When they departed from the Everglade they took everything they knew with them. No one knew where they went, no one could find them. *If they have returned it must mean... I don't know.*

Sail-Ro turned the corner to where the doctor's tent was. He waited to be cleared for admittance into the place of healing. Only when he was purified would he be allowed to enter.

The doctor greeted him with a smile. 'I was not expecting you today, sir.'

Sail-Ro looked at her with a pretend look of displeasure. 'I told you not to be so formal on our last visit. You do amazing things for us. You and your team. We are all in your dept.'

She blushed at his words. 'I am sorry, Sail. I will try to be less formal.' She picked up some paperwork and was about to walk away to tend to her next patient.

'I have not come for myself. I have come to see the two that were found in the plains.'

'Oh really? And here I was thinking you had come to just see me,' she teased. They both liked each other but they refused to court, due to their positions. They were of different races too, and they did not know how it would work.

'They are in the back. The male has not left his daughter's side.'

He left her to tend to the other patients and walked into the back. He knocked to alert that he was coming in. His eyes widened when he saw the two in the room.

The girl was a child about twelve years old and the man must have been in his late thirties or early forties. Their hair was dark and long. They had angular faces with sharp eyes. The male had a little more roundness to his features and his hair had a little streak of silver through it.

Sail had heard the stories of the race known as the Dal-Mai-Sai. As soon as he laid his eyes on them he could tell that these two matched the description he had once read in a book. Sail's mouth hung open; he did not know how to approach this now.

'Dal-Mai-Sai?' he mouthed.

'I am sorry, I didn't quite catch that,' the male said.

'Dal-Mai-Sai,' Sail said a little louder.

'You know of my race?' Danai responded.

The girl sat up and saw the man side on. 'You're an elf?' she said. 'Danai, do you remember the stories of the elves?' Marrisai looked at him with a puzzled look. 'I thought the elves were dead?'

'That is what I thought, too,' Danai responded. They studied him some more.

'So it is true? The Dal-Mai-Sai have returned?'

'Well, considering we were not from this world, we can't say returned,' Danai said.

'Why are you here?'

'Honestly, we do not know. I followed the stars. I imagine now it has something to do with the druids and how they have tainted the world.'

Sail-Ro was taken aback at the statement. *Druids, taint on the world?* The only druids he knew of were the boy Morace and the elven girl Shanrea.

'The only druids I know of are trying to help. They are in their sanctuary of knowledge.' Sail sat on a chair to speak to the two Dal-Mai-Sai.

Marrisai sat at the end of the bed and stared at the elf. She had been told of them by Danai. They were very distantly related to her own race. *Still alive?* The Dal-Mai-Sai thought them to be too far behind to survive. Somehow they had been kept alive.

'Did many of your race survive?' Sail asked.

'We have a city in the world we settled in.' Danai became cautious and did not want to give too much away. He needed to find out what had happened to the world first. One night he had noticed that it had two moons, which was strange. The stars said it should not have happened and that it was unnatural.

It suddenly became cold. Marrisai took hold of Danai's hand and squeezed it. With a look in his eye he could tell that she sensed it too. The same feeling as before when they battled the shadow creatures. There seemed to be more this time.

'It's back,' Danai said to Marrisai. Then he turned to the elf. 'We can help against what is coming.'

'What do you mean? What is coming?'

Danai looked at him perplexed. *Could they not sense the presence?* 'Can you not sense that? It is so strong.'

'I cannot sense anything.'

'I do not think he can feel anything, Danai.' In an instance Marrisai got off the bed and dashed for the door. As she passed Sail-Ro he saw a flash that looked like two blades appear from her hand.

'How many have you lost through not feeling their presence before they arrived?'

'How many what?' Sail asked.

'How many of your people have you lost before you realised the shadows had come to raid?' It was the only way

Danai could think to describe this. These people had no idea what was on its way. 'How many of your people were killed the last time the shadows struck out?'

'Thirty,' said the elf. 'We just have no idea when they are going to strike.'

'Well you do now!' Danai said. He ran out to meet with Marrisai. Her eyes were set on the sky. It had turned dark. None of the Kaartheans or elves seemed to be able to see this. *Damn, this is not good.*

'You!' He picked out a young man who became suddenly uneasy at being singled out. 'Where is your king? I must speak to him now.'

The boy pointed further into the camp, He ran off when he and Marrisai looked down the path. Danai looked at Marrisai for inspiration.

'The elf who was in the doctor's tent, he will be able to take us to the king,' she suggested. 'He seemed somewhat important.'

'Yes, go get him, Marrisai, and alert the king. I will meet with the shadows again.' He had not really gotten over the fact that he had actually been trapped and forced to use his druid-like powers on the shadows. Now that he knew what he faced, Danai knew he would be a match for the shadows.

'What about you?' Marrisai asked, concerned.

'Don't worry about me. I have a little pride to take back,' he said. He saw Marrisai's face change in to one of frustration.

'Damn you and your pride. What if...'

Danai shot her a look that told her not to go there. She would need to do as he asked.

'Fine, but I will be back, straight away!'

'No doubt you will, child.'

Marrisai turned around and ran to get the elf.

Now it is time for me to go up against the shadows again. Danai turned to where he could sense them the strongest. Just on the outskirts of the camp.

The sky had turned visibly cloudy and the members of the camp could now see that there was a shadow raid. This time, due to the presence of the Dal-Mai-Sai, they had yet to advance and strike out. They waited on the outskirts of the town. Danai could see them from the mouth of the camp as they watched. Some of them had distinguishable faces. Most of them were swallowed by the shadow that created them.

Seventy. Danai could determine that there were at least seventy different identities within the cloud of black. What made things worse for him was the fact that he could also tell they were using and projecting fear. He knew that he might not get much help from the camp's inhabitants. For a moment his concentration fell. He felt the light thud of someone approaching. When he looked up he saw that Lento stood next to him.

'It looks like your presence here has stirred something up.'

'I doubt it. These creatures were always going to come here. If anything, our presence has stopped an ambush. Right now they are waiting,' Danai explained.

'Can we defeat them yet?' Marrisai's voice peaked up.

Danai looked at her with a smile. She smiled back. She had the hugest smile that he had ever seen. For some reason she loved to fight. She was always determined to show him what she could do.

A lone shadow crept out from the rest. It was silent. Slowly other shadows began to creep forward and expand around the camp.

'Lento, please stand back.'

Lento looked taken aback. These two were going to try and battle all of these creatures on their own? *You're insane.* He did though as was asked. With focussed eyes he watched the battle unfold.

The shadows moved forward in groups of five or six. They were clearly on edge and did not want to be left to fight one of the two enemies on their own.

The first to meet one of the groups was Marrisai. From out of nowhere she wielded a short and long sword. They were thin and looked incredibly sharp. She sliced with precision; in a matter of seconds the five shadows she sought were down, with their heads rolling around the floor by her feet.

Is she dancing?

She did the same to five more of the little groups. The shadows had not managed to lay a scratch on her. With a grace that amazed him she danced from group to group dispatching them as they came. Lento watched on. His gaze turned to Danai.

Danai was a sight to watch too. When he pulled out his weapon from thin air he could see that it was a two handed sword in the style of Marrisai's.

Where are they getting these swords from? Can I learn this?

Not as graceful as his daughter but just as effective, he cleaved off the heads of almost every shadow Marrisai was not close enough to get to.

Just as things were working well, the shadows stopped all movement. A black swirl of shadow then took form in front of them. The shadow creatures that were still alive disappeared instantly. They were left without enemies.

The Dal-Mai-Sai looked at one another puzzled at first, but then they felt that same feeling as before. This time it was stronger and then it happened without them even being able to be ready for it.

Black chains shot out from the shadow that had formed. They sent Danai on a collision course through the air into Lento. With the force, the sleeve of his coat was torn. Lento could see his arm. It was not what he expected.

'Are you all right?' Lento asked. 'What is up with your arm? It does not look like flesh.' Danai's arm sparked as he got up.

'Take the girl.'

'Marrisai? Where is Marrisai?' He looked at the black swirling mass that was the shadows. It shot another chain out towards Marrisai. It wrapped itself around her waist and pulled her into its darkness. She did not scream as she was pulled through the dark abyss.

Chapter 32

Twak sat in his chair in the Crucible. He waited patiently to have brought to him what he had sensed a few weeks ago. He could tell it had come closer. Its presence was something he found strange; despite his lifespan in the worlds he had never felt anything like it. On the arm of his chair he tapped his fingers impatiently as he waited for the report that it had been captured so that he could examine what it was.

He could tell that it had power. His mouth was riddled with drool from the anticipation of what was to come.

A dwarf ran up to give Twak the news of the shadows' success.

'Of course they were successful! I don't need you to tell me that, you fool. Just bring it to me, now.'

A thick black chain rolled in from the entrance of the hall. It was bunched up where it held the captive. Without haste it unravelled to reveal something quite small.

Twak stood and craned his neck to see what the chain had bought him. His face fell. The creature he had waited for stood only a foot taller than he. It wore all black. Its black hair was long. It wore a scowl on its face. It was a girl. A little girl.

Twak circled the girl, taking her in. He remembered when he first felt her power. He could feel it here now. Her power attempted to escape.

'All this power comes from you?' Twak asked. He sounded unimpressed.

'So you have captured me for my power?' the girl asked. She attempted to use the fear on him. She was still a novice at this art though. It did not have much of an effect.

'Well, quite a bit of tongue you have there,' he said, looking hard at her face. The girl stood resolute in the middle of the room. 'Just how old are you?'

'Can you not see, scraggly beard? I am twelve.' She did not want to give him the pleasure of knowing that she was stuck in her twelve-year-old body, despite being in her twenties.

'I think you lie. I don't much like liars.' He put his finger along his neck to suggest that if she lied again he would kill her.

'You would not kill me,' she spoke with a confidence that rang through the hall. She knew that he had taken great care in her capture, even so to knock her father out of the way.

'Why do you say that?'

She leant in as close as she could. 'You want my power. You cannot have it if I am dead.' A light flashed in her hand. He had made the mistake of letting her get close to him. Next thing Twak knew, he was on the floor with two swords aimed to cut off his head at the neck.

'No way,' he said. 'I recognise those swords. You're a Dal-Mai-Sai.'

'Yes, and what of it? I presume you are an agent of the shadow empress?'

'Pfft. I am much more than that, bitch. I have grown stronger.'

'You say that, creature, but what of the fact that shadows dislike the light? I reckon you have not had much of a chance to save yourself against that. Have you?'

Marrisai took a ball that let off a little glow out of her pocket. She dropped it to the floor. It shattered everywhere and the glow became huge, blinding the little creature who thought he had her trapped.

Twak screamed at the brightness that overcame him.

Marrisai seized her opportunity to run. The dwarves who stood guard did not see her due to the light. She was free to run.

When she finally felt safe, Marrisai stopped to catch her breath. She scanned the area. There seemed to be a mishmash of different corridors. She made her decision and ran down one of them. At the end of it there was a door.

It opened easily enough, and with a little creak she closed it again. She decided to hide in this room. In the centre there was a large desk. To get a closer look she quietly moved to the table. On it was a map, which looked like the map of the world she was in.

The map was incredibly detailed, showing every last bit of Kaarth. Marrisai looked at where she and Danai had arrived. She traced her finger along the route they had journeyed. She could see they had travelled quite far. Marrisai followed the northern roads. Danai had told her that that they needed to find somewhere that was in the north of this land.

The stars had not told them much.

The north on this map was named *The Norse.* 'It looks cold,' she said to herself. 'And it's so big, too. How are we meant to find our way?' While she looked at how big the Norse was she noticed that there seemed to be a little mark on the map. To clean it she put her finger to it and began to rub. A spark came out of her finger. She was flung back and fell into something hard. With blurry vision she could make out some figures. She lost consciousness.

***

'My daughter!' Danai said with fury in his voice.

Lento sat with the man he had to restrain.

Danai had watched his daughter get taken away by the chains. He had been held back by Lento. Furious at the fact that he was forced to watch his daughter get taken away, he also felt ashamed that he could not protect her.

'Danai, the Shadow Lord has her. He is the one we battle against. He resides in the Citadel. No doubt you saw the black clouds over the city.' Lento sat back in his chair. He had not anticipated this. *He needs to calm down otherwise he will die.*

'I must get her back.'

'She seems strong, Danai. I imagine she also has some wits, too. You trained her, did you not?'

'I did, but she is still so young.' Danai sighed heavily.

'I am sure she will be fine. We will find a way to rescue her.' Lento looked at the man's arm, still unsure at what he had seen. 'Your right arm, Danai. What is it?'

'My arm?' Danai realised it had been seen in the battle for what it truly was.

'An accident when I was fifty took it off.'

'Fifty? You make it sound like you lived that age long ago. Just how old are you?'

'Me? I am one hundred and forty seven.'

'That is a long time to live,' Lento said. 'Is that normal for the Dal-Mai-Sai. His gaze did not leave the arm of the man.

'No... I mean, yes it is normal.' Danai realised he may have said more than what he had wanted.

Lento was aware that he had managed to get Danai to open up a bit, although he wanted to learn even more about him.

Danai added, 'In our race, some of the eldest live to exceed five hundred.' *I hope he believes that lie.* Danai's gaze lifted up. He had searched the foot of the door to see if he could gain exit from this room. He yearned to find Marrisai.

'Why is Marrisai so special?' Lento asked with a thought that he may have pushed his luck with that question.

'She is powerful, Lento. She has power, but if it reaches the wrong hands for example the hands of the druids, she might be used to cause destruction.'

'In your world you have druids?'

'We had druids, but I have killed every last one of their deceitful race. It seems though that one or two managed to escape into this world. I am sorry I failed.'

It is not good that he dislikes druids. I must not tell them where Morace and Shanrea are.

'I am sorry to hear that you have a dislike for the druids. I know of some from their order. They are good people who are trying to help.

'It is lies; they only look for their own gain. They managed to poison my world.'

'Poison?' Lento tried to probe further into the man's history.

'Yes, they sought to better it or so we thought. Now the air we breathe is poison and there is no cure.'

'So how do you live?'

'We live by staying in the confines of buildings.'

'What did the druids do?'

'They tried to become immortal.'

She lay in bed, on the swaying boat once more. She opened her eyes to find a woman staring at her. It was the same woman as before. She smiled.

'It's ok,' she said. 'You are safe here.'

Marrisai looked at her. The woman's smile warmed her soul. It was almost like she was enchanted.

'What is your name?'

As she tried to say her name, Marrisai realised she could not speak.

'Don't worry. The captain will come to see you soon.'

Marissai closed her eyes and when she opened them again she was on the deck of the ship. The captain was at the helm. She recognised him.

It was her birth father.

She began to walk to him, when all of a sudden her shoulders began to shake.

Marrisai's eyes opened to find a young girl looking at her. With a welcoming smile, the girl gave her some water and fussed at her not to get up when she tried. Her body ached all over. Gladly she accepted the water, realising her mouth was dry. The girl smiled and continued to sit with her while Marrisai woke up a little more.

There was a knock on the door. The voice from outside was a man's voice. It was deep and sounded strong.

'Nythe, has the girl woken?' he asked.

'Yes, she has, Morace. She looks a little scared but she has taken some water.' The girl who she now knew of as Nythe responded with a soft voice.

'Oh, that is great. May I come in?'

'Yes, but you are not to question her too much,' Nythe said forcibly, hinting that she was not to be tested on this matter.

The door was opened by a man in his early twenties. It was strange, Marissai thought he sounded older. He came to the side of the bed and sat on a chair next to the girl Nythe.

'My name is Morace.' He introduced himself with a softness that warmed her. He was attractive. She found herself drawn to him but she did not know who these people were. For all she knew they were not to be trusted. She remembered her father's training about not giving too much away about herself to people she did not know. *It's a good thing I look twelve, otherwise the slight lie I will tell would not work.*

'My name is Marrisai,' she responded. It would not harm to give them her name. It wasn't like they knew of who or what she was.

'Well Marrisai, it is a pleasure to see you. You dropped in on us quite suddenly.' He gave a little laugh. 'Yes, Lazon was most surprised when you landed on his lap.'

'Lazon? Lap?' she asked puzzled, unable remember much after the spark on the map in the Crucible.

'Yes, we were in the study when you quite literally fell through the ceiling. You landed on a young elven man's lap.'

Marrisai's cheeks burned red with embarrassment. 'Is he all right?'

'His pride is a little hurt as he screamed when you landed on him. Other than that, he is fine.'

She felt assured.

'Okay, I think she needs a little more rest now. You can come back later,' Nythe said. Morace got up and started to leave the room. He turned back.

'I hope you get better soon.' He left the room. As he closed the door he felt something strange, like a strong surge of power. He remembered the surge of power before with Lazon. This felt a little different but the core of it was the same. When he came to visit the girl he had left Shanrea in the room they studied in.

That was all they seemed to do at the moment, study. They had learned what was happening to the worlds they both came from, but they just could not find a way to either prevent it, or find a new world to live in. For a year now they had made little progress. They had finished reading the diary they had been given but they were stuck. It kept telling them about three.

Three what? It was too ambiguous, almost like the druid-wraith had needed to keep some information safe, so had written in code. Could they translate what the diary said? No, they could not. Morace, Shanrea, and Lazon had discussions, arguments and different theories but they just could not get their heads around the mystery. They needed to find something fast. The extra moon Kaarth had developed was creeping ever closer.

What also did not help was the fact that they had the shadows to contend with. He had not heard from his brother. The last he heard, Lento had been declared King of Kaarth. That had shocked him. He had even surpassed other lines of royalty and was voted in. Perhaps it was because he was so strong and great at battle. It was also well known that he had fallen into favour with a lot of the royal line for his rally against the shadows in the battle of the Citadel. No one held it against Lento for the loss in that battle.

The dwarves were also problematic. Where they had come from Morace did not know, but they were definitely not on the two worlds in hiding. Not that many people could hide. What also made matters worse was the fact that the shadows had somehow enlisted the dwarves. The three of them had come to the conclusion that the dwarves must have been able to remain hidden because of a truce with the shadows.

You did not, however, make a truce with the shadows. They created an opportunity to use you. It would seem that the dwarves feared this creature more than anything and that was why they were in tow.

That was not all that plagued his mind. Lorett was still unconscious. It had been a year and she had not woken up in all of that time. Morace was beside himself with worry. Nythe looked after her. She did all the healing as she was the most trained in that field. His niece kept him going. He knew that with her to look after Lorett, he could focus on what needed to be done. They would eventually find a way to get her better.

Morace entered the study. When he had left it had been a mess. With the appearance of the girl all of the books had flown everywhere.

Lazon looked at him still feeling a little stupid over what had happened. 'How is the girl?'

'She is awake. It sure is strange though.' Morace embraced Shanrea and gave her a little kiss. Their hands locked together and he sat next to her.

Lazon and Shanrea waited for Morace to continue.

'Well?' Shanrea asked impatiently.

'Oh well, she has power. Nythe clearly cannot feel it, but it is strong.' He looked at Lazon. 'It is the same as yours but there is a difference to it. Only slightly.'

'She is like me?' Lazon asked.

'She is. I think she may be able to help us.'

Shanrea looked at him with eyes that spoke of understanding. Lorett needed power. More power than any one of them could give her.

'Do you think that with Lazon, she could help Lorett?'

'I do. I think that the sort of magic that she could heal her.'

'Well what are we waiting for?' Lazon asked. He got up and was nearly out of the door when Morace called him back.

'We are waiting because that girl is only a child. She has also gone through so much trauma; it would appear she needs a little time to recover.'

Lazon had become impatient in his time in the druid sanctuary. Lorett had been the one to give him hope, reassuring him that he was not the cause of the plight they faced. It also seemed that the control she had helped him gain to stop his craving of the use of his power had started to waver. The urge had returned a few months ago. At the moment he fought hard against the urge, but he was weakening. *Lorett, please wake up soon.* 'We need to hurry up!' Lazon slammed the door and ran down the corridor.

Morace looked at Shanrea, puzzled. 'He seems a little on edge,' he said.

'He is keeping his urges away from us. He has been fighting the urge to use his power. Lorett was the only one that seemed to be able to stop him from doing so. I will speak to him.' Shanrea left Morace's side, kissing him before she left him alone in the room.

As he was on his own, Morace took the time to study the ceiling the girl had fallen through. It was whole. There was no sign to say that anything had happened.

His own power had grown in the year. It had gotten stronger and he had learnt some useful tricks through reading the books housed in their sanctuary. There were some that he found truly scary. He did not want to have to use them.

'It's your sister, isn't it?'

Morace looked up startled at the sudden voice. Marrisai stood in the doorway.

'I can sense her. I recognise her in your features. I have seen her before in my dreams.'

'Your dreams?'

'Yes, there is always a woman in them. She has your looks.' Her cheeks burned slightly. 'I mean...'

'I know what you mean. My sister and I have often been told we look alike. We are twins.' She walked over to him and looked into his eyes. 'You have power. I can sense it.'

'So do you,' he said. 'Would you like to see my sister?'

'I would. I would like to understand my dreams some more.'

When he gestured her to follow him she did. He felt as though she spoke beyond the age she looked. With her in tow, he could feel her eyes burning into his back. She had a focus that he had never seen in someone so young.

'How old are you?' he asked without looking at her.

To Marrisai, he seemed so strong. Entranced at his presence she forgot that she had decided to make herself seem younger. 'I am twenty six.' Suddenly she realised what she had said. It was too late to take it back. *Damn fool, why did I have to say that? Now he knows more about me.*

'Hmm.' Morace turned around to look at her. He studied her and smiled.

'What are you looking at?'

'You are older than I am,' he said. He turned around and started to walk on. *I knew there was something more about you.*

'Are you not going to ask any more questions?' Marissai asked.

'There is no need for more questions at the moment. I can already tell you have power. I expect something happened to you, when you were about twelve, and you became immortal?' He realised she had stopped in her tracks.

'What do you mean immortal?'

'It's like Lazon. He has immense power surrounding him like you. I discovered that he was immortal a while back. He does not actually know.'

'How do you know this just from looking at me?'

'I do not know. But I think you and Lazon can help my sister.' At this point he pushed open a door. It led into a bedroom. Marrisai could see a large bed in the centre and in its covers was a girl. Instantly she recognised her as the girl from her dreams. Marrisai circled the bed.

'She is your twin?'

'She is.'

'This is the girl I see in my dreams.' She seemed so peaceful. 'For a year she has slept? Not having a care about what happens in the world?'

'This is true, but alas she is needed in this world. I believe you can help her. Will you?'

Marrisai looked at him. 'I fear at the moment I am not strong enough. I just came from a horrific place. A Crucible.'

'You came from the Crucible? The one over the Citadel?'

'I did, I was captured by a creature called Twak. I managed to escape.'

'That is the creature that did this to my sister. How did you escape?'

Marrisai retold her story, leaving no detail out. Morace listened intently. He took every word in.

Once she had finished, he asked her, 'Do you have any more of these orbs? I would like to study one.'

'I do have some more.' Marrisai was about to pull one out when she realised she had just completely opened up to this stranger. She pulled an empty hand out of her pocket. 'I am sorry, it would appear that was the last one.'

Morace knew that she was lying. *Looks like some of Lorett's skills passed on to me too.* He gave a sigh. There must be a reason for her lie. *At the moment she has no reason to trust us. We need to find a way to earn her trust.*

'Marrisai, are you hungry?'

'I am.'

'I will ask Shanrea to make something for you. I think she went with Lazon to see you. As you are here with me she might have started preparing for dinner. I shall show you to the kitchen.'

They found Shanrea in the kitchen cooking some sort of hot pot. Shanrea's attempt at cooking was always to throw a number of vegetables into a pot. Every now and then she might put in one of the old chickens that had stopped laying eggs for them. The food she cooked usually tasted great and was filling.

'Shanrea, our guest is hungry. Is the dinner nearly ready?'

'It is. I am surprised to see her up,' Shanrea responded. 'Nythe was also surprised when she at one moment turned her back and the next you were gone?'

'I am sorry. I needed to find the girl who was in my dreams, but she is asleep.'

Shanrea looked at Morace a little puzzled.

'I will explain later,' he said with a tone to say she should steer clear of the subject for now.

'Right everyone. Go wash your hands.'

Lazon then entered the room with Nythe. They held hands.

'Lazon, if you think you could let go of Nythe for just a second so that you can both wash, that would be great.'

Lazon scowled. He hated it when she said things like that. Nythe blushed and let go. At the sink Lazon mouthed to her, mimicking his sister.

Nythe giggled, lightly kissed him on the cheek, and turned to sit at the table.

They ate their meal in silence, then they all went to sleep.

The Wayward mirror shimmered as it let through the group of twenty five Dal-Mai-Sai. They were led by one man. His name was Eld-So-Moi. Clad in black leathers, he had trained with these men and women for nearly fifteen years. These were the people he trusted the most. Their mission was to find the traitors and bring them back. Alive. To be tried and then executed.

Eld-So-Moi looked at the men and women he had brought with him. He could name them all. His lieutenant, Saishi, stood next to him. She wore a mask over her face that had slits in to allow her to see. The hood she wore covered her head. With the darkness she blended in to her surroundings.

'Commander. We are ready to move.' She stood waiting for more orders.

'*Hai* Lieutenant, I must look at the maps of this world first to see where we must go.' She handed the maps to him and he began to read them. 'I can see by looking at the map and at our surroundings, that we are somewhere in the south. There are five of what appear to be cities on this map. We shall split off into squads of three and watch over these cities.' He looked at the Lieutenant.

She made five squads of three move out. They each took with them a copy of the map and started towards their chosen locations. The ten that remained waited for their orders. They stood silent and still, in formation. Eld-So-Moi commanded that five of the unit would stay at the mirror and the rest would accompany him and the Lieutenant on a journey to the north of this land.

Now that every one of them were dispatched and knew their orders, the seven of them set off on their own journey. They had been given special orders by the emperor. They needed to find any druid and bring them to their world so that they could answer for what they had done to their own world. The lieutenant was their tracker for this. She had senses that could track druid magic. These were faint at the moment, but upon entry she could feel them up in the north.

The druids had caused their world so much pain due to their quest for immortality. They needed some form of retribution. All of their plans had come to fail when the main commander went AWOL in the line of duty some years ago. Every now and then he would be sighted with a young girl. Saishi hated her father for what he had done. He was the only one who could have truly saved them, but instead he seemed to have gone insane and had gone following stars.

Eld-So-Moi could see the frown forming over her face. 'Do not worry, lieutenant. They will be apprehended. Whatever demon has possessed your father will be squashed.' Eld had been a father to her in her true father's absence. He had promoted her so that she could be in this fight to get the help her father needed. That was not to say that Saishi was not without her own skills.

He looked at her with eyes that could burn living flesh. *I will get that traitor, and see that he is beheaded. The only downside is that I have to do it with his snivelling daughter in tow because of her power.* He smiled when he saw her gaze fall on him, to give her some reassurance. He still needed her on his side. Once he had rid the worlds of the two traitors he would finish her off too.

Chapter 33

Marrisai could not sleep. She needed to find out why she was here. All she knew was there was a woman she saw in her dreams and this woman was here in this very building and she had to awaken her.

'Uhh, I can't sleep anyway. I will go sit with her.' She took a candle out of its holder and made her way to Lorett. All the doors looked the same and there were so many corridors. It felt impossible to find one room in so many.

After about an hour of intense searching, she found the room the woman slept in. She pulled up a chair and took her hand. *Who are you? Why were you in my dreams?*

'You are like Lazon.'

Marrisai looked up, shocked. Lorett lay perfectly still and undisturbed in her room. *Have I lost my mind?* She did not know but it scared her slightly. Foolishness set in at that point. Next she would be scared of her own shadow.

'Why are you scared?'

Again someone spoke to her. It must be Lorett. Somehow she was managing to communicate with her in this state.

'I do not know,' Marrisai responded. 'I suppose it is because we are the only ones here and you are somehow speaking to me.'

'Do not fear. There are some things I need to tell you.'

'I am here to listen.'

'I need Lazon too. Can you get him?'

'I do not know where to find him. I am not meant to be on my own around this place. I still do not know what it is.'

'Don't worry about that, Marrisai. Please go and get Lazon.'

Marrisai went to find Lazon. After an hour, she found his room. He slept alone which surprised her considering his closeness with Nythe. She thought they would have slept together. She sighed. With the way she looked, despite being old enough, no one would ever look at her like Morace looked at Shanrea or Lazon looked at Nythe. *Damn this body.*

'Why are you here?'

Nythe had managed to get behind her without a sound. *How did that happen?* Since coming to this place it seemed as though all her training had completely gone out of the window. She had become weak here, almost like there was some sort of power that worked against her.

'I could not sleep, I went and sat with Lorett for a bit and she started to talk to me,' she said. She did not think that Nythe would believe her. It did seem a little foolish. 'I am sorry, I am tired and was probably hearing things.'

'She spoke to you, too?' Nythe asked, taking hold of her hand. She looked into Marrisai's hand, as though searching for the truth behind her words. 'She spoke to me the other week,' Nythe said. 'She told me we would be visited. I would need to be here to help that person and Lazon with something.'

Marrisai looked at the girl as tears welled up in her eyes. This must be something she has waited for; a chance to bring her aunt out of her sleep.

'We must wake up Lazon. We need to head there now.' Nythe gently shook him. 'Lazon, wake up.'

Despite being woken gently, Lazon sat up a little shocked. He stared at the two girls. He could understand why Nythe was here, as she visited every now and then. *Why was the girl that had fallen on him in his room?*

Nythe explained everything to Lazon. They went to Lorett.

'Lorett, we are here like you asked,' Marrisai said, a little unsure now at what was going to happen.

'Great. Now Nythe, I need you to get the futons and place them by the side of the bed.'

Nythe took two futons from the corner of the room and placed them with care by the side of the bed. She stood up and waited for more orders.

'Now Lazon, you go and lie on the left one and Marrisai you on the right.'

They did this. Once they were settled, they waited. Before they had even had time to think, there was a stream of bright colour. Nythe was blinded by the light. Silence created a pressure that she had never felt before. She slumped into the chair.

The sound of the waves hit the ship. It rolled on the wave of the tide though it seemed to go nowhere. There was no direction for the ship to travel. It was lost.

'This is my mind at the moment.'

Marrisai looked for the source of the voice. It could not be found. However, she did find Lazon. Instinctively, she clasped his hand as she had never really liked boats.

'Why are we on a ship?' Marrisai asked.

'There is often a commotion on a ship. At the moment, this reflects my mind.'

Lazon suddenly understood. He realised the reason that Lorett was lost, because she had so much running through her mind. It was no wonder she needed to retreat somewhere. A lot had been thrust upon her in the space of a few months. A lot had been thrust upon them all. Lorett had been the one to lead them. He had remembered her saying that she lived a carefree life.

'Where are you?' Lazon asked.

'I need you to find me, along with Marrisai. Together you hold the power to find me.'

Lazon looked at Marrisai. Just as they began to move and search the decks for her, someone from above shouted at them. They froze on the spot.

'You two, where are you going? You need to man the rigging.' It must have been the captain of the ship. Marrisai looked up at the man who stood at the helm.

'It can't be, that's...' she started to say.

'I said man the rigging.' The Captain swung down on some rope from the helm. 'Do you two not know how to follow orders?'

'Father?' Lazon said.

'What? I think you have me mistaken.'

'Wait, this is my father.' Marrisai turned on Lazon.

'What do you mean?' Lazon asked.

'I mean this was the man who helped bring life to me,' Marrisai said.

'He is the one who abandoned me and my sister.'

'What does this mean?'

They were both struck across the face and sent flying across the deck to land in a slump against the railings. They started to get up.

The Captain withdrew his sword. It was broad and long. 'This is why I abandoned you both. I knew you would be a waste of my time.'

The words stung them both. *If Shanrea was here, what would she do?* Lazon flicked his finger toward the Captain who still advanced on them. A spark ignited at his feet which sent the Captain back the way he came. He landed on his arse. He was back on his feet though a second later, enraged. He moved faster. His face turned red.

'I should have killed you when I had the chance.'

Lazon seemed stuck on the spot. The Captain was all but a sword's length away from him but Lazon could not even move. *What was this? Fear?* He suddenly heard a clang of metal. He closed his eyes and waited for the inevitable end to his life. When it did not come, he opened his eyes. What a sight. The twelve-year-old girl stood in between him and the Captain with two swords. The larger of the two was held at the Captain's temple. The other was poised at his neck.

'One more move and I will spill out the contents of your throat over the deck.'

The Captain started to laugh.

Weeks had passed since Tavener had been given the child. Tavener could not believe it. He worried that as they entered the colder region the child would surely freeze. The Norse's temperature had plummeted even more. It seemed like the severe weather was effecting the north just as much as the south now. His thoughts wandered over to the inn he had left behind in order to help the twins.

The girl seemed hardy and did not cry at all. Tavener looked at her as she slept in peace covered in blankets under a tree. Despite it being only a few months since her birth, she had grown. She now resembled a child of about six or seven. If it had not have happened in front of his very eyes, Tavener would not have believed it. He had seen children grow up before. This was something amazing. Other than that, the girl showed no other hidden talents, but he expected some to appear. He had seen enough of what he would have dubbed strange occurrences in the past few years to know that anything was possible.

The girl wore him out; he felt too old for this. The mornings were the worst. It was well known that Tavener was almost bear-like when woken too early, but the girl did not seem to care. He had picked her up and sat her on a tree stump. At this point, she had looked like a three year old. She just looked at him as he yelled at her. She had not a care that this huge man had shouted at her. He had given up.

One morning she had asked out of the blue where they were headed. It had been the first time she had spoken and Tavener was dumbfounded. It had been a silent journey.

'We are heading to some place safe for you to grow up,' he responded.

'I go up on shoulders?' she asked. Reluctantly Tavener agreed, it would not cause any harm to let her travel on his shoulders. She was light.

The morning came and they started to walk again. A blizzard had set in and Tavener's beard grew icicles. 'It's no good, girl. We need to stop; otherwise, we will get turned about,' he said as she tried to continue onwards.

'But safety,' she said.

'Will mean nothing if we do not find shelter. That is our safety,' he retorted. Over the night she had grown again. She seemed to resemble a girl in her eighth year. When she stopped suddenly, Tavener waited for her to turn around to him. She did not move. He walked over and knelt next to her. Then she turned around to face him. She put her hands to his temples and a warm glow emitted from them. When she relaxed the hold she had, Tavener got back up. She pointed out into the blizzard, but it seemed to him to be nothing but a few snowflakes now. What did she do? It had been a blizzard. Was this some sort of power she had? Had she finally exhibited some power beyond his comprehension?

'How did you... What did you do?'

'Magic!' she said and continued to walk.

It had not really answered his question as he already knew that it must have been some form of magic. What he wanted to know was what sort of magic it was.

As they walked on, she now led the way. He realised some of the chill had disappeared from his bones. He felt less fatigued too. They stopped to rest at a frozen pool. The child walked over to the centre of the pool and put her finger on the hard ice. Tavener watched as from her finger came a red spark. A circle from the tip of her finger gradually got bigger and the ice in the circle melted. Before Tavener could do anything, the girl had dived in. He ran to where she had gone. Unable to find her, he waited.

The hour he waited seemed like an eternity. Since he had been charged with this girl's care and safety, this was the first time he had come close to losing her. In front of him the same red glow appeared, this time from underneath the water. Tavener stood up and watched the circle form. He saw the girl's face with a smile on it. She held fish.

Tavener looked at her in amazement. He had wondered how he was going to feed them with the lack of game present. She had just provided them with enough food to last them for at least a week.

Her head came out of the water and she looked at him. 'Help,' she said.

Tavener helped her out of the pool. When he touched her he was amazed that she was so warm. They ate some of the fish and drank some tea that Tavener had the sense to bring. They continued their trek for the rest of the day.

The following morning she let Tavener sleep. She had become what appeared to be a thirteen year old. She had started to form more woman-like features. She also became leaner.

'Come on, old man. We are nearly there,' she said which stunned him slightly. This was the first time she had spoken in a proper sentence and she had even had a little joke.

'Lead on.' He followed her. As her legs were longer now her pace had quickened. It was easier for her to walk in the fallen snow and not be bogged down by it.

She stopped all of a sudden. 'Please can I have your sword?' As she said this, she turned and looked at him. He handed it over to her without hesitation. She walked a few paces forward. 'Duck!' she shouted. Tavener did as he was told. Once he had ducked she turned and threw the sword in the direction they had just come.

The sword whipped past his head, missing it by mere inches. He heard it cut the air. A thud from behind told him that it had found its target. He heard a noise from behind, someone had groaned. What had it struck?

'Wait here,' he said.

She walked passed him and out of his sight.

When she came back she had a creature hauled over her shoulder. Its deformed features looked grotesque. Its face was mangled and Tavener's sword jutted out of its back. It had gone straight through its body. This child had sent the sword straight through it. Somehow it was still alive.

She sat in front of the creature and gave it a little smile. 'Shadow creature, you have met your doom here today. You have followed us and now you are about to die.'

Tavener watched. The words from the girl he had been charged to protect chilled him. She scared him a little. 'Girl, I think we should just kill it. I doubt we can get any information from it.'

She gave him a sharp look that told him to shut up and let her deal with this. 'I would like to see what you have seen.' She put her hand on its head. It became rigid and did not move at all. Her eyes turned milky white.

A second later she came back to herself. Her hand gripped the sword at the hilt and she took it out. Then with a swing, she took the creature's head off.

'We are close to our destination. We need to walk faster; there may be more of them.'

Another four days of travel brought them in front of a large building.

'We are here, the druids wait for us.'

From out of the building a light came and surrounded the young girl. She disappeared from sight. Tavener was bewildered and looked for any sign of her.

The Captain stood laughing. 'You do not know what I am.'

Lazon looked at the Captain who stood on his feet now. He brushed away the two swords that were pointed at his neck. He then sent Marrisai hurtling into Lazon with a slap that could be heard below decks.

'Now let me show you where you are.' His face started to turn a greyish green colour. His nose started to stretch and his teeth became pointed. His neck started to grow longer and snake like. His flesh turned to scales and wings sprouted from his back. The limbs gained more muscle and a tail whipped from behind.

He became the dragon that Lorett had been forced to face.

'I need to defeat this dragon before I can come back. But I am too weak.'

'How are we meant to defeat this?'

Without warning a ball of light appeared in front of the dragon. Marrisai looked at Lazon a little perplexed. It became bigger and blinded all of those on the deck. Once their eyes had adjusted they realized there was a girl on board. She looked about fifteen. She seemed strong and oddly powerful. Both Marrisai and Lazon could sense her power. It was like their own.

'Who are you?' Lazon asked, ignoring the dragon that levitated behind the girl he questioned.

'Not important,' she said. 'Marrisai lend me your hand. I require your power for a moment.'

Marrisai looked at her. Apprehensively she wondered how this girl knew her name. Somehow though she knew it was the right thing to do. She walked over to the girl and gave her hand. The girl took it. There was no pain just light.

The next thing that happened shocked both Lazon and Marrisai. The girl gained the two swords that Marrisai summoned. She had taken the power that Marrisai had trained for a number of years to gain.

Marrisai tried to summon her own swords. Luckily they appeared. She was still able to defend herself too.

'Ready?' the girl asked both Lazon and Marrisai.

'Yes,' they both said in unison.

The girl led the assault. With precision and great agility she slashed at the dragon's legs. The dragon howled in pain. It sent fire in the girl's direction and the blaze engulfed her.

Marrisai stopped dead in her tracks, shocked at what she witnessed. The girl was totally unaffected by the blaze.

'Lazon, make it rain,' she shouted.

Lazon fumbled. He had not used weather magic for a long time. He had been told not to. Now he was being asked to do it.

'I don't know if I can.'

'Lazon, you can. You must to save me.'

Lorett's voice hung in his head. Her words formed courage in his heart. Delicately his fingers began to dance in the pattern to bring forth a storm. The storm clouds formed over the ship. It thundered, and lightning lit up the beacon on the ship.

The dragon raged as the rain hit its wings. It was no longer airborne. It tried to ignite the air with fire but it just sizzled and produced only steam.

'Marrisai now, you take the right. I shall take the left,' the girl said.

In unison the girls ran to the spots they were to target. They drew their blades and slashed at the limbs of the dragon. Due to the rain, the dragon had become weaker. When they cut into it, the wounds were deep and penetrated far.

As the dragon tried to escape, it limped. It was not fast enough.

The girl ran up the tail, onto its back and then summoned a long two-handed sword. The sword arched. When it made contact it went straight through the dragon's neck. The dragon's head fell to the floor with a thud. Its body lay limp and dead.

Lazon looked at the dragon.

'I am free. Please stand in the circle and you may return.'

The white light engulfed them and they found themselves back in Lorett's room. Nythe had woken up too and went over to them. They gathered around the bed and waited for Lorett to wake up.

Her eyes opened. She could see her three saviours, along with Nythe, as they stood with anticipation. With a warm smile she sat up. Lazon and Nythe gave her a hug to welcome her back.

Then the Nameless Girl suddenly remembered something.

'Tavener!' she said.

'Tavener? Who is that?' Marrisai asked.

'Wait, Tavener is with you?' Lorett said. She took the girl by her shoulders. 'Where? Tell me.'

The girl took them to where she had left Tavener. They needed to creep up. Tavener was surrounded by six shadow creatures with another two that held him in place on his knees.

One of the creatures held up a sword then brought it down. As it struck Tavener's neck, Lorett let out a scream.

Lorett nearly bounded over, but she held herself back until the creatures had disappeared. Then she rushed to Tavener.

He was dead. Tears flowed out of her eyes. She had come back to the world but Tavener had left.

'Come into my sanctum Rhean.'

The shadow agent's dove form flew into the room that the shadow empress waited in. Slowly she had gained some power. Her body had started to form more. It gained more substance with every day that passed.

'I am here, Empress.'

'Good, tell me what you have found.'

Rhean told the Empress of her journey and what she had found out.

'Mmhmm… looks like I need to teach him a lesson. I need to be prepared. In a few more weeks I will be ready to return fully.'

Rhean stood up. 'What aid can I give you?'

'I will tell you when the time comes for the aid I will need. Right now I need you to travel to the Norse. Something there stirs.'

Chapter 34

Lorett and Morace shed tears over the grave they buried Tavener in. He had been like a father to them both. They felt as though they had now buried two fathers. When he agreed to travel with them they did not think for a second they would ever need to bury him. The Nameless Girl he had brought with him remained silent as she watched him be lowered into the ground. Once the soil had been put on top she retreated back into the repository.

Marrisai stayed her distance. She did not know the man who died. It would have felt like an intrusion in a moment that was sacred. For the Dal-Mai-Sai to stand next to the grave of someone you did not know while they were lowered was bad fortune. She looked at the elven boy who she had discovered she was sister to.

Lazon held Nythe's hand comfortingly. When he turned around and saw that Marrisai was watching, he gestured to her to come over.

She obliged, after the casket had been lowered into the grave.

Shanrea stood resolute. She was the strongest in all of this. It looked like she needed to be. Otherwise, there would be no one to make sure they moved on.

'He shall rest in the ground and become life once again for the plants and the animals who shall feed on them.' Morace ended the ceremony with their traditional last words.

Marrisai walked over to Morace, but was unsure at what she should do now. In her world when someone died they did things differently. They would have burned the body.

'I am sorry for your loss, Morace. I truly am.'

It seemed to Marrisai that this was the right thing to say at this time. He just stared at her. He did not say a word.

Shanrea came over to him and gave him a hug. 'It's all right,' she said to Marrisai. 'This is the second man he has had to bury. This man was like a father to him and Lorett.'

It struck Marrisai then that they must feel for Tavener what she would if Danai was to die.

'Let's head back to the druid stronghold,' Shanrea said.

The word clung to Marrisai. It felt like a knot had developed inside her stomach. *Druid?* She stood still for what seemed like an age.

'I am sorry. Did you just say druid?' she asked Shanrea.

In her tracks Shanrea stopped. She turned to look at Marrisai. 'Yes I did, both Morace and I are druids.'

Marrisai fell to her knees.

'Why?' She seemed now to speak to herself.

'I am sorry, what's wrong?'

'Why? Why do you, who seem so nice, have to be druids?' she looked at them, tears filling her eyes.

Suddenly the swords appeared in her hands. She ran towards the two druids ready to strike. Before she got there, however, she was stopped.

The Nameless Girl still had some of the power she had taken from her. She held a long sword and pointed it at Marrisai's throat. The next thing Marrisai knew, she was on the floor, her vision blurred and distorted. She had been struck down.

Marrisai awoke in a soft bed. She had restraints round her wrists to stop her from escaping. As her eyes gained their focus, she realised that she was in the room she had woken up in before. In the chair next to her bed sat Morace. His face was vacant. He showed no emotion.

His eye flicked to the corner of the room. Nythe came and checked on the wound where Marrisai had been hit. As she changed the dressing Marrisai could feel her head ache. Once the dressing had been changed, Morace got up.

'You said that you could not be at the side of my late friend's grave due to your traditions.' Morace looked out of the window. It appeared to be morning as the low sunlight gleamed through the window's frame. 'May I ask? Does your tradition involve attacking people just as they have buried their friend?'

'You're druids...'

'It is a simple yes or no answer. The time will come later to explain.' He sat back down in the chair. 'Now answer my question.' He was so calm it seemed unreal. Marrisai wondered how he did it.

'No, it does not.'

Morace nodded. 'All right, then I can assume that for some reason you have some personal vendetta against druids. Is this so?'

'Yes, I do them...'

'Again, you will get to explain yourself once I have finished my questions. Do not test my patience again. You do not realise how calm I am trying to be at this moment.' He had been told to keep his calm. He had wanted to blaze in with no hesitation. The approach he wanted to take with this was dashed aside with the alternative approach Lorett suggested he take.

Morace did not want to do this. It had not even been twenty-four hours since Lorett had awoken. He really needed to talk to her and now this had happened. This needed to be sorted out first.

'Now tell me, why did you try to attack Shanrea and me?' he asked.

Marrisai explained in detail what had happened to her world. She admitted the fact that she and her father held no trust for the druids any more.

Morace waited patiently for her to finish. He walked out of the room to speak with the others who waited on the other side of the door. They needed to discuss what was to happen to Marrisai.

Lorett looked at her brother. She could not believe what she had heard come from his mouth. *How has he become so hard while I was gone?* She walked away from the conversation that had become too heated for her to bear. Tears fell from her eyes. Without paying attention to where she was going, she bumped into Shanrea who had just rounded the corner.

'Oh Lorett, you're here. I have been looking for you. I just spoke with Morace.'

'Did he tell you?'

'Tell me what?' Shanrea asked.

'Tell you that he intends to keep Marrisai, the girl who saved me, captive and chained up?'

Shanrea looked into Lorett's eyes. She could see both of their points. One of them was going to get hurt in this. Now she had been put in the middle.

'I do know. I do agree with him a little. But not to keep her restrained like she is at the moment.'

'She helped to save me,' Lorett said in protest.

'She did. It seemed like she had come here for that purpose. But once she had found out that Morace and I were druids she tried to kill us.' Shanrea tried hard to keep this from going sour. The attempt was a failure. Lorett, as she could tell by her face, was about ready to do something she may regret. 'Lorett.'

Lorett shot her a look that said 'do not stop me'. She walked away. *I need to talk to Marrisai. She will see reason with me.*

When she got to the room, she entered quietly just in case the girl was asleep. When she saw she was not, she gave a warm smile to make sure the girl felt safe.

'Hi, I am Lorett. I think you have met me before in your dreams. Is this true?'

Marrisai nodded. 'I have. I did not know what it meant at first. Do you think when we were inside your mind, the man that claimed to be my father truly was? I do not see how I killed my father along with my mother. They were druid Dal-Mai-Sai. They tried to use me for destruction.'

'I do not know. This is not what I have come to talk about.' Lorett looked at the water jug on the side of the bed. 'Would you like some? I imagine Nythe my niece has been looking after you, but it must have been a while since you had some water.'

Marrisai nodded. Lorett poured some water into the glass and helped her sip it.

'I would like to talk about my brother and Shanrea. They are druids.' For a moment Lorett paused to see Marrisai's reaction. 'I understand what you have been through at the hands of the druids in your world but...' Lorett gave her a little more water and caught the drops that fell from her mouth with a flannel. 'But they are not those druids. They have been trying to find a way to save both the elven people and our own people.' Lorett continued to explain what had happened to them and how they had got to where they were.

Marrisai listened carefully. Once she was finished Lorett asked her a question.

'We need your help. Will you help?'

She did not answer. 'Can you take off these restraints?'

'Why? I need your answer first.'

'I think the reason why will also answer your question.'

Against all reason Lorett did as Marrisai had asked. Marrisai sat on the edge of the bed and looked into Lorett's eyes. They were beautiful, so bright and full of hope. It warmed her skin through to her bone. She had got what she wanted. She had seen the truth.

Marrisai wrapped her arms around the shoulders of Lorett and gave her a warm embrace. It was the most difficult moment in her life because of what she had been taught, but she would help them.

Then it struck her hard in the head. *Danai. What would he do?* He had so much hatred for the druids; he only saw them as monsters. Surly, regardless of any tale they told him, he would not believe.

'Lorett,' she said still in the hold of each other's arms. 'My father may be more difficult to speak to about this. He will be looking for me.'

Lorett looked at her and smiled. 'Don't worry. It will be fine.'

A week passed and Danai tried hard not to worry. Since the disappearance of Marrisai there had been three more raids. He had managed to keep the shadows at bay but now he started to tire. The toll of using the fear had become too much.

'I need to rest,' he said to Lento. 'I do not think I will be able go through the next assault without getting an injury.'

'It's okay. You have done enough. Go get some rest. I will look to moving the camp.'

The shadow from the Citadel had also gained mass. It was slowly spanned more south every day. *At this rate we are not going to survive the shadow let alone the destruction of the worlds.* There were reports that villages had been consumed now and that the population of the world dwindled to the point where the Kaartheans were close to becoming extinct.

Lento still needed to handle the fact that he had been named king. This was all because of his exploits on the battlefield.

He started to walk to his tent to sit and ponder over what needed to be done when a raven came and perched itself on his shoulder. It was a raven from his brother and sister. It gave him his foot to take the attached message.

Brother, we have a girl named

Marrisai with us, she says she has

met with you and that her father is

with you. You must not tell him that

she is with druids because he hates

them. She is safe.

L

'How did she get to them? They are so far away.'

With the news of Marrisai, Lento went straight to see Danai. He found him asleep in his tent. *Do not mention about the druids? He hates them?* He remembered a story he had been told by Danai, and what the druids had done to their world.

'Danai,' he said quietly. This would be the sort of news any father would not mind to hear even if they had just been asleep.

The man woke suddenly. He looked at Lento with weary eyes.

He would welcome this news. 'I have news of Marrisai.'

Danai started to get up and grab his things. 'What news do you have? Where can I find her?'

'It's all right. She is with my brother and sister. She is safe up in the north. The shadows have not reached that far.'

Danai sat down on the bed relieved that she was safe. Now he wanted to find her. Fast.

'How do I get to them?'

'You will not be able to go just yet. The place they are in is a stronghold. It is protected. Marrisai found it because she was required.' Lento knew that much from what he had been told by Morace about the sanctuary. The people who find it are those who are required to walk its halls.

'I will wait for more word. Now I need more rest.' But Danai had no intention of staying. Marrisai was north and that was where they were headed. He would sleep through the night and then before dawn he would ask the stars for help.

Lento left the tent to see to his own sleep. His mind focussed on the matter at hand. He would send a message to Lorett in the morning. It was that moment that he realised the last time he spoke to Morace he had told him that Lorett was still asleep. Did this mean that she was awake? It looked like it.

He sent a letter back with the raven.

'I have sent a raven to my brother. If your father is still with him he will get word of your safety.' Lorett sat with Marrisai in her room. They had become fast friends and talked about growing up. It made everything seem a little normal in the strangeness of everything that happened. It became apparent to Lorett that Marrisai had only seen death and had not had the normality of family. Except her father who loved her dearly, but still they had never settled.

'Thank you, Lorett,' Marrisai said. It felt a little strange for Marrisai. She could feel herself soften and becoming less hard. Despite it being so cold outside, the confines of the stronghold were warm and she felt comfort. The only thing that did sadden her was the fact that Morace did not seem to like her at all.

She was truly sorry for what had happened and had tried to repent for what she had done. Morace, much to Lorett's shock, was a changed person. He had become so consumed with worry over her and also the fate of the world. *Is this what happens, brother, when I leave you for a while?*

Lorett left Marrisai to herself for the remainder of the evening. She went to find Morace. She found him in the kitchen, eating his dinner in solitude. He had even snapped at Shanrea and now they were in an argument.

'What has happened in your head, brother?' Lorett asked as she entered the room. He looked at her a little dumbfounded.

'What do you mean? I am the same as before.'

'No you are not.' She sat next to him and took his hand.

'Yes I am.' He tried to reassure her. The last thing he wanted was an argument with his sister. Shanrea had started to sleep in a separate room as she did not want to be around him at the moment. She said that he had changed. He was not the man she had fallen in love with.

'You are not. You have taken on so much. Shanrea says you do not share. What is on your mind?'

'I do. But then I get scorned for what I have said. So I keep it in now.'

'You used to listen to reason.'

'Well perhaps I am now the person I am meant to be. Who knows? Maybe I will have to make a decision that only someone with the mind-set I have can make.'

Lorett looked at him. This was what she had been told about. There will be a decision that Morace would need to make. One that might, no, *would* change him. It could be wrong it could be right. They would not know until the effects were shown.

'I am sorry. I know I am different. I probably do not seem like the same person any more. Please leave me alone.' He looked so sad. Lorett gave him a hug for comfort. She whispered in his ear.

'You are not alone. You do not carry the weight of the worlds on your shoulders alone.' She walked away. She knew that something needed to be done about his mind. *I feel like I have woken up from one nightmare and wandered straight into another.*

'I know.'

He needed to see it in front of him. She had an idea but did not know whether it would work. She needed to try it. She had to let him know that he had others to rely on too.

Lorett, for the first time in over a year, sang. She let her words fill the stronghold, every corner of it.

All who dwell within these walls
Come forth and heed my calls.
We need your strength
We need your wisdom.
To find our way to the end.

Within the hour all of the people who had come to the stronghold had met in the room Lorett had sung from. Shanrea, Nythe, the Nameless Girl, Lazon and Marrisai had all appeared.

'I am sorry to have to use my power like this to bring you all here, but I fear for my brother. He has withdrawn. He believes that this battle and struggle is for him to bear alone.' She stood tall and resolute. 'We are all here for a reason. We will survive this. But we need to be together. We are stronger together.' Instinctively they had all lined up to hear Lorett's words. 'I need you to follow me.' Lorett turned back towards her brother. The others were all in tow. They found him where she had left him about an hour ago.

'Morace, why did you not come to my voice?'

Morace looked up. 'I am sorry. I did not hear you.' He looked at the faces of all the people who were with Lorett; all of the inhabitants of the stronghold.

'You see us, don't you, brother? Every one of us. We are here. We are here to stay. We will provide you with support.'

'And what about the girl who tried to kill both Shanrea and I?'

'Marrisai is with us too. There is a reason she is here.'

Morace smiled then started to laugh. He then came over to them and patted each and every one of them on the head. Then with a movement of his hand he sent them out of the door. It slammed behind him. Lorett looked at the closed door.

'That is not my brother. His eyes were wrong.'

'What do you mean?' Marrisai said.

'I mean he is not my brother.' She tried to figure out what was happening. 'It is late. I am sorry for bringing you all here.'

They all left her, save for the Nameless Girl.

'You have lost a lot of your friends and family,' she said. The girl's growth had seemed to steady as she now resembled someone of twenty and had done so for a week or so.

'It is true. I have.'

'I have no name at the moment. I have not found what it is.' She looked at Lorett. Lorett still had no idea who this girl was. All she knew at the moment was that she had come with Tavener.

'How did you meet Tavener?' Lorett asked.

'My father entrusted to him my protection,' the girl said. 'I was born under half a cycle ago.'

'Who is your father?'

'He is a king of the free people.'

'A king? Of what country?'

'Evertere. He is called Caser Roccan.

'I am sorry. I just thought you said Caser? Roccan?' Then she could see it; her brother's eyes in this girl's.

'This is true. Your older brother is my father.'

What did this mean? Just as things could not get any more complicated another niece was thrown into the mix. This one seemed to have power too. Lorett's head rang with thoughts that bounded through her head. She needed to sleep.

'I think I am going to head off to sleep.'

'Wait. To tell you my identity was not just what I wanted to talk to you about.'

'Really? What else did you want to say?'

'There was a monkey here once, was there not?'

Lorett did not know. She had been out like a light pretty much as soon as she stepped foot in the stronghold. 'I don't know.'

'I think it has something to do with why you feel Morace is different.' The girl turned and walked away leaving Lorett to mull over the words that had been said.

Chapter 35

Lorett's investigation started in earnest the next morning. She went to ask Shanrea first about the monkey. It seemed a peculiar thing for someone who had only just arrived to ask about.

'There was a monkey,' Shanrea said. 'But I have not seen it for a number of weeks. It was quite attached to me. It disliked Morace though. I also think the feeling was mutual between them.'

'I think there is something weird about this monkey. Where did it come from?'

'When we first got here we were greeted by a wraith. He helped us find the repository of knowledge,' Shanrea explained.

Lorett took what she had learnt from Shanrea to think up what this could possibly mean. A wraith? What if the monkey was a manifestation of the wraith too? A part of it. Yes the wraith of the marsh was okay but that may not mean the same for this wraith.

'Shanrea, I think something has happened to Morace. I think the Wraith has taken him.'

'Really?'

'Yes. You have studied the books; do you know where to look about different creatures?'

The two women went to the study. They found the volumes that they thought would give them the information they needed quickly.

'I think I have found it!' Lorett said and passed the book to Shanrea.

Demon Wraith.

This is a being that has the power to take control of its host. It usually uses a familiar. It will trick the host into letting the familiar into the place the host would usually reside. It would then slowly learn all of the places the host would go. Its routines and habits. This is so that it can replicate for the people who know the host as cleanly as possible to avoid detection. The longest someone has survived with a host is five weeks. The way someone can find out if the suspected host is in fact a host is by the e....

The rest of the passage had crumbled to dust.

'How are we meant to find out?' Shanrea asked.

'The girl. She could tell there was once a monkey here. Perhaps she can see things that are no longer here by looking into the past?' Lorett suggested. It sounded farfetched but if her life had taught her anything, it was to expect the unexpected.

'Let's go find her.'

They found the Nameless girl. She was training with Marrisai. It was apparent that they may need to fight in the future so it would not hurt to practice. Thanks to Marrisai's ability to summon weapons they could train with a different selection. At the moment it was with two katana. The girl was as skilled as Marrisai at swordsmanship. It soon became apparent to Marrisai that despite her being older than the Nameless Girl she had learnt from her just as much.

When they two girls saw the others enter, they stopped. They took some water and came over to where the druid and the siren waited.

Morace held his head. It ached every day but he did not know why. *Damn, I must get this sorted out.* He looked at the papers he buried himself deep in to study. Everything started to blur. The need to stop for the night started to creep in. Rapidly he lost interest in the subject. This meant that he took nothing in.

'I guess I will go to sleep.'

'No, I think you should keep going.' The voice tempted him. The voice in his head had appeared a little over two weeks ago. Whenever Morace's reasoned mind came into play he realised that the arrival of the voice coincided with all of his problems.

'You are right,' Morace obediently said in response to the suggestion. Blood trickled down from his nose. 'I am bleeding again.'

'It is fine; it is a price you must pay for all your hard work.' *Now that you are tired I can finally take over.* It had always tried to get into the druid repository of Knowledge. The monkey trick worked. It loved that trick. Normally it would not work on druids but these ones were young. The female druid was so easy to trick. 'Now Morace, are you going to let me see more of your mind today?'

The demon needed Morace to be tired and less resilient. It would then be easier for the demon to do what it wanted.

'Yes you can.' More blood started to leak from his nose and some from his mouth.

The demon walked through his mind as though it was an open book. Morace had completely stopped in his research now. His eyes were wide open and milky.

'Can you tell if a demon has possessed Morace?' Lorett asked the Nameless girl.

'I can,' she said. Without hesitation, Lorett grabbed her hand and pulled her out of the room. They wound down the stairs and into the hallway.

'I think he has been possessed by a demon wraith,' Lorett explained to the girl.

'Please find out. Would you know how to get rid of it?'

'I can also do that.' They walked into the room where Morace had been left. The sight they saw made Lorett scream. The girl just looked at Morace. She closed her eyes to sense if there was indeed a demon.

'There is a demon.' Without hesitation she walked over to Morace whose face was now covered in his blood. With a clap of her hand a spark ignited. She touched a finger to his forehead and he fell limp. Seemingly lifeless, he lay on the table. 'He will need to sleep for a while. The demon uses tiredness to take over its host.'

So Morace was tired? Lorett looked at her brother lying on the table. *Why did this need to happen to us, brother?* She knew that asking that question was pointless. 'Please stay with him,' Lorett asked the girl.

The girl waited with Morace to make sure he was okay. She started to speak to him while he was slept.

'So you are my uncle?' she said. 'I could tell there was something wrong with you when I first met you but I did not say anything.' She took a drink of water from a decanter. 'I was a little upset, you see. I am not allowed to be upset, but I don't think even a stone could be that emotionless.' The girl started to pace the room while she waited for the others to return. 'The truth is I loved Tavener. I was with him longer than my real father so I suppose I loved him like a father. A little like you probably did.' She sat next to him and took his cold hand.

'I am sorry to see him go. I am sorry I need to seem so cold. I am just not allowed.'

The door clicked as it opened to let Lazon and Nythe in. Marrisai was in bed asleep as it had gotten late. The girl whispered to Morace as she got up and left the room. To the others it looked like a little kiss.

'Let's get him up to his bed. Lazon, can you help?' Nythe said. Lazon lifted Morace's body onto his shoulders. He had grown quite strong as he had also trained. It was Nythe that taught them all how to sword fight since she had been trained by her father. Now that Marrisai and the girl were here, they could spread the load to train the others. They seemed to hold skills that none of the existing inhabitants of the stronghold could fathom.

They laid Morace in his bed. He was so silent. So still. He looked peaceful. Lorett said goodnight to him and Shanrea, giving her a hug.

'I should have known there was something wrong,' said Shanrea. 'Why was I so blind to this?'

'Love does strange things to our minds,' Lorett whispered in Shanrea's ear.

Lorett closed the door and walked down the corridor. She bumped into Marrisai. 'Oh, I am sorry,' Lorett began to say. But Marrisai stopped her and told her to be quiet with hand gestures. They crept back down to the room where Morace had himself held up.

'The demon has not been defeated. I can still hear it,' Marrisai whispered. The girl summoned a sword with a slight glow to it. She handed it to Lorett and she summoned her own.

Thank goodness Lento thought to train me.

Lorett went the opposite way around the table to Marrisai holding her sword ready to strike. A noise came from behind the table. Lorett had rounded the table faster than Marrisai.

Marrisai already knew what was behind the table. She also knew that Lorett would be hesitant. She let her go first to distract the creature that now tried to hide.

Marrisai looked at Lorett. She watched Lorett's expression change as she saw the creature; it looked like her heart had melted.

The creature bared its teeth and started to advance on Lorett.

My plan is working. The creature is focussing on Lorett.

Lorett watched the little creature which looked like a deformed monkey. She remembered seeing the monkey before. Lorett lowered her sword. The monkey charged but it was struck down by the blow from Marrisai's sword. It fell to the floor in pain.

'How can such a small creature cause so much pain?'

The monkey began to dissipate into the air. After a minute it ceased to exist.

'Did you have to kill it? Perhaps we could have got some information from it.'

'No we could not. It was a demon from my world. They have killed thousands of our people. They were once druids consumed by hate and despair.' Marrisai looked at her with tears in her eyes. 'If they have come over into this world, what other things have come over here too?'

Lorett looked shocked. 'What sort of creatures do you have in your world?'

'Thousands, the druids created most of them. They called them chimeras. Beasts moulded together from other beasts. Horrible creatures. Pitiful creatures.' Marrisai took Lorett's hand in hers. 'It is the reason why Danai hates them so much. He lives to kill every last Druid to stop their blight. They took his wife and turned her into one.'

Lorett needed to sit down. *How could one race cause so much pain and suffering?* She was worried now for Morace and Shanrea. If Marrisai's power was anything to go by, what did this Danai hold?

'We need to find out how to prevent a war between your father and the druids of this world. There are only two of them and they are needed.'

'The father will not kill the druids.'

Startled, both of them turned to see who the voice had come from. It was the Nameless Girl.

'What do you mean?'

'The father will not kill the druids.' The girl came over to them both. She was dressed in night clothes. 'All the fathers will die in the rebirth.' The girl's eyes had turned white. It was like she spoke a prophecy. She fell to the floor. Lorett ran over to make sure she was unharmed.

'Help me get her onto the table.' Despite her size Marrisai was still quite strong.

'What do you think she meant by rebirth and all the fathers will die?' Marrisai asked.

The thought ran across Lorett's mind like a galloping horse. "All the fathers will die." She knew what the girl had meant. She realised it now. Her Pa had died, so had Marrisai's, and Tavener, who was like a father to both her, Morace and the girl. *How many other fathers were there? Or father like people in this?* Marrisai's adopted father? Caser, the father of the girl? Lento?

Lorett felt the weight of all this press down on her. There were people who had died and people who were going to die. Some of the people who were going to die, if the prophecy was true, had their children with them now. She was torn now with this knowledge. *Should I tell them? Or keep this quiet?*

Morace woke up. His head throbbed. He felt his face. The last thing he remembered was blood from his eyes. *Why does my head hurt?* Then he remembered the voice that had plagued him for the last few weeks. Every time he woke it was there. Now it seemed to be gone. At first Morace did not miss it, but the voice had been there when he felt down. It had given him a drive to move forward. What's more, it had told him of ways to increase his power. Some of the things he was told to do he had attempted. Others he did not because the idea of some of them scared him.

'Are you awake?' It was Shanrea. He remembered how he had treated her when the voice was around. It had scorned him for his relationship with her. It had told him that he did not need a woman by his side.

Her arm was draped over him for comfort. He turned around to see her face. It was stricken with worry. She leant in to kiss him on the mouth. The worry in her seemed to disappear as he reciprocated.

'I am sorry,' he said.

'It is all right, you were not yourself,' she said. She explained what it was that had taken over him.

Morace looked at her. It seemed more. Perhaps it only a dream but he was unsure. Shanrea moved to lie on top of him for a moment. Their naked bodies touched.

'Hold me for a while, like you used to.' She looked into his eyes. They had gained the life he once had. They had seemed dead lately. She kissed him hard on the mouth. Shanrea threaded her fingers through his hair as they made love.

Later, they got dressed and headed for the kitchen to meet with the others for breakfast. Lorett ran to give her brother a hug. He seemed to have returned to his former self quite quickly.

Once they had all eaten, Lorett stood up on the table. Morace looked at her and remembered the time when she was fourteen and very drunk. This time she had a look of determination set in her eyes. She scanned the room of people, all together. All of them had special talents. All of them were here for a purpose.

'I would like to make a statement.' Lorett sounded so powerful. Morace knew she had changed so much. 'We are all here for a purpose. At the start of the journey that purpose was unclear. Now it is coming clearer to me. One thing is for certain, the worlds cannot sustain each other. There needs to be a union. A collision of the worlds. I understand now that there is a third world involved and their world is also on the brink of death. Once the worlds have collided we will need to make something of the new world and bring the races together. Kaarthean, elven, dwarven, Dal-Moi-Sai and druid.' She stopped for a moment just to let what she had said sink into to everyone's mind. She also needed to drink some water.

Morace stepped up to the table.

'I know we have a lot of work,' he added. 'We still need to find out how to save the races. Somehow we will need to also convince some of them to join us.'

'How would we get the Dal-Mai-Sai to join us? Do they not hold a hatred for druids?' They looked at the only Dal-Mai-Sai in the room.

'I do not know. There are tensions everywhere with different races. It will be difficult,' Marrisai said. 'I think we should first find out how we are going to save the worlds.'

They all agreed to that and went off to find out what could be done.

Chapter 36

Danai left the confines of the camp early in the morning. He knew where he needed to go. He could sense it. The stars told him to head north to a place called the Norse. He had borrowed a horse without permission so that he could travel quickly. Lento had told him his daughter is safely with his brother and sister. Danai knew there was something Lento had not told him; something that he wanted to find out.

He was well into his second week of the ride when he realised he was being followed. They stayed well back and there was of three of them. He had no idea how long they had been following him for but it made him worry a little. If they could have remained undetected for so long they must have been skilled. The only thing that could be that strongly skilled was the Dal-Mai-Sai Advance team.

They were assassins trained in illusion magic. *Damn, they have found me.* He started to ride the horse harder. He only stopped to give the horse a little respite when it started to pant. It was about ready to fall.

Why haven't they attacked? If his judgment was correct and if they had been following him for as long as they had, he should be dead. He was not though. This meant that their orders were to keep him alive. It meant that he was to be made an example of.

Twelve years ago, when the stars had started to talk to him, he had been the leader of the advance group that now followed him. It felt like a long time ago but they despised him; they branded him a traitor. They pursued him throughout their world but Danai was too clever. He had taught every one of his attackers everything they knew. For a long time he had been their sensei. Every time an attack came, he remembered the face from his days in the training hall. It was because of this he spared the lives of the five that had come close enough to touch him. He had left them for the others to find.

The horse had started to pant and get out of breath a lot faster now. The brief respites for the beast did not replenish its stamina any more. He would need to stop and make tracks some way else. *I am going to have to end this pursuit first.* He knew the pursuit needed to end as he did not want the group to find Marrisai. Through association, Marrisai would also be apprehended and used to weaken him. Marrisai was his only true weakness.

Danai knew he would die for her. Despite his long life, he did not feel ready to die. But he would die today if it meant her continued safety.

It became no good. The horse started to stumble, throwing him off a couple of times. Danai drew his sword and slew the horse. 'You did well, my friend. You got me far. I am sorry it ended like this for you.' He took the time to bury the horse. The stars once told him to respect the things and creatures that aided him in his journey. Once he buried the horse, he began to walk in the direction the stars told him.

In his head he set a plan to catch the group off guard. The only problem with this was he did not know if they could tell he knew of their presence or not. He set about to demonstrate that he did not have a clue. Every now and then he would do things that showed he was not on guard.

The attack came one night after he had slain the horse.

He had pretended to sleep that night. One of them crept up to make sure he was asleep. The man or woman did not do anything. When they became aware he was not asleep it was too late. They had him surrounded.

'Oh, there you are. It only took you three days to actually try something with me.' Danai started to weave the fear through their bones. He wore a hat over his face like he always did to sleep. 'So who have they sent this time? I could tell they sent more than one.'

They all remained silent. There were actually four of them. They were frozen on the spot with their fear of him. Danai kicked up as though he was a youth. Slowly he walked around, inspecting the faces of the ones who tried to attack. This time he did not recognise them. *So they have sent people who do not know me this time.*

'Ha, fresh meat! I do not recognise your faces. This bodes bad news. For you.' A smile crept over his face. His face was shaded by his circular hat. He could feel the fear grow within them. He felt it, like a drug that filled his body too. It nourished him. This was the side effect of using fear to capture enemies. If you used it for a long period of time you started to become more corrupt with its power. You craved more. This was one of the reasons the druids became the way they did and they overused their power. 'Now how would you like to die?'

Danai did not give them a chance to respond to his question. He drew a small dagger and cut each of their throats. The pressure of fear dropped and Danai looked at the four bodies that lay on the floor.

You will need to do much better than that.

Marrisai woke up suddenly with a pain throbbing through her head. *He is using it too much.* She knew that Danai had just used fear to take over the will of his enemies. This was a sense she knew all too well. It was a great weapon but she knew its consequences and something was different this time. He had enjoyed it. The Danai she knew never liked using the power he had learnt. She shivered. *I was the one who helped him not get taken over by it.*

For a few days now Marrisai had felt the presence of Danai come closer. It brought her comfort that he was on the move, and that he was on his way. It meant that he was looking for her. This last surge of power also meant that he had met with a number of attackers. Every day she felt the pressure from his power, and she grew more concerned.

It was the early hours of the morning, and Marrisai could not sleep any further. She got up, got dressed and decided to train. It was well past ten o'clock before anyone found her. She still trained to take away her worry of her father.

'I think that practice dummy needs some rest, don't you?' It was Morace.

Marrisai looked at his face. She had been crying but she had not realised. He smiled at her and her knees weakened. To her he was quite handsome and strongly built. She smiled back at him.

Shanrea appeared next to Morace. Marrisai's smile dropped a little. *Morace would never like me. Not when I am like this.*

'I am hungry. I am going to get some breakfast,' Marrisai announced. She rushed past them.

'Something is up with her,' Shanrea said.

'You think? She just smiled at me.' Morace picked up the sword that Marrisai had used. It disappeared in his hand before he could swing it.

'Could you not tell she had been crying?' Shanrea said. She looked at him her eyes focussed on his.

'I couldn't, no.' He felt as though he should have.

'I can't imagine how she must feel. I know that if I was her age and trapped in a child's body it would be hard for me. Not to mention that her father hates druids yet she has become fond of us.' She picked up a training sword and started to swing it at another less battered dummy. 'She must be going through a lot right now. Just think, she might want love, like we have, but is conscious that she looks like a child.'

Morace looked at her. His eyes widened with realisation. 'Do you think she had eyes for me?'

'I do. Be careful. She is falling in love with you.'

Marrisai stood by the door, listening to the conversation. Perhaps she did like Morace, but he was with Shanrea. Besides, no man would have eyes for her despite her age. It was her appearance. *I really want to rid myself of this curse.* She resolved to find a way to get her body back.

Danai's head rang as his surge of power calmed down. It felt too strong. He knew that he needed to reach Marrisai soon. He needed to make sure that the madness that could claim him with the power of fear did not take over. Marrisai helped with that. She was the one who could stop him if needed.

The power to use fear as a fighting tool was developed by the druids. It was a cooperative effort. If you started to use it on your own it would damage your mind. You needed two people, so that the other could snap you out of it. The druids started to use it on their own and that was when things turned bad. Many people died from its incorrect use. The druids became oppressors.

Once he came back to his senses, Danai started to make faster progress. He had taken care of the enemy and now needed to get to Marrisai.

Danai looked on from the cliff he stood on. In front of him was the Norse. As far as he could see there was snow and huge trees. He could tell that this was going to be the difficult part of the trial. The provisions he had brought with him had slowly diminished. Although he could summon weapons at will, nourishment was a different matter.

The Dal-Mai-Sai had tried to find a way to create nourishment but it seemed it was impossible. Despite the fact that

Danai was unique in that he had lived for over one hundred and fifty years, he was not immune to hunger. He hoped that he could at least do some form of hunting here.

Once Danai had found a way down the cliff, the test started. The drop in temperature amazed him. It plummeted to freezing. His long coat kept him warm. On the first night he found a little wood and created a fire to keep warm. He had not thought it possible, but during the night the temperature dropped even more.

The sky was cloudless and he could see the stars. They spoke to him. They told him he was heading in the right direction and that in three days he would reach the destination. Warmth flowed through his bones. The stars protected him.

On the second day the stars led Danai to a herd of creatures that grazed on the taiga plain. They were quite large and cumbersome. They had long noses and three layers of different sized tusks. They were twice the size of him.

He wondered if these creatures were eatable. He needed food though, so he decided to risk trying. He summoned a bow. One designed to fell a beast of that size. He crept upon the herd and singled out a smaller one of the creatures. It must have been a young one, for its tusks were still quite small. Slowly he knocked an arrow to the bow and shot it into the creature's eye. An instant later he drew again and struck it in the other eye before the creature knew what had struck it the first time.

It fell to the floor. The other beasts ran in a flurry; they did not know what had hit them. It would appear that they were not used to being attacked, as they were very slow to react.

Once the other creatures dispersed, Danai dismissed the bow and brought out his sword. He had hunted enough times to know that when a beast like this was felled, scavengers would come. The sword was for protection. Danai

started to take a little bit of the meat from the dead creature. He made a fire and began to cook the meat he carved.

The flesh was tasty and filled him up well. It would be a
shame to leave this here. *Such a waste, but other beasts will
feed on it.*

Danai chose to walk during the night this time, as he felt
like he did not need to sleep. He had slept well the previous night. About halfway through the night he reached a
part where the trees became denser, it was very dark. He
made sure he had both his long and short sword out with
him.

The forest was tricky. The spruce had grown in a mass of
strange patterns. It was almost like the forest itself was a
maze. Danai walked for hours as he tried to find his way.
It was too dark though and he needed to stop. He decided
that it might be better to wait until there was some form
of light from the sun.

Danai dozed off. He was woken suddenly by a noise.
Damn, I should not have fallen asleep.

'There you are, traitor.'

Danai recognised the voice. It was his worst nightmare.
It was Saishi, a girl who claimed to be his daughter. Danai
had no recollection of this girl from his past. She stood in
front of him with a sword tucked under his chin.

'Are you not going to say hello to your daughter?'

'I have told you, you are not my daughter. I...' Danai had
repeated the same statement five or six times before.

'I told you to wait,' someone else said. Danai knew who
this was too. It was Eld-So-Moi . He just added fuel to the
fire.

'I see they have sent the two of you to apprehend me.
They must be desperate.'

The Dal-Mai-Sai commander picked Danai up by the
scruff of his neck. He locked eyes with him. Danai did not

have time for this, he needed to get out of the situation and fast. Marrisai needed him.

Danai started to add pressure by using a blanket of fear. It did not seem to work.

Like before, Marrisai felt the fear again. It was so much closer this time. *This means that he is close.* Marrisai ran to the room she knew Morace occupied with Shanrea. She burst in. 'He is close. I can feel him. He is in danger. We must go. Now!' Marrisai said everything so fast that Morace, who had woken up first had trouble figuring out what she had said.

'Hold on. Marrisai, slow down. I have just woken up.'

Shanrea was now awake. She tried to calm Marrisai down.

Marrisai's small fists were clenched by her side. If she tensed any more she would be a statue. She took back her breath and started to explain what she had felt.

About five minutes later the whole of the stronghold was ready. They had put protection on to find Marrisai's father.

'Lorett, you have a song for this, right?'

'I do.' Lorett started to sing a little to search for Danai. She found him. He was about an hour's walk south of where they were. They set out to find him.

When they found him, Marrisai's heart stopped. He had been beaten pretty badly. He had a limp.

'Danai!' Marrisai shouted. She ran to him. They exchanged an embrace and Marrisai started to tend to his wounds so that he could keep walking. Danai did not speak for a moment. He needed to make sure that Marrisai was okay. He checked her over.

Danai looked at the others who were with her. He judged them and took in their faces. 'We need to get out of here. Fast.'

'You did not kill the people you fought against?' Marrisai asked.

'No I did not. I knew who they were. I spared them.' He explained as he grabbed Marrisai by the hand. He started to walk to the others. 'Where do we need to go?'

Morace took the lead and after about an hour they reached the stronghold. The morning sun passed light over the structure and for the first time any of them had been there they could see what it looked like properly.

Danai dropped Marrisai's hand. 'I know this building,' he said. 'It is exactly the same. How did it get here?'

'What do you mean?' Morace asked.

'I mean there is one of these in the world where Marrisai and I come from.'

Rhean used the cloak of shadows to watch the group enter the druid stronghold. She needed to be able to gain entry somehow, but she imagined that she would only be able to do so with the acceptance of the druids. The man they just accepted would not have found the place if they not lowered the protections the druids had made. She needed a plan and quick. She had been hiding, looking to see if at any time one of the people who lived there came out.

Only two had left briefly in the week she had been stood with watchful eyes; the siren and another female, who appeared to have no power. The girl who had no power would be the most likely to be able to trick, but she did have considerable skills with throwing knives. It seemed as though she came out to practice her throwing on the trees as they provided more varied targets. She had watched her come out at exactly the same time every day. When the girl came to practice today she would set into motion the trap to trick her.

Once all of them were inside they went to the kitchen. Danai was still not hungry after what he had eaten the day before. They all wanted to discuss the meaning of what Danai had said.

'I have seen this place. It is strange though, it was created by druids. Well it was created by one druid. The one who once taught me what I know. He left for this world. He was known as the wraith druid.' Danai started to have a drink. Then he saw that both Shanrea and Morace's faces showed they knew something. 'Have you heard of this druid?'

'I think we met him. It was well over a year ago. He introduced himself as the Wraith of the Marshes,' Morace explained. 'He is the one that told me and Shanrea about our powers.'

Danai's ears pricked up at this. 'Your powers? You were trained by a druid?'

Marrisai watched with horror as the scene unfolded. Before anything else could happen Lazon created a shield that surrounded Danai. Marrisai had started to sense Danai using the fear but once the shield was up it was contained. Everyone looked at Lazon.

'That was really quick thinking, Lazon,' Morace said with appreciation.

'This is bad,' Marrisai said. 'Extend the shield to encase me too. I will talk to him.'

Lazon looked at everyone. There was no choice, it had to be done. Someone who knew Danai needed to explain everything to him. Morace gave the nod for the shield to be extended.

'I can only hold it this large for an hour,' Lazon warned.

'That power might come in useful, Lazon. How big can you make the shield?' Morace asked.

'I don't know. It is the shield I created to contain the weather magic.'

Morace looked into Lazon's eyes. 'I may have need of that power.'

Chapter 37

The girl, that Rhean waited for appeared later than usual. Rhean almost gave up, but decided to wait it out. She had a plan formulated in her head. She would use a little of her power to summon a couple of the shadow creatures to chase her. Then she would run into the path of the girl as she threw her knives.

As an agent of the shadows she would not be felled by the knife, but would be a little wounded. She would heal fast. Due to her guilt, the girl would then accept her into the stronghold. It was a great plan. One that was sure not to fail.

Rhean created two shadow creatures and told them what to do. They looked at her with puzzled eyes for a moment before they realised what she wanted. She started to run and like her plan dictated she ran straight into the path of one of the knives.

Nythe caught sight of the girl running in the path of the knife just as it came out of her hand. With fast reflexes she took another knife out of her belt and flung it at the knife she had just released. It struck the other knife and caused it to change direction slightly. It struck the girl but not as deeply as it would have done if she had not acted so fast.

The two shadow creatures then came into view and Nythe readied the knives to be sent in their direction. She hit the first one cleanly in its throat. It howled in pain as it fell to the floor. The second caught sight of the girl who felled its comrade and started a frenzied attack. This time Nythe had no more knives to throw. She had used most of them in practice. She picked up a stick and started to attack the creature as it advanced on her.

The creature was strong. If Nythe had not been trained by her father, who was probably just as strong as the creature, she would not have stood a chance. The stick broke and Nythe was left to fight using hand to hand combat.

Nythe started to tire. The creature seemed to have a higher endurance than herself.

Rhean looked at the fight. *Damn, the shadow is too strong.* From the floor where she lay, Rhean made the creature weaker. She turned the tide of the battle enough so that it looked like Nythe started to get the advantage on her own.

Once the Shadow creature was defeated, Nythe ran to the girl she had struck with her knife. 'I am so sorry!' she apologised and started to apply pressure to the wound she had created.

'It is fine. I am okay,' Rhean said. She tried to get up but Nythe made her stay down.

'No you are not. Please come inside. I will get you healed up.'

'Seriously, I am fine. I can be on my way.' Rhean wanted to make sure that she did not seem too eager to be inside. If she made a little fuss she could pull the wool over their eyes.

'I insist. I want to get you checked out and also you must be hungry. Don't worry you will be safe.'

Once they were safely inside, Nythe took Rhean into the room where she treated anyone who was injured. When Nythe was happy the wound was safe she asked for her name.

'Rhean,' the girl said. 'What is your name?'

'Seriously you have been watching me all this time and you have not learnt my name?' Nythe asked.

Rhean looked at her. *Did she really know I was watching all that time? Was I really that plain?* It had not been what she wanted.

'So why were you watching me train? I bet you were worried when I was late today?'

'I watched because I thought you were amazing,' Rhean lied, to make it seem as though she had been enchanted by the girl. 'But I was too scared to speak to you.' She needed to gain another foot hold.

'You really thought I was amazing?'

Rhean nodded. 'I did. I was not expecting to get attacked.' She looked at Nythe with sheer will. She hoped the lie had convinced her enough. 'Sorry for the interruption.'

'It is fine. It was good I got some practice on the shadow creatures anyway. The trees were getting a little boring,' Nythe said. 'Right, I am going to speak to the others about you. Please wait here.'

Nythe left the room. *Damn how am I going to explain this? I was not allowed to go out.*

She found everyone in the room where Marrisai conversed with her father. It had been hours since she had asked for the shield to be extended to let her in. *Poor Lazon, he must be tired.* He saw his face was now riddled with sweat. His eyes were getting heavy too. Nythe was worried for him. She went to speak with Morace.

'Uncle, I need to speak with you.'

'Is it about the girl you encountered in the forest?'

Nythe looked at Morace. He seemed so calm and collected. He sat in an armchair and waited for her response to his question.

'It is,' she said.

Morace got up out of the chair calmly and quietly. As he walked by her he patted her on the head. 'Follow me,' he said.

They both walked to the room where she had left the girl. While they walked he asked her to explain what had happened. As she did Morace said not a word to her. Once at the door he knocked and then entered.

He saw Rhean who sat on the bed. She had waited for Nythe to return.

'I hear you have had a run in with Nythe's blade? Let me see.'

Rhean took the dressing off that Nythe had put on. There was no wound, not even a graze where the knife had struck. Nythe looked a little shocked.

'It would appear that you are somewhat gifted. Or you are a shadow creature?' Morace stepped to the side of Nythe. He did not want to be too close to Rhean, just in case she did something unexpected. Rhean sat there. A tear began to form in her eye.

'I am sorry. I am an agent of the shadows, but not for the traitor Twak. I am on the empress's mission.' She looked at Morace. She had hard, cold eyes. Over this past year Morace had managed to harden his resolve. He had needed to. The tears of a little girl we're not going to stop him.

'So why is a minion of the Shadow Empress sent to us?'

'We need your help.'

'Help?'

'Yes, Twak, I have discovered, is quite insane,' Rhean explained.

'The last I heard the empress was locked away for her insanity that threatened the worlds.'

'Do not say that about the empress. She was once a druid like you, but something happened to her. She became poisoned.' Rhean had stood up. She shook with anger.

'I am sorry. So you say that the empress is willing to accept our help?'

'I am. The Shadow Empress had no knowledge of what Twak was doing. He had become maddened.'

Morace looked at Nythe. Was she taken in by this agent? He could not tell, but he would need to speak to her. She had gone out of the confines of the stronghold and potentially brought about in another agent of the shadows.

'How are we expected to help? If the empress cannot keep a leash on her subjects, perhaps she is too weak to do anything?'

'You have a siren. Twak despises them, he will do anything to rid the world of them. He is blinded by them. He would become vulnerable to them if he came close to one.'

'Are you mad? He damn near killed my sister last time. No, there must be another way.'

'No, I think this girl is right,' Lorett spoke from behind Morace.

Morace turned to look at her. He had not realised that she had arrived. Lorett came forward, past Morace, and looked at him.

'If it means the salvation of all our people, I am willing to risk my life. Brother, this is not your decision to make.' She looked hard into Morace's eyes. If Morace's change had been strong then Lorett's had leaped. She was physically and mentally stronger. It was as if she had grown up while she slept. 'Now we shall stop interrogating Rhean.'

Lorett took Rhean by the hand and walked her out of the room. Morace was dumbfounded. He had not expected that. When he realised that he still needed to speak to Nythe he found that she had gone too. *I think there are too many females here*. He walked out of the room.

Shanrea waited patiently with Lazon to make sure he was okay. The Nameless Girl looked on too. The shield started to weaken. Lazon became drowsy, due to the immense power he was using. He had said an hour but he was determined to push himself to help the cause.

The Nameless Girl then stepped forward and touched him on the shoulder. The shield became strong once more. Lazon fell to the floor disorientated. Shanrea ran to his side and made sure he was okay. The girl's eyes were determined and focused.

Inside the shield Marrisai spoke to Danai. Danai was furious.

'You are a traitorous bitch,' he spat with venom. Danai's rage had threatened to manifest in a fist to Marrisai's face five or six times now. There was no way to talk with him. The hatred he held for the druids was too much.

'Father, I am no traitor. I did the same as you. I understand though that the two druids here are...'

'Brainwashing you child, can you not see it? It is how they work.' Danai did something then Marrisai never thought she would see from him. Tears fell from his eyes. 'I thought I could protect you, but it would appear not.'

Marrisai could see this was going nowhere. She did not think she was going to get through to him at all. 'I am sorry father, I need more time.' Before Danai could see what had happened he was on the floor and knocked unconscious by his daughter. The shield fell when the others could see that the larger shadow inside had fallen to the ground.

'Are you sure that was wise?'

Marrisai looked at them with tears in her eyes. 'He always said that if either one of us stop seeing reason and are blinded by our hate to strike the other down, so that they can go through Shaik-lo. He warned me long ago that "when hatred consumes us, we perceive everyone as enemies"!'

'I am sorry, what is Shaik-lo?' Shanrea asked.

'It is the last resort. He is now deep within his mind.'

Chapter 38

The letter arrived a little after noon. It was handed to Caser who stared at the seal. It was unknown to him. It was black. He opened the letter and black smoke oozed out of it. He needed to put his hand to his mouth to block out the putrid smell the smoke gave off. Once the smoke had disappeared he unfolded the letter to read the contents. Caser began to read the letter out to his wife, Queen Galian.

Greetings, King I have yet to meet.

I am known to all as Twak. I was once an agent of the shadows but I am no longer. Over the years of the shadows decline, I became more powerful. This was unknown to all of the worlds. I was the voice inside of heads. I gave them ideas.

I am now here and in front of the world. This will be my domain. I have the Citadel as you are probably well aware. Now I have written this letter to you. I know you are king of a country you founded, but please heed my words. You will be better off joining your forces with me and bending your knee to my will. It will be less painful, not only for you, but your wife and your kingdom.

Come to me. Bend your knee and be protected.

'It would appear I must bend my knee if I want to survive; if this creature is as strong as he says he his.'

'You do not need to bend your knee, but you may need to speak with your brother,' his wife advised.

Caser stood up from his desk and walked over to the window. He had not spoken to his brother since the siege on the Citadel. Even though he did not want to, he knew it may be something he might have to do. His brother was now king of the Kaartheans by some twist of fate.

It felt a little strange for Caser. He was king of a people; His brother was king to another. Morace was a druid held up in the stronghold. Even Lorett was a siren. It seemed like the whole family had been put in strategic places. It seemed to him that someone had been playing a long game. Now the pieces had formed together and everyone was about to make their move.

It had been a number of weeks since they had sent off their daughter with Tavener-Doc. Tavener must have realised by now that his daughter was not as straight forward as he would have thought. If anything, she would be leading him. She should be with the twins now at the stronghold.

A servant had entered the room while Caser had been in his melancholy state of mind. He had not heard his wife trying to talk to him. When she touched him on the shoulder to alert him that he was being spoken to, he snapped out of his pensive thoughts.

'Dearest, your bath is ready. Shall we bathe?'

Caser nodded in agreement and followed the servant to the bath house. He took off his clothes and not only bathed himself in the bath but his wife's beauty too. It still amazed him just how beautiful she was. Every time he saw her it caught him by surprise.

'Our daughter should look like she is nearly twenty. Her growth would have been rapid. It may have taken your friend by surprise.'

'Will she be strong enough to do, it do you think?' Caser asked.

'Of course she would, she has mine and your blood.' Galian always sounded so confident. It was what made Caser take up the kingship of the people he had helped. 'In fact I can already tell that she has helped where needed. I just hope that she is not too focused on what needs to be done and let's herself have a little fun.' She tilted her head and gave a smile that warmed him up.

'I agree. She will have not had much time to be a child.'

The servant brought over a flagon of wine and poured some into a cup for the king and queen. They drank, continuing to wonder what their child was doing.

The Nameless Girl looked out at the stars from the window in her room. She mulled things over in her mind to figure out what needed to be done next. It seemed so simple before. Arrive at the stronghold, save the siren. Then what?

The answer had not presented itself to her at all. It was like she was trapped in an endless loop of possibilities. There were too many different people to consider. One thing for certain was when the large Dal-Mai-Sai arrived something he said struck her. *"I have seen this place before."* She knew that the man had not been in this world before. It meant that the stronghold must have been in his world too.

Before she took what she was puzzled over to the others, she wanted to research some more. It was not possible without talking first to one of the druids. They would be the only ones with access to the records she needed.

A star suddenly shot through the sky. She heard a whisper. *'All you need do is ask.'* It sounded like her mother's voice.

I can ask.

'Trust these people, child.'

I can trust them.

Perhaps her reservations at first were about trust. She would try. The Nameless Girl walked out of her door. She would ask the first druid she could find.

They would be in the bedchamber. It was night and they would be asleep. Without caring, she took her resolve to where she needed to go.

When she got to the door she needed she knocked on it lightly. There was not a sound. Still she slipped into the room silently and stood by the bed. She felt drawn to the girl; perhaps it was because they were both women that drew her.

The Nameless Girl tapped Shanrea on the shoulder to wake her up.

Shanrea woke with a start. 'Oh it's you. What time is it?'

'Late.' She was honest.

'Oh it's still dark out. Is something wrong?'

'No,' the girl said. She acted like waking someone up in the middle of the night was a perfectly normal thing to do.

'Why have you woken me up?'

'I needed help. Only a druid can help.' The Nameless Girl pulled on Shanrea's arm. She was strong. It must have been from the training. She let Shanrea put some clothes on. 'I need records of the stronghold. Only druids can gain access.'

***

The Queen looked at her husband. She knew how difficult the situation was with their family. He had been kept out of the loop about almost everything. He had not been told about his parent's death, or about Morace and Lorett. Nothing. It would be difficult for him to forgive them all for what had happened. He felt like they did not want to trust him with such information.

Galian knew why his family did not trust him. She knew of the stories about how Caser was before he became a king. Yes, he had been unruly and easily swayed, but now he was not. Lento in particular had reason to be distrustful of his brother. It was now up to her to show why they needed to be unified.

'Caser, you need your brothers and your sister onside. You need to speak to them and make them realise that unison is needed.' Galian looked into his eyes.

'I told you they do not trust me. I no longer trust them after they kept away the fact that half of my family is dead,' he said with defiance. He knew that she was right but did not want to believe it.

'Send a message to them. Tell them you wish to speak. Invite them to Evertere and show them what you have created.'

'It will not make any difference, Galian.'

'It will.' Galian got out of the bath. Caser followed and they put on robes.

'Make peace with your family then everything will be easier.' Galian took his hands and kissed him. They walked together to the study.

She led him to the desk and handed him a pen.

'Write a letter. Do it now.'

'Fine, I shall, but you will see what good it will do.'

He wrote the letter and dispatched it with his most trusted messenger.

Lento held the letter from the shadow creature in his hand. He wondered who else a letter like this may have been sent to. He handed it to the elven general who stood next to him as he read it.

'What will you do?' he asked.

'Well I for certain am not going to bend my knee to that creature.'

The general folded the letter with purpose and handed it back to Lento. In a sort of agreement he nodded.

'Good, that is the answer I would have expected from you. Now I am certain you have noticed that the shadow has completely taken over the south?'

The shadow that started from the Citadel had now covered the entire southern region. They had gained more men and refugees from the south. There were stories of people who had tried to stay in the place they called home. They were only horror stories, from people who had the misfortune of passing through the blackened villages. The south had become barren.

A group that had arrived from the south, sought Lento out. Lento recognised the woman who led them. She was from the inn that Tavener owned. They had needed to flee too. Lento also remembered the last letter he had last received from Lorett. It told of bad tidings.

The conversation was hard when it had to be retold.

'I am sorry, Dacy. I heard reports that Tavener fell victim to the shadows.' Dacy broke down. Lento held her as she wept. He let her sleep in a tent out of the way.

It was one of the hardest conversations he had.

He held the letter in his hand. *Would it be easier? Easier to just give in and let the madman take over?* The thought chilled him. No, he had seen the dwarves a number of times in battle. They were haggard and easy to fend off. They had no life. That may be another thing to consider. Perhaps the dwarves needed saving too. From what he could see they were on the brink of their own destruction. They had made a pact with the shadows but that must now seem a mistake.

Everything went silent for a moment then the general broke the silence.

'Lento? Are you there?' the General asked.

It snapped him out of his pensive state. 'Yes, sorry, did you say something?'

'I have been trying to say we have a break through. We have found another Wayward gate. Our scouts have just reported back.'

'Great! Where is it?'

'It is west in the woodland, near where we believe your brother resides.'

What had seemed to be good new now turned a little sour. *Brother.* 'Damn, I might not be able to go.'

'Do not worry about that.' The General handed Lento a letter. It had a seal he did not recognise. Evertere?

Lento opened the letter and read it.

Dear Brother.

> *It would appear I have a letter from our mutual friend. I received it not long ago. It invited me to bend my knee. It also implied you would receive one too. I have no intention of bending my knee to the shadows'. I have worked too hard not to have to bend my knee to anyone.*

Seeing as we have this mutual enemy, what do you say we put aside our differences for the moment, joining our forces and show the shadows the place they belong?

I assume you know where I am residing. Meet me at my Capital city in a week's time. If you get lost, head west.

Caser King of Evertere.

P.s Brother, please send a message to our siblings and invite them too.

'Where did this letter come from?'

'The scouts say they met a messenger at the Wayward mirror.'

Lento picked up his coat. Just as he was about to leave, he turned. 'Send word to my brother and sister. Tell them I will meet them at the Wayward mirror. I am leaving you in command in my stead.'

Lento always kept his horse ready to ride, just in case of attack. Luckily the shadows had not attacked recently. It would appear that the appearance of the Dal-Mai-Sai was enough to shake them a little. It was a shame he had left but Lento could understand the reasons why. It was wrong for Lento to ask him to keep fighting when his daughter was not with him.

I hope that he keeps his head when he finds out that two of the people who look after his daughter are druids.

Lento sat on top of his horse. Once he had issued out the necessary orders he kicked his horse to set it off. He knew he would need to take the longer route and go around the top of the Citadel as it was now impossible to travel the corrupted lands below. The shadowed clouds as far as he could see were slower reaching north than the south.

He rode with haste as he needed to move swiftly. If he stayed for too long in the same place he would get caught out. As it got to midday he stopped the ride long enough to eat and water the horse.

By nightfall he was a little north of the Citadel. He had made great time to get to where he was. The horse had to rest now for a while, and so did he. The day had been relatively warm but he could tell the night would be cold. He found a little shelter against the cold winds that were coming.

The night passed swiftly and without event. Lento felt refreshed and the horse was also less haggard. The next leg of the journey was westward It should take him four days to get to to reach his destination.

On the second day of the journey he realised he was being followed. There were four riders on horseback. They also carried the smell of the shadows.

Lento had realised that the shadow creatures had a distinct scent to them. They smelt metallic. The riders who followed had this same scent.

The creatures attacked when Lento entered the condensed woodland in the west. It was late into the third day after reaching the north of the Citadel. It turned out that they were not riding horses. From the waist down they *were* horses and the upper part they were human. Their arms were long and muscular and two held bows while the other two held spears. The creatures dripped with the same black that the shadows were coated with.

What are these beasts? Lento had seen nothing of the like before.

An arrow shot passed his ear. Then another. One then struck the horse. It fell, which made Lento land hard on the floor. As quickly as the horse fell, Lento was back up and had drawn a sword. Not from a sheath but from the air. It was curved like the Dal-Mai-Sai's blades.

'Thank you Danai, not having to draw a sword is so much easier.'

Danai had taught Lento how to draw the sword from the air. Lento had been a quick learner it had only taken him a week. Lento looked around for the horsemen. He fingered the throwing swords he had on his belt. He knew he needed to get rid of the bowmen first. When he found one he flung it at the horseman. It struck him in the throat and fell to the ground.

The second one was harder for him to find. Lento heard a twang from a bow from behind and arrow missed by inches. Lento turned to throw a knife but before he did the horseman collapsed. Lento did not have time to register what had happened when the other two horsemen had him caught with rope.

'We got the man. The master will be pleased,' one of them said. The other was about to say something in response but collapsed like their comrade had.

'What happened?'

It seemed Lento as though they had not realised the fallen bowman was not of his doing. From the grips of the ropes he hoarsely called out. 'Looks like you are on your own. It would appear I am no longer alone.'

'Shut up, you little man.' The half man half horse creature's eyes widened with pain. A sword jutted out of its sternum.

A man with long black hair sat on the back and looked out. 'Sorry for dropping in like that.' As the horseman fell to the floor he jumped off and bowed his head. 'Well, it looks like I have saved you.'

'It would appear so.' Now that Lento could get a better look at the man who had saved him and he could tell what it was. 'You're a Dal-Mai-Sai.'

'You know of us?' the Dal-Mai-Sai said.

'Yes I do, I have had the pleasure of meeting two from your race recently.'

'You have? That does sound like a tale to tell.'

Lento made the sword disappear in the way he was taught by Danai. The Dal-Mai-Sai saw this then pointed his sword at Lento.

'There is only one man or girl that I know of who could have taught you that little trick,' he said. The Dal-Mai-Sai moved a little closer, sword still pointed at Lento. 'You have either been trained by Danai So-Li or his daughter Marrisai Lin-Ji. Which one? Ah you said there were two you had met.'

Lento looked up at the Dal-Mai-Sai who pointed the sword in his direction. 'Judging by your reaction to this, I would say you do not particularly like these two?'

'That is correct, they are traitors.'

'Traitors you say? When I met them they seemed admirable and honest; hardly the look of traitors.'

'Danai is what we call a deserter. Looking at your uniform you must be in the military. You understand what that means? Right?'

'I do understand what that means!' Lento said. 'Danai also told me what happened, so don't try and make me think badly of him.' Lento stood up and took the rope from his neck off. 'I am sorry but I am going to be late for an appointment. You are free to accompany me.'

The Dal-Mai-Sai laughed. 'You are my prisoner, yet you command me like I am yours?'

A noise surrounded the Dal-Mai-Sai. The undergrowth rustled as people passed.

'You see, my friend, it is you who is wrong. I have two meet ups. This is the first.'

'Father!' Nythe exclaimed.

'Your daughter? The Dal-Mai-Sai asked. He could sense at least four people surrounded him and there was also Lento too. That made five. It would foolish to attempt an attack on the man now.

'Who are you?' It was another female voice. She had the accent of a Dal-Mai-Sai.

'I am a member of the advance attack group, Marrisai.' He said her name, knowing that it would raise more questions for her.

'How do you know my name?' she asked.

'I know your name because we are after you and your traitorous father. Or has he not told you of the other reason you and he fled to this land?'

Marrisai, as fast as anything, was in front of the man with a dagger drawn to his throat.

Nythe had never seen anyone move so fast. It was almost like she disappeared then reappeared in front of him.

The blade she held to his throat drew a little blood as Marrisai applied more pressure. The blood trickled down the blade to the hilt.

'What a ferocious little creature you are,' the Dal-Mai-Sai mocked. 'I suppose your traitor father never told you what you really are. Am I right?'

'No, but that is what we are here to find out.' Marrisai fought hard not to end the man's life. When she told Morace that the man who held his brother captive was also a Dal-Mai-Sai he had rested his and on her shoulder. He had squeezed it. She knew what it meant. In her ear he whispered.

'This is your battle. Keep your head.'

Marrisai looked up to see Morace. He stood watch without moving. He let her deal with it. The worst thing for Marrisai was the fact this man kept calling her father a traitor, when he was trying to help their world.

'I see you are restrained child.' The Dal-Mai-Sai raised his hand to strike her down. Marrisai was much faster though and swiped at his legs with her own. He fell to the floor like a sack of potatoes. The Dal-Mai-Sai's head split open where it had hit the floor. Marrisai threw a glance at Morace who still did not move. He waited to see what she would do next.

As Morace watched the events unfold from his vantage point. For him it was a test to see Marrisai's temperament. If she could exact restraint at a time like this then she would be of great use. Her father was still in his own mind to see the way. Lazon stayed with him as did Shanrea in the repository.

It was hard for Morace to leave Shanrea behind, but when they received the letter from his brother he knew what needed to be done. Someone in the keep who could access the knowledge there had to remain. The Nameless Girl was left to study.

Now Morace stepped forward along with his sister who stood with him to watch. She had been silent.

Lorett tried to figure everything out. She knew it would be almost impossible to speak to the people of the Dal-Mai-Sai, unless she went into their world as the siren of the three worlds. The Dal-Mai-Sai they had with them was pursued by her own kind. They would not be able to ask her to speak to her people.

'You can put back the dagger now Marrisai.' Morace said.

Marrisai did as she was asked. The unconscious Dal-Mai-Sai lay at her feet.

'Now what do we do with him?' Marrisai looked at Morace. Her face flared red. Why did he have to be so good looking? Morace looked at her and smiled. 'No don't smile that makes it worse.' She put her hand to her mouth as the words left her lips. She had not wanted to actually say them.

'Makes what worse?' Morace asked.

'Oh brother, you are a fool sometimes,' Lorett said as she wrapped her arm around Marrisai.

Lento watched his brother and sister in awe. They had grown up a lot in the year they had been apart. Both were stronger. Morace stood taller than he ever had and looked a little menacing. Lorett had become more beautiful but she was also strong.

Nythe ran over to him and gave him a hug.

'I see you have grown too, daughter.' He stood her in front of him and drank her in with his eyes. 'You have become a woman this past year. No longer the child I used to smack.

'Father!' Nythe said embarrassed.

Marrisai looked at them both. She smiled. Then the pang of sadness crept over her. *I wonder if Danai will be able to say that to me one day.*

'Lento we must make tracks. Are you ready?' Morace looked into his brother's eyes. He was determined to get to their destination as quick as possible. He had not seen Caser for many years. He claimed to be king of a country. This was something he was eager to see.

'I am ready Morace. Are you?'

'I am.'

The five of them walked on in the forest.

'Well, it would appear that no one has obeyed my letters. No one has turned up.' Twak sat in his seat in the Crucible. The shadow he had created was now over most of the south. To the west, there was something stopping him, which was troubling Every time he sent scouts out to that area they never returned.

At the time of his conquest, he recalled that horsemen had come out of the woods to take out some of his army. He had not known of their existence until then. *Did the shadow empress know of this?* It was probable he had been kept in the dark. Perhaps the empress had caught wind of his treachery even then.

How long she had known he did not care to think. It was time for his meal.

'Where is my food?' he asked. His tongue licked his lips in anticipation. A man was brought to him. An old man.

'Damn it! How is this old man meant to provide me with enough energy to last two hours?' He spat at the two dwarves who had brought in the old man.

'I am sorry master, but...'

'This will not do. Come here.' The two dwarves stepped forward and knelt before Twak. 'Now I shall show you what happens when you bring me weakness to feed on.'

'But master, this was all we can find...'

'There is a whole army out there, somewhere, with young men and women who will provide me with enough sustenance.' Twak stood up. A look of pure glee appeared on his face. The two dwarves became fearful for their lives. The Shadow Lord placed his hands on their heads and started to laugh. A dark glow flowed out of his hands and the dwarves' life force disappeared. They lay on the cold floor, dead.

'That is better. Now I will take this old man's life just because I can.' He did the same to the old man.

With the new power he had attained he moved to the room with the map. The whole southern region was covered with the dark shadows. He put his hand on the part of the map that had the Citadel. He moved his hand west-ward. There was still the resistance that had always been there. It stopped at the forest that bordered the land.

Twak's hand started to shake. A spark emitted from his hand, and like a rag doll he was flung across the room. He hit the wall with a loud thud. Damn this. The south was so easy. Why wasn't the west?

'I need to find out. If only we had dragons.' Twak limped over to the door. He needed to rest. Then he would fly out to the west and see what was there.

Galian stood at the window. She had managed to halt the progression once again. This time it was a little stronger though. *It must have eaten more today.* Galian needed to find a way to stop this once and for all. If there was a way she could put a poison in the mad Shadow Lord's next at-tempt, she might be able to use it to kill him. How she could do this, she did not know. It would require magic that this land had not seen.

She knew where this magic could be found. Hopefully with the coming of Caser's family, they would bring what she would need for this.

The main challenge for her was to keep what she was do-ing from Caser. It was strange; she had fallen in love with him despite it being forbidden. She was gifted by the stars to the world. It was told they would have a child. What was now needed was the reader of the stars to arrive with his daughter. Then what was written would come to pass.

The guide, the Catalyst, the power. Born of the three worlds.

The guide would need to gather all of the races. They would need to guide them to the safety.

The Catalyst would trigger and make everything move faster.

The power would control what would happen.

'I can see the two moons are brighter this night,' Caser said.

Galian was knocked out of her pensive thoughts. 'They are not moons, husband.'

'I know; one of them is the planet of the elves,' Caser said. She had told him the story a while ago.

'Yes that is true, but the moon that was always there is also a planet. It is a planet another race of people moved to.' She got undressed and put on her night gown. She slipped into bed with Caser by her side.

'Oh?' Caser said as he looked into her eyes.

'Yes, there are in fact three worlds involved in the collision.' She wrapped an arm around Casers body and started to unbutton his tunic. 'Caser, make love to me.'

Afterwards Galian dressed again and looked at her husband. A tear fell from her eye. 'I am sorry but I must now go.'

Caser sat up and looked at her. 'What do you mean?'

'I have done that which is forbidden for me to do. I have fallen in love.' She walked over to the window. As she looked out at the stars she felt Caser's hand wrap around her slender waist.

'I see, do you have to listen to the stars all the time?'

Galian nodded. 'I do, I was only here for one purpose. I am sorry for deceiving you.'

'You did not deceive me. I understand. Does this mean that the shadows will now be able to pass the forest though?'

'You knew about what I was doing?'

'I did. I also knew that it was probably forbidden. I should have stopped you.'

'It was something I needed to do, to protect the man I love.'

They kissed for the last time. Galian's skin glistened as she turned into silver dust. She flew out of the window.

Caser sat on the bed. He looked out of the window that his love had flown through and fought back the tears that had started to form. *Now, more than anything I need to keep strong.*

'It would appear that I need to act. I will need to make peace with my brother.'

Galian stood with her father on the star Galendril. He smiled at her. He was large and had a powerful presence that gave her a hard time standing.

'Daughter, you have done well. But you made it hard on yourself,' he said. He looked at her. He wore white robes that fell to the floor.

'I am sorry father. I know you told me not to fall in love, but it was difficult.'

'It will be more difficult for you now my dear. There is a reason you should not fall in love. It will put a pain in your heart that will make you ache for as long as you live.' He started to walk into a large hall.

'Is it possible? Can we do it?'

'Do what?'

'Can we ascend the King of Evertere when he passes from the world?'

He shot her a fierce look. 'You know that it is forbidden.'

'I know, but so was falling in love. But it happened any-way.'

'Hmm, you are right of course. And it is not the first time it has happened. Is this what you would want rather than his bones falling into dust?'

Galian rushed over, tears falling from her eyes and down her cheeks. She took her father's hand. 'It is, father.'

He looked at a figure in the corner, who also wore white robes.

'What do you say, Wraith of the Marshes? Considering this is your plan to rid the worlds of not only the shadows, but the certain calamity that was created by the use of weather magic.'

Galian felt a little uneasy when the wraith of the marshes stood up and walked over to her. Soon she realised that her father's presence was nothing compared to the wraiths'. The look on his face chilled her too. It was like he was about to say something that could change the world. Her world.

He paused for a moment. He took her in his gaze.

'There will be a consequence, child. Are you sure you are willing to pay it?' he spoke calmly.

She looked at the Wraith of the Marsh. She nodded.

'Are you sure?'

'I am. Tell me, what would be the consequence?'

'To ascend this man, you will need to return to his world once its dust has settled. You will be able to meet each other for one more day before you head back. His ascendance will mean that you will become mortal. You cannot spend the rest of your lives together.'

'So either way we would not be able to stay together?'

'That is correct.'

'Then I say let him ascend. So long as I know he is alive I will be happy.'

The Wraith of the Marsh looked at her father for his approval. Her father nodded.

'Very well. I will set in motion what is needed to be done. Remember child you will not be able to return. You will also die one day of old age.'

'I do not care. I would much rather live a shorter life and know that Caser is alive than live forever and know that he has passed away.' She stood up and left the room. She was happy and satisfied with what had happened.

Caser, for one more day we can be together. I will be planted with your seed again and live with our son or daughter.

Nythe looked at her father during the meal they ate together. She had not seen him since the war. It was known to her that he had become king of their people, though it was a title he would much rather not have.

That means that... I am a princess.

'Father, how are you?' She took his hand.

'I am fine daughter. I am still just amazed.' He smiled. 'You have grown up. If there was not all of this happening you would be ready to marry someone.'

'I know. Father, I think I have found the person I would like to marry.'

'You have?' He looked surprised. They had often talked about her marring someone and she had always shrugged it off. She had said that she was not ready and still had a lot that she wanted to learn.

'I have, do you remember the elven boy that was with Morace and Lorett?'

'I do, do you mean to marry the elf?' He looked at her, a little worry in his eyes.

'I do. Are you happy for me?'

'I am worried. I do not know how intermarriage would work.'

'You mean you do not know if we will be able to marry?' Nythe stood up. She had not even realised she had raised her voice. All of the others looked at her then at her father. 'Morace and Shanrea have...'

'That is true. Do you know if they will be able to have children?'

'No but...' Nythe's fist pounded the table.

Lento waited for her to calm a little. He was happy for her; happy that she had found love despite all the strife in the worlds. He was merely worried that because she had fallen in love with an elf they might not be able to have a family.

'I know I have pushed for you to get married before,' he said as he stood up. 'Now I am a king, all be it reluctantly. You are my daughter. The child you would give birth to would be a future king or queen of the Kaartheans.'

'If I cannot marry the man I love then I will not marry at all.'

Lento looked saddened. This was not a conversation he wished to have with his daughter. Nythe stormed out of the tent. Lento was about to follow when Lorett seized his arm. He looked at her. Her grip was strong.

'Not now, Lento let her think.' She let the grip on his arm lessen for a moment. She could feel him relax. He sat back down at the table.

No one noticed Marrisai quietly leave the tent and follow Nythe. She knew how she felt. It was hard for her too; she had fallen in love with someone she could not have. She understood that Nythe had potentially fallen in love with someone she may or may not be able to be with. *I must catch up with her and speak to her.*

'Nythe?' she called out. 'Where did you go?'

'Go away,' Nythe shouted back. 'Do not follow me.'

'I am sorry I cannot do that.' Marrisai picked up her pace. It was quite dark, anyone else may have found it hard to run in the woods like this. Not Marrisai. She gained on the girl.

Nythe stopped suddenly and it took Marrisai a lot of effort to stop before hitting her.

'Why are you following me?' Nythe turned around a looked at Marrisai. Tears filled her eyes.

'Because I know how you feel.'

'Do you?'

'Yes. It is a similar situation with a different ending. There is a chance you can have the man you love, for me it is impossible.' Marrisai looked hard at the Nythe. 'I am twenty six years old. I could be married right now if I wanted to. I could have children and be with the man I love. But look at me. What do I look like?'

'You look like a twelve year old.'

'Exactly. I am unable to be with anyone I love. When they look at me they see nothing but a child. How do you think I feel, looking at people who are in love? Reciprocated love.'

Nythe understood. *It would be worse to be in her situation.* 'How have you managed for so long?'

'I learnt that there are things other than love. But it has become harder since I fell in love with someone from this world.'

'You have fallen in love with Morace? Am I right?'

'I have, but he is in love with Shanrea and his love is reciprocated.' Marrisai sat on a fallen log. Nythe went and sat with her.

'I am sorry. Your love plight is worse than mine. There is a chance I can still be with Lazon. Whereas you have not really any chance at all.' Nythe put her arm around Marrisai's small frame. 'You're looking for a way to become older in your body?'

'I am.'

'That is great. When all of this has ended, with the worlds colliding and everything, and the shadows destroyed, I will help you and Danai. If he is still around or onside.'

'Thank you,' Marrisai said. Tears had started to fall from her eyes too.

'Now let's go back. I need to apologise to my father.'

They made their way back to the tent. Morace stood at the entrance. Nythe went in to speak to her father. Marrisai stood in front of Morace with a look that showed she was determined for something. *I can do this.*

'Thank you,' he said.

She wiped away her own tears. 'Morace. There is something I need to tell you,' she said.

He led her to the outside of the tent so that they could talk. 'I know you have needed to say something. I am sorry I had not seen this before,' he spoke without the cold attitude he had developed, but with warmth.

'I think I have fallen in love with you. I understand that due to my appearance at the moment you will never love me.' She took his hand in hers. 'I also know that you love Shanrea and that even if I was older looking I would not have a chance.' Marrisai dropped his hand and walked into the tent.

Morace watched her. It was not the conversation he had expected. He had been told that Marrisai liked him, but she used the word love just now. He felt a little sorry for her. Her situation was not nice for someone of her age.

Lento received the apology from Nythe and apologised back. It was hard for him as he was her father. Her mother had died years ago. He needed to bring up a teenage girl in the city on his own. He was at that point the guard captain of Darth City. It was a challenge.

'When do we head to see Uncle Caser?' she asked after they had exchanged a warm embrace.

'We are to leave once the camp has been disbanded.' Lento replied. He walked over to where the prisoner was held. He had regained consciousness. 'How are you, Dal-Mai-Sai?'

'I would be better once I have that traitor and his child brought to justice.'

'Oh that is not going to happen. Now tell me what your name is?'

'My name is of no importance. You will find out whose name you need to hold with great import however. Soon enough.'

Lento looked at Marrisai, who stood watching the conversation. 'Are your people normally this dramatic?'

'No, not really. I imagine this one has been somewhat brainwashed by someone.'

'You lie, you little piece of trash.'

'No, you lie. My father was discharged from service when he started to hear the stars.'

'Ha, now look who is the brainwashed one.'

Marrisai drew a sword from the air and pointed it at the throat of the prisoner. 'Tell me, how would you like to die?'

'I do not believe your comrades agree with you about my death. At the moment I am too valuable to you all alive.'

'He is right.' Morace said. He put a hand on Marrisai's shoulder. She trembled a little but then stood firm. The prisoners face relaxed a little. He felt safe. 'Oh I would not relax too much. I have learnt a way to make people who will not talk, talk.' Morace looked at Marrisai and she realised what was about to happen. The same sort of pressure that she felt from Danai started to build up around them.

Marrisai looked hard at Morace. 'Are you sure you know what you are doing?

'I am sure. I will need you to help me though!'

'I will. I am used to this power.' Marrisai held out two swords. Her long black hair fell past her shoulders.

'Now Dal-Mai-Sai, I am sorry that you have forced me to use this power, but you have left me no choice. I should say this is the first time I have used it. I do not intend for you to die, but if it were to happen I am sorry.'

'You can't use the power of fear to trick me. I know your game, druid.'

'Oh do you? Well I am not using fear. I am going to use terror. That is something worse than fear. It is what fear develops into.'

'Morace you can't. Not even the druids of our world were so reckless.' Marrisai started to protest.

'I am sorry Marrisai, but it is necessary.'

'No it is not.'

'It is, now please be quiet.' The pressure deepened and the form of the Dal-Mai-Sai became blurry to all except Morace and Marrisai. He started to scream with terror. He shook and his skin became blackened.

'So this is what you fear? Death itself. Well my friend you will see it all. All the ways you can die.'

'Morace, don't do this.' Marrisai pleaded

'Just watch, Marrisai. He will change his mind soon enough.'

Steam started to rise from the Dal-Mai-Sai's body.

'Now tell me your name,' Morace said coldly.

'Captain Zen-Lu,' the man replied.

'Good, tell me the truth behind the warrant for Danai's capture.'

'He was called a deserter. From the reports he was commanded to do something, but then he refused. He mentioned something about stars and a child.'

'What was he ordered to do?'

'I do not know. It was classified.'

'So you could have been brainwashed?'

'No our government would not do that.' The captive started to scream as pain now coursed through his body.

'Believe me governments can do whatever they wish.'

The pressure gained even more of a hold on the prisoner. Marrisai could sense that Morace may have started to lose his grip on it.

'Morace?' Marrisai try to see if he was responsive.

'Yes, Marrisai?'

'How long are you going to keep this up? I think we have enough from him for the time being. Let go of the power.' Marrisai held the sword ready to strike, just in case Morace could not control it.

'You are right. I will stop now. I can see why the druids needed a partner with this power.' The pressure started to drop and Marrisai looked at Morace. He looked like he had aged a little. The prisoner was now unconscious.

Morace dropped to one knee and Marrisai held him up. She looked for the others and gestured for them to come forward. She was still small; she would not be able to hold him for long.

'Quick, get him. He is so heavy,' Marrisai said.

The others took him. Lorett looked saddened. She had not wanted him to use the power he had. She feared it would be too much for him.

Once Morace had regained his strength they set off on their journey. The prisoner had died soon after his encounter with the terror. Just in case he was not alone they burned his body so that his fate could not be found. *It looks like that power was a little too strong.*

Lorett was concerned for her brother. It was bad enough that he had used the power, but now he had killed with it. It may have been an accident but nonetheless sometimes accidents turned into nightmares. She watched him like a hawk but he seemed the same.

'You are concerned for him Lorett,' Lento said. She had not realised he was walking beside her. It shocked her when he spoke.

'I am. He has changed a lot. Too fast. I grow ever concerned for him.'

'As do I, for the both of you.' Lento looked at Lorett. 'Give me your hand.' She gave him her hand and he squeezed it. 'I am your brother too. I will protect you as much as I can. I also thank you for your hand in helping my daughter grow.'

'What do you mean?'

'Do not think me stupid Lorett. I know Nythe has missed the tenderness that is having a woman around to bring you up. She was young when her mother died. She has only known training, which is why I was pleased when she said she wanted to be a healer. I was worried that she would never love anyone. I know it will be hard if the man she has fallen in love with will not be able to take her as a bride.'

'I would not think too hard on that brother. The elves and man were once one race. As were the Dal-Mai-Sai.'

'You mean that they could be compatible?'

'I do. I would not have let them fall in love if they were not.' She winked at her older brother. It reminded him of when they grew up.

'Why did you not say anything before?'

'Because, brother, I am siren. There are certain things I am bound to do. One of them is to observe. I also thought it would be a little fun to see how you would react,' she added cheekily.

'Why, you little...' He ruffled her hair.

'Hey, you know I dislike it when you do that.'

'I do. So does Nythe and pretty much any other woman or girl with long hair,' he jested.

Lorett walked off.

In the slumber that Marrisai had put him in, Danai could still sense the power of the druids. One of them had used the power of terror. He could tell that Marrisai had been with him. She did not know it but she emitted a calmness that stopped the user of such power get consumed. It was within her, it always had been.

He knew that if the druids here had learnt how to use the power of terror, there was no hope. Or maybe there was... If Marrisai was with them to help, then maybe it would not go that way.

The power always consumed in the end though. With the use of power came the craving you get all the time. Danai needed to find his daughter. Clearly the druids had poisoned her mind somehow. There were others, though they were not druids. He had sensed them. A siren. Someone with a lot of power. Others too. He could not tell who they were. He needed to get his way out of here.

In the dream state Danai sat up and looked around at his surroundings. It was white. The colour blinded his eyes. He began to walk forward. His mechanical arm was out-stretched, feeling for anything that might block his path. He stubbed his toe on things he could not see. Thank goodness I have my hand stretched out.

He walked on like this for what seemed like hours. There seemed to be no end to this forever whiteness.

'Damn that child, when I get my hands on her I will...'

He then looked ahead. He saw her standing there in her black tunic and trousers. She smiled at him.

'Welcome father. Here you shall learn the truth. Marrisai turned around and beckoned him to walk forward with her.

'Wait; are you the true Marrisai, or the one who has been brainwashed by the Druids of this place?'

'I have not been brainwashed father, I am truly the girl you remember. I have just realised you cannot pass a judgment on a whole race due to a few individuals.'

'Do you think to teach me about acceptance child?'

'I do.'

'Then you are wasting your breath. I will never accept any druid.'

'Dear father, you have been led to believe that any druid will turn into a maddened figure. Crazed by the fear they have inflicted and the terror.'

'Well it is the truth child.'

'Father, I will show you that the two you now seek to de-stroy are in fact two people that will save the people of all the worlds. They will need us.'

Danai spat on the floor and walked in the opposite direction to his daughter. 'Insolent child. Do you forget that it was I who brought you up?'

'I do not forget father. You once told me that if any of us went on a path of revenge and became blind, we were to use this method to bring them back. This is what I do now.'

'I know what you are doing. The only reason you have used this is because you know that I am defenceless in here. You probably wish to kill me.'

'No, that is not true. I would never want you dead.'

'Ha, you have a funny way of showing it.' Suddenly the scene changed. It showed the time when she had fallen through the ceiling after she had touched the map. The scene then flashed to where she was lying in a bed asleep. The druids stood next to her bed.

'See how much they cared for me when I was hurt.'

'Pfft. Lies,' Danai spat.

'No, not lies. In this space there is no room for lies remember?'

'Look at this next scene.'

The scene whizzed to where Marrisai had learnt of what Morace and Shanrea where. He watched Marrisai fly at Morace with the blade. Then she was subdued.

'Ah, so the brainwashing started here,' Danai said. He looked at her.

'No, not brainwashing. This was where I realised the truth. Both of us were blinded by hate. Sure the druids in our world tricked us but we let ourselves both become blind.'

'Well you have fallen for one of them, I can see.' The scene whipped to the moment near the tent where she declared her love for the male druid.

'Wait what are you doing?'

'I am seeing the scenes that you do not want me to,' he said coldly. 'I need to know the extent of their damage to you so that I can repair it.' The scenes from all her time with the *druids blurred passed in almost an instant. Then it stopped upon the scene where she realised that not all druids were bad. That scene was replaced with another, Danai's eyes widened.*

'I see. So you are no longer in the stronghold? Looks like it is my time to return.'

'Wait, what are you doing?'

'I am leaving. But don't worry I shall rescue you.'

Everything went black.

Chapter 39

Marrisai woke up with a start in the bedchamber with Lorett and Nythe. They had made it to Evertere during the night. She had woken up suddenly because she felt the place that held Danai collapse. She also knew that his mind was still bent on revenge. She had a nightmare it seemed. One where he still believed she was brainwashed by the druids. Except this was not a nightmare and Danai had promised to rescue her.

She hoped the others still in the stronghold would be safe.

Marrisai did not know what time it was but she was hungry. She left the room she shared with Lorett and Nythe and worked her way down a number of different corridors. Marrisai looked around for a sign of a kitchen or a dining room that looked to be set up for breakfast. She found none and after half an hour of searching, she was truly lost.

While she looked around she bumped into a young boy. He was about fourteen. He dropped what he carried. Marrisai's cheeks flushed red as she helped him pick his items up.

'I am so sorry,' she said.

'It's okay. I am sorry I should not have gotten in your way.' They turned to go their separate ways. He turned back and said, 'You're very pretty by the way.'

Marrisai stood fast in her tracks. She realised that to the boy she would appear to be around his age. Did he like her? To her he was just a boy. It was too weird.

'Thanks,' she replied, and ran off. Back at her room she closed the door a little too loudly. *Damn.* For a moment she did not realise that Lorett was awake. When Lorett spoke it startled her a little.

'There you are. I wondered where you were.' Lorett looked at her.

Marrisai smiled. 'The strangest thing has just happened to me.'

'What happened?'

'A boy just said I look pretty. An actual boy. Not a man saying it because I look like a child. A real boy.' She spun around in a circle for a moment then fell in to Nythe's arms who had come over to see what the fuss was.

Both Lorett and Nythe gave a little laugh.

'What? Why are you laughing?' Marrisai got up. She was back to her usual self, as hard as nails.

'It's nothing really,' Nythe said.

'We have just never seen you like this. Usually you are so serious.'

'What do you mean by serious? Is that not a good thing? I am focused that is all.' Marrisai became agitated.

'Calm down Marrisai,' Lorett said. She sat next to her and started to brush her hair. 'It is just nice is all. We have not had much of a chance to act how we should.'

'So if this suitor asked you if you out for dinner, what would you say?' Nythe asked as she sat on the opposite side of Marrisai.

'I would say no.'

The other two looked at her surprised.

'Please, I may look like a twelve year old but I am much too old for him. I am attracted only to men.' She stood up to look at her hair. It was in two braids like Lorett's and Nythe's.

'You mean like my brother?' As Lorett asked she gave Marrisai a little wink. Then she dodged the cushion that was flung at her face by Marrisai. One was about to be thrown back when a knock sounded at the door.

Nythe opened the door. It was her father Lento. *Time for a little joke.* She winked at her father as if to say follow along.

'Marrisai, I think it is for you. Did you say that boy had black hair?'

'No! But he did have black hair.' She looked down at the ground, embarrassed that she was so excited.

'Well then it must be for you and look he has brought flowers.' In the next instant Marrisai was at the door. Her face dropped when she saw Lento standing there, looking little perplexed.

'Oh,' she said.'

Lento shot a look at his daughter that suggested that the joke was a little low.

Nythe apologised to Marrisai who had become quite quiet.

'Breakfast is ready. Please follow me to the dining hall.' Lento said.

They followed Lento. When they got to the big hall doors that were decorated with intricate designs, Lento halted. He let them go past except for Nythe.

'What was that all about?' Lento said.

'It was just a joke father.' She explained the story of what had happened.

'I see. The face that I saw when she realised it was an only a joke was a little disheartened. She may be mature but remember she has held this burden for a very long time. It must be hard for her.' Lento let her go into the hall. *Damn children, they never stop needing to be scolded.*

Lento really wanted to see his brother but he was yet to present himself. Upon their arrival Lento was informed that Caser's wife had passed on to the next life a number of days ago. When a servant appeared at the door Lento asked for his brother to be sent. The servant obliged. Lento then went to eat some breakfast.

The servant arrived an hour later.

'The king would like to see you now,' he said. He escorted them to where the King waited for them.

The room the king stood in was circular. It had been furnished with a lot of wooden workings. There were pictures of people they had never met.

'Brothers and sister, I see you have brought my niece too,' Caser said. 'And who is this pretty little thing?' He looked at Marrisai.

'I am Marrisai, I am a Dal-Mai-Sai,' she said. She did not take too kindly to being called little.

'Oh yes the Dal-Mai-Sai. I remember we had some of them here about a month ago. They were looking for someone of your description.' Caser spoke with a calm tone.

Marrisai could not judge this man. He seemed a little strange to her. Then she saw it; the Nameless Girl had some of the features as Caser did.

'You're the girl's father?' she asked.

'Yes, I am the Nameless Girl's father. Her mother was from the stars.'

'Wait, the stars? My father is a reader of the stars.' Marrisai got up and walked over to the man Caser and took his hand.

'What was she like? The Lady of the stars?'

'She was beautiful,' he said. 'She said she was here to help. Help she did. My daughter who I sent with Tavener has extraordinary power. She will find what it is we need. The Wraith of the Marsh said so.'

Morace stepped in. 'You know of the Wraith of the Marsh?'

'I do, he was once a Druid but like every man he is flawed. He fell in love with another druid who became corrupted. No doubt you have read the diary he gave you?'

'We have, both Shanrea and I, it does mention of this love story.'

'I know, you would not have found the stronghold if you had not read the diary.' Caser walked over to the window and looked out into the sky. He sighed. 'I should not have fallen in love with her. She should not have fallen in love with me. If that had not happened she would still be here now.'

'Love is powerful; it can create an amazing being or topple a whole world.'

'We could not have our child born without love. Otherwise it would have become rotten. She would have been no good to anyone.' Caser looked at Marrisai. 'Your father you say is the star reader? Does he still hold a disdain for druids?'

'He does,' Marrisai responded a little disheartened.

'Why are you disheartened?'

'Because people who I have grown to like are druids, my father thinks me brainwashed by them.'

'In a way we are all brainwashed. Your father will learn eventually,' Caser said. With a grace that came from being a king, Caser walked over to Lento. 'Now brother, we have both received letters, we are both kings.'

'I would like to say that once all of this is over I will renounce my crown. I am not meant to be a king; I was only appointed because I am strong.'

'That is what this world will need once the dust has settled,' Caser said.

'No, I wish to retire completely after this, I am getting too old. I wish to retire with my family.' He looked at Nythe, who was watching the two kings in admiration. Both her father and uncle were kings. Her father had told her that their family were simple fishermen in a little village. But now they were rulers of two kingdoms.

'Life usually has a knack of stopping what we plan brother, you should know that.' Caser directed his head towards the twins. 'It would appear our family are meant to be leaders. We were once all Kaartheans, granted I have chosen a different name for my people, but it is where we started.'

'I give you credit brother. From the bandits you once lorded over you have created something truly amazing.'

Caser shrugged off the compliment. 'Don't presume you can flatter me! I am still bitter over what you did to me. I have just been informed that this is the way we must go. Once the shadows have been defeated and the world's inhabitants are saved, I will take my people away.'

'Then you side with us only for this brief time?'

'I am, I don't think I could ever forgive you for what you have done.' Once Caser had finished what he had to say he left the room. They were all a little perplexed and dumb struck.

'Why is he so bitter?' Lorett asked.

'He was not told of Pa's death or of the death of the rest of our family.' Lento explained.

'But the former King of Kaarth said he would dispatch messages to both you and him.'

'Caser was known as a criminal to all in Kaarth. The chances are the king just said that as lip service.' Lento turned to leave too. 'I need to think on what needs to be done. We somehow need to defeat the Shadows or keep them at bay until we find a wa...'

The ground shook with a huge force. It felt like the palace was about to fall to pieces. It seemed as though it lasted for ages. It threw books off the shelves and caused some windows to smash.

Everything settled for a brief moment, but then the same thing happened again. This time it felt like the earthquake was much closer.

Lento looked at the others in the room. He told them to get under the large table and wait for the quakes to stop.

'What is happening?' Nythe asked. He voice was quiet compared to the sound of the destruction.

'It must be the weather magic's effects again.'

A fireball then shot through and shattered the remaining windows into pieces. One of the shards caught Lento in the leg.

Lento realised what this must be. 'I think we are under attack!' Lento managed to catch a glimpse just outside the window. Sure enough, the black clouds that formed the reach of the shadow creature Twak, had extended its grip over Evertere. Before Lento could even tell the others to get their weapons Marrisai was next to him with her two swords drawn, ready to fight. Lento did the same and looked at her. The fierce determined little girl stirred him up for battle.

Marrisai was astounded when she saw Lento draw the swords from the air. *Danai must have taught him.*

'Morace, can I assume you have learnt some battle magic?' *Lento asked.*

'I have some in my arsenal,' Morace responded.

'Nythe, are your throwing blades sharp?'

'Yes, I practiced every day.' Nythe stood forward ready for battle.

'Lorett is there a song you can use to quell the foe?'

'I know of something,' Lorett replied.

'Great, I trust you all know how to protect yourselves if needed?'

They all responded yes together. Lorett started her song.

Into battle the men and women go.

Give them strength and let them know.

Protected they shall be,

Protected they shall be.

A light from Lorett's heart started to shine bright and out of the window. It blinded the gathered Shadow creatures. She heard their yells as they fell to the group.

She knew she had done all she could to help as a siren. She started to leave the room when a black hand reached around her waist and pulled her out. A giant put her in front of its one eye. It seemed to smile. It put her down on the roof top.

'I have found you Siren. It appears that my last visit was not enough to kill you.' Twak stood tall next to her.

Nythe saw the giant put its hand into the room and pick up Lorett. Instinctively she pulled out her knives and flung them at the beast. They had no effect. It turned around empty handed. *Damn, it must have felt the blades.* It started to walk over to her. It was slow and was easily over twenty meters tall. It stood on the solders that were round its feet.

Marrisai saw the giant too. She looked for Morace; he held the purple Druid fire in his hands. He poured the fire into the faces of the attacking creatures. They howled in pain.

'Morace, you need to use fear to destroy that one.' She pointed to the giant. She knew it would be difficult but Morace had survived using terror to fight before. Once she saw Morace nod in agreement she set off to kill their quarry. The pressure of fear started to build up. It was quite strong even for a master of fear. *Morace, I hope you can handle this.* She advanced on the creature. It looked too big even for a man twice her size to battle. Marrisai was an ant compared to the giant. Sometimes though, ants have big bites.

The giant now had its hand on its head. It was screaming with fear. The only way that Marrisai could get to the beast was to climb onto the roof of a building. She found one close enough to the creature to leap onto its shoulder. With any luck it would not notice her and leave her be.

With ease she scaled the wall then drew her swords. She jumped onto the giants shoulder. It did not move. It had not noticed her. She spun around, her long sword opened up the flesh on its neck then the short sword penetrated it, causing black blood to spew out all over the battlefield.

To get down she buried the short sword into its chest as though cutting through fabric. She slid down using the resistance of the blade in the giant's chest. Once was safely on the ground she ran to Morace. She could still feel the pressure from the fear that threatened to overtake.

She put a hand on his shoulder and she started to feel the fear stop.

'That was a close call,' she said.

Morace looked up to the rooftop. He could see Lorett. Twak was with her. His hand was around her neck. The next thing he saw was her body become limp. Twak threw her body in front of them. It was lifeless. Once he had discarded Lorett's body he transformed into the griffon and flew.

Morace ran to his sister's body. 'No, you bastard!' he screamed on top of his voice.

Marrisai looked as Lorett's body. She felt the pressure build up once more. Morace's power threatened to overwhelm her.

Suddenly a man jumped from a building that had toppled over. He landed on the ground, and with a speed that meant he had trained, he stood in front of Morace. It was Danai. Morace could see the madness in his eyes. He gave

Morace no time to react; with the hilt of his sword he hit him round the head.

Marrisai fell to her knees unable to believe the turn of events. The Shadow creatures they fought were either dead or had disappeared.

Chapter 40

Danai stood over the druid. It would not be right to kill him now, while he mourned his sister. Even Danai was not so hell bent on revenge to kill a man like that. He had needed to strike Marrisai too. She was not herself. She needed to be saved.

Fear had been used to subdue the other members of Morace's family. His brothers and niece were now locked up in dungeons underneath the city.

Evetere's people were consumed with fear he had created, so that he could roam around freely. In their heads they played the same scene over and over again. What would happen if they played up? The death of their king, Caser was enough to keep them at bay.

Marrisai started to stir. When she woke up she found she was bound.

'I am sorry daughter. I needed to bind you for your own safety.'

'Do not be such a fool father,' she begged. 'Please understand these people are trying to help.'

'Do not presume me to be a fool. This druid has started using the power of fear. He has even moved onto terror.' He walked over to her and looked her in the eye. 'I warned you this would happen. Now I have a battle on my hands to help you see your senses.'

'I have seen my senses, I was bent on retribution. There are good people out there, people that can help. This druid is trying to find a way to help.'

'He will turn out like the rest, mark my words. There is no stopping a druid when their minds are set.' He untied her to make her comfortable.

Marrisai felt her wrists. She was still tied at her feet so she could not get away if she wanted to. 'I think you have turned crazy in your hell bent fury,' she said- tears welled up in her eyes.

He slapped her across her face. The tears began to flow. 'The only way to stop a druid is their death.'

From the star, the Wraith of the Marsh watched the events unfold. Galian watched with him.
'Is this how you expected events to unfold?'
'I did not expect anything. What will happen will happen. I can only hope for the outcome to be good.'

Galain's hand touched the Wraith's shoulder. 'You can speak your mind here.'

'I think I need to show Danai the error of his ways. He will not listen to his daughter because she looks like a child. When it reaches night I will make sure the message is loud and clear. It will be up to him then to make his mind up.'

Twak flew back with the tied up prisoner on his back. He was annoyed a little. The Dal-Mai-Sai man who was not supposed to be there had stopped part of the plan. The Druid was meant to implode and release his uncontrollable fear. It had meant to end there and then. But now he would need to resort to his next plan.

What was more he had risked everything with this venture. It was the flaw of creating a crucible. The further away you became the less power you would get from it. It was a double-edged sword. Twak was vulnerable. Had he been caught there and then he might not have survived.

It had gone so smoothly until then. Now he needed to think. It would not take long to get back to the Crucible. He had left it a day's flight away. You do not bring the most valuable weapon into the battlefield. That had been their downfall. The siren was like a poison to him. Her voice disgusted him.

The prisoner started to wake up and move around. Twak struggled to keep it on his back. *Damn, you are going to make me stop.*

Twak found a place to land then unbundled the prisoner. He transformed back into the stunted man. 'Now you need to be still.'

Lorett looked up at the man that had her captured. She was unable to speak because of the gag that was over her mouth.

'I would not bother trying to sing either.' Twak laughed. 'You do not know this but to your family and friends you are dead!' He touched his hand to her head so that the memory could be played. A tear fell from Lorett's eye. This might mean that rather than try and save her, Morace would seek vengeance. His head would not be right.

'I presume you already know what this means?'

Lorett nodded. Morace would be less responsive to reason. He would put his life on the line and not think rationally.

Twak transformed back into the griffon and flew off with Lorett in his talons.

Unknown to Twak, Rhean watched him fly away. She needed to decide what to do. She had been forgotten by pretty much everyone who mattered. This played into her plan well. It would be easy to manipulate all of them. *Which one would the Empress want manipulated the most?*

It would be best to have good faith with the Druids and help them destroy the traitor. She went to where the battle had just been fought to get a sense of how Morace handled the news of his sister's demise.

'I have found it Shanrea! It is here, what we needed to know.' The Nameless Girl looked at the Druid. They had worked in silence for most of the day and the sudden outburst made Shanrea jump.

'You have?'

'I have.' The Nameless Girl's growth had steadied now. She looked like someone in her mid-twenties. She walked over to Shanrea and showed her three books she had been looking at. In each of them there were pictures. The pictures were of the stronghold they sat in. Each book was about each of the three worlds. The girl pointed to the author's name; they were all written by the same person.

"W.o.t Marsh"

The diary that Shanrea and Morace had received from the Wraith of the Marsh sat on the table. It started to glow. The pages spun and then stopped. Shanrea looked at the girl. She was shocked. They both were.

'What was the surname on those books again?' Shanrea asked. She looked at it. 'No way! It is the author of the diary. He wrote these books.'

'What could that mean?'

'It means that the Wraith of the Marsh has been working us hard,' Shanrea said. 'I do not know what his game is, but he is centred in all of this.' Shanrea started to read the passage the dairy had opened up on. As she read the passage she realised that it was a new one. 'This was not here before.'

'What do you mean?'

'I have read every inch of this book. This was not here.' Shanrea started to read the passage out loud.

Entry C

Aside from the Shadows that threaten to engulf (although I have managed to subdue them for the time being), I must highlight an even greater threat to the worlds. Yes, please note that I did not mention this before, but there is a third world that is under threat due to the elven use of weather magic. No doubt, you the druids selected for this, will have realised this by now otherwise you would not be reading the passage.

The three books show the same building on the same world. At the moment they are unconnected except for the room that you will be reading this passage in. Please note, if you leave the room this passage will disappear. In this room you are the only one who can read this.

They are also the only place that can house all of the three world's inhabitants and keep them safe. You would have realised before that you needed to find a way to save the three worlds, but not the means how. I am sorry I could not run the risk of this falling into the wrong hands. I needed to be careful.

Once the stronghold is full and members from all the races inside, there should be five in all. Then will the races be saved...

The passage ended there. Shanrea looked at the girl. *How could they get word to the other races? And tell them?* Shanrea knew she needed to speak to the others. Luckily she had made sure they had taken one of the Siren stones with them. If not how would they have communicated?

'We need to speak to the others. Follow me.' Shanrea ran to the room where the connection needed to be made. She took out one of the stones and willed it to life. Lorett had taught them the song. She said it was not just her that could sing to the stones. That they were made to make sure everyone could communicate if they knew the right song for it.

There was no answer.

She tried again frustrated. 'Damn it! It won't work,' she said.

'Let me have a look.' The Nameless Girl took the stone. She disappeared suddenly.

Shanrea stared at the empty space the girl had just occupied.

The Nameless Girl reappeared in the cell that Morace and the others were kept in. They all started at the appearance of her. She saw her father with them. He back at her. At first she was a stranger to him, but then he saw the resemblance.

'Galian.' He walked over to his daughter.

'I am not mother, father. I am not named yet.' She gave him a warm embrace as she could tell that was what he wanted.

'My, you have grown fast.'

'They always do,' Lento said.

'I have news from Shanrea. We have found what needs to be done. Everyone hold the stone.'

They all took hold of the stone and disappeared the next instant. The last to touch the stone was Morace.

'I cannot come. I need to avenge my sister.'

The girl looked at Morace. 'She died?'

'Yes at the hands of the Shadow lord.'

'No she didn't.' They turned to see Rhean, the girl that Nythe had bought into the stronghold. 'I saw her. The traitor Twak tricked you into thinking she was dead.'

'What? How did you find her?'

'I will always be able to find the traitor as it is my mission to bring him to justice for his crimes.'

The thought that she worked for the Shadow Empress still chilled Morace, but she was here to help them. It was like she tried to prove she was with them. He decided he would keep an eye on her.

'Where did they go?'

'To the Citadel.'

'I can take you using the stone,' the Nameless Girl stated. 'I will help.'

'I will also assist,' Rhean added.

The Nameless Girl changed the tone to reach Morace's sisters stone. They all felt a weird sensation creep over them as the magic took hold of their bodies.

The next thing they knew they were in mid-air. They plummeted to the ground.

'What is this?' A voice screamed as it fell with them.

Twak had not yet made it back to the Crucible. He was a few hours away still. They all landed hard on the ground.

Twak attempted to fly away, but he felt considerably weekend. *How is this so? Damn it.* He looked at the people who had fallen out from the sky. Then he saw her - the same girl that had dared threaten him.

'You!' He started to advance on her but he let go of Lorett.

Morace ran to Lorett and ungagged her. She started to sing instantly. Morace then attended to the bind but Lorett gestured with her head towards Twak. Morace left her to sing and went to battle Twak.

Twak had fallen to one knee to one knee.

Twak transformed into Morace's sister just as he was about to plunge the druid-fire into the shadow agent. Morace halted for a moment unable to move. Forced to think about what he was doing. Twak it would appear was still cleaver. Knowing that Morace would find it difficult to send the fire to the face that was depicted.

'Morace it is not me,' Lorett screamed. 'Kill the beast that is Twak. Rid the world of him.'

Snapped back into action, Morace created his purple druid fire and plunged it into the face of Twak. The creature flung back in pain. The fire Morace conjured weakened slightly and Twak made it back onto his feet. He attempted to transform into a bear. However, it was deformed and had an arm missing. He charged at Morace with a blood-curdling scream. Morace's fists enclosed by fire struck at the Dark Lord as he tried to slash with bear claws. Morace dodged the wild swipes from the bear, as he dodged he timed a strike to the creatures face, causing it to howl in pain.

The attack was the dying shadow agents last attempt at survival. In its eyes, Morace could see defeat reflected in them.

I need to finish this. Morace let the power build up at his finger-tips. The bear staggered now. In the corner of its eye, it could see Lorett. In its rage, it flung at her. Morace let loose the powerful druid-fire. It landed right into the bear's sternum.

As the fire hit and burned through Twak's dark flesh he went through different transformations. The stunted man and the griffon. Eventually he settled on the Elf Shanrea had known as Gragio.

This would make it easier for Morace to kill him. The fire had died down. The face was disfigured and gnarled.

'Do you have any last words?'

'You will not win,' Twak sang with fury. 'I will reign supreme.'

'I shall not kill you with magic.' Morace took out his sword and sliced off the head of the Shadow agent known as Twak. His body fell to the floor. It started to turn to dust and disintegrate.

The Nameless Girl looked at Morace. 'He is weakened when he is away from the Crucible. Sirens make him even weaker. We needed to trick him out.'

'Did you set this all up?' Morace asked.

'Yes sorry, Lorett was in on it too.'

Morace turned to Lorett. He helped her up and unbound her. He gave her the longest embrace and then looked into her eyes. 'Why did you not tell me?'

'You would not have let me do it.'

'Damn right I would not have let you do it. The whole plan was flawed from the start. 'What if he had actually killed you?'

'Somehow I knew that he would not.'

The Nameless Girl stepped in to interrupt the brother and sister moment.

'I am sorry, but now is not the time to have this talk. If you remember, the Dal-Mai-Sai had you captured. He is likely to have found out you have all gone now.' She held out the stone. They all touched it and disappeared back into the stronghold.

Now that the threat of the rogue shadow agent Twak had been defeated they needed to find out how to get the people of the races into the stronghold. The Nameless Girl read through the books. She learnt how it could be done. What needed now was to find how they could get all of the races to agree to co-operate. It seemed an impossible task.

They knew three of the five races would agree. It was the other two - the Dal-Mai-Sai and the dwarves that needed to join. With their leader dead would they be willing to accept? Or would they go back to war? They could not tell. One thing was for sure, they needed to act fast.

The diary said that they had only three months to go before the worlds would collide.

The Nameless Girl would not sleep, she was so focussed on what needed to be done. Morace put a hand on her shoulder. He told her to get some sleep. Her eyes were starting to blur under the weight of it all.

'Go to sleep, now,' Morace said to her in the end. He said it with authority, as though the answer no could not happen. The only acceptable answer would be yes. In the end she did go to sleep for two hours. She then snuck back into the room to continue her study without Morace's knowledge.

'Morace is right you do need to sleep.' It was Shanrea. 'If you die from exhaustion before have done what is necessary, your birth will have been for nothing.'

The girl looked at her with sleepy eyes. 'You know?'

'I guessed. I have read the texts like you. You are a child born of the stars right?'

'I am. We are born when there is immense energy required. Such energy is only found at the birth of a planet. Sure there will be some when the three worlds collide but not nearly enough to sustain a planet.'

Shanrea started to pour some tea. Once it was done she sat down with the girl.

'The same happened with the start of these three worlds. A girl like me was born in order to keep balance with the worlds. She should have lasted longer.' The Nameless Girl started to weep a little.

Shanrea took out a tissue and wiped the girl's eyes. 'But the Elven people started to use weather magic.'

'Indeed, you know they were told ages ago that its use would damage the worlds. Do you want to know who by?'

'Who?'

'The Dal-Mai-Sai. That is why they left. They are a race of star readers. They were meant to guide the races. Then because their words were not headed they gave up and left.'

'But they left for a world that would be equally affected by the use of weather magic.'

'Correct.' She took Shanrea's hand and gave it a squeeze. 'Please, I am not going to die. I can live forever if weather magic is never used again. If it is I will die.'

'I will do everything I can to make sure that your sacrifice does not go to waste. But seriously go to sleep. We will handle the diplomacy.'

Shanrea led the girl to the room where her bed was. She made sure the girl went to sleep then went off to her own bed.

Rhean left the stronghold in the night. She held onto the stone she had salvaged from the fight with Twak. When Lorett was dropped to the floor the stone she carried had fallen out of her pocket. Rhean had picked it up. This was what she needed to bring to the Empress. She now had news of Twak and also a way into the Stronghold for her empress.

She knew it would be pointless to try and spread the shadows over this world. It would be destroyed soon. Twak seemed to have forgotten that. Eventually the worlds would collide and Twak would have died, but now at least the Empress would be strong enough to enter a world renewed.

It would take two weeks for her to fly to the empress as the dove. Time would run out fast. She needed to think what would be best to do. Given that she would need to keep the empress hidden in one of the strongholds she needed to decide which would be the best one to send her to. During the flight to the empress she would be able to think it over. Then she could give her idea to her to see what the empress thought of it.

Chapter 41

The dwarves watched as the Crucible disintegrated. They also felt the pressure they had on them lift. It was like they were free from an endless nightmare. They looked at one another for some sort of sign that they were safe. Their master was meant to have been back by now.

They were still perplexed and unsure at what had happened.

'What happened? Are we free?'

'I do not know.'

'What do we do now? We have no leader.'

'Well it looks like we have a city... we need to find ourselves a king,' one of the dwarves suggested. Who was next in line? The shadow creature had killed all of the successors.'

They looked to where the king's tower stood. Where the Crucible once was. They started to make their way to the tower.

When dwarves were without a ruler they needed to find the strongest. The battles were usually bloody and messy. Hundreds of dwarves took up arms. It looked like some had already started at the top of the tower, as some dwarves were flung from it like a discarded toy.

At the top of a tower, a larger dwarf who wielded a war hammer stood on top of a pile of his kind. Still he smashed at those who dared get in his way. His armour was black obsidian. Two dwarves stood at the door, not daring to move. They threw down their arms and bowed to the new leader.

The melee was over quickly. A new leader of the dwarves was crowned.

Agrue T Ged was sworn in as the King of the Dwarves that afternoon. He stood on the tower to give his first ever speech.

'I am your new king. I remember what the dwarves were meant to do in this land.' The king swung his war hammer across his shoulders. 'We are conquerors. Yes, we were tricked, but so was every other race that encountered the shadows. Now we will reign supreme.'

Chants filled the air.

The king turned around to view the man who stood behind him. 'Don't you worry, I shall lay waste to the Druids too,' he assured him.

Danai stood out of sight of the army. *Good, now I shall be able to bring my daughter back from the madness that has claimed her.* 'You will have my power, King Agrue.'

'I intend on using it,' the king replied.

Once all of the dwarves had disbanded, the king had private council with three people sworn in to help him make decisions.

The other looked at the Dal-Mai-Sai with unease. They had never seen any one of his race before. They knew nothing about him. They feared him.

That was good for Danai. It was what he needed. Fear was his weapon. He resolved to beat the druids at their own game. These dwarves did not know it yet but fear was what was drove them. It was subtle. It was deceptive. It was discreet.

The shadow agent used pure fear. The fear Danai created was enough to create unease.

'We need to take stock of our supplies. Who knows what we lost in the time it has taken for us to come to our senses and get on the right track,' a rather plump dwarf said. His mace tucked by his side.

'I agree, but we also need to make some sort of statement. For too long these people have not feared the dwarves. We must remind them who we are,' a younger dwarf with red hair said.

'No, no no. We must make peace.'

All in the room looked at the dwarf who mentioned the word peace. Before another word was said his head rolled on the floor. Danai moved back into his position near the door.

'Peace cannot happen while there are druids walking this world.' Danai said as he looked at the dwarves who had fear written all over their faces. He started to like how it felt. With the knowledge that he fed them fear on a daily basis made him want to do it more.

It was the fifth day since the council of the dwarves convened. There had been five deaths in that time, at any mention of the word peace. One of them had even been killed when they mentioned it was not allowed.

'Just in case the idea brews in your head. No talking of it,' Danai said.

Shanrea, Marrisai, and Lazon stood in the room where they would be able to transport to the Dal-Mai-Sai world. Marrisai was undoubtedly nervous. She did not know how she would be received. If she had been branded a traitor along with Danai, it would be difficult. These talks needed to happen though. At least they would get transported to where they needed to go.

'Are you sure you want to go Marrisai?' Shanrea asked one last time before they were to depart.

'I am sure, I need to do this.' Guilt overwhelmed her for a moment. She did not want to leave Danai behind. She wanted to help him.

'Lorett we are ready for the portal to be opened,' Shanrea said.

Lorett sang to let the portal open. It would be the last time Shanrea, Lazon, and Marrisai would hear Lorett sing for quite a while.

'Before we go, I should warn you our race is a quite advanced. Sure there are some of us who still use swords, but some use other things. We must be careful.'

'That is fine. I am sure we will be safe.'

The portal opened up. They walked through.

Morace had spoken to Shanrea the night before to make sure she did not mind them being separated for so long. She told him it would be fine, but deep down Shanrea had wanted Morace to come along too. But they knew that because he had used the power of fear the Dal-Mai-Sai would seek to contain him.

The Nameless Girl looked at Morace and patted him on his back to reassure him. 'It is the way it is needed to be.'

'How do you know so much?' Morace asked her.

'I know so much because I have been told. When I travelled with Tavener, he felt the same way as you do now. Whilst I was too young to know where to go, he led. Then I led him.'

'Did you love Tavener?'

'I did, he helped me get to you. I was sad to see him go.'

'Once, when we were children, Lorett and I made so much noise one morning and woke him up. He was in such a rage it scared us.'

'There was one morning where I woke him up,' the girl said. 'He was in a rage when I did that. I was not scared though.'

'Well you must be the only one who has witnessed Tavener's wrath and not been scared.'

They both laughed together. Lorett came in to the room to see them laughing.

'We were talking about Tavener.'

'Have they set off yet?'

'They have, have you seen the girl, Rhean?'

'I have not and one of the stones is missing too.' Lorett showed them the remaining stones. 'I think she has taken one.'

'When?'

'I dropped it I think, when you rescued me from Twak.'

'I don't imagine we will find her anywhere now. Unless we can find where she keeps the shadow empress.' Morace said. 'It would appear keeping you here Lorett was a wise decision.'

The portal shimmered as it changed to allow passage to the Dal-Mai-Sai world. The three who were to travel stepped through. When they arrived they were blinded by the sun. As their eyes adjusted to the brightness they realised they stood in a ruin. The building they had expected to arrive in was barren. The air was hot too. They scanned around and saw that this was not like the Norse they had arrived from. It was a dessert. It looked to be devoid of all life.

A huge gust of wind suddenly drove them to cover their eyes.

'Take them prisoner,' a harsh cold voice said. 'I want to question them.'

Lorett was just about to close the portal behind them when she sensed that something was wrong. Without warning and a determination, she stepped through the portal. As she did, she saw Shanrea, Lazon and Marrisai captive on the ground in chains. Instinctively she moved to go to them.

Suddenly a sharp pain ran through her whole body. She fell to her knees as her blood painted the ground red.

Shanrea saw Lorett. With the tip of a spear jutting out of her body. She screamed out, she tried to go to her but was held back by a strong hand.

The portal became inactive.

Epilogue

Rhean slipped into the cave where the shadow empress stayed safely hidden. She knew her mistress would be pleased that she had a plan to make her safe. She walked into space where the Empress was left to gain her strength. It was a great sight.

The empress was more whole now. She was still too weak to function on her own but there was more of her.

'Child you have returned. What news do you have?'

'I managed you get the people of the stronghold to let me in. It was relatively easy, all I needed to do was pretend to be hurt.'

'That is good. I sense that the Traitor is no more?'

'He was defeated by the druids with my help.'

'Good news. Tell me, why have you returned? I am sure it would not only be to tell me this.'

'I returned because I have secured a way to save you. The worlds are going to collide. This stone...' she took out the stone, '...will take you to where you can rebuild your strength and wait out the collision.'

'Speak to me of your plan.'

Rhean explained what she felt would work to keep her safe. The empress asked to be left alone for some time so that she could think over what had been said.

The young Dal-Mai-Sai looked at the energy reader. It read that there was a huge spike of energy in the North. There had been no trace of anything there for years but then it spiked. He knew this needed to be reported. A spike of magical energy this huge had to mean something.

He pointed it out to the woman who sat next to him. 'What could this mean?' he asked her.

'I don't know. But I think you should be the one to tell the emperor.'

The male Dal-Mai-Sai responded and left the room. He took down the hall to where the emperor would be seated at this time of the day. The guards tried to slow him down but it was a futile effort. If anything it made him speed up.

He reached the large iron doors. The two guards looked at him. They let him catch his breath before they interrogated him.

'I...I need to speak to the emperor.'

The guards laughed in his face. They mocked him.

'Everyone needs to talk to the emperor. Go awa...' They stopped when they saw his insignia. It meant that he was granted permission to interrupt whatever the emperor may be doing if he felt it necessary.

'I am sorry I have to flash this, but I need to speak to him.' He spoke with authority now.

'I am sorry my lord, please forgive us. Enter.' They dropped to one knee and bowed.

'Thank you.' The man entered.

'Emperor, I am sorry to trouble you at such a late hour but the need is of great importance.'

The emperor looked up at him. He was feasting with his family. It was a great feast, one that the millions who went hungry would be jealous of.

'Well, tell me what you must.'

'Emperor.' He walked over to the table. 'I will introduce myself so that you know who is speaking.' It was customary to announce who you were to the emperor.

'There is no need. I know who you are. Dalmein Lin.'

'Yes sire. There has been a reading. In the north.'

The Emperor stood up, his feast over. 'Are you sure?'

'I am.'

'Then it means activity? Ready the council, they will need to be made aware. Remember what we discussed Dalmein.' He looked at the man to make sure he understood.

'Ey emperor.' He left the room and headed to the reading room.

About the Author.

A.J. Van-Rixtel, born and raised in the East Midlands of England, always liked to be imaginative and started writing during college. A.J.'s passion for writing developed when he found a novel by Terry Brooks on a bookshelf in his local second hand bookstore. He still has ties to that store and visits regularly. His writing really took off in 2012 when he took part in National Novel Writing Month, where most of the first draft of *A Collision of Worlds* was written.

Other passions include drawing, the maps, which you see in the novel *A Collision of Worlds* are all drawn by A.J. The book cover is also designed by A.J. He also performs in local pantomimes with an amateur dramatics group and dances a number of disciplines. He is an avid reader and enjoys the works of Terry Brooks and Karen Miller.

A.J. also writes poetry and will be looking at publishing in early 2015 his first poetry book, titled *Sinful Souls.*

For more information about A.J. Van-Rixtel visit his blog on- www.fantasyfictionauthorslife.blogspot.co.uk/

ALBAR
Publishing.

81587808R00212

Made in the USA
Columbia, SC
04 December 2017